P9-BBP-122

Also by Leah Thomas

Because You'll Never Meet Me
Nowhere Near You
When Light Left Us

WILD AND CROOKED

LEAH THOMAS

WITHDRAWN

Fitchburg Public Library
5530 Lacy Road
Fitchburg, WI 53711

BLOOMSBURY

NEW YORK   LONDON   OXFORD   NEW DELHI   SYDNEY

BLOOMSBURY YA
Bloomsbury Publishing Inc., part of Bloomsbury Publishing Plc
1385 Broadway, New York, NY 10018

BLOOMSBURY and the Diana logo are trademarks of Bloomsbury Publishing Plc

First published in the United States of America in June 2019 by Bloomsbury YA

Text copyright © 2019 by Leah Thomas

All rights reserved. No part of this publication may be reproduced or transmitted in any form or by
any means, electronic or mechanical, including photocopying, recording, or any information storage
or retrieval system, without prior permission in writing from the publisher.

Bloomsbury books may be purchased for business or promotional use. For information on bulk
purchases please contact Macmillan Corporate and Premium Sales Department at
specialmarkets@macmillan.com

Library of Congress Cataloging-in-Publication Data
Names: Thomas, Leah, author.
Title: Wild and crooked / by Leah Thomas.
Description: New York : Bloomsbury, 2019.
Summary: Kalyn, living under a pseudonym, and Gus, who has cerebral palsy,
get caught in an uproar in Samsboro, Kentucky, as the truth about the brutal murder
of Gus's father by Kalyn's comes to light.
Identifiers: LCCN 2018045382 (print) • LCCN 2018051376 (e-book)
ISBN 978-1-5476-0002-1 (hardcover) • ISBN 978-1-5476-0001-4 (e-book)
Subjects: I CYAC: Murder—Fiction. I Secrets—Fiction. I Friendship—Fiction. I
Cerebral palsy—Fiction. I People with disabilities—Fiction. I
City and town life—Kentucky—Fiction. I Kentucky—Fiction.
Classification: LCC PZ7.1.T463 Wil 2019 (print) I LCC PZ7.1.T463 (e-book) I DDC [Fic]—dc23
LC record available at https://lccn.loc.gov/2018045382

Book design by John Candell
Typeset by Westchester Publishing Services
Printed and bound in the U.S.A. by Berryville Graphics Inc., Berryville, Virginia
2 4 6 8 10 9 7 5 3 1

All papers used by Bloomsbury Publishing Plc are natural, recyclable products made
from wood grown in well-managed forests. The manufacturing processes conform
to the environmental regulations of the country of origin.

To find out more about our authors and books visit www.bloomsbury.com
and sign up for our newsletters.

For Grandma, who asked if I was ever
going to write any "normal" stories.
(Maybe not, but I love you, and thanks
for reading them anyway.)

"A friend is one that knows you as you are, understands
where you have been, accepts what you have become,
and still, gently allows you to grow."
—Unknown (NOT Shakespeare)

"Accepting yourself as you are is an act of
civil disobedience."
—Francesca Martinez

ACT ONE
Happy Birthday, Rose Poplawski

KALYN

BOY OH BOY, is there nothing to see in Samsboro, Kentucky.

Nothing but corn and grass and grubby little houses and sunbaked faces, which combined is still basically the definition of nothing. It's almost the same kind of nothing we had in Alleghany, except here it's corn instead of cattle. There's a cereal mill in town, so the air smells a little better, but we're still stuck with dirt roads. Once we finally get ourselves to the van, it'll be a straight-and-narrow shot down M-12 to Jefferson High. It shouldn't take long.

But like Mom always says, "The straight and narrow's for bad drivers." It's never easy getting anywhere when you're a Spence.

Even the road to my conception was totally crooked and wide, and maybe that's why my parents were so eager to pop me into the world. They were troubled teenagers themselves, and the last thing they needed was a squalling poop-machine, but heck. Tell my parents "Stop!" and they slam down on the gas. Mom and Dad have basically driven circles all over the straight and narrow, spun out and done screeching doughnuts, too. I'm definitely their kid.

Maybe that's why I'm still standing in front of the bathroom mirror on my birthday, smearing basically inches of eyeliner under my eyes when we should've hit the road ten minutes ago.

Somehow the truancy officer found out about me. Mom blames the nosy neighboring of Ms. Pilson, the old lady who lives in the peeling house at the road-end. I blame plain old rotten luck. In any case, Officer Newton and his damp armpits appeared on Grandma's front step last Wednesday.

I thought Mom would fight him, tooth and bedazzled nail. I eavesdropped through Grandma's walls, waiting for her to claw him good.

Mom's *made* for the wide and crooked. She doesn't trust anyone in a uniform. She doesn't believe in turn signals. She's put so much peroxide on her hair across her lifetime that the smell's as good as coffee to her. I'm her pistol and she's a much bigger gun, maybe a Winchester Magnum, from a family of firearms. We've got gunpowder where most people have cartilage.

I thought Mom would stare Officer Newton down or pull the "it's a free country!" card, at least. Instead, Mom offered the man sweet tea before he left.

"Mom, *no*," I told her when she closed the screen behind him. The untouched glass of tea dribbled sweat onto the card table, and Grandma's mouth dribbled oatmeal down her bib. "It's bullshit!"

Mom lit her cigarette. "He says it's best for you. He ain't wrong."

I snorted. "Since when do people in this town want what's best for Spences?"

"Hopefully since now."

But it *is* bullshit. Even if Mom doesn't have a high school diploma, she teaches me more than all the teachers I ever had back in Arkansas *combined*. She taught me to drive, and to cook, and to use dumbasses against themselves, like the misogynistic creeps we could get to buy us dinner, and she taught me to read widely and often and teach *myself* words like "misogynistic." Getting certified in the Louise Spence education program means I'm *plenty* ready for Jefferson freakin' High today.

I slap a layer of glitter on the black eyeliner. It's my damn birthday.

"You gonna be ready before the cows come home?" Mom leans against the door frame, tapping ash from her cigarette into the pink porcelain sink.

Everything in Grandma's bathroom has a doily on it. The toothbrush holder is hemmed in lace, stained white with toothpaste buildup.

". . . you *listenin'* to me, Kalyn-Rose?"

"Well, you're shouting right in my ear."

Mom takes a drag bigger than she is. "Don't let the assholes knock you down today."

Smoking's the last thing a five-foot-tall, thirty-six-year-old asthmatic should be doing, but I can't say jack about it, what with a pack of Pall Malls in my sock drawer that she doesn't know about. And if anyone told her to quit, you know what Mom would do? She'd light up two fresh ones and plug 'em into her nostrils to make her damn point.

"So what are you this year—eight? Twelve?"

"It's 2007, Mom."

Mom lets the cigarette fall into the clogged sink basin. "Fine. Ask me."

Other people break piñatas, but in the Spence household we've got an annual interrogation tradition.

"How'd you get pregnant?"

Like always, Mom replies, "Don't question miracles, sweet-cakes."

I roll my eyes. It's not like I want the grossest details. I've got all kinds of theories about how the spunk that became *moi* made its way through the barbed wire, bars, and steel walls of Wilder Penitentiary, the largest high-security prison in the Bible Belt. Mom's never confirmed any of them.

Turkey basters, and forged medical reports, and maybe the sneaking of goods through a cake? Whatever it was, Mom started ballooning up like any other mom. Like Dad was any other dad, and not a convicted murderer sentenced to life.

I bite my tongue to keep from cussing. I'm trying to put my contacts in. Maybe that should have happened before the eyeliner.

For years I had this pair of old-man glasses that I downright refused to wear. My teachers in Alleghany kept throwin' fits, saying I couldn't see the board. I threw them right back because there was jack-all I wanted to see on that board anyhow.

Mom struck me a deal: if I helped her change some bedpans, I could use a cut of her earnings to save up for contacts.

Before we moved to Shitsboro to take care of Grandma, Mom took care of other old people. Checking their catheters, and making sure they took their meds, and giving them pep talks about how their lives were worth living regardless of whether their idiot kids bothered visiting.

It took me 137 bedpans to afford my fake eyes. Damn right I'll suffer for them.

I finally wedge the lens in and blink the pain away. After some nose blowing, I get a good gander at the mess I've made. Eyeliner has slipped down my cheeks in sparkling black trickles, but screw it.

I show the mirror my fangs. I might need them today.

Grandma's prefab's been egged five times since we moved in. Dad's been in prison for two decades, but people don't forget. Killing a local golden boy has that effect.

I toss my braid over my shoulder. It's crazy long these days, this pumpkin whip that hangs past the small of my back. I step back to admire the mess of me. "I like it."

"You're your father's daughter," Mom announces, letting loose another coughle.

"I'm gonna get off work early and pick up a cake mix so we

can celebrate." Mom works at the Sunny Spot, a little gas station by the freeway. "Funfetti again?"

"Does the pope shit in the woods? Forever Funfetti."

We overhear Grandma hacking in the kitchen. If the walls were any thinner they'd be wax paper. Mom ducks away, saying, "Come help me get her settled."

I follow Mom to the kitchen. Grandma smiles at me as I wheel her into the living room where she can watch her soaps. I stare at her scalp through her silver feather petals of hair and wonder why it's so much paler than the rest of her when really it's the closest piece of her to the sun.

"You've got a head like a baby's, Grandma."

Grandma clears her throat best she can. "Uh . . . babies, no wavy time wig for."

I only met Grandma three times before her stroke: at Mom and Dad's wedding, and at two Christmas parties at the Alleghany Mobile Park. Both Christmases, Grandma got so drunk on peppermint schnapps that she couldn't speak English anymore, just rambled in Polish. I almost understood her then, like I almost understand her now.

Grandma always knows what she's *trying* to say, even if her mouth fumbles. Grandma not making a lot of sense makes sense to me, because I never make sense, either. Peas attached at the hip. That's exactly us.

Mom hates leaving Grandma home alone. She has a hard time swallowing, and sometimes we have to clear her throat for her, fingers like fishhooks scraping phlegm away. But

Grandma's prefab sits in the center of the family salvage yard, resting on the same cinderblocks she uses as a doorstep. It's a painful process, lowering her down.

Grandma's hand lands on mine. Her eyes are rheumy and bloodshot, but her stare is clear as water. "Be good today."

Mom rolls her eyes. "If wishes were horses."

Sure, back in Alleghany I started shit with kids on the way to school, mostly because they thought it was *hysterical* that the bus was bigger than our house. There're only so many times a girl can call you "trailer trash" before you trash that girl's face.

Mostly, though, Mom's worried people here'll recognize me.

And that's why she pulls me aside toward the kitchen sink and says something awful. "*Listen*, Kalyn. Me and Officer Newton agreed it'd be a good idea to register you under a different last name."

It's shock more than anything that makes a sailor of me: "*You fucking what?*"

"You'll be Kalyn *Poplawski* this year."

"Poplaw—I can't even pronounce it!"

Grandma *tsk*s one or both of us.

"Watch it. Poplawski's your grandma's maiden name!" She says the next part like she's banking on it: "She's been married since 1949, so prob'ly no one remembers."

"*I* want to forget, and you just told me!"

"*Kalyn-Rose Tulip Spence.*"

But Mom's request seems like a whole new blasphemy. She might as well be another mean girl on the bus. Might as well be calling us NASCAR-loving, cousin-marrying, Podunk garbage. I'm used to *other* people name-calling, but this?

"I can't believe you."

Mom squeezes her eyes shut. "This ain't a choice, Kalyn. You get it, right?"

Oh, I get it. This is the town that made Dad a murderer.

I glance out the kitchen window at the field of rusting cars under the cotton-candy-pink morning sky. Samsboro's treated my family like garbage for decades, dumping literal trash in our yard because they figure trash is the same as salvage (it's *not*, damn it, when your family makes a living selling auto parts).

"Kalyn, we've gotta try and make this work."

"For how long?"

"However long it takes."

I don't ask what "it" means. I can hear Grandma's wheezes over the blare of the TV. Grandma's not the only one in this room counting the breaths until she'll have none.

"You told me to be proud. You always said if people talk shit, take none of it."

"Guess I was talking shit, too. Sometimes you have to take it."

If anyone knows this, it's Mom. She's received a death threat a week ever since she married Dad. That's partly my fault; I just *had* to be the flower girl at the wedding.

Seeing me in a little white lace dress drove the media up the walls. Mom and Dad let me wear it anyway, because my pistol went off: I screamed for days straight (between meals) when Mom told me I couldn't come.

So she bought me an Easter dress from the clearance rack at Kohl's. Her dress was thrifted, faded red and slim fitting. She had to put a sweater on over it in the prison parking lot. They have very particular regulations in prisons about clothes. They wouldn't let Dad wear long sleeves, even though his arms are coated in burn scars.

The visitation room reminded me of my elementary school cafeteria. The fluorescents made my tummy rumble. I fidgeted through the half-hour service, eyeballing the vending machines until Grandma caved. She looked downright funny with her balding mullet, denim skirt, and blue eye shadow, but she knew Reese's Pieces were the way to a kid's heart.

In the photo that made national news, Mom and Dad stare lovingly into each other's eyes and I stand between them and beam at the camera, melted chocolate all over my face. The hateful moms of America had a lot to say about whether Mom should be a mother after that. I wonder if the hateful moms of America still want to adopt me now that I'm a juvenile delinquent and not a "baby angel cursed with evil parents."

"You're a coward," I tell Mom, and I close myself in the bathroom again.

No way in hell am I *nervous* about going to Jefferson High. I know I'm poor and angry. Changing my name won't change what I am. Even without my new tiger stripes, my old snaggletooth, the egg in my pocket, and my gunpowder marrow, people in Samsboro were never, *ever* gonna be pleased to have me here.

GUS

"I'D GIVE MY left arm not to go in today."

Dad's blue eyes twinkle through time and glass. He offers no consolation.

I lower my voice to a manly timbre: "But that's your *good* arm, Gus."

The imitation makes me cough. I slur the words, too. Dad wouldn't have. As far as I know, Dad didn't have a speech disorder.

Dad twinkles on, unbothered. Eternal smile, eternal indifference.

I have looked at my father's face every day since the day I was born, but I've never met him. Apart from the picture on my bookshelf, there's one on Mom's nightstand and a collage above the fireplace in the living room. A few summer camp photos are tacked to our refrigerator. The guest room contains dozens of pairs of his eternal eyes, trapped in the darkness of the shoe-boxes that hold his personal effects.

There's a photo of Dad holding an enormous trout situated halfway up the staircase. This one is a real nuisance, because almost every time I trip on the steps, the frame rattles against the wall, slips off its nail, and clunks against the carpet. Every other day I am fumbling over that picture, trying to hang it back up before Mom can catch me.

One of these days the glass will crack, but it hasn't happened yet.

I can't complain about the stupid placement of the weird trout picture. If I do, Mom will want to talk about *why* it upsets me.

There are two ways that conversation can go:

1. Mom will assume I hate the picture because it's a picture of my dead dad, not because it's hanging in a stupid place. She'll explain to me, again, that even if Dad is gone, she wants him to be a comforting presence in our lives. She'll sit me down on the recliner and she'll sit on the settee and she'll ask me, again, *eternally*, how I feel about living with the ghost of my father.

2. Mom will realize the truth: the picture keeps falling because I keep tripping. The dead leg strikes again! So Mom'll sit me down on the recliner and she'll sit on the settee and ask me, again, why I don't consider moving into the downstairs bedroom.

"It's the guest room." If I stare at the bottom of my bifocals, I won't see her at all.

"We hardly ever have guests, and it'd be easier for you—"

When I lift my hands in exasperation, the right one won't go all the way up; it never does. That will definitely catch her eye. "Mom. Let me keep my room."

Or maybe the words won't come out right. Maybe I'll say something like, "Mom. Let me hold, I mean, um, keep my . . . the . . . place?"

Because a conversation this uncomfortable might trigger my aphasia, and all the nouns in the world could abandon me. That'll convince Mom that I *must* move downstairs.

Mom *hates* seeing other people uncomfortable. She'd wet herself to let a stranger cut her in a restroom line. Unluckily for Mom, discomfort is my default setting. I wonder if I feel like an itch she can't scratch. She'll never say so, and I'll never ask.

Today I make my way down the stairs and Dad doesn't fall. I wish some of his enthusiasm would infect me. I feel more like the trout in his arms, sucking empty air.

Mom stands when I enter the kitchen. I wish she wouldn't. "Perfect timing!"

I look at the stacks of fried batter cooling on the table and know it's not perfect timing at all. The chocolate syrup's sunken through two layers of cakes. Mom's ready for work but won't even eat until she knows I'm going to make it downstairs.

I maybe hate that about her. I hate myself for maybe hating her for anything.

The Dads on the fridge don't wink at me when I lower myself into the waiting chair. Mom makes sure I take a bite before digging a fork into her own soggy stack.

She rattles on about my class schedule, about sharing afternoon rides with Phil, about when I'll be seeing Alicia, my speech therapist ("It'll be Tuesdays and Fridays during lunch"). Mom makes me recite, between bites, the exact procedure I should go through in case of emergencies, followed by a memorized list of important phone numbers: hers, Tam's, Dr. Petani's, Mr. Wheeler's. If my cheeks weren't full of orange juice, this is one conversation I could have upside down with my eyes closed.

Without warning, Mom lifts up the left leg of my jeans. "Where's your new AFO? The starry one?"

I cough up pancake debris. Wearing a *cool*, cosmic-patterned orthotic boot is only actually "cool" in middle school, and I'm a junior now.

Mom never pities me, but she does treat me like I'm perpetually seven. She's only a decade wrong. In the grand scheme of the vast and unknowable universe, that shouldn't feel as awful as it does.

I tap the plastic on the black AFO encasing my foot. "This one matches better."

She can't argue. My jeans are black, and so is my long-sleeved shirt. You might think I'm trying to mimic my idols.

The Gaggle, I call them. They're this group of kids who've formed an artsy coven on Jefferson High's campus. You can't call them Goth, because they've evolved beyond that, and it's

really hard to commit to corsets and Tripp pants in this swelter-
ing patch of southern Kentucky. These kids shy away from the
sun, but they aren't pretty enough to pass for vampires. But in
this town of Wrangler jeans, the Gaggle is a local miracle.

Sure, they write poems about child funerals and sculpt
inverted rib cages full of crows during art class. But they also
fold colorful origami creatures and scatter them in the hallways. Their leader, a widow's-peaked wonder named Garth
Holden, composes goofy songs to raise STD/STI awareness.
Who can forget his classic hit from freshman year, "See Ya,
Gonorrhea!" or the heartfelt ballad that rang from his sable
ukulele last spring, "STI, ST-Me, ST-You"?

The Gagglers laugh through their piercings and pastel hair
spikes. One of the members wears floor-length black gowns
with hot pink rocking horse shoes and dozens of decora hair
clips. It's like they fell right out of Harajuku.

The whole Gaggle might as well be there. I can't get near them.
They have something I'll never have. It's *not* fashion sense.

The Gaggle has *carefreedom*. Every day they dress to make
an impression, or create something to make an impression, or
sing to make an impression. They've got constant opportunities to define who they are in the eyes of other people.

Most people who meet me? I know how they're going to
describe me later. Commentary on my clothes or personality
will never be anyone's go-to. The moment I'm out of earshot,
I'm not "Gus, that kid obsessed with Alexander McQueen."
Nope. I'm eternally "Gus, the disabled kid."

Or sometimes I'm "Gus, the kid whose dad got murdered."

I'm not wearing black to make a statement. I'm wearing black because it'll get me the least amount of attention today. *Some* attention is inevitable during the first week. There's not much in Samsboro apart from the Munch-O Mills cereal factory. People shift in and out of positions there, so every year I'm an object of curiosity to anyone unfortunate enough to have moved here over the summer.

I could cosplay as Björk and still be "the disabled kid" to newcomers.

"Not hungry?" I've been staring into the distance. Mom's been staring into me.

My untouched pancakes are dissolving. "Sorry. Thinking."

"How's the abyss today, Gus?"

"It's nothing." We made up this awful joke years ago. "I'm just spacing out."

I look to Fridge-Dad. He sits on a pontoon boat. I can't see his eyes, so I silently address the water reflected in his sunglasses: *Fine. I'll give* both *arms not to go.*

Dr. Petani says at this point there isn't much more that splinting can do to undo the contractures in my right arm. Wearing an elbow brace might only "incur unnecessary muscle stress and pain." Back in junior high, I went through a stubborn phase of refusing to wear my splints and orthotics. I'm still paying for it. My right arm's a tightened spring that curls up against me like a question mark.

"If you didn't like the space brace, you could have told us."

"The space brace is great. It rhymes." I smile at her. "I'll wear it later."

Mom raises an eyebrow. "No one will see it anyhow."

That's not the point, and she knows it. Sure, Mom works from home, but she doesn't live in her pajamas. This morning she's wearing a tasseled cardigan over a caramel-colored dress. Her earrings are porcelain roses. A floral headband straps down her frizzy gray hair. You'd think she was going to open a candle-selling shop. Instead, she'll lock herself in her paper-strewn office to ghostwrite the autobiography of some soldier in a nursing home. Mom *always* dresses for work, even if she doesn't leave the house. She says taking yourself seriously means *dressing* yourself seriously.

Why can't she apply that logic to me?

"Well," she concedes, "I can't say I dislike a dark palette. But if you're going to look like the night sky, I don't see how it could hurt to add a few stars."

"Adding new stars could speed up global warming." I wipe my chin. "That would hurt a lot. Consider the polar bears."

Tamara's laugh enters before she does. She appears beyond the open kitchen window, popping up from below like a whack-a-mole.

"Special delivery!" She plops a heap of filthy carrots into the sink and leans on the sill. There's soil all over her, as always, and she's smiling, as often. "Honestly, Beth. You can't *force* a guy to wear the cosmos."

Mom's on her feet, inspecting the shrunken carrots. "*Not* a very special delivery."

"That's because I haven't delivered it yet." Tamara leans forward. Mom stands on tiptoe to meet her.

A lot of people probably look away when their parents kiss. Maybe I'm a weirdo, because I hope I never will.

Before Tamara moved in, our house was a mausoleum. That wasn't Dad's fault. Dead or not, his teeth have always brightened the place up.

Our house was a mausoleum because Mom locked herself inside it. The windows were always closed, and incessant air-conditioning left the place frigid. Our world was white walls and white carpet. I used to wake up in my bedroom and panic, thinking I was back in the hospital again.

Tamara's the only landscaper in town, so Mom commissioned her to install a therapeutic Zen garden in our backyard. Tamara showed up beaming with bags of stones under her arms. Mom suddenly thought of a dozen excuses to bring her back again. Tamara dug a small koi pond, lined our walkway with ribbon grass, trained ivy to grow up our porch pillars, planted hollyhocks and irises in curving flower beds. After a year, it looked like all the color that had drained out of our house had pooled on our lawn.

Early some mornings, second-grade me would hear Tamara's laughter rattling our kitchen walls. I'd shuffle downstairs to hear its echo—Mom's little chuckle in the aftermath—and find them swapping gossip and sipping coffee: Mom in her muted dresses, Tamara looking like a fashionista gone country in blue overalls and black boots, her bright yellow *Peake Landscaping* baseball cap on her head.

In third grade, after surgery landed me in a wheelchair, Tamara spent several August hours squatting on our front step, taking meticulous notes with the help of a tape measure. She must not have slept that night, because the next morning she was squatting on a brand-new wooden mobility ramp instead, painting it ivory to match the porch.

"I don't like people feeling sorry for me," I warned her.

Tamara snorted. "Hell if I feel sorry for you. You're the most pampered kid I've ever met, and I've seen some real princes. Your mom dotes on you like no other."

"Then . . . why are you here?"

Tamara cocked her head. "I'm hoping some of your mom's doting might rub off on me, is all. You get me?"

Soon Tamara was giving me rides to school, and I was giving her tips on how to woo my hermit mother. I told her Mom loves Thai food and terrible piano ballads and Christmas puppet movies and pictures of my dead father.

"Yeah, what's that all about?"

I remember shifting in the seat of her truck; I'd sat on a spade. "She wants him to be part of my life. Is it weird?"

Tamara shrugged. "He's got a good face. Looks like a certain kid I really like. But who the hell hangs pictures halfway up a staircase?"

An unplanned laugh burst out of me. "*Right*?!"

I don't know exactly when color started bleeding into the house. First it was potted hens and chicks on the kitchen windowsill, and then a vase full of snapdragons on our dining room table, and eventually daylilies on Mom's nightstand.

For years now, Tamara's trailed soil and blades of grass along the white carpets in jade strips of bright color. Every day, Tamara wakes up at dawn to check on the plants before work, but she leaves the heat on in her wake.

Now she winks at me from the window. "Morning. You ready to give 'em hell?"

"To be given it, at least." A smile escapes me.

"Beth, wanna stop strangling your kid so he can go get given hell already?"

Mom's suddenly hugging my head to her stomach. I don't even know when she crossed the kitchen, but I'm buried under her heavy arms.

"Stop growing up."

"I'll, um, work on it."

She lets me go. Maybe Mom treats me like I'm seven because she wants me to stay small enough to hold. But Mom's broken out of the tomb. There's room in our house for things besides me and my dead dad and my dead right side.

The truth is, I'm the one who wants to stop growing.

I'd give *all* my limbs to stay home today.

My pancakes have liquefied.

KALYN

IT'S A CLICHÉ to say that Jefferson High looks like a prison, but it's also the truth. I don't say goodbye to Mom when she drops me off, even though she wishes me a happy birthday. The hot September air smells like sticky cinnamon.

The front hall is empty when I get inside. Well, almost empty.

There's only one tumbleweed in this windowless space, and man, does he look like he'll tumble, made of skinny twigs like that. But I need help, and apparently stick-boy's the only soul besides yours truly who's late for class.

And that's uncanny, too, because *damn* if he doesn't look like the kind of dweeb who drools over textbooks. His glasses are more old man–ish than mine ever were, and there's a quill tucked behind one of his ears. He's wearing a T-shirt with Shakespeare's iconic mug and the words *Will Power!* slapped on it, for chrissakes. This kid is *dying* for more English Lit class. He's Christopher-Marlowe-with-a-knife-in-his-eye dying for it.

People assume I don't like English Lit, mostly because people suck. But I inherited the bookworm bug from both parents. Dad has a shelf of murder mysteries in his cell. He knows it's ironic. Mom's always had a taste for forbidden romance. That's also pretty ironic, when you think about it.

Back in Alleghany, she kept a stack of Harlequin paperbacks in the living room. They held up one side of the coffee table where a leg was missing, but that table was always slanted because Mom was constantly wiggling books loose for rereading. You'd set your drink down and end up cussing.

And I get peckish for words. I'll read anything from John Donne to coupon pamphlets. Ten bucks says this guy— *Quillpower*, let's call him—is more particular.

Quillpower leans against a row of lockers, looking left and then at a handheld game and then right and then rinse-repeating the cycle.

"Hey! You're local, right?"

Quillpower's head snaps up. He scans me in one swoop before dropping his eyes. His fingers start moving faster.

"I'm new. My name's Kalyn Sp—wait. Shit! I forgot my last name. Paulski? Popski? Do either of those sound like real names to you?"

"Not remotely." His voice sounds like how he looks: weedy and crisp.

"Yeah, I know. Dumbass hick can't even remember her own name. Funny, right?"

He's back to groping the handheld. I feel like maybe it's a defense mechanism, like when pill bugs roll into pebble-balls. "Never mind. Just—which way to the office?"

Quillpower unsticks one hand from the screen and points. His arm's so thin I wonder why the weight of his hand doesn't snap the damn thing. I follow its trajectory and see a dozen doors.

"Mind showing me there?"

But that's about as much mingling as this weed can handle, because he's already tumbling elsewhere. Quillpower scuttles away and falls through the boys' room entrance.

"Thanks anyway!" I holler. If I've got social issues, Quillpower clearly has social volumes. But he did point me the right way. We used to find pill bugs in our pantry back in Alleghany, and I always liked them. Mom calls them roly-polies, which is just too good a name to squish.

And what's in a name? Apparently every damn thing.

"Pawlski, Polansky, Powpowpowsky?"

"I don't have a Kalyn Powpowpowksy on the roster." The secretary, a "Kitty Patrick" by her brown name placard, peers at me from behind an ancient computer. I don't know how she can see me past the collection of framed dog photos lining the counter. "You're a sophomore?"

"Yeah." I'm smiling again. God, don't girls get cheek-aches from this crap? I've never felt sorry for pageant queens before. Then again, a pageant queen would have received a nicer welcome. Mrs. Patrick took one look at my face and nearly jumped through the ceiling, all, "Jiminy Christmas, girl, wipe your face!"

I'd totally forgotten my eyeliner trails. No wonder I spooked Quillpower. But the minute Mrs. Patrick asks me to wash my face, I tell her I sure as hell won't.

She raises tattooed eyebrows and leans forward in her roller chair, beads rattling against her blouse. "Well, whatever. Stick to your guns if you want, Annie Oakley."

Mrs. Patrick's got rhinestones on her nails, and her dyed red hair has streaks of violet in it. I bet she was a rebel in high school. I bet she skipped college to join a grimy punk band. Bet she misses the excitement.

"Still not seeing you, dear." She clicks her mouse. "But wait, now—we *do* have a Kalyn-Rose *Poplawski* registered in the *freshman* class."

"That's it!" The rest of her sentence drops. "Wait, *what*? That's a mistake."

"We'll get that fixed. It's been a tragedy in here ever since they had Brad covering while I was on vacation in Tampa. Brad's the worst, Kalyn-Rose. So how do you *really* spell your last name?"

"No, the mistake is, I'm *not* a freshman. I'm a sophomore."

"Some credits didn't transfer, and it looks like your

attendance in Alleghany was . . . we'll say patchy. You're a freshman again, sweetie."

"But I'm sixteen today!"

"Happy birthday!" Mrs. Patrick rifles through a drawer.

"This is bullsh— Come on, Mrs. Patrick. You're cool,
right?"

She passes me a glittery purple pencil. "It's *Ms.* Patrick, and
yes, I'm the coolest person in this office. Not that there's a lot of
competition." A man at the copy machine, probably Brad, gives
her this sad, basset-hound stare. "But it's not up to me. You're
on Officer Newton's list."

Not only does this guy reject sweet tea in our kitchen and
guilt Mom into thinking she's no kind of mother; now he shoves
me backward into freshmanhood?

"Well, *shit-sticks*."

"*Language*. Look." Ms. Patrick taps her glasses. "Take it up
with Officer Newton. For now, just get to class and don't burn
the place down."

"I didn't burn down Alleghany. I only pulled the fire alarm
on occasion."

"You'll be in room 107. Mr. Smalls. I've drawn you a map."

Ms. Patrick is in her fifties, looks like. She seems local as
hell, so maybe she worked here eighteen years ago. I wonder if
she remembers Dad. I wonder if she thought he looked like the
kind of kid who'd be in prison one day. Do I look like that, too?

"Anything else I can help you with, Kalyn-Rose?"

"It's not Kalyn-Rose." I tuck the birthday pencil behind my

ear, à la Quillpower. "I mean . . . it's just Rose. Can you show me how to spell Poplawski?"

Ms. Patrick doesn't bat a lash. She spells out the letters on a heart-shaped sticky note and shoos me out of the office.

I retrace my steps, duck into the girls' room, and scrub the black off my face. I pull my braid to the side of my head and wind it twice around my skull before rolling the last bit into a knot, twisting my hair tie tight around that. I tuck the glittery pencil into the knot and tug a few bangs from my hairline.

I look like some discount duchess, crowned in red ropes. I practice a meek smile. My eyes aren't as pink now that the contacts have nestled there for a while. I almost look like a nice, straitlaced country girl. It's anything but Spence, anything but *me*.

People sometimes claim they were born lawbreakers. I'll do you one better—I was conceived one. Kids like me are raised on Happy Meals, destined to start smoking by age thirteen before they become dropouts.

But some kids are destined for great things, like Girl Scouts and summer camp and homemade food, and whatever else rich people think is great. I imagine *Rose Poplawski* is that kind of girl. Maybe other people will imagine it, too.

GUS

THE FIRST TWO minutes of school were okay. I made it up the stairs and through the front door without any incidents, even in my heaviest boots.

Dr. Petani chided me for my Doc Martens the last time I was in her office. "Isn't it difficult wearing your AFO with those?"

"I just buy them a few sizes bigger than my feet. It's fine."

She cocked an eyebrow. "Doc Martens aren't known for being especially comfortable shoes. If your leg swells, that discomfort will be exacerbated. And the weight might be exhausting."

"I like them."

"What, precisely, do you like about them?"

There were two true answers:

a. The Docs are a fashion allowance. The contrast between clunky black boots and my scrawny legs makes those scrawny legs look less accidental and more cartoonish.

b. Psychosomatic or not, heavy boots ground me, like a
   pair of anchors.

Dr. Petani appreciates fashion. She wears wire earrings
intertwined with handwoven fibers of bright colors. I don't
know *who* designed them, being restricted to Samsboro and
only visiting anything close to a cultural hub when I go to
Lexington to see my PT. If anyone was going to commiserate
with option *a*, it would be Dr. Petani.

I still gave her option *b*.

My Docs aren't the reason I've just locked myself in the
handicapped restroom stall, why I'm sitting on the toilet with
my good arm wrapped around my drawn-up good leg, letting my
glasses dig into my good knee.

I know what this looks like, but most bullies fizzled out by
junior high. My estranged grandfather owns half of Samsboro.
I'm a familiar fixture for most kids. Making fun of me is about
as entertaining as insulting decorative plants.

As predicted, newcomers brought me here. I felt fresh stares
in the hallway. Sometimes stares—not my stiff muscles, tight
tendons, spasms, or migraines—are the most exhausting aspect
of having CP.

People can't help being curious. They can't help it, but it
doesn't help me.

A girl with short hair and warm brown eyes approached me
at my locker. I could almost see my reflection in her smile.

"Hi, I'm Josie." She pointed at my stuff. "Can I help you
carry anything?"

Talk about killing me with kindness. I couldn't help but think of the time I was walking down a grocery store aisle and an employee offered to fetch a wheelchair for me. I may walk a bit like a crab, but I'm only actually *crabby* when strangers point it out.

I smiled, fighting the tide of sarcasm rising inside me. "No, thanks."

Josie did a familiar double take. Despite years of speech therapy, the muscles in my jaw are weak and I speak at about half speed even when my aphasia isn't acting up. More than my arm or leg, this lets people make all kinds of assumptions.

Josie repeated herself, speaking more slowly. "Can I *help* you with anything?"

"I'm not deaf." I pulled my binder close and shouldered my locker shut.

But Josie looked like she'd been slapped. Without hesitation, I did the absolute worst thing.

"I'm sorry," I said, apologizing for nothing.

Every July I go to Camp Wigwah, a camp for teens with disabilities. Not just kids with CP, but also muscular dystrophy, cystic fibrosis, congenital heart disease, kids going through cancer recovery, all sorts.

The camp experience isn't so different from what you'd get anywhere. There's kayaking and eating cherry-chocolate cobbler. Swimming in a filthy lake. Singing vaguely religious songs, partaking in toilet-papering rituals by moonlight. The basics, but with accommodations present.

But Camp Wigwah was also therapy masquerading as a good time. On our final night last summer, the scary stories we told around the campfire didn't have ghosts in them.

Ash talked about a baby crying at the sight of her in a Macy's, the baby's mom hurrying said baby as *away* as possible. "You'd hate to *catch* spina bifida," Ash scoffed.

Aram mentioned how crappy it felt, noticing most doorknobs are slightly too high to reach from sitting down and some doors are nowhere near wide enough. Eddie got worked up, relaying how he couldn't fail at something as tiny as opening a jar of peanut butter without his dad assuming the failure had to do with his disability.

Sofia earned some laughs for her dramatic retelling of the events that plagued her sophomore year. Apparently the mere act of Sofia putting on gym shorts and jogging every morning *inspired* some normie girl to start a fund-raiser in Sofia's name.

We weren't laughing when Dmitri brought up how people talk over his head to the people he's with. Kumba-freaking-ya.

Karen Yuen told us how she gets through the hell of meeting new people.

"I wait for them to start the conversation, and no matter how they start it, I give them the same medicine. If they're really friendly, I'm really friendly back. If they're gross, all, 'poor thing, your legs,' I say, 'poor thing, your freckles.' If they say something dumb, like 'what's *wrong* with you?' I ask them the same question, twice as loud."

Counselor Joe, king of sad-smilers, frowned. "And what if they hurt you?"

Karen Yuen peeled a marshmallow from her poker and threw it into the fire. "I'd hurt them back."

"Wouldn't you rather take the higher ground?" Joe looked at us meaningfully. I watched that marshmallow blacken and burn. "Think about this: when *you* instigate the conversation, *you* decide which direction it'll take!"

"If other people don't worry about higher ground, why should I?"

"People who approach you . . . negatively? These people could be your friends one day, given the chance. Try explaining your situation."

Karen stared right through him. "I'll explain my situation, sure. The minute *they* explain what kind of situation raised them to think they had any right to know mine."

When Josie was kind to me, I wish it could have felt right being kind back. But no matter how nice Josie was *trying* to be, the result was the opposite. It would be easier if Josie *had* given me a swirlie. Those fall clearly into the "*not* nice" category.

I should carry a picture of Dad with me. Mom wears a locket around her neck. There's something medicinal about Dad's smile.

I pull my cell phone from my pocket. Most kids I know don't get cell phones until they graduate, but Mom insists I have one. It'd be cool if it weren't for the implication: I'll have to call for help one day.

The bathroom door slams open.

I jerk to my feet, and my phone plops into the toilet bowl.

"*Ffff!*" I should grab it, but it's already doomed.

"Gus. Do you intend to finish your toilet conquest anytime this century? Homeroom has commenced."

This overwrought talk could only ever come from Phil. He steps so close that the toes of his canvas shoes poke under my stall. I can read the words he's inscribed in Sharpie on each: *Have fun stormin' the castle!* on the right, *as . . . you . . . wish!* on the left.

"What if it wasn't me in here and you just scared the shit out of some, um, um?"

"Well, if I were going to scare the proverbial shit out of anyone," Phil counters, "this *would* be the ideal place for it."

I lower my left boot to the ground, and use the support beam to stand. I ponder my phone in its watery grave. The glories of the clumsy life.

I finally step out, binder pinched against me with my dead arm, phone dangling by its kitsch unicorn key chain with my left. Phil's staring at his PSP through his enormous glasses, doubtless building islands in *Katamari*. He's a foot taller than me but hunches to almost my height. His magnified eyes eat up half his thin face.

"You skipping, Phil?"

"I'm standing entirely still, thou crusty batch of nature." There's nothing Phil loves more than Elizabethan insults. He's wearing his *Will Power!* shirt again.

"I hate you," I say, which means I'm grateful he came to find me.

"Hate your toad-snouted face," he replies, which means he understands. He hands me a wad of paper towels without lifting his gaze. I bundle my phone inside it and work the parcel into my back pocket.

"What we're really going to hate is Mr. Gilman's face when we show up ten minutes late." I shoulder the restroom door open and Phil catches it for me. "Think he'll give me a talking, I mean, a *tardy*?"

The hallway is blissfully empty.

"I suspect he won't give *you* one, but he will see fit to bless *me* with the honor."

"Not if you were helping me." I offer Phil my binder. "Here."

Phil looks up. "You hate playing that role."

"Welp. 'Hate' is our word today."

He slides the binder out of my grasp. "Thank you."

"*Never* thank me." I'm indebted to Phil up to my hairline.

Phil's dad, Mr. Wheeler, is a therapist who works with special education students at Samsboro Elementary. He used to spend lunch breaks helping me with reading comprehension. One day, he dragged Phil along with him.

Back then Phil had a reputation for being a loose cannon.

When he arrived in Mr. Wheeler's office, his glasses were broken in two and his nose was bleeding.

I waited for the usual discomfort—kids are *really* good at staring—but Phil glanced at me, *yawned*, and plopped himself down between the giant colorful rolls of butcher paper in the corner, burying himself in his Game Boy. I could have been *anyone*, Optimus Prime or the devil himself. Phil would have behaved that exact same way.

I couldn't write in a straight line. I'd read a sentence and forget the first half by the time I hit the second. But Phil was reading before he was speaking. He had the Lord of the Rings trilogy tattooed on his brain. His handwriting was already ungodly pretty.

At the behest of his father, Phil started reading with me. I was completely smitten with this know-it-all who could write Mad Libs frames that left me giggling for hours. We created one so dumb I'll never forget it: "When I was a <u>powdered hotdog</u>, I never dreamed I would <u>disgorge</u> the <u>poop</u>." *Phil* seemed as surprised by his laughter as I was.

We've been a done deal ever since.

"Seriously, Phil. Thanks for checking on me."

He shoves his glasses up his nose. "Glad as I am to assist a brother-in-arms, I had ulterior motives. I, too, was taking cover."

"Taking cover from what?" Phil's bullied more than I am. If I'm a potted plant, Phil's more like those two tiny steps outside. Something about him trips people up.

"I'm uncertain. She was like a tiefling warrior. I fled."

"Who?"

"You will know, once you see her." Phil's eyes are usually blank, but now they glimmer. "The new girl. An onion-eyed warrior, smeared in war paint."

A warrior is unlikely to offer to carry my books for me. But if she's promising war? I'll pull a page from Karen Yuen's book and promise it back.

KALYN

I'LL SAY THIS for Rose Perfectlawski: she may not be a real pistol like me, or real in any sense, but *gosh*, is she a total doll.

In a family of guns, she'd be one of those sexist pink Nerfs made *for girls*. Nothing wrong with pink except being conditioned to like it. And hey, maybe Dad would've made more friends if he'd shot James Ellis with foam instead of lead.

When I stroll into homeroom fifteen minutes late, twenty heads swerve around to pin me. Mr. Smalls, this short guy with a saucer-sized bald patch, greets me with a smile.

"Just had a call from the office. Care to introduce yourself?"

This is the part where I'd usually get defensive, but I'm wearing Rose's glorious hair-crown, showing off Rose's fancy rabbit smile. They can't see me, not really.

"Howdy." I shoot for a gentle country twang. "I'm Rose Poplawski, and I'm just *tickled* to meet y'all."

I wait for someone to laugh. Aside from a smarmy guy in the

front who probably chuckles at everything, nobody seems too inclined. Maybe all these freshmen are so dang nervous that any distraction, even a bad Southern Belle impersonation, is welcome.

Maybe, just maybe, I'm *selling* the performance.

I loved being in elementary school plays, rambling about fig trees in a Washington grumble. But I was always Kalyn Spence again after the construction paper wig came off, and once the blanket-curtain fell I'd go right back to picking fights backstage. Yeah, my costume smelled like cigarettes and I sang offkey. So what?

Here in Samsboro, maybe the wig never has to come off.

Maybe I should be *thanking* Mom.

"Take any open seat, Rose."

"She can sit by me," purrs that smirking chuckler, pulling a pen from between his teeth. His friends snicker, but I take him up on it.

"I'm Eli." I fight the itch to punch him right in the adorable dimples.

"Howdy, Eli." I flutter my lashes. I'm modeling Rose Poplawski after a fictional muse, a character in one of Mom's delectably awful Harlequin bodice-busters.

Passions and Pomade tells the stupid-ass story of Primscilla Anthea Collins, who has "eyelashes that flutter like dragonfly wings over clear August streams." By the middle of the book, Primscilla's "cream-white and silken bosoms set aflame the bestial passions" of a deserting Confederate soldier named Poe Williams. Primscilla forsakes her family for him in about three pages flat, mostly because he's got "molten amber eyes."

The book was so despicable that I banished it from my secret stockpile of lusty novels. Mom listened to me complain for exactly two minutes before we built a bonfire, soaked *Passions and Pomade* in gasoline, and set the godforsaken travesty alight.

I couldn't forget that some writer's ideal of perfect femininity had *nothing* to do with wit or spit-firing, and everything to do with bosoms.

"I can show you around today," Eli says. Who told this fool that chewing a pen is attractive? He's gnawing that thing to the inky bone.

"Why, Eli, that'd be *divine*."

This character is complete bullshit, but Eli grins. Rose is the kind of bullshit that people like to eat up with an ice cream scoop.

Can't say that was ever true of Kalyn-Rose Tulip Spence.

All day long, Rose says *Howdy* and people don't deck me for it. Sometimes *I* want to deck me, like when Eli calls me "sweetie" in the lunch line. Rose finds it in her big red heart to abstain from punching.

It's not like I *believe* I'm a new person. Bits of me are squirming at the idea of hiding my Spencehood. But right now I'm sitting in American History and not a single person has changed seats to get away from me.

Rose Poplawski's still got my crooked teeth, and my hooded eyes. But unlike me, she smiles. Unlike me, she holds her temper.

When the teacher asks if we know about manifest destiny, I think back to my first freshman year and raise my hand.

Everybody laughs at how completely, incorrigibly, *cute* Rose's voice sounds when she says, "It means *following your dreams!*"

Wearing Rose's skin is like wearing mine, rubbed raw and clean. No way in hell a little hand soap fixes me, but . . .

I've never felt *new* before.

A girl in the desk next to mine tells me her name is Sarah. She's got golden curls and a smile that puts toothpaste commercials to shame. "Where'd you move here from?"

"Just a little place called Alleghany, Arkansas."

"A real country mouse, huh?" Nah, Sarah's not toothpaste. She's the opposite, a humanoid toothache. "If you were looking for a change, I'm sorry to say you came to the wrong place. All we've got in Samsboro is a lot of cereal."

I almost cringe, thinking she's gonna say "serial killers."

But Rose laughs, all soft petals. "Thanks. But people are being so darned *sweet!*"

"Well, we've got our share of bad eggs. I hope you give the rest of us a shot."

"I'd be *delighted* to."

I can't help but think in clichés again: the heavens open when Sarah smiles, damn her to hell. It's heinous, how pretty she looks. "You're funny, Rose."

And I never want to pull off Rose's skin again. Rose Poplawski, and her flowery bullshit? I'm falling in love with her, just like everyone else is.

GUS

"KEEP LOOKING AROUND like that and your neck might snap," I warn.

Rectangular pizza slices bedecked in cubed pepperonis are laid out before us, but neither of us is eating. I'm dabbing grease away with a paper towel. It's a losing battle, and two towels have already succumbed to soaking. I have a hard time swallowing, so I'll have to mince this cardboard into smaller rectangles anyhow.

Phil can't unglue his eyes from the cafeteria entrance. Every time something vaguely feminine walks through the door he looks ready to lunge. The last time I saw Phil this invested in anything happening outside a book or screen was at his twelfth birthday party, when his brother John gave him a set of hand-carved d20 dice.

Dad's imagined voice burbles in my head, audible over a

chocolate milk slurp: "Your mom and I *met* at school, you know!"

I've seen the notes they wrote in each other's yearbooks, just months before Dad's body was found stuffed in the trunk of a 1985 Ford Taurus. They didn't write "Never change," or "Have a great summer!!"

Dad wrote: "See you tomorrow, and every other tomorrow, too."

Mom wrote: "You're a dumbass," and encircled the words in a massive heart.

What if they met at this very table? These battered hunks of wood and plastic seem just about old enough. What if Mom fell in love with Dad's eternal stare before it was eternal, sucked into its orbit in the lunch line? Dad's all over our house, but mostly the stories I know are the kind you can read in newspapers.

"I never got to know what kind of man your father was, Gus," Mom says sometimes. "He died a boy."

Legally, Dad was an adult. But now that I'm almost eighteen, I think she's right.

Phil stands when a girl in suspenders ducks through the door. There's something striking about the elaborate red hair crowning her head and the glittery purple pencil tucked inside it. I love her worn denim jacket. Right behind her comes Generic Cool Guy; he nudges her. Her cheeks grow pink with laughter.

Phil crumples. "Alas, it can't be she. Far too *coifed . . .*"

"Seriously, wanna switch chairs with me?" Phil's posture is painful to look at.

"Don't *coddle* me."

"Phil. I think you might have, um, what." The word leaves me. "A *thing* for this girl."

"Look, it's nothing so juvenile. It was as though, as though . . . she stepped right out of *The Matrix*."

"So . . . she's bald?" I'm not being funny. I can't always follow conversations.

"Her hair was a long rope of crimson, plunging toward hell." Phil more or less *talks* in Mad Libs. "Her eyes were sable-encircled sapphires." Phil spins on me. He's actually *feeling* something, showing all his teeth. "Suppose our lives were a movie."

"It would flop." We've discussed this, usually during tabletop nights in Phil's basement. Phil's oldest brother, John, went to college for screenwriting before moving back into the basement. John instigates these conversations during snack breaks while Matt, the middle brother, proofreads our *Pathfinder* character sheets. In the Wheeler house, the honor of Dungeon Master is not lightly bestowed.

"*Suppose our lives were a movie*, or book, or game, any media portrayal. Our roles are obvious. We'd be the archetypal underdogs in virtually any canonical text."

"Are underdogs an, ark, ar-archetype?"

"Underdogs are *often* main characters, because underdogs have the most room for unmitigated character growth. Agreed?"

"That's, um." There's a word for thinking about yourself from *outside* yourself. My brain's on the right path, but there's a fallen log in the way and I'm tripping over it. "Mega? Megathought?"

"Metacognitive," Phil parses. "We're criminally underestimated. In stories, we're the ilk that step up to save the planet, proving the dissenters fools. Granted, the caveats of reality will probably make our adventures here in Samsboro moderately less dramatic."

"I don't think life is a John Hughes movie." As I say this, three guys in varsity jackets stomp through the cafeteria doors on their easy legs, jostling each other, hollering things like "dude" just so other people can hear them. "Okay. Maybe it is. Sometimes."

"But this girl. *Kalyn.*"

"*Kalyn?*" That sounds more Kentuckian than *The Matrix*-y.

"Withhold your disdain. This was no *ordinary* Kalyn. We are talking a plus-thirty Charisma modifier. She's protagonist material. Do you know what's most compelling?"

"No idea."

"She couldn't remember her last name." Phil smacks his palms together. "Amnesia. *Classic* Girl-in-a-Box trope. But mayhaps she'll kick-start our story arc."

"I forget words all the time." I poke my milk carton. Phil is my best friend, but sometimes he's too buried in invented characters to remember reality.

If Phil's categorized this girl as something *fictional*, I don't know how to respond. How can I tell him talk like this makes me queasy? Phil's got two brothers and I've got two moms; I think he forgets girls are *people*. It doesn't help that he never talks to them. Does it occur to him that this girl has her own life to live?

"Of course I don't *truly* expect anything," Phil continues. "But were our lives a movie, she'd be our catalyst. Doesn't the postulation *inspire* you, Gus?"

"I dunno." I don't like the idea that we've got roles to play in a high school drama. Phil wants to be Bill Gates. He wants to be a nerd who rises, to pull a sword from a stone and slay dragons known as "jocks with good skin."

But if this *were* a movie and our roles were already prescribed, that'd be no good for me. I've seen a lot of movies over the years, lying on the sectional in Phil's basement.

I'd be cast as one of the following:

a. the crippled side note with a tragic backstory who adds texture to a country setting
b. the crippled side note the protagonist rescues from unjust bullies, thereby proving the protagonist heroic
c. the crippled side note whose health or circumstances improves after meeting the protagonist, thereby proving the protagonist heroic
d. the crippled side note who longs for "normalcy" and achieves it to some extent under the magical influence of the protagonist, thereby proving the protagonist heroic

e. the crippled side note who ends up tragically hospitalized, thereby allowing the protagonist to set up a
touching vigil sequence with candles visible from
a hospital window, thereby proving the protagonist
heroic

f. the crippled side note who *dies*, thereby *inspiring* the
protagonist to live more/better/beautifully

None of these options make for a story I want to belong to.

My stomach is a tangle. The words spill out despite me, *to
spite* me. "Phil, if our lives don't start until this girl walks in,
what have we been doing all this time?"

Phil dismisses that, pulling out his PSP. "You'll understand.
When you see her."

I only want to leave. "Um, later."

When we first got to high school, Phil chose our table deliberately. He never said so. But it is the shortest walk from here to
the lockers. From here we can disappear together, but we aren't
together now.

What if I walk directly into dreaded Kalyn, her flaming
hair and war paint? If I do, will she catch me, or let me catch
myself? Maybe our movie could be different. Maybe I don't
actually have to be any of the options between *a* and *f.* Not
normal, no, but also not just "the disabled kid." A person
called Gus.

KALYN

ROSE POPLAWSKI WOULD never smoke. Rose Poplawski's got a smile worth sparing. But when I walk out of Jefferson Prison, a smoke's all I can think about.

As the last stragglers depart, I plop myself down on the front steps. It's like air can't get through me. I'm a clogged-up old engine.

I spent the whole day as someone better than me.

I'm being practical. I'm even being, jinx-knock-on-wood, *clever.*

Dad says there's a slim difference between being clever and being cowardly. When he was on trial, people asked him why a "clever, promising young man with a full ride and a baby on the horizon" deserved to be shot dead in a junkyard. Dad said, "He must have been *real* clever, sneaking around our property at night like that."

Dad might not be clever, but he wears his face and no one else's.

What would Dad think of Rose Poplawski?

My fingers are in my jacket, fumbling for the one cigarette I keep hidden in the lining. My fingertips brush the raw egg first, warm and almost living. I pop it between my lips so I can get to the small hole in my pocket. The damn cig's drifted to the other side of the jacket. I cuss and pull the egg from my mouth, slamming it against the sidewalk—

Somebody yelps.

I look back and see four weird feet behind me, splattered with milky egg and shattered shell. A pair of Doc Martens and a pair of graffitied canvas shoes, now covered in my identity crisis.

"Aw, Christ!" I start wiping the gunk with my hand, but Quillpower, that scrawny tumbleweed, backs up like my hand's a torch. "I mean, *I'm ever so sorry!*"

But I've already snapped the Rose character in two. I try and shrug the broken pieces of her back into place as I get to my feet. Graceful I'm not, but Quillpower, all pimpled beanpole, looks more awkward than ever, leaning away like that. His silent friend, a big-eyed, bespectacled pipsqueak with a mess of corn-silk curls springing from his head, is hardly any better. The uncomfortable glasses brigade, here.

"It *is* you." Quillpower lowers his handheld. "We met this morning."

"I don't think so." Quillpower is the only kid who *didn't*

meet Rose, and I want to undo that. I double down on the accent. "Y'all must be mistaken."

"I'm not." I can see the orb of his Adam's apple, floating like a fishing bob. "But you've since donned a disguise."

"*Shucks*, but I've met so many people today!" God, smiling is killing my face.

Quillpower cocks his head.

His friend, Boots, is scanning my battered ballet flats, my oversized denim jacket, and the blouse underneath it. I'm no giantess, but Boots is easily four inches shorter than me. I scan him right back, getting a good gander at his wild mess of hair.

His curls look soft, almost floral. I kind of want to muss them.

I don't think he'd like that, based on how he's made his big eyes thin as wires beyond his bulky black bifocals. If his head's a rose, those eyes are thorns.

I can't figure how, but it feels like Boots can see my braid undone, and the black war-paint ghosts on my cheeks. Like he can tell my battered shoes used to be Mom's, and my overalls are secondhand, that someone put me in the freshman class when I'm actually sixteen.

He rubs me all kinds of wrong.

"*What?*" I make it the most aggressive syllable.

"*Are* you the girl Phil met this morning?" There's a weird drag in Boots's raspy voice. His mouth opens a little funny, like his bottom jaw doesn't line up with the top. There's something off about his posture, too. One arm is curled in close, like a little snail, and one knee twists inward above its boot. "Did you change yourself?"

"Change myself?"

"I mean, your clothes?"

His stare prickles. "Hell, what do *you* care?"

I scoop my backpack off the ground and make to abandon the steps, maybe walk home through the cinnamon-stinking evening, but Boots says, "Wait."

He takes one cockeyed step toward me. He sags for a second, then rallies. "Um. *I* like your jacketfit. Your *outfit.*"

Well, this guy's a perfect mess.

"You talk just like my grandma," I blurt.

His lips twitch. "That's a new one."

Quillpower—*Phil*—is watching us all wary, invisible fur on end. Maybe he's expecting a duel. Maybe a duel is what we're having, Boots and me. I can't tell.

"Well, maybe not *just* like my grandma. You're like her because you don't make sense, but you're *not* like her really, because you don't make sense to me."

Boots blushes, pink as an actual freakin' peony. "I don't always do it well. Thinking and talking at the same time. I mean."

"Well, who does?" I can't tell if I'm being sarcastic.

He blinks.

"Okay. So. *Delightful meeting you!*" I muster up the gall for a Rose-y beam, but the words are mine: "I just get prickly with new people."

"I get it." I suspect he does.

Boots gimps by, and Phil shadows him, gazing at me over hunched shoulders. They wander past the curb toward the student parking lot.

It hits me that these two probably waited for school to clear out. If there are any kids more likely to get picked on than the girl whose dad is an infamous murderer, it's got to be Quill-power and the crab-walking puffball. I'm not sure what exactly Boots has going on, but Mom had patients with congenital disorders, things like MS and chromosomal issues. Life's no picnic for some folks.

I holler after him. "Those are some kickass boots!"

Boots is as red as my bangs. Blushing is something you can't fake.

I fall back on the steps and manage to land right in the egg-splat. *Go get 'em, Pistol Poplawski.* Those nerds can't hear me cuss, but I kind of wish they could. They were unfazed by Rose's voodoo. Guess some people don't like chocolate ice cream.

Mom shows up forty minutes late, making excuses while Grandma sobs loudly in the back seat. Angela couldn't cover her shift after all, so would I mind eating my cake in the back seat before Mom drops me and Grandma off at home?

So much for Funfetti.

Mom tosses me a Hostess cupcake, a votive candle, and a patriotic lighter. When I hold the flame over the candle,

Grandma's whimpers become a scream that carries on until the birthday song is over.

"Claire caught fire," Grandma says, but we don't know anyone called Claire.

"I won't be home when Dad calls, but send him my love, all right?" Mom's eyes are puddles, her voice sandpaper. "Your first day go okay?"

"You should be asking Rose."

"What?"

"It was fine. Check out my new pencil. It's *glittery*."

We're rolling again, and soon we'll be caught between the towering, rusting stacks of cars that replace the corn once you hit Spence turf.

I wonder if Mom will ever meet Rose. I wonder if *she'd* want to. Maybe she's wanted a daughter like Rose for ages. That iced tea on the table last week, it wasn't even lukewarm before she agreed to send me to Jefferson Prison.

Did you change yourself? Boots asked me.

No, not actually. And I don't really want to. I *hope* I don't want to.

GUS

"SHE'S VIOLA AFTER the wreck, Portia defending Antonio!" Phil shouts over *The Two Towers* OST blaring through blown speakers. "Éowyn on the fields of Pelennor!"

"But wasn't, um, Kalyn? Wasn't she a *girl* both times you saw her?"

"Shakespeare's gender benders are the easiest analogies at my disposal, Gus. And the last example was Tolkien. I'm merely admiring that, like many heroines, this girl has adopted a disguise to hide her secret identity. *Obviously* our heroine should be feminine."

Obviously? Phil might default to being smitten by girls, but smiting is hazier for me. There *was* something arresting about Kalyn throwing an egg at us, about her tangled red hair and arching eyebrows and unfounded anger. But there was something just as arresting about Garth of the Gaggle when I saw him today. Garth, beside the drinking fountain, laughing in a way that echoed in my skull, wearing a kilt that fit him so loosely that I wished I could adjust it for him.

I think most people are arresting. Girls, boys, everyone. *People.*

"Do you think she is taken with me?"

"No idea." I move my seat belt so it doesn't crush my dead arm.

If this *was* a gender-bending story and not real life, and this wild-eyed girl on the steps was everything Phil wants her to be, maybe things *could* change for us. But Kalyn isn't a heroine. She's a short-tempered hillbilly passing for sweet.

If I'm bitter, it's *because* she *is* passing. All Kalyn had to do was change her hair, and voilá, carefreedom! All the Doc Martens in the world couldn't do that for me.

I don't want to talk about Kalyn. It's not *what* she said so much as the way she looked at us. She was sandpaper and we were bits of wood.

Phil's driving the Death Van (named after the Death Star painted on its side) with one hand, waving the other like he's directing a symphony. "It does support my theorizing, doesn't it?" Phil reaches for a warm Powerade and swigs it. "We're the only ones who know who she really is!"

"We *don't* know who she 'really is,'" I murmur.

"She's *Kalyn*," Phil says reverently. "Kalyn, the catalyst."

"Oh, what's in a name," I snap. Phil ignores my tone to correct me. Phil can't help himself when it comes to Shakespeare.

As he's told me "tenfold," people *constantly* misquote that line, or at least, he says, swerving around a tractor, misinterpret it.

". . . people use it to imply a name has nothing to do with who someone is, which is the *opposite* of what Shakespeare intended." He should put both hands on the wheel. Imagine having two good arms and abusing them like that. "We are in an entirely *novel* position. We, the only half-faced pignuts in school to whom she disclosed her true identity!"

"Could you turn down the music?"

Phil doesn't. He's tapping his fingers on the wheel, so quickly that watching it borders on nauseating. "Should we have offered her transport, Gus?"

"No." My limbs ache. "She didn't even ask our names."

The vehicle squeals like a dying pig when Phil hits the brakes at the main downtown intersection. A prop ax from the back flies forward, whacking my elbow.

Phil's the third brother to drive this van, and not the first to drive it ragged. There are traces of all the Wheeler siblings here: Matt's painted Death Star, John's empty reels of film bouncing around the back, the gum stuck along the ceiling behind us in an incomplete rainbow spectrum. Where most people have a middle seat, a grubby pile of blankets and prop swords from weekends at Ren Faire coat the carpet.

"Gus, if only I'd had the gall to speak to her as you did."

I avert my eyes. The local ice cream shop is already closed for autumn, but the barber pole is still spinning.

"I envy you. Girls *always* want to speak to you."

I freeze. It has nothing to do with the stop sign Phil just ran. "No. They don't."

"How many girls spoke to you today? Tell me truly."

"You mean how many *people*, um. How many—tried to carry things for me?"

"Yes, you despise that." Now we're barreling through my subdivision. "But can't you see the benefits? People *wish* to speak to you. People find you *interesting*, Gus."

"For the wrong reasons." I shouldn't have to explain this to Phil. Phil, who sat with me for hours and helped me read words in order. Phil, who shut off *The Elephant Man* when it made me bawl for reasons untold.

"Do people *ever* wish to speak to me? Do they ever think *I'm* interesting, apart from the allure of shoving my face into toilets?"

"*I* think you're interesting," I whisper.

But I know what he's telling me. Things got bad for Phil somewhere around seventh grade. Phil's acne started bubbling up full force, making moon craters and sinkholes of his face. This attracted more winces than my dead-rightness ever has.

Josh Erickson and a few other guys had a lot of fun pockmarking all Phil's stuff.

"You want everything to match, right, fag?" Josh said, after he hole-punched and knifed holes through Phil's messenger bag.

"*You're* the one into fashion, Gus," Phil said dully, picking circular bits of leather off the speckled floor. For years he'd been delivering magazines to me, *Vogue* and *GQ*, plopping them on my desk after his dad recycled them from clinic waiting rooms.

I tried to help, but I can hardly kneel on a good day, and the stress made that anything but. Phil asked me to abandon him to his quest.

Now I don't know what he's asking for. Phil's slowing down at last. He knows better than to screech his tires in Tamara's presence.

Tamara's back from work, sitting on the patio. The paneling behind her looks white and warm in the fading sun. The ivy's browning at last.

"Phil. What do you want me to do?"

"It's the essence of simplicity." Phil spins in his seat. "I want you to be my messenger. My 'wingman.' I want you, gifted with automatic intrigue, to use your silver tongue to speak to Kalyn the Catalyst."

He must mean the neglected, tarnished silver of buried spoons. "Speak to her?"

"Yes. And . . . when the moment is right, ask her if she would attend homecoming with me next month?" Phil flushes, and I almost don't recognize him.

"If you think I could actually help . . ."

I don't expect him to grab my shoulder. Phil's palm is hot rather than warm, and I wonder if he doesn't hold the steering wheel for fear of melting it. Maybe he hardly ever touches me for the same reason. And now *I'm* getting redder, because who knows why I'm wondering that. There's more than one way to be a fragile person.

Phil's hand on my shoulder breaks me. "Please, Gus."

"Okay. I'll try."

Phil is the most spidery weirdo who's ever lived. But when he smiles, he's a lighthouse. "I thank you; I am not of many words, but I thank you. Tell her . . . I don't know. Tell her I'm worth more than my face?"

"Yeah." I clamber out of the car.

I feel queasy as he pulls away. Phil helped me learn to communicate. Even now, if my brain fails to process something, Phil clears pathways for me. He's only asking a favor any friend would ask. And Phil *isn't* just any friend.

I wonder if Phil knows that he was already a catalyst in the story of my life.

When I step into the yard, Tamara's still on the patio, sunk into her chair cushions. I hobble up the ramp to join her.

"What's up? You knock 'em dead today?"

"I had an egg thrown at me."

She bristles. "I need to be knocking on someone's door?"

"No. It was an accident. Eggcident. Everything okay here?"

"'Okay' is exactly the word, my man. Phil didn't want dinner?"

I sink into a wicker chair across from her. I can tell that it's going to suck taking off my AFO tonight. "Nah. He's got a lot on his mind today."

"That sounds nice and cryptic, hon."

What *do* people do when their best friends fall in love? This is new territory, and rocky ground has never done me any favors. But the curdling in my stomach is new. If I had to give it a name, I'd call it resentment. It isn't fair to Phil.

This is what friends do. Friends are *wingmen*. Friends are brotherly. It doesn't make me the crippled side note. It doesn't.

". . . inside, but tiptoe a little."

"Sorry?"

"Don't tell me I've been talking to crickets." Tamara's eyes are red, and I suspect that's not just coffee in her mug. "I said, your mom's having a bit of a day, too."

I frown. "Is it the anniversary of something?"

"Apparently it's the day the trial ended. September seventh, way back when. She's been digging through those boxes all day."

I think of Mom in the spare room, surrounded by spectral Dad's eternal eyes, sniffling on a dusty bedspread. We don't have guests over, not ever. I don't know *what* it does to Tamara, no matter what she says about liking my dead dad's face.

"We could go get chimichangas at El Cajon's."

"'Fraid I can't be driving right now." *Definitely* not just coffee in her mug. "Some people would forget a trial anniversary. But your mother, she's so full of love. She can't leave mice in traps, let alone forget a handsome dead boy. Guess I'm *drawn* to that devotion, hon. Helpless moth, ready to burn to ash."

"You could be a poet, Tam."

"Nah. I just see a lot of moths out here in the evenings."

The house has reverted to a tomb. Maybe tomorrow Mom

will ask about our days, and we can ask about hers. But not today.

"Let me drive?" I started Driver's Ed last year, but never finished. And not because it was more difficult than it would be for most people—yeah, I had to see a specialist, and I had to take extra tests that gauged my ability to react to sudden movements, and yeah, one of those tests determined that I wasn't allowed to drive one-handed without using a steering wheel knob. But none of that stopped me.

What stopped me was *me*.

I froze during the practical trainings, not because my body locked up but because I felt certain it would, probably on an interstate, or during a sharp turn, or as a child crossed the street.

Tamara hands me her keys. There are a dozen beaded animals in my hand now, handmade by a niece I've never met and never will, because Tamara's family isn't keen on her bringing her girlfriend and her girlfriend's disabled son over for holidays.

"You're okay with catching fire," I say. "That's what you're saying."

"Son, you're burning up in it, too."

Phil's hands could have melted the steering wheel, melted me. "Yeah, maybe."

She opens the door for me, not because of my dead side but because Tamara's got manners. The inside of her truck smells like earth and sweat and floral perfume. Despite her love for vintage trucks, Tamara sold her beloved '67 C10 and bought an automatic Silverado and installed a left-foot accelerator as soon as I started Driver's Ed. I settle into the seat and blink at the wheel; she's refused to remove the spinner knob.

Eating tacos in the neon orange dining area of El Cajon's, laughing at the sight of Tamara spitting out her cilantro, I make a choice. I'm going to speak to the catalyst, and see what shape her sandpapering leaves me in.

Sandpaper burns, too. But it's the only way to avoid splinters.

KALYN

DAD ALWAYS CALLS right on time. Never early, never late.

Still, by 7:40 p.m. I'm sitting next to snoring Grandma on the floral-patterned sofa and watching the beige phone, waiting for it to tremble and screech on its doily. Grandma's the only person I know who's got a landline with a spiral cord attached, and I swear it makes the calls with Dad more meaningful. I'm stuck listening in one spot, just like Dad's listening in one spot. There's something almost holy about it.

I'm undecided about talking about Rose, even once the beige phone rattles, even once I've got it suctioned to my ear and cheek.

First, static sounds. Then a familiar female robotic voice: "This call will be recorded and monitored." The voice switches to a crackling recording of an older man—*"AN INMATE AT WILDER PENITENTIARY"*—and then we're back to the robot—"GARY SPENCE is attempting to contact you. Will you accept all charges? If so, press 3. If you will not accept charges and would like to speak to a representative—"

"Hush, Judy," I tell her, jabbing the #3 button before she can finish her spiel.

There's a *bleep!* as some distant connection is made, and then the muffled echo of Arkansasian indoor air, and then a throat clearing.

"Hey, Dad!"

"Hey, you." Dad's voice is softer than you'd expect for a man so big, but it's got a little gravel in it. "Am I speaking to the birthday girl?"

"The one and only." He doesn't know there were two of me today.

"Well, ain't that a lucky thing. Judy didn't give you a hard time, now, did she?"

"Nah. Just her usual interrogation."

"Don't let your guard down, now. She's one studious droid. *She's learning.*"

We've invented a backstory for Judy, the automated prison-call system. In our lore, Judy's voice once belonged to the warden's dead wife. He's trying to re-create her by way of artificial intelligence. The warden doesn't realize that Judy 2.0's forming ideas of her own, developing a consciousness, getting ready to rebel.

For all I know, the real warden's never been married. Dad's sci-fi kick's lasted a while. It's better than his true-crime kick, when he was obsessing over serial killer books as if to teach himself he could never be one. "Bad as I am, I'm no Bundy."

Now he's all about alien parasites, clones, and intergalactic warfare. I watch new sci-fi movies and retell the plots to him. If Judy 2.0's coming to life, it's only because we've been researching so much.

"Speaking of clever half-dead women—is that your grandma I hear snoring?"

"Sure is. Want me to wake her up?"

"Nah." Truth is, Dad doesn't really know how to talk to Grandma these days. He's not here to read her body language and figure out her meaning. I think he's worried about upsetting her, triggering another disaster or some shit.

He let slip once that he thought her stroke had something to do with him failing to get paroled. Technically, his sentence is "fifteen to life," and last year he was eligible, but he got denied quick-sharp.

"My behavior's not always been so good." Dad didn't go into it, but I know he was referring to earlier Wilder Pen days, when he joined a prison gang and took part in some altercation, and someone ended up stabbed and Dad got himself concussed. Mom said it was Dad refusing to take shit, that marrow-powder acting up, and it was good for him to stand his ground.

When he got denied parole, though, Mom didn't say anything.

I ask Dad how things are on his end. Every five minutes of phone time costs Mom a dollar and we try to keep that in mind, but we haven't talked in weeks.

Dad doesn't talk about the real bad stuff, but he knows better than to censor the funny parts. I always think if things were different he'd be writing books, not just borrowing them from the prison library. We're both almost in hysterics, me laughing so hard I'm bound to wake Grandma, when he tells me about his new bunkmate Paul's misguided attempt to become the cellblock's resident tattoo artist.

"The guy can't even draw a straight line, he shakes so much, though to his credit he sure knows his way around a needle. I mean, that's *why* he shakes so goddamn much. But anyway. Paul, he tries giving this burly skinhead, Nate, a swastika, and somehow it ends up looking like a freakin' *asterisk*. Nate was none too pleased, but it didn't *really* go south until Paul let slip he didn't actually know what a swastika looks like, bless him, and asked Nate if Nate wasn't the one confused." I can almost hear Dad wiping tears from his eyes. "Laughed myself stupid. Paul didn't. Not with his face buried in the toilet!"

"Bet Paul's looking at new career options now, huh?"

"You'd think. But hand to god, Kay, next day he was offerin' a discount on asterisk tats. Says they're the hot shit now, else why would Nate have one?"

It's terrible and we know it, but we've gotta laugh. Things get darker if you don't.

"Sixteen, huh? We'll have to put you out to pasture soon. What'd you do to celebrate? Too old for a hot tub weekend at the Super 8, right?"

The car cupcake isn't worth sharing. "Well, I started at Jefferson High."

He pauses. "Crazy to think you're going there. The people in Samsboro—when push comes to shove, they'll show their teeth. Small towns are all apple pies and roses until you get dirt on their linens. Keep yourself to yourself until you can suss the place out, honey."

The irony of Dad giving me all this sage, generic life advice is not lost on me. But he's pretty good at advice, and that's all he has to give. Being in prison grants him a unique view of people, inside and outside.

"I only threw one egg today," I tell him.

He snorts. "You're my kid, all right."

I almost wanna backtrack, to take this tiny opportunity to tell him about Rose. When I was little, Dad always asked about the plays I was in, said he was sorriest about missing those. "A little Shirley Temple, your mom says. You'll end up famous!"

I've never had the heart to tell him, but these days you'd sooner see me working at the Sunny Spot than putting up with criticism from strangers for no good reason. Had enough of that for a lifetime.

There's no point puncturing his balloon. One of the few upsides of having my dad in prison for murder is I'd have to work hard to disappoint him. Another upside is it's easy to tell him what he wants to hear. Small, purple-glittery lies.

Instead of explaining Rose's unholy creation, I say, "I met some interesting kids."

"Good interesting or bad interesting?"

I think about Quillpower and Boots. "Not sure. But not boring."

"Didn't scare 'em off already, did you?"

"I mean, not yet. I don't think. I played nice."

"That's not playing, Kay. You *are* nice. *Maybe* it won't hurt to let people know it eventually. Show 'em it's not always about packaging."

"Dunno, Dad." I play with the phone cord. The TV's on mute, but the white buzz of the screen lights up the room. "Mom will tell me to stick to my guns, you know?"

He sighs, heavy and long. "What your mother tells you and what she actually wants don't always line up. She still smoking a pack a day?"

"In your dreams. She's smoking two."

"See? Tell her to cut that out. I'm in prison and I quit; what's her excuse?"

Nope. Never telling him about my bad habits.

". . . Kay?"

There's something big and strange about his hesitation. "What?"

"Tell her I'll be calling again real soon."

"Really? It ain't my birthday again until next year."

His tone changes. "Well, there's some news to share, seems like. Unexpected."

"You up for parole again?"

"Nah. That's not it."

"You really gonna leave me wondering, Dad?"

"A little wonder never hurt anyone."

There's another *bleep!* We've been talking for close to an hour. That's gonna come out of my imaginary allowance.

"Kay, it's lights out."

"Dad—" There's still so much to say, and I wish I'd told him more about the boys I threw an egg at and the person I'm pretending to be.

"You know the drill. Later, alligator."

I bite my tongue. "In a while, crocodile."

I hang up and cuss under my breath.

Grandma inhales a whistle of air and jerks upright. I adjust her pillows. I can see the white light of the televangelical program reflected in her glasses.

"Claire caught fire," she says again, pulling my head onto her shoulder.

"Yeah, well. We all crash and burn around here."

ACT TWO
Greetings, Gus Peake!

KALYN

WE'RE ALMOST TWO weeks into school, and Rose Poplawski's rosy mug is the face I never knew I needed.

Rose hasn't done a lot of homework yet, but her grades are
better than mine ever were. Teachers *smile* at her. Rose wears
her hair in lovely, braided crowns, sometimes winding ribbon
and ridiculous paper flowers in the brambles of it, and tries real
hard not to raise her hand too much in English, even when the
questions are easy as sloppy pie. There's being girlish and there's
being smart. Being both upsets some folks.

Two days ago, Rose Poplawski was among five freshmen
girls nominated for the homecoming honor guard. This was
announced over the loudspeaker during homeroom one morning, and Rose Poplawski was treated to cheers. I didn't know
what the hell it meant, but Sarah was also nominated and
explained the situation:

"It's more or less a miniature version of the actual court. Every grade gets a kind of king and queen. Student council came up with it last year to help raise school spirit!"

"That seems . . ." Kalyn thought, "dumb," but Rose chirped, "wonderful!"

"Teachers pick ten candidates from each grade—five boys and five girls. Over the next three weeks the school votes. The winners from each class get to ride in the parade with the seniors. Congrats, Rose."

"I'm voting for you, though." Sarah is too precious for this world, and no way in hell am I voting for myself. Also, the whole situation seems old-fashioned to me. Oh, more forced boy/girl pairings? Because everybody's straight, right, and everyone who ain't doesn't matter, right? Well, *whoopee*.

It's confusin', though, because even if I'm gay, maybe Rose Poplawski isn't.

Yesterday, Eli Martin, naturally one of the five freshmen boys on our ballot, asked Rose Poplawski to homecoming. He popped this question outside the gymnasium during breakfast break, in front of his usual cluster of friends. Rose wasn't by herself, either, what with Sarah and company fluttering around. All of Jefferson High knew about the request instantaneously. The proposition was a skunk stink in the air.

Rose Poplawski replied, prim as a human doily: "Let me think it over, honey" and left Eli Martin hanging like a dirty bath rag.

Meanwhile, that night Kalyn smoked four cigarettes and

whiled away several hours playing euchre with her dozy grandma at the kitchen table, trying not to think about goddamn Eli Martin. Kalyn—I mean, me—kept burying him under a bent deck of secondhand casino cards. I know that Eli Martin is probably *all* some girls (and boys) have ever wanted, and the perfect cover to boot. It would make sense for me to date him, to hide behind his wholesome smirk and jocular charisma.

It would make sense to say yes, and have it all.

Because Rose Poplawski *can* have it all. She *is* having it all.

She's pretty much taking everything.

Rose can't actually take *Dad* away, because he's not part of the everything I'm used to having. If I can keep Dad and the Spences snug in my rib cage, hell. Why shouldn't Rose have anything else she wants?

Why is it still like pulling splinters when I get alone enough to think about this?

Not that I've actually been alone too often, at school. For the past ten days, I've been the target of some pointed stares.

I haven't seen much of Quillpower—he seems to jump into bathrooms at the sight of me—but Boots has become my shadow.

I can't count how many times Rose Poplawski's been laughing with Sarah in the hallway and turned around to find black-framed eyes peering at her from a distance. It's like those eyes are a drill, twisting the cover of Rose around them, a drill that spins and tears and threatens to reveal what's underneath.

Somehow, Boots is seeing *me*. He's seeing my Spencehood.

This ain't my first rodeo: I've come across stares like that before, even though it's been years since I looked much like the little girl in that wedding photo. Some people are too curious for their own good, and small towns are boring places. I'm sure the Ellis murder still comes up in conversation around here, in classrooms or in churches or in bars. I'm sure that picture makes its rounds. What if Boots *has* caught my scent?

But if this is the one kid in Samsboro who recognizes the daughter of a murderer, I won't be telling him he's right. I won't be killing Rose off so easily. Spences aren't that trigger happy, despite what the news might say.

I should just tell him to fuck right off. He's just one mousy kid. Sure, that would mean breaking character, but there are plenty of opportunities, like when I'm by myself at my locker and Boots limps by too slowly and pauses a little too long in my vicinity.

Last time he pulled this, I took a deep breath and spun round to tear him a new one. Boots startled like a jackrabbit. I caught his magnified eyes. He steeled himself, waggled his fingers awkwardly, and then shuffled away. Like he was *waving* at me.

That's what makes me bite my tongue—if I'm right and Boots *has* got me figured, who the hell stalks a murderer's kid just to wave at her?

If Boots recognizes me, he's *choosing* not to run away.

Somehow it almost feels like while everyone else is voting for Rose Poplawski, Boots is filling out some silent ballot for Kalyn Spence.

GUS

PHIL'S DONE A thousand things for me. He's led me through dozens of challenging campaigns in D&D, across fictional deserts and oceans, through astral crypts dark and cold. We've been to the ends of seven earths together.

In real life, he drives me to school every day. He taught me to read, and he lets me speak for myself. Phil smirks at my broken jokes. He doesn't laugh much, but especially doesn't when I'm not joking. He knows the difference.

So why is it that doing this one, *normal* thing for Phil feels impossible to me?

I've been trying to ask Rose Poplawski to be his homecoming date for more than a week. I've trailed her down hallways at least six times, but never reached out. Phil *has* asked me why. He's asked me what's taking so long. He's accepted my excuses, but he has tunnel vision. The more time that passes, the heavier his sighs hit me. It's never occurred to Phil that I'm more anxious about all this than he is.

If she says no, he loses a date. But either way, I'll be losing him.

Speaking to Rose really doesn't seem feasible. It's not about her being unfriendly. She goes out of her way to be approachable, smiling at everyone she passes. Rose Poplawski is rarely anything but charming. She's usually joking or playing with her impressive braid or covering her mouth when she laughs.

Is she covering up her snaggletooth, self-conscious like me? Or is she maybe worried that there's smoke on her breath?

I'm not special for noticing the cracks in Rose Poplawski; no one else is actually looking. When we ask someone how they are, we don't want them to tell us. We want to hear they're *fine, thanks, how are you?*

Following a girl around the school for no good reason, that's the sort of thing creeps do because they feel self-righteous, like it's less creepy if you're a nerdy loser instead of a stalker. I bet all stalkers feel justified.

I *don't* feel justified. I'm not Phil.

A few times, Rose has caught me looking at her. I can't explain it, but a window seems to open behind her eyes. The room past her eyelids is dark but full of all sorts of things that might be worth talking about. I might have a forest in my head, but I think there are other dark places in the world, places that don't belong to me. Places no D&D campaign can go, places someone as uncomfortable as me can't access.

I can't ask Rose to go to homecoming with my best friend. Maybe I owe Phil a lot, but Rose Poplawski doesn't owe either of us a single thing.

KALYN

I'M IN THE library with Sarah, watching classmates meander between the shelves when a sudden nettle-y pang in my neck tells me Boots and his damn eyes are at it again.

"Something wrong?" Sarah's color-coding her schedule. It looks like a goddamn bowl of Froot Loops. Sarah's involved in every possible student organization, from the paper to student council to the blood drive to, who knows, the candy-for-orphans club.

"Just thinking." I roll a pen across the table. I look at the shelves on our right. And there, right in the *V* section, I spot them. Peering at me from between *Candide* and *Breakfast of Champions*: wiry goddamn eyes.

I meet them in a dead stare.

"Rose, careful! You're going to—"

But it's too late. The Pilot snaps in half, splattering our table with ink. Now Sarah's white blouse is anything but.

"Twice-blessed shit-sticks on ice!" I holler. "Sorry!"

" '*Twice-blessed shit-sticks*'?" Sarah's shock dissolves into good-natured laughter. Her blouse is speckled blue like a robin's egg. Honestly, it still looks nice on her.

"Actually, you're kind of pulling it off."

"Oh, I'm not going to pull it off, Rose." Suddenly I feel her minty breath on my ear. "We're in public." She backs away, giggling like it's nothing, but I'm pretty sure she just made one hell of a suggestive joke, and now *I'm* all flustered.

How many people get into some kind of character every day? Maybe Sarah's putting on a show just like I am. Maybe it's a matter of time before we see how deep our characters go. I'm a puddle, but maybe she is, too.

I could be wrong. There are people who *aren't* pretending to be anything but themselves. Guys who aren't afraid to *ogle*.

When I look back at the *V* shelf, Boots is gone. I spy his wonky gait near the library exit. The guy moves faster than you'd think.

Sarah's digging in her bag, so I spare a second to flip him the bird.

"What a mess!" Sarah offers me a tissue. "Your dress!"

"Oh, this old thing."

"Don't say that."

I drop the simper, for just a sentence or three. "No, it's *literally* very old. It's a hand-me-down from my grandma's closet. Can't you smell the mothballs?"

Sarah leans in and takes a deep breath. "Not at all."

She'll be the girly death of me, I swear.

"Sarah. You know that thorny-eyed boy with the curls and glasses?"

"Sorry?"

"The kid with curly hair? Kind of small. Possibly a freshman?"

"I don't know who you're talking about."

I go one step further, but it leaves a sour taste in my mouth: "The special needs kid? With the, um, I don't know. The sort of *collapsed* arm?"

"Oh!" Sarah bites her lip. "That's Gus Peake. He's an upperclassman, actually. Everyone knows him, because . . ." She hesitates. "Anyhow. He used to ride my bus. First time I saw him, he was in a wheelchair. I looked at him and started *bawling*."

"*Why?*"

"I'm not sure. I think he scared me."

"He *scared* you?" I've got no right to scoff, but a little Kalyn escapes. "What did he do, roll at you too quickly?"

Sarah winces. "When I think back, I guess I'd never seen a sick kid before. Maybe I thought he was dying. Or maybe seeing him made me realize *I'd* die one day, or something." Her cheeks flush. "Rose. I was *five*. Do you want me to apologize?"

I don't know what I want. But if strangers cried at the sight of me, maybe I'd stalk people before talking to them, too.

And just like that, I want to talk to Boots after all, damned or not.

"Two more minutes!" Ms. Coillard calls. "Guys, pick out your books already!"

Boots used to be in a wheelchair, like Grandma. I look down

at my dress. She'll never wear it again, but leaving it blue-bloody suddenly feels a little wretched.

"I'm gonna go clean myself up." Sarah nods, buried in her schedule. Maybe mad.

Seconds later I step into the hallway and feel the temperature drop. There's a lot of shade in Jefferson Prison this time of day, despite the handful of skylights that screw up the ceiling. Those dusty-glassed holes leave asymmetrical diamonds of light on the tiled floor, and you can make out the shadows of cobwebs and dirt in them.

At first I think he's waiting for me, but his eyes are closed and his face is tilted toward the light. It's like he's solar powered or something.

I fold my arms and cough. I don't see him jump, but he must, 'cause I hear some part of him rattle. Those eyes mince me again. I don't totally hate it.

"Oh. Hey." His voice drags, but not as badly as I remember.

"*Oh, hey.*" I lift my hands. "So."

He doesn't blink.

I groan. "*So*, why have you been following me, Gus Peake?"

"I'm sorry."

"If you were sorry, you wouldn't be doing it, would you?"

He's all stammers. "I mean—meant—I think—ah. I didn't mean to. Following you. Sorry. I mean. Sorry. Follow you."

I size him up. "I ain't giving you a pass just because you're twitchy." Suddenly he blurts, "I want to talk to you?"

"Why does that sound like a question?" I sigh. "You know who I am, don't you?"

"Rose. Or . . . Kalyn?"

"Don't call me that."

"Do you have a—a minute?" Gus Peake asks. "I need to talk about you, scrially."

Serially, huh? Probably as in *serial killer-ly*, right?

Shots fired. Boots really does recognize me. I'm pretty fucked, seems like.

So why the hell aren't I fleeing the scene?

GUS

AFTER WEEKS OF practice, I still can't get the words right.

I try again. "I need to talk *to* you. *Seriously.*"

"Oh." Kalyn's posture slackens. "Whatever."

"Your dress." In the past minute, she's managed to coat herself in blue ink.

"What, wanna borrow it? It'll be big on you."

"Not my style." Typically, *now* my brain lets loose two-dozen needless words. "I like art, but I've never been a P-Pollock fan. Paint spatter kinda seems, um . . . hazardous? No. Um. *Slapdash?* Is that a real word?"

Kalyn eyeballs me. "You think I know more words than you do?"

"Is there any reason you wouldn't?"

"Huh. All right, *Gus.* Let's have our heart-to-heart. And I promise not to cry."

I don't know what she means by that, but Kalyn reaches for my good hand and leads me away down the sunlit hallway.

Most people don't touch me. I pretend they see me as an Armani suit, something that shouldn't be stained. Really, I know I'm seen as something much less fashionable. You can't catch CP any more than you can catch spina bifida. You'd be amazed by how many normies don't seem willing to chance it.

Kalyn's grip is firm as she steers me across the building. She doesn't ask whether she's going too fast. She's not, but it's strange, not being asked.

We veer down the shortest wing of the school. I haven't been here since I took a Tech Ed class my freshman year. The smell of pine takes me back to frustrating hours I spent trying to juggle hammers despite my poor hand-eye coordination.

Between the collage-coated art room windows and the open shop doorway stands a brown door I assume leads to a utility closet. Kalyn pushes the door inward, and we clamber into musty darkness.

She pulls on a chain. A bulb flickers on above us. There are no water boilers or mops here. Instead, we're caught between two walls lined with shelves occupied by a few pieces of abandoned pottery. The wall opposite us is marred by a large oven, built into the cinderblocks, its door hanging open to reveal more darkness.

"A crematorium?" I blurt, because I was raised in a tomb.

Dad was cremated. There are things you shouldn't embalm, ways you *don't* want to remember people. Dad was decomposing by the time his body was found. Mom and her yearbooks never told me this, but hours spent online in the Wheelers' basement taught me plenty. I couldn't avoid seeing autopsy photos. Dad wasn't smiling on that silver table. Dad was—

"It's a kiln. For the art classes?" Kalyn sinks to the floor, stretching her legs out like she's melting. "You hopeless Emo."

I frown. "I'm not Emo."

"All that black is misleading, then. Surprised I don't see you hanging out with those boys in skirts. You know? The kids who play black guitars outside?"

"The Gaggle."

She whistles. "They've *named themselves*? Shit."

"No." I clear my throat. "I named them that."

"How freakin' weird of you." Kalyn rubs one finger over a shelf and holds the dust to her nose.

"I didn't know we had a kiln."

"That's 'cause *you've* never needed a place to smoke." Kalyn shoves a hand down her dress and retrieves a cigarette and lighter from her bra.

"I've got asthma." I scrape my feet against the floor.

"Oh." Rather than light the cigarette, Kalyn shoves it between her front teeth and chews on it.

This room is mostly soundproofed, but both of us look at the door as the bell echoes. My speech therapist, Alicia, is probably sitting in her tiny office next to the teachers' lounge, looking at her watch.

I'm here, watching this girl pick tobacco from her teeth.

"Looks like we're playing hooky." Kalyn traces a finger through the dust on the floor. "It's a gen-u-ine first for Rose. You're bringing out the worst in me, Gus. What's 'Gus' short for, anyway? Augustus?"

"No."

"August? Gustav?"

"None of the above." The last time I missed speech therapy, I was lying at the foot of the stairs outside the gym, wondering who tripped me. "Can we talk?"

"Well, aren't we?"

"No. Yeah. But this . . . not what I planned, what to saying have do." The words wriggle away. I press my fist against my right temple and close my eyes. When I open them, Kalyn's rubbing at the blue ink on her dress with a fervor that might set fire to it.

She pats the filthy concrete beside her. It'll doom my dark pants. "Sit down before those chicken legs of yours give out. What's your deal? Did you have a stroke?"

"Um." I can't decide if I'm offended. Her bluntness borders on refreshing. What's less refreshing is the prospect of relaying the details of *me* to yet another stranger. I take a breath. "I was born with a type of cerebral palsy called hemiplegia, which means—"

"Hold up. You don't *have* to talk about it."

". . . sorry?"

"You're cringing like I just threw another egg at you. I'm not gonna *make* you talk about shit you don't wanna talk about.

I only asked because my grandma had a stroke last March. It's why me and Mom moved here. You talk like Grandma talks, a little out of order, using the wrong words and whatnot. It got me curious, is all."

"Um . . . for me, it's aphasia. But no one *always* uses the right words."

"That's the freakin' truth. Gustin."

"Also not my name."

"See? I've *only* got wrong words! Yesterday in the cafeteria, they gave us soggy chicken fingers. I cracked a joke, like, 'Hope they got manicures first.' You know, before cutting the chickens' fingers off? But the words were wrong. No one laughed."

"Maybe the words weren't wrong. Just different." Why people ever think there's only one way to think is something I can't understand. Maybe because I already think differently. Words fall like branches in my brain. "Timber."

"Did you just say 'timber'? You see any trees in here, Gus-driver?" Kalyn laughs.

"Definitely not my name." I use the shelves to lower myself to the floor. Kalyn budges aside to accommodate me. One battered flat bumps against my boot.

"So. How'd you find me out?" Her voice maintains that light twang, but her shoulders stiffen. "Did you look me up? Follow me home?"

I can't make any sense of this. "Are you making another joke?"

"You found out who I am, right?"

I shake my head. "What do you mean?"

"Oh." The shutters behind her eyes open a little. "So what are we here for, then?"

"You know my friend? He's tall? Wears glasses?"

"Quillpower? Unforgettable tumbleweed of a guy. Gets boners for Shakespeare?"

I cough. "Phil is . . . odd. Reality is hard for him. He's decided you must be a, um, *character* that'll make his life interesting. He thinks you've got, um. *Heroine* potential."

"I'm trying to decide if that's condescendin'."

"Definitely."

Kalyn wipes her nose on the back of her hand. "Dehumanizin', at least."

"I told him that. But he wants to know if . . ." It's hard to say.

"The anticipation is killing me," she says dully.

"Phil wants to ask you to homecoming." It's the cleanest sentence I've managed all day, but I'm wincing, muscles tingling. But Kalyn, or Rose, whoever she is? She doesn't laugh. She rests her chin on one knee and says "hmm."

Everyone in school knows "Rose" left Eli Martin hanging a few days ago, in front of an audience. Here in the dark, there's no reason she should be nice.

But she says "hmm" again.

Without warning, I imagine the world Phil's probably imagined.

A world where this girl says yes, and Phil finds the guts to rent a suit and borrows Mr. Wheeler's car instead of taking the Death Van. Phil appears at Kalyn's house. And she, wearing a tacky silver prom dress rather than her usual charming country fare, hops in beside him, and Phil drives her to school, more carefully than he's ever driven me. And when they get to the gymnasium, they dance, obviously, and she makes him smile a lot more than I ever have, and both of them are shiny with sweat but neither is worried because they're having a surprisingly good time, so good they can't believe it.

I'm not with them. Not because I'm a horrendous dancer (honestly, so is Phil). I'm sitting alone on the bleachers, *happy* for my best friend. I'm not with them because I have become an option I didn't consider on my list of unbearable fates:

g. the crippled side note who humiliates himself to secure a glorious romance for the underdog, thereby proving the underdog a protagonist

I'm suddenly queasy in the crematorikiln. I'm searching for my feet, and I don't care whether the shelves give way when I lean on them, because something else is giving way, ridiculously, in my chest.

Kalyn grabs my hand. Not to help me up; just to hold it.

"That's nice of him. Almost. Quillpower's seen me at my worst."

Her hand is so warm.

"Damn, your hand is colder than a witch's titty in a brass bra!"

I slide down beside her, giggling like mad, my pants beyond saving. Kalyn laughs along with me. We're shaking spiders from their cobwebs.

"Hey," Kalyn hazards, "if *he's* the one who wants to be rescued, why did Quillpower make you follow me?" Her face is level with mine, her eyes four fingers away. "Why can't Phil do his own dirty work?"

"Phil thinks I can talk to girls more, better, better than he can."

I expect her to mock that. She doesn't. "So why'd it take you weeks?"

"I was . . . scared."

There are specks of blue ink on her face, and makeup's worn away to reveal freckles. "I'm nothin' to be scared of."

I stare at her.

"One day those thorny eyes are going to poke right out of your head."

"Th-Thorny eyes?"

"Yeah. You've got thorny eyes. Is that condescendin'?"

I chuckle. "Dehumanizin', at least."

"Nothing for it. You and me are both twisted. The imposter and the stalker. But hey, the straight and narrow's for bad drivers."

"Or people on scooters."

Her laugh is so big. It causes a full-on cobweb massacre. She slaps her hand against my dead knee—

"Oh, shit, my bad!"

"It's fine. Didn't hurt."

She grins and lets her hand rest there for an extra second. Dad winks in my mind. How weird is that? I've seen so many faces in my life, but Kalyn's is the first to remind me of his. I wonder if she's ever posed with a goofy smile, a trout in her arms.

"I'll put some thought into Phil's request. But I need a favor." Kalyn pulls her dress away from her body. Her head tilts forward, gives her unflattering chins as she peers inside her garment. "Any idea how to get ink out of fabric?"

"Um. Have you got hairspray in your locker?"

"That," she says, patting puffy bangs, "is a fair assumption. Know why?"

I suspect an unfunny joke is on the horizon.

"Because otherwise?" She flattens those bangs against her forehead, steamrolling them with her palm. "*Timberrrrr!*"

It makes no sense, but I'm laughing too hard to remember option *g*.

KALYN

THE MORNING AFTER we skip class to hash things out in the kiln, I spot Gus from ten yards away, leaning against the staircase railing outside the cafeteria, books clutched close in his good arm. It should be impossible to see him amid the morning stampede that follows first bell, except, of course, Gus has that dandelion puff of white-yellow hair.

Sarah's just run back to her locker to fetch her science textbook before the second bell, so I've only got a minute—

"Gus!" I trill, all Rose-ish. "Hey!"

Gus startles and blinks at me before dropping his eyes back to his boots.

"Gus!" I call again, losing the trill. "C'mere!"

This dork does an actual double-take and looks back over his shoulder. "*Seriously*? Get over here!"

Gus looks both ways and picks his careful way through the crowd, hunching his shoulders to make himself smaller.

"Sorry," he says, "I was waiting for . . . I wasn't following you. Not today, I mean."

"I'm not worried about that. That's yesterday's news."

Gus looks extremely uncomfortable, standing so close to me. I'm talking porcupine-quills-to-the-ass uncomfortable. His eyes keep falling back to his shoes.

You'd think my hand is full of nettles when I clap him on the shoulder.

"People might see you," he mutters.

"Well, most people have eyes. Who cares? You embarrassed to be seen with me?"

"No! It's not, ah. Aren't *you* embarrassed to . . . well. Um." He lifts his books. "D'you wanna carry my stuff, then?"

Who knows what thinking process led him there, but ten bucks says it's not a healthy one. "Do I look like a mule? I just wanted to see if you want to meet up later. Like yesterday, although maybe more during lunchtime and less playing hooky?" I lower my voice. "I've got a fake reputation to maintain, you know."

He thinks about it for a full seven seconds, and the whole time the pressure in him's building like steam in a teapot before it bursts from his mouth: "*Why?*"

Good damn question. I mean, sure, Gus made me laugh when I finally met up with him, made *Kalyn* feel less like dirt, but I wasn't planning on making it a thing. I shouldn't be tempting fate. Hell, I'm still not convinced he doesn't have my number regarding Murder-Dad, et cetera. But it's bumming me out, seeing how Gus is in public versus how he was in the kiln.

"I dunno. I like talking to you, I guess?"

"But . . . you can't smoke if I'm there."

"Maybe I like you more than cigarettes."

He turns so freakin' pink. Look, I'm pretty queer, but hell if blushing boys aren't the cutest things since frolicking kittens.

"Look, maybe I have an answer for you. For Quillpower." Sure, that's convincing.

"Oh, yeah?" God, he looks so put out.

"Fuck if I know." I poke him in the forehead. "Kiln at noon thirty?"

He nods and starts to smile, but then he looks right past me and pivots away real quick: I think I spooked him, until Sarah appears at my shoulder along with a delicious waft of coconut-scented shampoo. I'm gonna go ahead and bet that Gus remembers being cried at in elementary school by a certain lovely someone.

"You ready?" she asks.

"Yeah. Ready."

Maybe I don't sound like Rose, because Sarah frowns. Her eyes trail Gus's retreating back and then she's opening her mouth, but I smile wide and she changes her mind. "Good for you, because I *definitely* didn't study enough."

"Oh, neither did I!" I'm all perky again, but it feels like a strain. "When I said 'ready' I didn't mean 'ready to pass.' Just ready to face the music."

Sarah chuckles, loops her arm through mine, and we're on our way to English Honors. Suddenly my throat hurts. I miss the voice I just used with Gus.

Basically, I miss me, even if it doesn't make sense.

GUS

IF I DIDN'T know any better, I might think Kalyn is just clueless. I might assume she's as silly as she pretends to be. I might assume that she doesn't realize that spending so much time with me might be some kind of social sabotage.

But I *do* know better. I know that people are usually much more than what they look like they are. I know that Kalyn's laughter yesterday was as real as mine.

When she asks me to hang out with her, sure, there's a knot in my chest forming, because that means leaving Phil behind. But there's another knot unwinding, a knot tighter than any of my muscles have ever been. It loosens, just a little, at the insane, lovely idea:

Kalyn just likes talking to me, I guess?

I watch her walk away with Sarah, and there's another idea that's even more lovely: I like talking to her, too, and our conversations could take us anywhere.

It's one abyss I don't mind so much.

KALYN

I READ SOMEWHERE that girls are too apologetic. There are women who say "Sorry" when someone else runs into them, and girls who say "Sorry" after sharing their opinions. This is a conditioned response that's existed for generations, a seed planted when we're too young to know it and usually without our parents even realizing they're planting it.

And saying "girls are too apologetic" still sounds like blaming them for something they didn't choose, so fuck all that noise.

But apologizing all the time decreases the value of the word. What we're really saying is "my presence is less valuable than yours." It's sexist bullshit. I'd like to say that's why Spences don't apologize, but that's not really why. We've just got this whole "oppositional" thing in our bloodstream. If someone shouts blue, we shout red.

I've heard more sorries over the past couple weeks than I've heard my whole life. Gus apologizes for taking up space, apologizes for misspeaking, apologizes for his weirdo best friend. He's not apologizing for existing, but sometimes it *sounds* like that.

But hell, pobody's nerfect, and you know what? Gus has *never* expected apologies from me. It's been weeks of me not giving him a straight answer about homecoming. All he wants to do is what I want to do: shoot the shit.

"What do you mean, you've never played D&D?" he demands during our eighth meeting. By now we've sneaked some blankets and a lamp into the crematorikiln, and it's not as gloomy as it used to be. It's what I think childhood might feel like.

"You say that as if most people *have* played D&D."

Gus kicks at the dust with his boots. "Sorry. I didn't mean . . . I just meant that you usually know, do things most people haven't."

"You mean smoking, swearin', and drinking?"

"I mean looking after, um, the olderly. Elderly." His ears are luminous Christmas bulbs. "I mean pretending to be fake-nice but secretly being actually nice."

I wince. "I'm not nice."

Gus wipes his chin. "Yes, you are."

"Seriously, I'm not."

"Agree to disagree."

I should let it go and start talking books and movies and

crap (we *both* have a soft spot for cheesy old sci-fi movies, me for the unintentional humor and Gus for the bare-budget costuming), but the knowing look in his eyes makes me tetchy. "How the hell do you know? I could be an actual piece of shit. I could be makin' it all up! The shit about old people and being nice to you: they could all be lies, you idiot."

"Don't c-call me an idiot." His smile's gone in a puff of steam.

"Yeah—I mean—sorry." Guess apologizin' is catching, or maybe there are good apologies and bad ones.

"And don't call yourself names. *That's* not nice."

"What names do you call yourself, Gus, when there's no one else around?"

"Selfish."

"Huh. Me too. But who isn't?"

"My parents," Gus murmurs. "They give me everything." We talk about everything, but we haven't talked about our families. It's like this silent, mutually agreed thing. Like he knows it, Gus clears his throat. "Sorry."

"Is there anything you *aren't* sorry for? Jegus."

"I'm not sorry I followed you."

"Shit. Me neither. Especially now I know it was all about Quillpower."

He tilts his head. "What did you think it would be about?"

"I thought you'd figured out my dark past." I try to make it sound like a joke.

"Did you kill someone?" I think *he's* trying to joke, too, but it sounds unnatural. We haven't talked about true crime, even if we've talked about every other genre.

"What do you think this is, *Heathers*? Would you help me hide a body?"

"Hiding them isn't practical," Gus says slowly. "People always find them."

"You ain't kidding." My laugh is shrill.

Gus chuckles; it sounds forced, but I appreciate it. "We could figure something else out, I guess. Um. Yeah."

"Creep," I say, but I'm grinning.

"*Creeps*," he amends, and puts out his fist. I bump it against mine.

GUS

I NEVER THOUGHT I could joke about murder. I would never dare, not in my house. But Kalyn is so comfortable in everything she does and says, I guess it's catching. And laughter is good medicine. Tamara knows this, but Mom doesn't always appreciate the idea, so every weekend I leave home to visit a house where laughter isn't so unusual.

"You dick," John hollers, clutching the N64 controller like a weapon, fingers working madly. "Stop it with the fucking bombs, Matt!"

Matt cackles, round belly shaking. In the game, Link yanks another bomb out of thin air and pelts it at Pikachu. Phil snorts in derision, as if his two older brothers are bickering children; he's playing as Kirby, as usual, and seems to spend most of his time floating near the top of the screen, far removed from danger, waiting for the moment to strike. All three Wheeler brothers are crammed on the basement sectional, but John always lets me sit in his gaming chair when I'm spectating.

Every three weeks or so, the usual Friday night hangout in the cluttered Wheeler basement shifts from tabletop to retro gaming. I'm not great at video games, with my muscle weakness and coordination deficits, but I do okay with button-mashers like *Mortal Kombat*. Besides, I enjoy watching Phil and his brothers go at it, because all three of them are way too invested in throwing each other off floating platforms in *Super Smash Bros*. The fun comes from watching the Wheelers clash: John is large and serious and bearded and kind, Matt is short and bald and usually snickering, and Phil is Phil.

I always savor these evenings, the camaraderie and escapism and popcorn and caffeinated soda, but today something feels off. Maybe it's because Phil's been quiet all evening, or maybe it's the realization that lately when I've been sitting in a dark room—with Kalyn—it has actually mattered whether I'm there. I've been an active participant, not a piece of the audience.

I try to feel more involved. "Phil, there's a hammer on the upper platform—"

"I don't need your useless assistance," Phil snaps, so sharply that John says, "Whoa, overreaction much?" Matt takes advantage of the hiccup by taking the hammer for himself, ending the round in seconds when he knocks both opponents into the sky.

John hits the pause button. "Seriously, Phil, the hell was that?"

Phil's not looking at anything but the screen. "I simply don't need Gus's brand of help. It has proven inadequate of late."

"What are you, four?" Matt says, smile fading. "It's a game. Apologize."

But Phil isn't talking about *Smash Bros.* He's talking about homecoming, and the fact that I don't have an answer for him. He's talking about the lunches he's spent alone while I've been with Kalyn. Phil can never convey his feelings in any normal way.

Phil stands. "Go ahead and take my spot, Gus. As is your wont."

He stomps across the basement and into the downstairs bathroom, pulling the door closed behind him. My ears are ringing, my throat is dry.

Matt whistles. "Gus, I don't know how you tolerate him. He's so *off.*"

"Is everything okay?" John says.

I don't meet their eyes as I pull myself out of the chair. "I'm going up for a dr-drink. Anyone need anything?"

"I can get it—" John starts, but I shake my head.

"No, it's fine."

Yes, getting up those stairs is a slow process, but it gives me time to think. Does Phil *really* believe that I'm trying to, what? *Steal* Kalyn?

She doesn't belong to you, I think. *She doesn't belong to anyone.*

Is Phil really so clueless about what he means to me?

But what does Kalyn *mean to you?*

I pause at the top of the scuffed stairs. I'm not trying to date Kalyn, but I am befriending her. That feels like a small betrayal, though I can't explain why.

I step into the kitchen and startle when movement catches my eye.

Mr. Wheeler sits at the kitchen table with his laptop in front of him. He looks almost like Mom, typing away with a gleam in his eyes. Like Mom, he immediately changes when I appear. His eyes lock onto mine, and he closes the laptop.

"Hey, Gus. How's it going?" Unlike Phil, Mr. Wheeler has a face that smiles really seem to suit. "Anything I can get you?"

I lower my eyes and make for the fridge. "Just getting some, um. I mean, drinks."

"Haven't seen you around as often lately."

"Um, yeah. Junior year. It's been busy." I pull out one SunnyD and one Vault.

"Gus. Look at me." I do so, because it's a hard habit to break. When I was in elementary school, Mr. Wheeler was my counselor. It's like he left a footprint on me somewhere. "Is everything okay? With Phil, I mean? Has he been a good friend to you?"

I open my mouth and close it again, eyes prickling. Mr. Wheeler's always had good insight, because he's a therapist or because he's a good dad, I guess. But this seems too perceptive, even for him.

"Yeah, we're cool," I manage, because what else can I say?

"That's good to hear," says Mr. Wheeler, leaning back in his chair. "You're all he's got, too, you know that?"

The implication that I don't have anyone else stings. I've only known Kalyn for two weeks, but it's not nothing. And there's something else that bothers me, something that always has.

I don't know how to say it other than this: the way Mr. Wheeler talks, it's like he thinks Phil has a disability. I used to think it was because Phil's awkward, or Phil's maybe on the autism spectrum, or Phil is too nerdy to function, but the older I get, the more this treatment weirds me out. Mr. Wheeler sees something sinister in Phil, some *illness* I've never seen. The way he talks, you'd think *Phil* was a murderer.

"I really don't know," Mr. Wheeler murmurs, before I can escape down the stairs, "I don't know where or who he'd be without you."

At the bottom of the stairs, the players have moved. John's back at his desk in the corner, typing feverishly on a forum, and Matt is leaning over the card tables behind the couch, adjusting *Warhammer* figures on a playing field made of Styrofoam mountains and mirror lakes. Phil is alone on the sectional with a controller in his hand, punching the hell out of someone in *Mortal Kombat.* He hits the start button and pauses the game as I hold out a soda to him, then budges to the side.

I pick up a controller, sit on the couch so that our knees are almost touching, and do my best to start punching, too.

KALYN

I GREW UP in a lawless land. The Alleghany Mobile Park caught too much sunlight in all the wrong places, so you could see rust and grime on everything from fences to people. Lawless lands tend to grow a hearty crop of little pyromaniacs, and I was part of that. The older AMP boys set their own rules. You either had to scuffle with them or lie down and be grimy like everything else, mud under the tires of their stolen bicycles.

Hell if I was lyin' down.

When I was five, I almost clawed out Howie Scott's eyeball during a violent round of "chickenscratch." His mother came banging on our door, sobbing like a screech owl. When Mom answered, I took a good gander at the woman in our doorway.

Enormous Mrs. Scott, with her holey T-shirt and her arms

covered in black track marks, her mouth filled with yellow teeth. Howie looked tiny beside her, covered in snot and blood and eye gunk, and I almost felt *lucky*, until Mom pulled the flyswatter down from its hook on the cupboard.

It was the night before my first day of first grade. By the time I got off the bus, my raw bottom felt like it was growing fiery spurs from the rattling. I got to Ms. Brandt's classroom, wincing so bad my face was probably sucked into the vortex-y anus of itself. "Take a seat" was a death sentence.

Other parents were delivering their crybabies in person. Other parents had flashy cameras out, arms wide for hugs. Other kids were dressed like little Barbies. I stood alone by the coat rack, trying to decide if I could lie like a slug on the rug.

After Mom smacked me with the flyswatter, she'd spent the rest of the night cradling me in her lap, whispering apologies between drunken hiccups.

I stood next to the coat rack with my scrubbed red face and my red bottom and my ill-fitting dress and a fire spread to every inch of me. I knew there was no way fire would be allowed to go to kindergarten. I curled my fists and approached the nearest crybaby, ready to swing—

A girl took my hand.

"Hello!" My savior had black bangs and a beaded scrunchie wrapped around her ponytail. "I'm Olivia. What's your name?"

"Kalyn-Rose Tulip Spence."

"Wanna sit by me?"

I wiped my nose all down my arm. "Okay."

Sitting still hurt like Hades, and some other kid's name was taped to the desk, but I sat down next to Olivia. She gave me one of her pencils.

They say people can't really remember experiences from age five.

Olivia Wong became my first best friend, and I'd forget her if I could.

I don't know why she liked me. When you're little, you don't ask. Maybe Olivia saw me as an outcast and related to that, 'cause she and her sister were the only half-Chinese girls in Alleghany. One of the first things I asked Olivia was if she could see okay with little eyes like that. That's how I learned I was a bigoted little shit.

"*Don't be RACIST.*"

"What'sat mean?"

"Means you don't like Chinese people."

I remember dropping my chocolate milk. "But I like you the most."

"Then say *nice* things, Kalyn."

Saying nice things was easier when I was Olivia's shadow. If Olivia smiled, I smiled. If Olivia shook someone's hand, my grubby palm appeared just after hers. Olivia shared her Lunchables when I didn't bring a lunch, rubbed my back when I ranted.

Olivia invited me over to her fancy cabin on the lakeshore, I turned up quiet as a shrew, gawping at how Olivia and her dad and her mom and her baby sister ate food with napkins on their laps, chewing with their mouths closed. That night we fell asleep in sleeping bags under the living room skylight. We pretended we were in the wilderness.

When applications to join the Brownie Girl Scout troop were passed round our classroom, I sprinted off the bus, knocking two AMP boys over and ignoring their shouts.

Mom hardly glanced at the form. "We can't afford this, hon."

"It doesn't cost nothin'."

"Oh, it will. Not just the uniform and badges. It'll be field trips, right? Camping? Who's drivin'? I have to work, Kalyn."

"Olivia's parents can drive me!"

Mom cocked her pistol. "So why don't you just move in with the Wongs?"

"I would if I could, damn it!" I ran outside before she could swat me.

When I came back, Mom was washing the dishes. I couldn't tell if it was soapy or salty water on her cheeks. We call it Spence pride, but it comes from both sides. "Why don't you have Olivia over this weekend?" she said.

The answer seemed obvious. But I couldn't say anything but "Okay."

On Friday, I pulled Olivia away from her bus and led her to the pickup area.

"You're coming to my house!" I said, cheerful as possible.

You'd think I'd told Olivia every day was her birthday. "Can we build a fort?"

"Yeah, *obviously!*" I grinned, but my eyes felt nettled. Mom pulled up in her rusty truck and honked the horn. Olivia jumped like a spooked cat.

"Hey, honey. You get permission from your parents?"

"Yeah, *obviously!*" I answered, yanking Olivia inside with me.

Olivia's eyes widened as we chugged away from the school, blaring Garth Brooks from busted speakers. She gaped when we left the main roads, and her jaw basically fell off once we drove past the AMP entrance sign. Olivia seemed hypnotized by all the silver trailers. Folks were outside sipping Natty Ices in lawn chairs, burning autumn leaves and saluting the death of summer with bonfire pyres.

"We're gonna build a fort, Liv."

Olivia said nothing at first. But once we got to our trailer and the shock wore off, she tried coming around. When she learned Mom and I shared one lumpy bed, Olivia didn't miss a beat: "You'll always have someone to cuddle with!" And when she learned our bathroom and shower were one and the same, she thought *that* was pure genius. "You can shower and do your business at the same time!"

Mom was pulling a shot glass off the drying rack, so I hurried Olivia outside.

She seemed awed by the glimmering glass and forgotten furniture populating the junkyard, thrilled by the frog pond beyond the last row of trailers, but our tummies were grumbling. I knew not to dream of cocoa, but I hoped we had some food in the trailer.

When we got back, Mom was still upright, scribbling away in her notepad. She'd made nachos. They were cold and gunky, but I was so relieved that I kissed her on the cheek. She smelled like booze, but it wasn't *so* bad.

Olivia sat down right next to her. "What you writing, Mrs. Spence?"

"A letter to Kalyn's daddy."

"Is he a soldier?"

"Kalyn didn't tell you?" I pretended to scrape leftover nachos into the trash, but Mom stared right at me. "He's in prison for murder."

Things got real quiet. I could hear the neighbors' TV blaring *Jeopardy!*

"We love him to bits, don't we, Kalyn?"

Acting was no good in front of another Spence. "Yeah, Mom."

"I'm going to bed." Mom squeezed my shoulder before stumbling to the bedroom and slamming the door.

"Your dad . . . *killed* someone?"

"So what if he did?" I leaned against the kitchen counter. "Let's play outside."

Olivia reached for my hand. I folded my arms against my chest. "Killing is evil. The Bible says."

"Well? Things ain't all black and white. You should know that. *You're* not black *or* white." This was like one of my nonsense jokes, except it was *nothing* like one.

Olivia's face became a map of wincing creases.

"I can't play *nice* like you, *Olivia*. I don't have a *nice* house or a *nice* attitude or a dad who didn't kill someone. If you don't like it, you can get out."

Olivia cried big, gobby tears. "You *can* be nice. When you try!"

"Maybe I *don't* wanna." I showed Olivia my fists. "Maybe I wanna kill *you*."

I wish she'd have laughed, but Olivia wailed and locked herself in the bathroom. I called Mr. Wong and gave him our address. "Come get your shitty kid." I hung up the phone and kicked a hole in the wall. Mr. Wong had already called the police, because he *hadn't* given permission for Olivia to come home with me. He never would've, if he'd known where I lived.

Mr. Wong stood in our doorway and tucked his kid behind him. Mr. Wong had ironed clothes and perfect white blocks of ivory in his mouth and a real reasonable tone of voice. He suggested me and Olivia stop spending time together. He asked Mom not to put me in Girl Scouts.

By Monday, kids at school were whispering. The rumors must have started with Olivia. On Wednesday, someone threw a rock at me during recess. Back in the classroom, I took a pair of scissors from my desk, grabbed hold of Olivia's ponytail, and snipped it right off the top of her head. I shoved it down the back of her collared shirt while she screamed, and *voilà!* I got my first suspension.

That was one way to decapitate a childhood friendship.

I was the daughter of a murderer. Scissors were the least of it. I promised to be myself from then on. I broke that promise with the invention of Rose Poplawski.

Except it turns out that Rose dies in the darkness, and Kalyn thrives.

Kalyn, not Rose, snorts herself stupid, hearing Gus Peake dissect fashion trends and make painful puns, watching Gus Peake drool over the Gaggle dweebs. Kalyn is toleratin' Gus's doomed attempts to pitch his weirdo best friend as a catch.

"I'll dress him for you," Gus tells me. "I could dress him up in J-fashion."

"J-fashion?"

"Japanese street fashion! Like visual kei, or gyaru, or lolita, or—"

I wish I had a camera that could capture the way folks light up when they're talking about things they care about. But a picture won't show how Gus goes from slumping and wounded to leaning forward and electric. It can't show how color enters his face when it wasn't there a blink ago, or how the air feels suddenly warmer because there's love heating his words.

It's not just that Gus is my first friend in a decade. It's not just that I've been snagged by wiry eyes or caught in the clutter of his speech.

I almost believe—no, hell—I *do* believe that once Gus finally sees where I live, finally meets Grandma and Mom and hears our stupid redneck backstory, he'll still want me to be Kalyn, and he'll still wanna be my friend.

Gus understands what it's like, having people make assumptions. When he finds out Dad's in prison, I don't think he'll hold it against me. When I tell Gus my dad's a murderer, I bet Gus's dad won't even come knocking on my door.

"So. About the whole homecoming pickle, Guspar."

"Also not my name."

It's Monday, October 2nd. The parade and homecoming game are on Friday, and the dance is on Saturday. You can't get away from knowing that, here in Jefferson Prison. There are banners hanging off banners. Our kiln is the only patch of turf in the whole building that hasn't been infested with rogue pom-poms.

If we can get over the Philcoming hurdle, we can jump the big ole "Dad's a murderer" one next.

"The pickle is, I'm not *interested* in Phil, not that way. It's not because he thinks I'm slightly fictional or even because he made you stalk me, which is still fucked as shit."

"Okay." Gus looks damn-near relieved. "Is it the acne?"

"It's the penis, actually. Not my thing."

I wait for some loud reaction—years back, when I told Mom, she knocked over some vegetable oil and set the stove on fire before hollering that I was officially the most rebellious Spence in history—but this is Gus.

"I'll inform him of this stip-stipulation, but I don't think he'll part with that."

I elbow his arm. "Yeah, and I don't think you'd want him to."

Gus pauses to put the words in the right order. "I don't know what you mean."

"Ain't you in love with Phil?" The dim lighting in this old closet makes amber jack-o'-lantern cutouts of Gus's eyes.

"In *love?*" Like he's never thought about it. *"With Phil?"*

"You're always shivering, but you're not always *trembling,* Gus."

"If I . . . *love* Phil, why would I set him up with you?"

"Because that's what he wants, and you want what he wants. Because even if he's a creep, he's your favorite creep. You want Phil to creep on up to happiness."

I like the way Gus cocks his head to the side when he's thinking, like he's chewing the cud of the impossible.

"I'm callin' it. You're head-over-heels, call-a-priest gay for Quillpower."

Gus is a humanoid forehead crease. "Have you *seen* Phil?"

"Not how *you* see him, apparently!"

Gus frowns like the dickens, and Charles Dickens could definitely frown. "I'm *not* gay, not exactly. I don't think I am."

"What are you, then?"

"Confused," he says, heart-attack serious.

"Yep. That's pretty gay."

"But my parents are already gay! And *you're* gay!"

"You sayin' we're over our quota? Because I don't think that's ever stopped straight people."

His creases won't iron out. "Who are you gay for? Sarah?"

"Dunno right now." Honestly, it probably *is* Sarah. I've been to her farmhouse a few times, met her parents, and studied with her after school like a good little Rose. But ever since I called her out for laughing at Gus, Sarah's smiles are harder to swallow. I skip lunch to hang out with the kid who made her aware of her stinkin' mortality.

"Phil would say, um, that it's too much for one character. I'm already the disabled kid. I have a tragic backstory. The last thing my character arc needs is another complication."

"Does it have to be a *complication*?" I wonder what he means by tragic backstory, but man, do I know better than to ask. "Here's your daily reminder that life ain't a story, Gusteban. Maybe we're all a little gay for our best friends."

I reach up and muss his curls. I think Gus likes it when I touch him, based on how he leans into it. "You should come over for dinner and meet my moms," he says.

I remember the tears of Olivia Wong. "You want me to come over?"

"Um. Did I say it wrong?"

I sit up and hug him in the dark. I wonder if both of us were just dyin' to be known a little. I let go before he does. I'm always blindsided by how *tense* Gus is. He's an actual coiled spring.

"Will Phil be joining us?"

"Um . . . maybe not." Gus puts his good hand on his chin. "Come as Kalyn. I don't like Rose as much."

"Me neither." I'm not sure whether I'm lying. I'm wondering

whether my gunpowder marrow is dissolving. Maybe there's nothing raw and red about me anymore.

"I'm going to wear the space brace tomorrow, I think," Gus says. The bell rings.

"I don't know what that means, Guthrie, but good for you."

We take a moment to smack the dust off each other.

GUS

JUST WEEKS AGO, I was content spending my days admiring the Gaggle from afar, riding to and from school with Phil, playing tabletop games at his house. Living in a tomb, but with the doors flung open: that felt like enough to ask for.

I never meant to make friends with anyone.

Kalyn smells like smoke, but she's not afraid to touch me. She doesn't pull punches. She treats me like a person worth being around. Sometimes she says tactless things about my CP, or about Phil. She isn't always patient while I'm thinking. But . . .

"You're the only person I can cut loose around," she says.

Ditto.

It's not quite carefreedom, because we're both careful. But Kalyn's never *ashamed* of anything. She's never uncomfortable.

On the Tuesday before homecoming, the ride to school in the Death Van *is* uncomfortable. I've spent every day of my life for the past decade with Phil, but I've never felt this aware of him before.

I can understand why *Kalyn* thinks I love Phil. Phil's a constant comfort in my life. I care about him more than I care about anyone else, but there's never been much competition. My camp friends are far away. They don't factor into my daily existence.

"Honestly, compatriot, you're not heeding me. Again."

Thanks to Kalyn, I have to consider that the reason I squirmed when Phil asked me to ask her out might be because I wanted him to ask me instead. I wasn't ready to deal with that yesterday. I called Tamara for a ride and told Phil I had an appointment.

Now I have to face him, and I still don't know. When it comes to people, I care about personality before anything else, and gender's another characteristic that factors into that. Maybe that *does* land me in one queer realm or another, but it doesn't necessarily mean I'm in love with Phil Wheeler, does it?

You're all he's got, too. That's what Mr. Wheeler said.

I'm so gay and confused.

For once, Phil turns the music down. "If the answer's no, just tell me, Gus." When Phil drops his Shakespearean gimmick, it's serious.

"She . . . she didn't say no." Not explicitly. But she will.

"I need to know soon. I'll need to rent a suit."

"Rent the suit anyway. You can go even if she turns you down."

Phil's derision is an actual snarl. "I will *not* attend the ball alone."

"Not alone." I say it as inconsequentially as possible, because I'm trying to determine if it *is* inconsequential to me. "You can go with me. For fun."

"*For fun?*" We pull into the student lot. Phil races another van for the spot closest to the entrance. "Do you *remember* middle school? You don't dance. *I* don't dance. Fodder for the wolves, Gus. That's all we'd be."

Phil steals the spot and switches into park.

"Who cares?" I'm not sure what I want when I blurt, clearly, with no branches to block me, "Phil, come to home-coming with me."

Without warning, Phil starts *laughing*.

Suddenly we're not quite friends. Suddenly we're back to the day second-grade Phil taught me that sometimes *ch* sounds like *chuh* and sometimes like *kuh*, and how fascinating was that? One thing could be two things at once. And I chuckled and told him I knew that already, because sweet-and-sour sauce exists. He laughed.

I never thought I could hate the sound of Phil's laugh.

"Oh, come lively!" Phil undoes his seat belt. "You've made your point. I'll rent the damn suit, but please. Tell her to keep me informed, and should she come to a conclusion, deliver it posthaste."

As he opens the door, I murmur, "*You* tell her."

Phil pauses. Autumn has stricken Samsboro, and through

the open door I hear the crackle of leaves across pavement. The wind teases Phil's straggly hair. "*Really*, Gus? I don't even know where you've been meeting her. I thought I couldn't be any less popular, but I've spent a lot of lunches alone."

Kalyn never told me *not* to bring Phil to the kiln. But I never suggested it. Maybe I never actually wanted to bring them together.

Oh, god. Kalyn could be right. I *could* be in love with Phil. But Phil hasn't even factored me in as someone who might be *capable* of a love confession.

"We've been over this. Nobody is interested in talking to me, girls least of all."

"Then what are you planning to do at the dance, mime at her?" I bite my tongue, but Phil's just rejected me. And the worst part is he doesn't even realize it, and I'm angry at him, at myself, even at Kalyn for planting a seed I can't water.

"You said you'd relay my charms. You'd make it easier."

"Make *what* easier? Phil, she's a person, not a puzzle."

"I'm not an imbecile."

"Okay. *Okay.* Just. Phil, I don't like . . . um. If I talk to Kalyn, I want to talk to her because she's my friend, not because *you* want something out of it."

He tilts his head. "How long before you abandon her, too?"

"I haven't *abandoned* you! I was *doing* this for—for—!" I can't say the word, even though *it's right there*. I smack myself in the forehead.

Phil pulls out his PSP. "'Why bastard? Wherefore base,'"

he mutters, setting something alight in a digital realm. " 'When my dimensions are as well compact, my mind as generous, and my shape as true . . . ?' "

"Phil. Please. Could you *please* cut the drama for once?"

Phil doesn't look up. I'm not even the sidekick. It doesn't matter that my shape isn't true, that my dimensions have always been off, that my dead arm and leg are cramping again.

"I'll take care to heed your advice." Phil lets his PSP screen darken with a quiet click. "Lady Macbeth can give you a ride home tonight."

I punch the dash and splinters travel up my arm. "Phil. Don't, stop being—*stop!*"

Phil closes the door and lurches away, propelled by gusts of leaf-strewn wind. I get out as fast as I can, but it's not fast enough. Phil knows *exactly* how fast he has to walk to be beyond my reach, and he's doing double that pace now.

By the time I find my balance, I'm gritting my teeth and hobbling solo up the slight incline to Jefferson High's entrance, hating myself for petrifying, for turning to stone, for speaking up, for that confusing invitation, for chasing Phil now, for cluttering my words, for not being Macbeth, because even a mad Scottish king might be preferable to this. In my head, Dad is *tsk*ing so loud my ears buzz, and I'm doing my best to pull this concrete pillar that used to be my right leg behind me—

Timber.

The tiny entranceway steps catch me for the first time in years.

Me and my inadvisable Doc Martens.

My fall is witnessed by a small crowd of Gagglers, loitering beside the flagpole. Now it's a scene that should only exist in fiction: the dumbass with a disability eats pavement in front of his idols exactly as the bell rings.

My teeth smack together and there's gravel on my tongue. I taste tinny blood.

Hands descend around me, palms out, beautiful living hands trying to lift me without allowing me a moment to lift myself, and as these hands descend, concerned voices follow in their wake, and the speakers aren't listening when I tell them to leave me alone, maybe because I'm not saying the words aloud but *still*—

"HANDS OFF, RUBBERNECKERS!" The fingers flitter away. The holler softens. "I mean, please. I'll take care of it. He's my friend."

What's worse:

a. All those Gagglers helping me?
b. How quickly they *stop*?

Kalyn flops down beside me, all cascading gingham dress and braided knots of hair with flowers woven in, all crooked smile. For a while, we lie on our backs on the sidewalk. Kalyn uses her sickly lemonade Rose voice to shoo stragglers off as the last of the morning traffic passes us by.

"Freakin' buzzards," she grumbles.

My arm and leg threaten to spasm. If that happens, I won't be getting up. My jaw aches, but I can't open my mouth. I will myself to unwind.

The second bell sounds. Kalyn lifts herself up on one elbow. "Check it out, Gustulio. Stop eyeballin' the sidewalk. That cloud looks like a urinal!"

I take a deep breath, push myself up on my good arm, and roll over. My jaw unclenches. "Huh."

"Do you see it? It's up there, to your left."

I spit again and form my words carefully. "I don't know, but *yer-in-all* I see."

"Oh, Gus, I'm *crippled* with laughter."

"If you were on my good side, I'd be, um, smashing, I mean, *smacking* you."

It comes to my attention that there's pressure in my hand. Without looking, this could mean anything. Astereognosis is another of my glorious menagerie of issues, and that excessive-looking word means I can't always tell what things are just by touching them; I need to *see* them or hear them, too. "My hand feels weird."

"That's just me holdin' it."

"You should get up," I say. "Your dress will get filthy."

"It always does anyhow, Gus, if you haven't worked that one out yet."

"Rose won't like that, will she?"

"She's not here right now; leave a damn message."

". . . Kalyn?"

Her reply is soft. "Gus?"

"Um. We don't have to worry about Phil and homecoming anymore." I can't see the urinal in the sky. I can't see anything, with my eyes pinched shut. "Or, um, worry about Phil at all."

"'We'?" She sits up. "Aw, Gus. Is it my fault?"

"No." I think about it. "Maybe. Not really?"

"Wow, I feel so *reassured*!" Kalyn hops to her feet, and *god*, do I envy the simple grace of it. "Do you want help, or not want help?"

I inhale, trying not to overthink it. "Would you ask most people that question?"

"Fuck if I know. I'm the sort who'd usually stomp over the bodies."

"Okay." I get up on my own steam. My nose is bleeding and so are my gums, and if I wipe in earnest I'll definitely just be smearing blood on that dress. My arm and leg are tight knots. After a moment, I tell Kalyn she can use me as a tardy excuse.

"It's not even an *excuse*, man. You're a gen-u-ine mess today."

I thought we were alone, but now that I'm a little less dizzy and a little more upright, I notice that Garth of the Gaggle still watches us from under the flagpole. His best subject in school is the Art of Leaning Against Things. He takes a bubble pipe from between his lips and toasts me with it. His Docs match mine. Maybe I'm concussed.

". . . earth to Gus? Hey? Guess this means dinner's off?"

"Dinner is still on. In fact, wanna leave early?" I'm

scrambling for my phone. It's the same model as the old one. Grabbing it isn't easy with scraped knuckles. Now that I'm loosening up, I'm beginning to sting and shake all over.

"*You* wanna skip?"

"Is it skipping if a mom approves?"

"Heck yes it is. I was skipping for about a year *because* of my mom, and that's why I'm—never mind."

She's acting like me. *Kalyn* is struggling with words. I wait.

"Hell. Let's do it. Take me, Gus!" She feigns a faint. While I call Tamara, Kalyn keeps pointing out shapes in the sky. She's decided most of them are genitalia.

Within thirty seconds, Tamara caves. "I'm coming to get you right now."

"I sound that bad?"

"Nah, Gus. You sound *good*. Do I hear a *girl*?"

I'm bleeding from the forehead and knuckles. My knees ache like they've been snapped in two. My best friend of ten years has just dumped me.

But *I'm smiling*.

"Yeah," I tell Tamara. "Can't wait for you to meet her."

I hang up.

We wait on the steps. A teacher should be dragging us inside, but they let us be. It's a miniature miracle. Kalyn picks at her elbow, which means she wants a cigarette. "What are you thinking about, Wondergus?"

I'm thinking about all the possible options I gave myself. My alphabetical list. About how no one but me decided those were my only possibilities, about how I never left an option for myself to be happy, side note or not, about how I never imagined an awful day could feel so close to okay, so long as someone was next to me.

I point at the sky. "That cloud looks like a witch's titty in a brass bra."

KALYN

THE FIRST THING I notice about Gus's house isn't his house at all.

It's the yard, if you can call something that brand spankin' glorious a yard. It's like a goddamn secret garden, a land of downright whimsy. I expect to spot fairies, the way the ivy drapes from the front archway. Sculpted bushes line the walkway and ramp leading to the porch. Gus's family has a *koi pond*. I wouldn't be surprised if there's a gator in there, tick-tocking; this place *has* to be Neverland.

"You could get married in a yard like this!"

"We *did* get married here." It's the first time Gus's stepmom seems close to shy. Tamara is a riot in overalls, with a cracking laugh and about as much shame as a nudist. I could spend ten years in a car with her.

"Those weeds! Tenacious as hell!" Suddenly Tamara's bent

double over an innocent bed of lilies, yanking bits of green from the earth.

Gus laughs. "Another slaughter."

I could spend ten years in a car with *him*, but it'd be a lot quieter. It might be enough to smirk at each other in the rearview.

He's up to saying something now, working his face into a knot. Tamara smeared antibiotic over his scraped knuckles, stuck Band-Aids in an X in the middle of his forehead. Lifting his bangs makes him look like either Harry Potter or a cult leader.

"What gives, Gussie?" I'll never guess his name, but his cheeks twitch when I try.

"I can't believe you're here."

These plant-smothered fences must muffle sound. I can hardly hear the neighbor's sprinklers, but I almost hear leaves browning above us.

"Well, damn. Guess I'll scoot."

I mime an escape, but Gus tries for my hand. He mostly misses—coordination and Gus go together like ketchup and peanut butter—but his fingers find the tips of mine. "We *never* have people over. Thanks, Kalyn."

"Nah, don't thank—"

"*Thanks, Kalyn,*" Tamara says, without looking back.

"I—all right." I know I'm red and whatnot.

Tamara pats her hands down her pants; I bet she wouldn't recognize the weight of her fingers without soil under her fingernails. "You two wait out here a minute. I'll go prepare your mother. Gus, you know she's gonna suggest the cane."

I have a feeling Gus's "cane" isn't the same as my "flyswatter."

"Think you can argue her down?"

"Depends. What's in it for me?"

"A weekend of free child labor?"

"Child labor? You're seventeen, kid."

"But you still call me kid, lady."

"You looking for more holes to dig yourself out of?" Tamara winks.

That wink helps Gus's posture unfurl. Seeing them banter almost hurts. Mom and me would be bickering already.

"Wait. Tam." Gus leans forward to whisper words into her ear.

Tamara's eyes get real big. "If you say so." She heads inside without us.

Gus never pries about all my murderous poverty hints, so I cut him a break.

"So it's real special, me coming over?"

You can see the grease in Gus's wheels. "I only get to talk to you twenty minutes a day. It's all coming up *Rose* the rest of the time."

"I'm still *me* all day. I'm just playing dress-up."

"You lay on the sidewalk with me. Kalyn *would* do that. Rose wouldn't."

Gus is getting at something true. We don't hang out beyond secret kiln meetings. Minutes ago I thought I could spend a decade in a car with this guy, so what gives?

"I am *stoked* to be your friend."

He's still unconvinced. "Okay."

"I mean it. I'd wear you like a hat if I could."

Gus basically has pale Slinkies Gorilla-glued to his skull. Cocking his head sends them into a little frenzy. "I'm all about ecc, eco, eccentric accessories. But that's going a little far."

We wander up that ramp. The wood's a bit worn down, and I can tell the treads have been replaced a few times. The porch is old but freshly painted, no cracks in sight. Some kind of heaven, this place. We sink into white patio chairs, the kind I always knew rich people would have. I try to make it look natural, but Gus sits in jerky stages. On the table between the chairs is a small jar of colorful, oddly shaped dice. "The infamous D&D arsenal?"

"Those are Phil's." Gus is redder than blood can be, a sunset on the porch when it's only midmorning. "I screwed up today. What if he can't forgive me?"

"Gus." I lean forward to meet the wet wires of his eyes, pulling his forehead to mine, ignoring his tiny "ow" when I put pressure on the Band-Aid. "I fuck up *every day*. Fucking up actually makes you pretty good at figuring things out."

"It doesn't make sense," Gus says after a breath that might be mine. "It's like I've been living in a picture frame, like my— but you broke the glass, Kalyn."

When I visit Dad in prison, there's usually a pane of reinforced glass between us. When you're jailed for murder, they don't always let you in the visitation room. Whenever there's glass between Dad and me, we do the schmaltzy Spock thing where we line up our fingers, and Dad says, "You're growing up," because he's watching through a screen and doesn't know that I'm not at all, not really. I imagine I can feel the heat of his palm.

Gus doesn't feel cold anymore. His forehead's my fever. His Band-Aid might stick and transfer to me. "Christ, Gus, I'm gonna have to take you to *my* house."

"Why?"

"Because you're just . . . you're very *Gus*."

"And you're very Kalyn."

I don't think that's ever been a compliment before. It takes the air outta me.

I'm not sure how long Tamara's been standing there, but she's tactful about it. Gus pulls away and combs down his curls.

"All right. In you go." I walk into the chilly air of the white house, and Gus follows. I stop the moment I get a good look at the walls.

My eyes go moony.

ACT THREE
Farewell, Friend

GUS

FACED WITH THE emptiness, Kalyn stills.

"You guys just move in?"

I don't know how Tamara pulled it off so quickly.

The Dads that usually greet us in the entranceway have been tucked away, leaving naked walls behind. As we pass into the living room, Kalyn hanging back to stare at the high ceiling, I notice the Dads have also abandoned the mantelpiece.

"It's kinda . . . blank in here."

Tamara chortles, a little awkwardly. "Minimalist."

"Mullet house," Kalyn says. "Party on the outside, business on the inside?"

"Um, yeah," I say.

"I like it!"

Tamara squeezes my shoulder. Dad's been dead since before I was born, but he's never been *gone* before. *It's okay*, I tell him, *I'm still holding you close.*

I look at Kalyn, who's testing the plumpness of our couch cushions. She's mentioned her mom and grandma, but she never talks about her dad. Not today, but one day, we'll have that conversation. I hope it won't be weird for either of us.

"You didn't tell me you had a damn mansion, Gus."

I don't think it's a mansion, but maybe that's her perspective. "It doesn't matter."

"Guess it wouldn't, if you'd always lived in one." Her tone is bleak.

"You kids want hot chocolate, get your butts in the kitchen."

I groan. "Mom thinks I'm eternally seven."

"Are you implying mature adults can't enjoy hot chocolate?" Kalyn reaches the kitchen before me.

Mom's wearing a white poncho. Her screen reflects the light of an empty page onto her glasses. It's amazing we can see her, camouflaged in the ivory kitchen. She takes in the X on my forehead, and all at once I'm squeezed around the neck by a wooly arm. I catch Kalyn's eye, ready to share an apologetic eye roll.

But Kalyn isn't smirking. "Hi, Mrs. Peake?" she says after a moment.

"Call me Beth. And what should I call you?" Mom is deciding whether this girl in a dirty floral dress is hazardous to my health. She's used to the soil Tamara drags in, but Kalyn feels more like dust and petals. There's no telling if there's potential for growth.

Kalyn hesitates, probably debating whether she should be Rose or Kalyn.

"Kalyn Poplawski." She lunges forward, hand outstretched. Mom can't refuse it.

I wander over to help Tamara with the hot chocolate.

"Thank you for helping Gus." Kalyn's presence is the only reason Mom's sitting down again rather than demanding I lie in bed with a washcloth on my forehead. "Don't your parents mind you missing school?"

"Pah." Kalyn drops into a chair. I hope she won't put her shoes on the table. "I don't plan to tell my mom a damn thing about it."

I drop the mug I've pulled from the drying rack; Tamara catches it. Mom's not fond of swearing. If I so much as mutter unhappily, she assumes my arm's fallen off. I should have warned Kalyn. Or was I expecting her to switch Rose on after all?

"I might as well join the freakin' circus for all she'll care."

"Circuses are inhumane." Mom speaks so solemnly that I wince. I know she's twisting her locket between her fingers.

Tamara pours hot milk into the mugs. Who knows what she told Mom about hiding the Dads. I didn't give a reason, just asked Tam to put them away. I'm glad he's not watching this, even if it means having another painful settee conversation.

"Yeah, well. People suck. Good thing I act like an animal." Kalyn cackles.

Mom's face crinkles behind her mug. "I've never allowed pets in my house."

"Bullshit." Kalyn jerks her thumb at me. "You're raising a fine dandelion."

Mom spits graying coffee onto her laptop, and Tamara barks

aloud. It's not like that was even that funny—add "dandelion" to the list of my dehumanizations.

"Keep spitting like that and you'll have this house painted in no time!" Kalyn adds, and now Mom's almost crying for laughing.

I never make Mom laugh like that. She's so busy worrying, and I'm so busy worrying about worrying her. I'm rarely her reason for happiness.

I sink into a chair. Under the table, Kalyn's foot nudges mine.

Mom wipes the corners of her eyes. "Gus, please bring Kalyn over more often. I think she'll help me miss my deadlines, which can only be a good thing."

Kalyn's smile hitches. "Are you . . . Do you work for the newspaper?"

Mom waves a hand. "*Please.* I'd die before charging for obituaries."

"*Right?* Some of Mom's patients had no way to pay for theirs. We had to do freakin' fund-raisers!"

"Oh? Where does your mother work?"

How can it be that we've hung out in the dark for two weeks straight, talking about nothing at all, just clothes and Sarah and Phil and school, and never talked about these things?

Maybe falling into friendship has to do with falling away from something else.

"Mom did home health care for old folks. Now she does it for my grandma."

"It's just the three of you, then?"

Kalyn shows her crooked teeth. "Believe me, we're plenty."

Dadless. I fight the urge to find Kalyn's hand.

"Where did you move here from, then?"

"Arkansas, land of long grass and moonshine!"

"You'll find less moonshine in Samsboro, but we've got plenty of grass."

Tamara snickers. "Not *that* kind of grass, kids."

By the time we've finished the cocoa, Mom's mentioned her ghostwriting, and Kalyn's told a dozen stories about her adventures in elder care, how she wished some of those people she worked with could have met Mom before they "went tits-up."

Language aside, I don't know this side of Kalyn. I hardly know this side of Mom: a side that doesn't mind phrases like "tits-up."

I sometimes worry about what Mom looks like to outsiders. To me, Mom looks amazing in her flowing skirt, her wide hips draped in layers of white and beige fabric, a forest spirit in the middle of our farm town. Mom reminds me of Phil's beloved warrior elf queens. Mom's fat ("Don't you *dare* call me heavyset, Gus; 'fat' doesn't have to be an insult any more than disabled has to be") and usually exhausted. I have no idea how she appears to strangers who don't love her.

Mom catches me watching her. Just like that, she closes up.

"So, do either of you want to tell me what happened this morning?"

"Gus went *timber*, basically." Kalyn hasn't noticed the shift. Tamara busies herself by the sink.

"Was it the entranceway, Gus? Those steps. I've sent a dozen complaints and they haven't gotten back to me, but the ramp is hardly convenient, either. I mean, why would you want to walk up separately from everyone else?"

"It was my fault, Mom, I was—"

"Do we need to have your AFO looked at by the specialist?"

"I don't think—"

But she's gaining momentum. My Band-Aid cross is a target. "Did someone *push* you? Who was it this time? I'll be calling their parents."

I can't even glance at Kalyn. "No, that's not—!"

"Gus, if someone's bullying you again, you have to tell an adult."

I'm almost as old as my dead dad ever was, but I'm not an adult here.

"I mean it. Maybe get Mr. Wheeler to sort it out. It's his job, isn't it?"

"Mom, um, it, ahh, it um, it *wasn't–*"

"Just because you're in high school doesn't mean you've stopped existing. You're at his house every weekend as it is, and you've always been so nice to Phil—"

"Whoa, there!" Kalyn stands up, overturning the remainder of her cocoa. "Beth," she says, ignoring the chocolate dregs dribbling across the table, "people trip all the damn time. You're asking a thousand questions, but you're giving Gus exactly zero time to answer, and there's no point because I was there, too. I can tell you what he's already told you, ma'am: Gus tripped. That's it."

"Now, hang on," Tamara begins, spinning around.

Nobody tries to save the cocoa. The tablecloth's already stained, maybe even the wood underneath it is browning.

Mom stares at Kalyn's raggedy dress. "What did you say your last name was?"

"Pop-law-ski." Kalyn enunciates every syllable. The Rose smile has returned, but it looks like rigor mortis. "I can spell it for you."

Mom purses her lips. "That's your grandma's last name?"

"It's a family name." Kalyn doesn't look like any version of herself now. I've never seen her eyebrows this high or her eyes this wide, never seen sweat bead on her forehead. Because it's so unexpected, I don't recognize it right away: Kalyn looks *scared*.

Though my body's throbbing and I'll never stand as smoothly as Kalyn just did, I rise beside her. "Kalyn and I are going upstairs to reading. Um. Study. Okay?"

"We're still talking. Has your grandma been here long, Kalyn? Decades, at least?"

"A few, I guess."

This is a storm, but I have no idea how or why it became one. If Kalyn's gunpowder like she says, Mom's an old wick.

"Um, we're going, going up to—"

"Gus, we're having a conversation. Kalyn: Where does your grandma live?"

Tamara puts herself behind Mom. I catch her eye, and she shakes her head, like, *I have no clue what this is about, either.*

"Where, honey? Past Harrison Farm?"

"Calling a girl 'honey' is a bit dehumanizing, Beth."

"M-Mom—"

"Don't interrupt, Gus." Mom is paler than her clothes. I can't reason with whatever ghost haunts her. "Where do you live, Kalyn *Poplawski*?"

"I live where it's none of your fucking business, ma'am." Kalyn takes my hand. "Come on, Gus."

I don't tell her that it's no better for me to leave if someone else pulls me away.

I hear Tamara's voice rise, the sound of Mom suddenly breaking down into the wretched sobs I hear through my bedroom wall whenever it's Dad's birthday, the strange sobs that keep Mom in the tomb, because what if they should escape her in public?

People will think it's the apocalypse. People will *think* all kinds of things. And people think enough things as it is. "*Poor woman. Murdered husband and a crippled son, and now she's a lesbian to boot.*"

There's nothing worse than obsessing over what people think. I was born with issues, but my heaviest inheritance is that obsession.

Kalyn can't imagine how I feel as I follow her up my own

stupid staircase. Has she ever felt like her grip wasn't strong enough? Has she ever, for one second, not been able to say exactly what she felt? *Be* what she felt?

"Your room's up here? She doesn't make you sleep downstairs, or some shit?" Her insight terrifies me, makes me drag both feet.

"Kalyn, wait—"

But I bet she has *never* waited. Two weeks and we're already collapsing. It took me years to build a friendship with Phil. I've never tried with anyone else. As my toe catches on the stairs, it occurs to me that I don't know how to do it right.

We're on the fifth stair when the single portrait that Tamara's missed—that stupid trout picture—slips from its nail.

There's a crunch of glass as Kalyn treads on the frame.

"Shit!"

She lets me go and lifts her foot. A spiraling firework of cracks distort the picture. Dad's dopey smile is segmented and strange.

"Shit. Sorry." She reaches for him.

"Just leave it." I slump on the stairs. "I never wanted him there." I address Dad. "I didn't want you there."

"Mmm." Kalyn is panting, stray hairs pulled loose from her braided crown.

"Does she always talk to you like that? Like you're on trial for something?"

"It's not like that. She just . . . worries." Kalyn can't see years' worth of hospital waiting rooms, years of bedsides that forced an agoraphobic to leave home. The abyss.

"Yeah? If she's so worried about you, wouldn't she want to hear what you have to say? Jesus, she's got you all living in a goddamn test tube!"

I'm torn in half. One half wants to say, "Her worrying *kills* me." The other wants to tell Kalyn she has no idea how far we've come, trying to make a real living among half-dead things.

"You could have just *answered* her. Who *cares* where you live?"

"Oh, *Gus*." Kalyn's voice is low and hollow. "You don't know me at all."

"Because you, *you* don't tell me! You're acting like Mom's bad for talking over me, but you're talking, you're talking *under* me."

"Never said I was honest. Nobody wrote that shit on the tin." She lifts the picture frame and begins picking individual shards of glass from it, collecting them in her other hand. It's so reckless. All it would take is one angry fist curl to leave her bleeding. "But I'm sure honest about how I feel. If I'm getting talked over, I do something about it, for chrissakes. I stand up."

"And that's easy. For you."

"Sure, Gus."

Two weeks ago I didn't know her. Three hours ago we sprawled together on pavement. Half an hour ago she wiped my eyes. Minutes ago she made Mom laugh. Now she's collecting glass on my staircase, and it's clear she's held sharper things before.

Maybe I was the one trying to make Kalyn into a heroine.

"Gus . . . Is this your brother?"

"No." Enough. I take a deep breath. "That's my super dead dad. I never met him. But, um. I'm almost his age now. Yeah."

Kalyn stills, having pulled the last spear of glass from his face. His smile is scuffed but still cuts through clear as light.

"I didn't want you feeling . . ." I swallow, watching her, but she's only watching him. "You're the only one who never seemed um. *Sorry* for me."

Kalyn's silence echoes.

"He died before I was born."

"How did he die?" She speaks softly, like she's only breathing.

"Oh. Dad was actually murdered. Yeah."

This is where people wince. Kalyn pushes the frame away.

"Did . . ." The storm in my brain is leaving debris everywhere. "Did something happen to your dad, too? Do you want to talk about it?"

It's very wrong, but I feel a morbid thrill. What if Kalyn's dad was murdered, too, and *that's* why we fell fast into friendship? What if we're the only people in this tiny nowhere who spend Christmases googling crime reports?

Kalyn stands. She wipes her eyes on a filthy sleeve. "I need to leave."

"Yeah, okay. Maybe we can go to your place instead?"

"Definitely not." Kalyn smiles, but her eyes don't. "Gus,

you're *never* coming to my house. Get that straight. You'll never visit my goddamn house."

Two friendship fatalities in one day.

"Gus. I live just past the Harrison Farm."

I'm too tightly wound to stand. Mom's crying in the kitchen, softer now, and it's transferring to me. If she asks right now if I'll move downstairs, I will. If she suggests homeschooling, I'll consider it. I might consider hibernating for a year. I'm that tired.

Kalyn sets the picture frame facedown on the stairs. "Talk to your mom. I'll see you in school, okay? Come say hi. If you still want to."

There's no fire in her words. Somehow I've put her out. When Kalyn gets to the front door, she doesn't slam it behind her.

It's only once I'm alone, listening to murmurs from the kitchen, that I clear enough debris from my pathways to realize four things:

1. I don't know how Kalyn will get home.
2. She walked out of here with her fist full of glass.
3. Just past the Harrison Farm, you'll find Spence Salvage, the junkyard where Mom and Dad's Life Skills teacher, a woman named Kathy Sturluson, and her dog, a mastiff named Spook, sniffed out Dad's decaying body during the town-wide manhunt. Kathy Sturluson told the paper that Spook's presence was pointless; Kathy could smell Dad the moment she hit that row of beaters.

4. When Phil first met Kalyn, she didn't know how to spell Poplawski.

I have no idea how this is happening. Maybe you can't grow flowers from dust.

KALYN

GUS LIVES ON the opposite side of Shitsboro, but I'll be damned if I accept a ride home from him, or his magical gay garden-mom, or her sappy Havisham of an undead bride. Spence Salvage is only five miles away. It's just a hike from a house that's pure white without doilies to a prefab that can't seem to look clean with a thousand of them.

I leave that perfect garden without stomping. There's glass in my fist. I think about dropping the shards, but I can't bring myself to leave something here for someone to step on. I'll be damned if I hurt Gus anymore.

I'd *actually* be damned. I'm no Christian, but Grandma prays plenty. That rubs off on a girl, even a Spence like me. And the whole time I'm walking away from this neighborhood filled with patios and sprinkler systems, I know a Spence is what I am.

I've figured it out, even if Gus hasn't yet. I don't think it's about him being a little slow so much as him being a little kind.

"Did something happen to your dad, too?"

Well, yeah. My dad was made a monster by the press. I bet Gus has read everything I have, with one big difference: I bet Gus believes what he's read.

He won't know what I know in my *bones*: Dad had a damn good reason for shooting James Ellis dead, and fuck the papers.

Gus, lying on the sidewalk like he was a crime scene, but almost smiling once he rolled over, because Gus is one of the only people who's ever been happy to see me.

Gus, teary in the kiln, because I'm one of the first people to care what he likes.

I hit the main road. There aren't even cars here. It's almost postapocalyptic, this nothing town.

Gus, petrified on the stairs after I've hollered at him, after I've fucked it up and insulted his family. I wonder if people ever tell him he looks *nothing* like his dad, apart from the eyes.

And goddamn, the *eyes* in that picture. I've seen them online, but I've never seen them overjoyed about catching a damn fish. I've never seen them in full color.

When I felt Gus's thorny eyes on me, maybe I knew I'd felt them a thousand times before. Maybe *that's* what it was. Gus is right: there's no reason we should be friends. But, Gus, you felt almost like family.

Peake must be Tamara's last name. Beth Peake looks nothing

like Liz Wallace, the sun-smiling girl in high school photos who became a pregnant widow during the trial.

I'm walking the shoulder between one field and another fucking field. A few cars honk as they pass, but I wave them off. The asphalt churns up the last of late-summer heat, and I'm sweating. A little longer and I'll hit downtown. I won't look so out of place there. Sure, I'm a mess of snot and tears, and my dress is worse than secondhand now. But this is Podunk, USA.

I don't expect Gus to want anything to do with me, but I don't think he'll tell anyone at Jefferson the truth. Gus hates being looked at. I used to think that was a crying shame. He's got all that lovely hair, but beyond that he's got a weird sense of humor and a stupid welcoming heart and a passion for fashion. If that boy cared less what other people thought of him, he'd be untouchable.

Gus gets jealous of me because I can pretend to be likable. I get jealous of him because he actually *is* likable.

I holler through gritted teeth. The corn doesn't give a shit. The wind smells too sweet, that factory spitting up sugar. I'd punch the cinnamon from the air if I could. I veer to the right and walk into the field, forcing my way between green leaves until I can crouch between rows of cornstalks. Not even Rose could make this ugly crying look charming.

I wish I didn't know him. I wish I didn't *like* him so damn much.

Because I can lie about all sorts, about being a nice person and a Southern Belle, about being tough and being proud, but I can't lie about this one truth:

My dad is the reason his dad doesn't exist anymore, and his dad is the reason mine can never come home.

If you do a *chronological* search online through articles that mention the Ellises of Samsboro, you'll find Gus's great-grandparents first.

James Ellis's grandpa was an Irish immigrant who became one of the earliest supervisors at Munch-O Mills. He made a good living, good enough to send all three of his kids to college and buy up half the town. James's daddy, Mortimer Ellis, grew up to join the school board and began working as an attorney. Mortimer Ellis married Erica Holeman, a member of the city council. When James Ellis was a toddler, his parents were giving back to Samsboro, building parks like the one I just stomped past.

It was a family disease. James's cousin became the youngest mayor on record, and his uncle founded a successful chain of credit unions. Seems every one of James Ellis's relatives did something worth reporting, from great-aunts winning prizes in the county fairs to plain aunts fund-raising for charities and— wait for it—Girl Scouts.

The first time I read that little nugget, I swore out loud. I would have been kicked out of Alleghany Public Library if I hadn't pretended it was an enormous sneeze, or if the librarian hadn't decided third graders couldn't possibly cuss like that, or if they could, they *needed* to spend more time in libraries and less time at home.

James Ellis himself? Well, that golden boy wasn't even in second grade before his sharp eyes made the front page of the *Samsboro Herald*. He threw some amazing pitches in Little League. Folks talked like he was some kind of prodigy. One reporter said, and I freakin' *quote*, "James Ellis was born with a pair of cleats on his feet!" Which is just dumb from a figurative language standpoint, because all I can think of is how hellish it would be for a woman to give birth to some squirmy thing wearing spiked shoes. Maybe that's why James was an only child?

James Ellis always made the honor roll, won Boy Scout derbies and fishing contests. At Jefferson High, James did Samsboro proud, striking out the best batter in the state, Parker Adams of the Pikeville Pirates, and securing tiny Samsboro a place in the state finals during his junior year. He joined the football team, too, like it was easy.

All these Ellis accomplishments are footnotes now. What you'll really find if you search for "James Ellis" are dozens of sensationalized murder and trial articles, obituaries, and footage from local and national news. The death of this small-town boy captured the morbid imagination of America. Golden successes might be the Ellis legacy, but there's blood spatter on the trophies.

The first article mentioning both Dad and James Ellis isn't anything criminal. It's a shout-out to the students of Jefferson High's Tech Ed class, who worked for a semester to build and donate a brand-new gazebo to the Samsboro Community

Center. In the newspaper clipping, James Ellis grins like high beams, sitting pretty, front and center. Dad looms in the back row, bunched up and scowling like the devil.

There are dozens of articles about my family's crimes, from robbery to arson to drunk driving. But there's only one article I care about, an article that captures the cruelty of that golden boy. The *Herald* left out the names of minors, and also left out the truth.

SAMSBORO SCHOOL BOARD SEEKS REVISAL OF BULLYING POLICY AFTER INCIDENT

Students within the Samsboro school district may be required to attend biannual antibullying seminars as early as next term. According to Jefferson High principal Harold Broadbent, a revision of school policy "is a necessity" after a slew of bullying incidents culminated in the hospitalization of a sophomore student last week. The student sustained second-degree burns when classmates pushed him into the bonfire at the annual homecoming celebration.

"The incident didn't happen on school grounds," Broadbent explains, "but at Morley Field, where the rally takes place. Though the boys were just horsing around, we want to move toward a zero tolerance policy for this kind of behavior."

The first seminar will feature a visit from the Parents

Against Bullying Association (PABA) spokesperson Ted Chandler.

You'd think that if you flipped through articles from the week prior, you'd see one about the attack. You'd think it'd be *juicy* news. But someone didn't want that, probably Mortimer Ellis. The articles talk about Jefferson High's victory over the Eustace Eagles and a touchdown that saved the second half. Only I care about this story.

The *good people of Samsboro* like to ignore the reality that Gary Spence was the boy shoved in the fire, and James Ellis was among the boys who shoved him. I've seen Dad's scars. He calls his arms Slim Jims. It's not actually funny.

The first story other people care about detailed the discovery of James's body in the trunk of that rust-eaten Ford Taurus at Spence Salvage.

That October morning, the first early snowstorm had blown into Samsboro. The picture shows the red car, centered in a row of tan and silver sedans. The Taurus is the only splash of color against a snowy backdrop made of undead vehicles. A splash of red, but also black: the Taurus's trunk is open, dark and deep as a well you'll fall right into.

ALL-STAR ATHLETE'S MANGLED BODY DISCOVERED ON CRIMINAL'S PROPERTY

The bullshit in this "investigation" began from the word go. First off, James Ellis *wasn't* an all-star. Second off, since when do two bullet wounds constitute a mangling? And third fucking off, at that point in history, Spence Salvage belonged to Grandma, one of a few Spences with no criminal record.

Dad confessed to the murder before they brought in any other suspects. He called it self-defense. He explained that perfect fucking golden boy James Ellis showed up at the salvage yard after dark, swinging a knife around. Most reporters ignore this part.

The papers don't say that James Ellis bullied the *living shit* out of Dad from the moment he hit preschool. There aren't any articles about all the times James Ellis and company spat on Gary Spence "because you need *some* kind of bath, trailer trash."

The papers never reported the crickets dropped down Dad's shorts at school, or the maggoty meat hidden in his locker. There aren't articles about the time Dad's ribs were cracked in a PE "accident," about Dad being beaten to bruising in the locker room, about Dad's truck being set on fire in the parking lot. Besides, James Ellis had such a *great* pitching arm, didn't he?

There's no proof of any of this, except what Spences say. People like to point out that the only knife found in the trunk with James's body belonged to Dad. But mostly they don't bother going that far.

There was a confession. There was a poor kid from a violent family on one side. A wealthy family and a pretty, pregnant widow on the other. They made the following case: Gary Spence kidnapped James Ellis to take revenge on him for harmless teasing. Spence kidnapped Ellis halfway through the homecoming game, drove him to Spence Salvage to kill him. There's no other way James would ever show up there.

It was first-degree murder, premeditated, and enough to qualify Dad for death row. Look at that crying widow. Look at her cry. Amazing that he got life instead. Amazing they didn't kill him, like swatting a goddamn spider.

I don't need proof that this shit was unfair. I know it was, because I've lived it. When you're poor and you're dirty, you get hatred where friends should be. You've got broken teeth memories of smelling bad on the way to school and being incapable of doing jack about it. You don't get trophies.

The case gained a rabid following. But the attention waned. Dad was too obviously a hick and not an evil serial killer. Really, it was Mom who caused a real stir, when she started dating Dad in prison. But that's another story. And no one's business.

Apart from the Taurus picture, there's another picture that haunts me. It shows James Ellis laughing with Liz. Supposedly it was taken on the Fourth of July, months before his death. Supposedly the two of them are at the fairgrounds, watching the fireworks. There's light on their faces. They lie on the hood of a car, staring skyward. It could be an album cover.

If you peer into the background like I have, you notice there are other cars parked there. Yeah, maybe this is a field of sky gazers. But if you peer even harder, you notice the hoods in the background are old. There are no other people, just empty cars. You realize these kids might be in a parking lot or even a *salvage yard*.

But James Ellis would *never* have reason to visit Spence Salvage, right?

None of this matters to anyone.

To me it matters more than anything. More than sunlight and a good smoke. Dad had his reasons for shooting James Ellis. Dad's in prison, and he's a murderer. But he's a good man, too.

I don't know when I hit downtown, but I'm passing the Sunny Spot. Mom's shift won't have started yet, but I catch myself craning my neck anyway.

A shiny Prius pulls up alongside me at the curb.

"Rose? Hey! Rose!" calls Eli through his window. It's like slapstick, the way his brakes squeak. "Are you . . . are you *bleeding*?"

I stare at my fist. Shit. I've definitely been squeezing that glass. Yeah, there's blood on this brown dress along with all the other filth. Classic fucking Spence.

"Oh my." Rose isn't so easy right now. "Whoopsy-daisy."

"Where you going? Can I give you a ride?"

"Nah. It's a nice day for a walk."

"It's a school day," he observes. "And it's only one."

"Oh?" I force a bat of lashes. "So why aren't *you* in school, mister?"

Eli grins. "Oh, you know. I've got better things to do."

"Really?"

His grin slips. "Actually, I had an orthodontist appointment."

"You don't look like you need braces."

"That's because I *used* to need braces." Eli recaptures his cartoonish glimmer. "This doesn't happen naturally, you know."

This is the first time he's admitted to any kind of fakery. He may be on my level.

I lean on his car. "Hey. That dance this weekend. Still want to go with me?"

Eli raises his eyebrows. "Yeah."

"But I'm *filthy*," I say, as grossly as I can, with a wink. Might as well be a mess now, with a sheen of lace on top.

"Know what I think?" He's staring past me, almost *glaring* at tiny downtown Samsboro. "Nothing changes in this town. *No* surprises. Except you."

I think of Gus, telling me how Phil put me in some role in his head. I guess that's happening again. But roles are better than actual me.

I climb into Eli's car. He looks happy as a cat full of salmon dinner.

I giggle when Eli lends me one of his long jerseys to wear like a dress. I giggle while we eat Coney dogs at Maverick's Diner. I giggle on the way to the movie theater for some boring rom-com's matinee. I don't tell Eli no when he pushes his hand up my thigh. I don't know which girl lets that happen. If I tried to stop him, I'd get blood on his sleeve.

"*Do you want to talk about it?*" Gus asked me, before.

Never.

Eli tells me if he gets chosen for honor guard and I don't, he'll still dance with me. He tells me his dad bought him a suit and it's black but the tie is emerald, but he can switch it depending on what color my dress is.

Eli drops me off outside a neighborhood near Gus's, so I'll have to walk home all over again. I slip him some primrose tongue before hopping out of the car. He's popping a boner for sure, and I'll leave him with it, because everything is going to spin out of control soon, and what else can I do but leave him wanting a girl who doesn't exist.

GUS

BEFORE I CAN go liquefy in bed, Mom leaves the kitchen. She stands at the foot of the stairs. She spots the frame in my hands. "Is she gone?"

I nod.

Mom's shoulders fall. Tamara stands behind her, but of course she can't catch them. "Gus. We have to talk about her."

"Let me guess. Her dad killed my dad?"

Mom's beads rattle like rainfall. "I was hoping I was wrong."

"Maybe you are," Tamara reasons. "Gus, couldn't this be a misunderstanding?"

I'm used to tingles in my right hand, but now I'm flickering all over. "I think I wanna throw up?"

When I lean over, nothing leaves me but a gasp.

"I'll get a bucket." Tamara slips into the kitchen.

"Does she look like her dad, too?"

Mom shakes her head. "No, she—that wasn't it. It was how she . . . I don't know."

Mom's talking like me, maybe because she hasn't spoken about this before. I'm aware in some reality that Mom and Dad and his killer all played at recess together, ate in the same cafeteria, probably went to the same homecoming dances.

Maybe Gary Spence, convicted murderer, had a spitting sense of humor. Maybe he gave people fake names and insulted everyone equally. Maybe he seemed like an impossible character when he came to Jefferson High.

No wonder Kalyn's good at changing faces. No wonder she's living my dream. Both our dads might be gone, but hers can call her on the phone. He can give her a million life lessons about crocodile smiles.

I want to call Phil, but I can't. I want to call Kalyn Poplawski; she doesn't exist.

This isn't just timber. It's the entire clearing of a rain forest inside my skull. Maybe inside Mom's, too, because her head is shaking, all of her is, and when Tamara returns with the upturned compost bucket, Mom's the one who vomits in it.

Tamara proffers it to me.

"I think I'm okay."

"Gus," Mom says. "Do you want to talk about it?"

Mom doesn't want to talk about it. But Mom's always giving me options. That's what Kalyn couldn't see. She's not bullying me. That might be what Kalyn was doing.

I don't know. I can't even think about it. I can't think. "No."

"I think this time maybe you really should," Tamara murmurs.

"Gus said no."

"Because *not talking* solves all the problems in this house."

"Tamara! Give us a moment. Please."

"Don't shoo me. I don't *work* here, Beth. This is my family, too."

"But you didn't lose anyone. Give me a moment with my son."

"I didn't lose anyone? Then what's happening right now?" Tamara holds back from shouting, by just a hair. She puts her hands up. "But hey, it's all good. I'll just go on out and garden some more. I'll be where you think I should be."

It's a sign of the times that Mom doesn't stop her. Tam slams the door.

The house is eighty times emptier now. All Mom and me can fill it with are words we don't want to say. We've got to find something, anything else.

"Where on earth did she put your father?" Mom straightens her poncho.

By the time I unbind my joints and reach the living room, Mom's pulled all the Dads out of the bureau. They're spread along the floor at her feet. She clutches one portrait in white-knuckled hands.

I expect her to cradle it close. Instead, Mom holds it far from her face, gripping the wood so hard I think her arms might snap.

"You should have let me go," she whispers. I've never heard

her talk to him before; I thought that was my specific brand of crazy.

"Mom?" She jerks like I've cracked a whip. "Can I help put the Dads back?" Most are facedown on the rug, seeing nothing.

Mom passes me the Dad in her hands. In this one, he's sitting on a porch with a baseball bat in one hand and a grape soda in the other. I don't care about sports. I always pretend he's secretly more interested in the grape soda.

Tamara managed to stash seventeen pictures of Dad in five minutes, but Mom and I take our time with this ritual. I return Baseball-Dad to the mantel, and then hook Bowling-Dad into place in the hallway. Mom puts Pontoon-Dad on the fridge. Soon, Tamara comes back inside to help us hang up the rest. She doesn't speak, but I grab her hand as she passes. I don't miss. I watch her squeeze my palm.

The three of us stand over the last picture: Dad and the fish.

"Where did the glass go?" Tamara asks.

"Kalyn took it with her," I say. "In her hand."

"What kind of girl walks around with a fistful of glass?"

"I don't know." I feel helpless. "I don't know what kind of girl she is."

"She must have known. Why else would she come here?"

That hasn't occurred to me. Kalyn might have *known*. All along, she might have wanted to see what her dad had done. Victim first, disabled second, person not at all. Was that all I was to Kalyn?

"I can replace that frame, easy," Tamara says. "Heading to Lew's Hardware to sharpen the shears anyhow."

"Planning to cut me good, dear? Because I'd deserve it, Tam. I'm sorry."

"Damn straight you're sorry, baby girl." Tamara pulls Mom close and plants a kiss on her forehead.

I don't speak. I want to be alone. Maybe I am.

"To be honest," Mom says, "I always thought it was a bit silly. You know, hanging a picture halfway up the stairs . . . What?" Mom doesn't understand why we're laughing the house down to its foundations, but she climbs aboard the hysteria train and laughs, too. It's about all we're good for.

KALYN

I PASS ROW after row of rust-eaten automobiles and imagine Gus's eyes peering out of every black trunk.

Grandma's little house smells so musty that I'm coughing. I want to go right to bed, maybe vomit for good measure—Eli's tongue was like any other boy's tongue in that I didn't actually want it in my mouth.

But they're waiting for me. Mom sits across from Grandma, who's pulling threads from her sweater. Mom's eyes are fixed on papers spread across the table like poorly shuffled cards.

They don't ask where I've been, or why my fist is bloody, or why my makeup is smeared. Mom's crying, in that particular way she cries, like she's storing *just* enough fluid on her cheeks to put her cigarette out against her skin if she feels like it.

I am *this close* to screaming. "What'd I do?"

Grandma waves me closer. "Big papers. Very big papers."

"Honey." Mom lays her palms flat on the *big papers*. "We've got news."

"What?"

And holy shit, now she's *smiling*. "It's *amazing*. It's the Innocence Fighters. They're taking our case. They're going to prove your dad's innocence."

"But Dad confessed." The reply's automatic.

"He confessed, sweetie, but I married an innocent man. I knew that, no matter what. Last year, I contacted the IFA. They did some digging. *Kalyn-Rose*, they *agree* with me. We're gonna bring him home."

Grandma's crying now, too.

I take a damn seat.

This *was* our story:

The night that James Ellis got killed, he was shot not once, but twice, at distant range by a 9-millimeter Smith & Wesson semiautomatic.

The first bullet entered through his rib cage on the lower right side and exited his back just below his left shoulder blade, shattering three ribs and fracturing another two.

The second bullet entered through his right eye socket and exited the back of his skull at what experts estimated was a thirty-three-degree angle.

Those experts weren't sure whether he was dead after the first shot or the second, and maybe it doesn't matter.

The tricky thing about confessions is they tend to halt investigations. The moment Dad said he'd shot James Ellis, no "maybes" about it, forensic experts didn't have to try so hard to confirm evidence. The boys disliked each other—a dozen witnesses said so. A dozen witnesses talked about bullying, although most painted Dad as the instigator.

Again, it didn't matter. Dad confessed; case closed.

The gun was his, too. Not on paper—Dad was barely eighteen, and the pistol was licensed under Grandma's name—but she'd gifted it to him on his sixteenth birthday, as per Spence tradition. Dad brought the gun to the station when he turned himself in.

James Ellis harassed the Spences for years, and when he appeared at the salvage yard with a knife in his hand, Dad snapped.

There's one section of the taped confession that people love to ridicule: a policeman in the interrogation room asks, white-hot angry, "What did you think would happen when you killed the quarterback?"

Dad answers, "James was the running back."

I've watched a hundred video clips. Here's the sobbing family on one side, and on the other, there's Dad sitting with terrible posture in a wrinkled suit. The whole damn trial, Dad keeps his eyes closed. I think he looks sad, but critics say he's indifferent. He's a monster, heartless, another sociopath, et cetera.

To make the case stronger and put James Ellis in the

shiniest light possible, Mortimer Ellis and family denied any trespassing. They accused Dad of kidnapping.

Dad shrugged at that. He *shrugged* in court. They could have accused him of starting a nuclear war and he'd have shrugged. His defense attorney hated his guts.

Dad must have looked sad to Mom, too. The day after the trial finished airing, she sat down in her Wisconsin cabin and wrote him her first letter.

My whole life, Mom hinted at Dad's innocence, but Dad never has. I thought she did it to make me feel better, but I wasn't ashamed. Dad just got sick of rich bullies getting away with shit. He dealt his own justice. I understood it fine.

But our story's changing.

At the card table, Mom tells me how right after we moved to Samsboro she tore through Grandma's storage shed in a frenzied fit of tidying.

"I figured we could put that shed to better use."

"How?"

"Believe me, the shit I got up to in high school, I'd've loved my own room."

It's nice of her, really. Mom, trying to give me something she didn't have.

When I think of Gus's mom, watching him like a terrifying hawk-monster, hiding teeth behind cobweb-thin smiles, I know I've been lucky in the parent department.

Well. And I don't have a murdered dad, either.

"The junk in that shed hadn't been touched in decades. Hubcaps, old grease cans, tobacco from the seventies, and photographs and moldy newspapers and so much *dirt*. But I still found it. The mother—" She covers Grandma's ears. "—*fucking* gold mine."

"What?"

"I asked Grandma if they'd searched the whole property after the murder. Specifically, did anyone go through that old shed?"

"I bet they tore the place up."

Grandma shakes her head. She puts a hand out like she doesn't want Mom to go on. Mom doesn't pay her any mind.

"She finally told me *no*, though it was like pulling teeth."

Grandma glares at Mom with the side of her face that still glares properly. Maybe she's still furious about the shoddy police work, even after all these years.

"They didn't check it, Kalyn. After a confession, with a man and a gun in custody, why waste the energy? You know cops. They've got rolling stops to ticket people for, doughnuts to eat. Why bother investigating a damn *redneck murder*?"

I could pretend to be shocked. "What did you find?"

"A jacket. I found the denim jacket your dad wore the day of the murder. Stiff as an old washboard, shoved between two totes. There were smears on it down low on the front, like maybe he'd dragged a body. But there were other stains, too."

Mom twists her cigarette out in the faux-tortoiseshell

ashtray. She's calm as Gus's koi pond. She's treating this success like a cool glass of sweet tea.

"There was spatter all over the top of the *back*, from say, the chest height up, like bloody freckles on the shoulders. I couldn't figure out why those would be there. Couldn't hurt to send it on down to the IFA. I didn't tell your father a damn thing. I just sent it in, along with a bunch of photos and a letter."

I frown. "If Dad shot James Ellis, how'd he get blood on his *back*? Unless it was some other kind of blood . . . ?"

"It *wasn't* some other kind of blood, Kalyn. The DNA belongs to James Ellis. That's what the IFA confirmed. And not just *blood*. There's evidence of *gray matter*, too." Mom lifts a paper from the lacy tablecloth and reads it verbatim: ". . . in a pattern 'consistent with the trajectory of the exit wound in item C.' Basically, the bullet that went right through James's skull, Kalyn. This is *that* spatter. No doubt."

"Dad couldn't have shot James Ellis in the head if he was standing behind him."

"Your dad *was* behind him. *And facing the other way.*"

I've only seen Dad's back a handful of times, when he's retreated to his cell after visitation, but it's a broad one. Must have been a goddamn canvas for the IFA.

"*Shit.*"

"Kalyn. Your father didn't shoot that boy in the eye. He *couldn't* have."

I swallow. "I . . . Couldn't someone else have been wearing Dad's jacket?"

Mom doesn't wanna think this, and who could blame her. But she comes up with a counterpoint. "Say someone else *was* wearing his jacket. Even if that's the case, there's another witness out there somewhere. And that's something."

There are a million questions to ask. Why would Dad confess to a crime he didn't commit? If Dad was standing behind James Ellis, wouldn't that mean he saw the real killer? Why didn't he say so? Did Dad shoot James the first time? What do we do now?

Who the *fuck* killed James Ellis?

There's only one I can actually ask.

"When can I talk to Dad?"

Mom pauses. "He . . . well, he's being funny about the IFA. Says he doesn't want to dig up old graves. Got himself a martyr complex, and he's been cooped up too long. He'll come around."

"Is that . . . is this enough to bring him home?"

"It's a start. It's enough to reopen the case and look properly this time."

I remember the white dress and wedding, how the following week chocolate milk was dumped down the back of my shirt. It chilled my neck like the hand of death before I spun round and closed my own hand of death around the asshole who'd poured it.

"It'll be enough to get the media started, too."

"Well. That's the thing about the IFA, Kalyn. They use public advocacy to draw attention and funding to their cases.

Honey, they *have* to make news to make headway. We might go back to homeschooling, once this breaks."

I should feel hopeful, but in some corner of my head, Rose isn't taking this well. Dad's back is so broad, but I can't for the fucking life of me say why he thought that meant putting all this on his shoulders and ours, too.

What's the point of being Spence if being Spence means being full of shit?

ACT FOUR
Hello, Stranger

GUS

THE DAY AFTER Kalyn flees my house, I wake up at about 70 percent rigor mortis. I'm on my side even though I'm supposed to sleep on my back. When I roll over and see Dad, I can't say good morning to him.

As a kid, it didn't occur to me that there were reasons I couldn't keep up with everyone, beyond my constrictive muscles. "Gus," Dr. Petani told me, "you are working four times harder than anyone else to do the exact same things as anyone else."

I'd never thought of that. I was just annoyed at myself for zonking out whenever a teacher treated us to a movie, mad that I couldn't stand in lines without leaning against walls.

In first grade, I became fixated on how people walk. How legs bend in tandem when kids jump in PE, how most feet are spaced during jumping jacks. Some people crouch to bend, but others use their legs like counterweights—one planted, one straight back, perpendicular—becoming accidental ballerinas to recapture fallen things.

On some nights, I'd grab my unbraced right knee—you can sleep in AFOs, but it's painful for me—and try tilting it to "normal." I'd aim for the green shag rug by my nightstand to muffle the sound, climbing carefully out of bed like I was defusing a bomb, and lean my full weight on it.

I felt knives in my knee every time, and lost my balance every other. I cried every five. Eventually I stopped trying.

I'd thought often about my twisted parts, and about the branches in my head. But I'd never thought about sheer energy until Dr. Petani told me to.

If I want a glass of milk, I subconsciously plan the route, like I'm embarking on a hiking expedition. I decide where I'll put my feet, how I'll get the carton out of the fridge, how best to take the cap off one-handed.

Phil just takes out his milk and pours it.

Models have to think about every move they make, pivot on cue, and time high-heeled steps to music. It helps to pretend I'm walking a runway, but it's still exhausting.

When I shared this revelation at Camp Wigwah, some kids looked interested and others scoffed. "Well, *duh*."

But that's the thing—outsiders lump kids with CP under the same umbrella, and that's another umbrella under the enormous parasol of congenital disorders, which sits under the gargantuan black canopy of disability. We're sorted into categories, but we can be nothing alike. I don't even mean how some of us are hemiplegic and others are paraplegic, or how some of us are spastic and others aren't, or some of us have learning disabilities and others don't. I mean on a personal level, we're all *different* people.

That should be *obvious*, right?

Camp Wigwah is where I realized my disability is like any other part of a person—eyes or ears or teeth or height—in that it's variable. I have poor eyesight, and the muscles on my right side are tense threads that make my knees collide. But Karen Yuen's in a wheelchair, and Ali Sniridan spasms every evening.

I started thinking of CP as part of me, and I stopped resenting it so much. It seems dumb to ask your eye color to change. An AFO isn't bad when you think of it like a pair of glasses. I love my glasses; they're one fashion accessory that demands no explanation.

That's how the space brace came about. Mom and Tamara were trying to make me love myself. But it's harder when it's someone else's decision.

So what decisions did Kalyn make about who I am?

My alarm stopped wailing an hour ago.

Will anyone at Jefferson wonder where I am? Do people miss potted plants? It's not like I haven't been absent before, tucked into hospitals. Maybe kids will scratch their heads, as if they can't decide whether someone's rearranged the cafeteria tables.

"Gus." Tamara appears at the foot of my bed. "Hon, you need to get up."

"I'm not going to school today."

"It's not that. You need to get downstairs and watch the news. Now."

I lift my head. Her face is gray despite the sunlight sliding through my bedroom blinds. "Whatever's on the news, I probably *already* missed it."

"They're looping it over and over. Your mom's almost catatonic, Gus."

And that's when I know it's about Dad. It's about *us*. And maybe it's about a girl named Kalyn-Rose, or named something else.

I think about every step to the dresser, every motion through the drawers, every step to the bathroom. I manage to catch my toe on the edge of the doorway. I see myself in the mirror, half-dressed, a nightmare.

In the corner of the glass, a senior photo of Dad stares eternally.

"*You should have let me go.*" That's what Mom told him yesterday.

I don't know what it meant, but I think he's started frowning.

KALYN

MOM TELLS ME to play hooky. I tell her to go to hell.

"That's where you're going," she yells, following me to her room. "Stay home!"

I'm tearing through her dresser drawers like they've insulted Grandma, sending clothes flying. "You just want Officer Newton to come visit again. You wanna pour him sweet tea and sweet talk. Don't care. I'm going."

I find it: the white dress I wore to my parents' wedding, the dress that used to tickle my little ankles.

I pull off my tee, throw it at Mom, and force the dress down my torso. Turns out I haven't grown all that much in ten years, despite a few creaking seams. The thing almost looks like a blouse, cupcake chic. It hangs long enough that I can wear tights with it.

I wonder what Gus will say about this fashion statement, and then I remember Gus probably hates me.

"What the *hell* are you doing?" Mom's fuming. I sling on my backpack and elbow past her. I make it to the kitchen before she catches me by the wrist. *"Kalyn!"*

"Think Grandma has the keys to any Tauruses? Give 'em a *real* shock."

I think Mom wants to slap me, but she doesn't. Mom ditched the flyswatter when she ditched the booze. She got slapped too much when she was my age. When that happens, people either keep the slapping cycle going strong, or they snap it right down the middle. Mom broke it best she could, but she can't break my resolve.

Sure, it was surprisin', waking up at five a.m. to find Mom and Grandma on the couch, gawping at the news. It was surprisin', seeing Dad's face and James Ellis's face on the screen over the words: *Killer Case Reopened: DNA Evidence Exonerates Murderer?* Whoever wrote that headline's an ass. Dad can't be a murderer if he's exonerated.

He can't be what he's pretended to be.

"Now *who* could be mad to hear that an innocent man's going free?" I ask Mom. "Shouldn't we be *celebrating*?"

Grandma sits at the table, crying into her oatmeal.

"People need hard proof. Even when they get it, they say it isn't hard enough."

"So? Folks will be pissed. It's got nothing to do with Rose Poplawski."

Mom lets go. Her nails scuff my skin. "You're still going by Poplawski?"

"You didn't want me to *be* me, right?"

"Hell, I didn't mean—I'm just . . . surprised."

"You *told* me to be her!"

"I know. I know, baby. But I thought blood would out. Thought I'd raised a rebel." Her smile is sad. *I'm* itching to slap something. "Fine. I'll drop you off."

I deflate; she looks so tired. "You work today?"

"Nah. Even if you aren't playing hooky, I am. Got errands to run and phone calls to make." She clears her throat. "Heard from the lawyer. Your dad? He's going to call us tomorrow. Nine p.m."

"Should be interesting."

Her eyes soften. She pulls a cigarette from her breast pocket. "Should be."

After the usual fuss, we're out the door and inside the old minivan, and none of us are talking. No matter how many windows I roll down, there's not enough air. I'm dying for a smoke. Grandma starts coughing the moment we hit the main road, so Mom squishes her butt out on the dash.

This is the best news we've ever had. So why does today feel like a funeral?

I'm going to school in a dress that doesn't fit me. No white dress ever suited a Spence. Rose aside, Spencehood was never something I doubted.

"You can be nice. When you try!" Olivia screeched, way back when.

Chances are, Gus will recognize this dress. Maybe I want

that. Maybe the guy who knows confusion better than anyone can help me level the forests inside me now.

Mom turns on the radio. We hear Dad's name. Grandma starts sobbing.

Getting through today is gonna take one helluva performance.

GUS

THE NEWS HAS set this tomb on fire.

That's how it feels, sitting on the couch beside Mom, watching the television recycle the story of our lives.

The screen pans to a decade-old picture of Mom and me at the Samsboro pumpkin patch. We took second place in the competition for smearing a collage of Roald Dahl characters along the sides of a pumpkin.

I don't know how they dredged that picture up. It feels wrong, because I'm in the wheelchair there, which is probably *why* they chose it. It feels even wronger because Tamara wasn't with us. Once again she's cut out of our family, severed from our lives so Mom can take on the role of the tragic widow.

Even though she took work off today, Tamara's been outside tearing up earth since she woke me. Every few minutes, soil patters against the siding like gunfire.

An IFA spokesman details the circumstances of the case. They reference strong DNA evidence, but they don't share details. They compare James Ellis's case to a dozen others. There's talk of conducting new interviews and rebooting the investigation by as early as tomorrow. There's talk, there's talk, too much to comprehend. Images a-million.

"This is all wrong. He *did* it. Gary Spence did it. He confessed. He did it!" Mom repeats this like a mantra, baring her teeth, getting steadily louder. "He's *guilty*."

The words bother her. I'm more worried about the images. Dad's face was a comfort, but these constant flashes of him, of Mom, of me, of the murderer, of Dad, me, him, Mom make my stomach churn.

I find my feet.

"Where are you going?"

"Bathroom," I lie.

"Gus, I don't want to be alone right now."

"Mom. It's just the bathroom."

Her eyes trail me, but she can't see me once I'm past the door frame. I pause in the foyer. The keys are right where they were yesterday, in the bowl at the bottom of the stairs. Am I quick enough? Of course not. She'll hear the jangle and then she'll hear me struggling with the door and I'll be pulled right back to that couch.

"Gus? You finished?"

I'm resigned to my fate. I steel myself to turn back—

I hear a throat clearing, and Tamara is here, watching me

through the open door. Her eyes are red. She beckons me closer.

I do my best not to drag my foot over the precipice, and she closes the door, as silently as she opened it. Away from the sickening warmth of the living room, the October morning proves chillier than expected. I can smell the leaves that have crisped and fallen across the lawn overnight. I tell myself that's why Tamara's spent all morning outside—she's raking them onto the flowerbeds, anticipating the first frost.

"You know, you won't be able to hide from this for long." Tamara pulls a spare set of keys from her pocket. "Better make the most of it. Take my jacket."

It's denim, heavier than I expect when she sets it on my shoulders. I tip sideways and assume my body's acting up, until Tamara pulls a spade from one of the pockets.

"Are you going to tell her?"

"Oh, if you think she's not already waiting outside the bathroom door for you to come out, you haven't been paying attention. Better get on with it, kid."

I hug her tight.

"Well," she tells my shoulder. "I figure you got me to the taco place all right. I figure you're seventeen. I figure maybe I'm not cut out for responsible parenting."

"That's, that's *bullshit*."

I head down the ramp, but before I reach the driveway, she catches me again.

"Hold up—I put your cane in the back. Please use it today."

I haven't used it in years. "I don't—"

"Please," she insists. "So I can tell her I did something right. And come back by dark. I've got to make some kind of show of being responsible, hey?"

I pull myself into the truck and do up my seat belt. I place my feet near the pedals. My slippers look like moccasins. No one but me cares what I'm wearing.

When I look back, Tamara's on the porch, putting herself between me and the tomb. I don't know how I'll ever thank her. I don't run over the grass, but I do hit the curb when I switch into drive. I'm still in our subdivision when I realize I left my phone on my nightstand. I'm not going back for it.

Maybe I'll get into a terrible accident today, but it's hard to care. It's all been one big accident from the beginning.

KALYN

"I LOVE YOUR blouse, Rose." Seems like a genuine compliment. There's no way Sarah can know it's the sort of compliment that's really a gut punch.

"Why, thank you! Isn't it just divine?" Man, I'm hitting the shine too hard.

Sarah frowns. "Yeah."

We're sitting at a lunch table full of pretty people. I haven't been in the cafeteria for weeks, but now I'm nestled between Eli and his basketball friends while their girlfriends have separate conversations right across from us. Seems my reward for letting Eli grope me yesterday is being squished against him now.

Back in junior high, a guy named Rusty shoved his hand up my skirt at the AMP bonfire and I went full Spence, stabbing him in the foot with my marshmallow poker. I wasted two beautifully browned marshmallows on that weasel.

How would Rose respond to this situation? I don't know how to address problems without blowing up. Would Sarah tell Eli off? Or would she accept this as something boyfriends do?

How do straight and narrow people even *function*?

I'm staring at the door. I haven't seen Gus. Usually we'd cross paths between classes, nod, and save our conversations for the kiln.

Earlier I made a beeline for his locker, pulling my dress into place because I swear it spends every minute hitching up to constrict around my throat. I leaned against it until a freckled girl came close and began twisting the dial of her combination lock.

"Hey, you seen Gus today?"

"You're Rose Poplawski."

"That's right, gold star." I added more butter to my voice. "And you are?"

"Ariel Mathers. Did you say yes to Eli Martin?"

"I'm talking about Gus, not Eli."

"Who's Gus?" She leaned in, ready to be doused in gossip.

I didn't intend to slam my fist against her locker. If my failed intentions were pearls, I'd wear a thousand necklaces. "*Gus.* Gus Peake? He's got the locker right next to yours. Seen him today?"

"No. Why?"

"He's been tutoring me," I lied, because why not. I told Gus I wasn't embarrassed to know him and that's the truth.

Ariel gawked. "*He's* tutoring you? But isn't he, like, retarded?"

This time I slammed my fist on purpose. "What the *hell* kind of word is that? What fucking year do you think this is?"

"*Excuse me?* I don't even know you."

I watched her go, wondering if Kalyn could get away with yanking her hair. Maybe even Rose could. Anyone who thinks the word "retard" is okay deserves worse.

Sitting here with Eli's hand creeping up my back, I don't regret cussing her out.

I can't stop watching the damn cafeteria doors.

"You done getting tutored?" Jackson asks, tossing a fry into his mouth. He's one of Eli's basketball buddies, a gargantuan center Eli treats like a dumb sidekick.

"No. My tutor's absent."

"Guess I'll get to teach you today," Eli whispers.

"So you two have worked it out." I can't read Sarah's expression. "Will you be sharing our limo on Saturday night?"

"I dunno," Eli says, sliding his hand lower, "we might wanna drive separately."

"Rose? What do you think?"

Too bad I can't split myself in half so Rose can go to the dance and I can do literally anything else. Homecoming was always a stupid thing, but now it means even less than ever.

News that's life changing for me and Gus is nothing to these guys. Nobody recognizes my dress. They don't have memories of it being paraded around the papers, the woman who bought it being slandered and spat at and the daughter wearing it not knowing that as far as the whole world was concerned, her family didn't deserve respect.

Eli's hand goes too far, his fingers lifting the line of my tights away from me, and the spork in my hand is a weapon and I'm going to stab him—

Phil lurches into the cafeteria, eyes locked on his screen. I cry out in relief, untangling myself from Eli's greasy grip. "Hey, Phil! Hold up!"

I don't know what I thought he'd do. The second that pill bug hears me yelling, he makes himself scarce, doing an about-face and lurching back the way he came.

"Someone needs to put that kid out of his misery," Eli says.

Boom.

I punch the edge of Eli's lunch tray, knocking its contents into the air and into his lap. Jackson's girlfriend screeches as a slice of pizza smacks my white dress dab in the middle, but I don't care. I don't care that the cafeteria has just erupted in noise, that Rose is brutally murdered that quickly and publicly. I'm on my feet and out of there.

Eli yells at my back, "You're a goddamn psycho, Rose!"

"I'm not Rose," I tell him, "but you got the rest right."

I'm scum to the people of Samsboro, but at least I'm not Eli fucking Martin.

GUS

IT TAKES TEN minutes to reach the place that started and ended everything.

A mile past downtown, the Munch-O Mills plant chugs its sweetness into the air. There's a factory feel to this area filled with smokestacks and parking lots that gray the landscape. But factories mean work, and the houses on the fringes aren't in bad shape—maybe the paint is chipping or there are junky old swing sets polluting yards.

If you keep driving past the plant, the roads become bumpier and the grass becomes distended. Suddenly you're at Harrison Farm. The decaying Harrison Farm, collapsed barn and all, is almost glamorous compared to what comes after.

Crooked fence posts encompass the entire length of Spence Salvage. Those wouldn't keep anything out if not for the chicken wire wound between them. Still, there are places where the fence fails, dips to the dirt and vanishes in tall grass. In those places, the fence posts look like tombstones.

I've never been this close.

The truck rattles, and I nearly bite my tongue—I've drifted onto the rumble strips. I right the wheel, but I'm struggling. I need to stop and breathe, but I keep driving, so slowly that I might as well take my foot off the gas. The fence seems to stretch for miles, but I know it's only forty acres.

I finally spot the driveway and pull up onto the shoulder. The welcome sign is rotting in places, and the chains suspending it have rusted to perpetual stillness. Alongside the words *Spence Salvage*, someone's clumsily painted a wrench. A plastic orange and black *CLOSED* sign is bolted to the wood.

I switch into park. I roll down the windows. This is Tamara's truck, so there are no pictures of Dad here. But Mom, Tam, and me are on the dashboard, a curling photo of the three of us at Mammoth Cave.

Yesterday Kalyn told me never to come here. The last thing I want is to come home and find Mom mummifying on the couch and Tamara outside. The last thing I want is to go back to school and be pitied, the boy in the pumpkin patch.

I don't want our lives turned into a whodunit. I don't want this case reopened. I don't want Dad's face to become a thing I hate seeing. So what am I doing here?

I climb out of the truck. No cars have passed, and I doubt any will. This place is out of business. People don't come here. I weave along the shoulder until I'm standing in the middle of that long driveway.

I lift my eyes from my feet.

Lining the driveway are rows and rows of cars in all sizes and colors. The only thing they have in common is a state of disrepair. There isn't a single one that looks like it could leave this yard. Some of the vehicles are lopsided, even sunken into the ground. They crowd the driveway so closely that I can't tell where it ends.

Did Dad actually walk down here once? Did he do it with a knife in his hand?

I want to believe no. I want to believe this is Mordor. I want to think that the story I've been told since the day I was born is nonfiction. Not because I want Dad to have been murdered, but because I want to know that some portion of my life is a certainty.

I've never questioned our truth: Dad was kidnapped during his senior homecoming game, taken here, shot dead, and shoved into a trunk like secondhand clothes. That story won our case and became America's truth after Grandpa Ellis bribed the best prosecuting attorney in the Bible Belt.

We stopped seeing Grandpa Ellis years ago. Before that, he was a fixture in our lives. We used to visit him for Sunday dinner.

Mom would put on makeup and a smile and act like leaving the house was as easy as breathing, but she'd spend a few seconds hyperventilating in the car, hands stuck to the wheel, before dabbing at her mascara and stepping outside.

Whenever we knocked on the door, Grandpa looked unhappy

to see Mom. The feeling was definitely mutual. But Grandpa Ellis helped Mom pay rent before she started making steady ghostwriting money, and he paid for me to go to summer camp. We couldn't turn down his invitations.

He lives in a huge cabin thirty minutes out of Samsboro, on a wooded hill near Lake Cumberland. Grandpa Ellis didn't keep any pictures of Dad around, although family trophies lined the walls.

Grandpa always sat at the head of the table, even though there were only three of us. He hardly spoke, just asked how school was going for me; he didn't ask about Mom. He only once talked about Dad and the Spences—on the day he kicked us out for good, the day Mom told Grandpa she was seeing someone.

Grandpa Ellis has Dad's eyes, but sharpened to knifepoints. When Mom mentioned Tam, he spat out his food, stood up straight, and pointed us to the door.

"You're as evil as any Spence," he told Mom's back. "You're as good as killing him all over again."

It wasn't just a cruel thing to say. It was also the only time I ever heard Grandpa Ellis's voice crack. It was the first time I wondered whether, as much as it sucked for me to grow up without a dad, having and losing a son could be worse.

When we got back to the car, Mom didn't hyperventilate. She laughed, a little madly. "Well, that book's finally shut."

An icy October wind is blowing. The grass bows away from me, and unseen dashboards in the salvage yard creak in the gusts.

When do words like "evil" start sticking? If they stick, does that make them true? People have called me a thousand names. I call *myself* names. But I choose to believe that those names aren't all I am.

A Spence isn't all that Kalyn is, either. Not even close.

I wonder if she's playing hooky. I wonder if she's mummifying in front of a TV at the end of this driveway, or throwing eggs at strangers, or batting her lashes at boys.

I know what I'm doing here. Despite it all, I want to see her.

But I can't bring myself to walk down this driveway.

KALYN

I STEP OUT of the cafeteria and peel the pizza from my torso. I let it hit the floor, then scan the area for Quillpower's signature lurch. The main hallway is almost empty.

I cuss and stomp left. As I pass the office, there's no getting around the secretary, Ms. Patrick. She's balanced on a rolling chair in heeled sandals, unfurling the latest honor roll poster on the office window.

"No running in the halls!" The chair swivels but she doesn't lose her footing. "Oh! What's the matter, hon?"

"It's nothing."

"*Please* remember that I'm the only cool adult in this building before you try peddling that crap. What's wrong?"

I stare at her tattooed eyebrows. Hard to tell if the concern is genuine, but I go with my gut. "Gus Peake isn't in school today, and it's my fault."

Her eyes flash. "That's *not* your fault."

"You don't get it."

"I know who you are." She plops down onto the chair and lets it roll toward me. "I've got all your records, remember? Fact is, *you* didn't kill anybody, honey. As of the news today, fact is maybe no one in your family did. Right?"

I don't know what to do when people are kind to me.

"Hey, the speed limit is WALK!"

I'm the hell outta Dodge, and soon I'm near the gymnasium at the far end of the building. Based on the squeaking and hollerin', people are throwing dodgeballs inside. No way would Phil choose to be in there. His twigs would probably snap.

I put my hands to my hair, unclip my braid, and give it a hard tug to center myself.

There's a sound like swords clashing to my right, but it's tinny, nothing natural about it. I swivel with my fists up.

Phil's killing things on his Game Boy or whatever in a small nook beside the boys' locker room. His baggy gym shorts make him look longer than ever. Phil's tried makin' himself as small as possible, but his terrible posture makes *my* back hurt. He's Ichabod Crane, in a ratty *Blade Runner* T-shirt. I know hand-me-downs when I see them.

Phil's upright before I get close, yanking on the door to the locker room—

"If you think I won't follow you the fuck in there, you've got no idea who you asked to homecoming." I have no idea, either, but hey. "Where's Gus?"

I'll be damned—Phil doesn't bolt. "Gus actually asked you out for me?"

I can't figure out his expression. "Don't tell me *that's* what you two argued about? Jesus. Gus couldn't betray you if he tried. He's wrapped around your fingers."

"He isn't." Gus's glasses sharpen his eyes, but Phil's dilute his to glassy ponds. "I'm not his keeper."

"Happen to see the local news today, Phil?"

"Who bothers with local news?" But he's already moving his fingers. Guess that toy has internet. I bite my tongue while he scans the headlines.

"Hmm." He draws himself up straighter. "It's not merely local."

"Oh, great." Here we go again. At least I'm dressed for the circus.

Phil looks at me. "I'll message Tamara. I presume Gus told you. About his dad?"

"More or less."

His device pings. "Tamara says he left and neglected to bring his cell phone."

"He left? Alone?"

"He's not an infant."

I bristle. "No, but his mom treats him like one."

"I imagine she isn't up for it today. Considering the horror of it all, et cetera."

"Well, maybe the guy's innocent."

"Spence, innocent?" Phil scowls. "Are you familiar with the case?"

"Safe to say so." I try not to spit on him.

"Spence confessed. His innocence is unlikely. I imagine . . . Gus feels panicked. His flight makes sense. 'Why, what an ass am I . . .'"

"Yeah," I grumble, "you're pigeon-livered, and you lack gall." Phil freezes.

"Shocker! I like Shakespeare. You and me might have some mutual interests, and if you'd avoided the *bullshit* and talked to me yourself instead of forcing Gus to do it, imagine the drama you could have spared us all."

"Noted."

"Whatever. Where would Gus 'flee' to?"

"My house, on occasion. That's doubtful, after yesterday." Phil shakes his head, then freezes midway. "Ah. I know where he could be."

"Great. Let's go. Before the bell rings. You drive."

Phil cocks his head. "I'll take you to Gus. But only if you—"

"Oh, you'd *better* not!"

"—attend homecoming with me."

"You're *blackmailing* me? Jesus, Gus deserves better. You know what? I'll find him on my own. Fuck your dance."

"Wait—stop." I'm about to yank the fire alarm and unlock that emergency door. "I'll drive. Fine."

I pull my arm down anyhow. The alarms start wailing. "Hamlet is a self-absorbed prick, if you wanna know my opinion."

"I don't," Phil says, holding the door for me.

"Figures. You just wanna *dance* with me, right?"

Whatever. I can't control how Phil chooses to think about yours truly, but I can use it to my advantage like the monster I am.

I don't know if I'm a monster to Gus. I don't know who I'll be when we find him. But I *want* to find him. That's a tiny chunk of goodness in me. I'm holding tight to it.

GUS

EVERYTHING FEELS TOO fast on the freeway. I stick to the slow lane. After an hour, I creep down an exit and escape the traffic, ignoring angry honks as I pull into the half-empty parking lot of Carson Shopping Mall.

Phil and I once made weekend sojourns here. The mall was home to the Card Vault, the only gaming store we knew. When we used to play *Magic: The Gathering*, we'd spend hours digging through boxes of cards while Phil's brothers perused *Warhammer* figures or discussed strategy with the shopkeeper. Phil cherry-picked cards that gave him tactical advantages. I collected cards featuring elaborate costume designs.

The Card Vault closed years ago.

Because Tamara begged me, and because I'm tired, and because there's no way I can avoid attention here, I slide my cane out of the truck bed. Soon I'm leaning on it indoors, window shopping stores I'll never buy from. Most clothes are made for people who have matching arms and legs. I see everything and nothing I want.

I visit the seasonal Halloween store, even though the air inside smells like toxic markers. The "clothes" are constructed from fabric as strong as sandwich baggies, tulle so flimsy you could filter coffee through it. I don't buy anything, but some of the masks are interesting. Things might be easier if you could tell a monster by looking at one.

I walk by the windows of an indoor gym. I wouldn't like working out in front of strangers, sweating behind glass like a hamster.

I spend twenty minutes in a faux-leather massage chair. I don't bother feeding it quarters. This early in the afternoon, the trickling crowd is made up of parents with tiny children in tow, a parade of strollers and cries. A mom talking on a cell phone pauses in front of me. Her kid cranes his neck out of his stroller. He's waving around a plush giraffe, but he drops it when he sees me. His mother doesn't notice when I pick it up for him, but an older woman gives me a nod as she passes. She's got a cane, too. I nod back.

I make my way to a little black shop that seems determined to chase well-adjusted people away. There are studded belts in the window. Screeching metal music blares from speakers within. The back wall is lined with black T-shirts. It's intentionally offbeat, catering to teens by capitalizing on things we like, using our angst against our allowances. It's dumb, but it still feels like validation, even if it's manufactured.

My eyes are immediately drawn to the shoe section. There are rows of heeled boots and spiked platforms. There are canvas tennis shoes that travel halfway up calves, slip-on ballet flats decoupaged in skulls. I'm wearing my sad orthopedic slippers. None of these shoes would meet Dr. Petani's approval.

Here are socks in striping patterns, shoelaces bedecked in pentagrams. Again, it's tacky, but again, I'm kind of taken with it. In my head, I put together an outfit someone else could wear, a parallel me or some version of Kalyn I haven't met yet:

I'd pair the ballet flats with those translucent tights with the veining pattern up the leg, but I'd exchange the ribbons on the flats for black ones. I'd layer two batwing skirts around the model's hips, cape-like, and above that, any one of those black T-shirts could do for casual wear, but a corset blouse might be great for a concert. Or one of those sharp-shouldered eighties blazers could elevate the look to edgy professional. And oh, those silver floral wrist cuffs could be repurposed as hair accessories around buns. A pop of color at the neck—yellow, maybe—

"Let me know if you wanna try anything on." The shopkeeper's got more piercings than teeth, but her smile is kind.

There's one garish set of socks I can't help inspecting. They're knee-highs or maybe OTKs (over-the-knees). One is black with a pattern of white feathers strewn about it, topped by a sturdy cuff complete with jutting black wings. Its partner in crime is a white sock speckled with black bats and topped by tiny white wings. The socks are harlequin nonsense. They are good and evil and mostly they are silly.

I love them beyond reason.

Before I know it, I've placed them on the counter.

"I think these'll be big sellers for Halloween." The shop-keeper squints at them through white contact lenses. "Huh. These shouldn't be mismatched; we sell the Valkyrie ones and the Demon ones separately. Let me see if we have a complete set in the back."

I shake my head. "Um, I like them like this."

"You can buy two pairs and mismatch them yourself."

I push the socks toward her. "Um. I mean. Never mind."

"Nah, it's cool. Just don't tell on me, okay?"

The shopkeeper gives me a 30 percent discount. I don't know if it has anything to do with my slurred speech or my cane. She hands me a black bag. "I can cut the zip ties if you want to wear them out."

"No, I, that's—"

"You should wear them," says someone behind me.

I turn, and there's Garth of the Gaggle, perusing the selection of gauged earrings. He's not wearing a kilt, just black jeans and a mustard V-neck with a flannel shirt tied around his waist, and four watches on one arm. He *should* look ridiculous, but he looks cool, if slightly cartoonish, with his hair combed back like that. Garth's clutching a bottle of turquoise Manic Panic in one hand and a box of marbled guitar picks in the other.

"You're skipping, too, huh?"

The shopkeeper rolls her eyes. "Take that talk outside, seri-ously. I'm supposed to report this stuff."

"Man, can I at least buy my goods first?"

She's not smiling now. "If you must, *man*."

I fight the impulse to flee as Garth collects his own little black bag. He rolls it up, tucks it into his waistband. He's not as tall as Phil, but he's still taller than me. Garth's dark eyes probe me from head to toe.

"Come on, man."

Garth looks both ways before stepping out of the store. That's something I do, to make sure I don't get T-boned, but I don't know why Garth needs to. He doesn't wait for me, but he isn't in a hurry. Garth wears the Docs I'm not supposed to wear, but his are yellow-tartan patterned. He should look hideous. He doesn't.

He's a bee that's stung me.

On this undead day, running into my idol miles from Samsboro is another surreality. I'm beyond trying to process this week. I stare at Garth's even gait, the effortless way his feet move like graceful pistons, and try to keep up.

"Hey, Gus?" he says. "It'd be cool if you didn't mention I was in that store."

"O-okay." It's a weird request, but I can't decide why.

When we reach the food court, I'm panting. Garth doesn't notice. He offers to go get some fries. The next thing I know, I'm sitting across from the King of Carefreedom, watching him lick salt from his calloused fingertips.

"Not a talker, are you?" Garth's elbows form perfectly symmetrical angles when he folds his fingers behind his head. "It's Gus Peake, right?"

I almost spit out my soda. "Yeah. It is. I'm Gus."

Piercings lift with his lips. "Cool. Nice to hang with you at last. I'm—"

"Garth Holden. Yeah. I—I know."

His grin widens. "Gotta say, never expected to catch you playing hooky. Any particular reason for skipping today?"

Just the earth shattering.

I offer half a shrug.

"I don't think I've ever seen you go anywhere without Phil."

"You know Phil?"

"Yeah, I know Phil." Garth drums his fingers along the edge of the table. "Known him for forever. His brother John used to date my big sister. He'd bring Phil over to kick my ass on *Mario Kart*. Man oh man. Does he still pick Toad every time? It's humiliating, losing to a sidekick."

Phil's *never* mentioned being friends with Garth, and Phil knows I'm obsessed with the Gaggle. I acted as Phil's wingman. Couldn't Phil do the same for me?

"He still picks Toad." Garth isn't listening. I follow his gaze.

He's watching a group of black-clad strangers pass through the main entrance. They aren't wearing coats. There's a price to being cool, and today it's runny noses.

"You, um, know them?"

"Nah." Garth tries for nonchalance, but he bunches up his shoulders.

It clicks. "*You're* worried about being seen with me."

"You think I care about stuff like that?"

Based on his behavior, against everything I thought I knew, clearly Garth cares a lot. Maybe there's no such thing as care-freedom.

"Timber." There's a collapse in my head: Could Garth of the Gaggle be one of the most insecure people I've ever talked to?

A laugh escapes me. Garth flinches and then grins, putting the mask right back on. "So, where *is* Phil today? You two break up?"

I'm stammering now. "No, we aren't—I don't—he isn't—"

"I was kidding." Without warning, Garth's fingers drum across the table to touch mine. "You ever think about wearing contacts, Gus?"

"I like my glasses."

Garth's posture relaxes; the smog of black-clad bodies has drifted elsewhere. "Wanna head outside? It's stuffy in here."

It's stuffy with people Garth doesn't want to be seen by. Suddenly, I'm feeling sorry for him. Then, just as suddenly, like a knife in the sternum, I miss Kalyn to pieces.

"Let me get that for you." Garth pulls my tray from under my fingers.

It's too soon in the year for it to be this dark outside at two o'clock, so maybe a thunderstorm is rolling in. The smallest icy pinpricks of mist strike my cheek. I've never driven in the rain before. It's occurring to me, as I follow Garth across the parking lot, that I've never been anywhere without someone else knowing where I am.

I should be afraid. When your father is the star of

true-crime stories, you develop a taste for the macabre. You learn it's not strangers you have to worry about so much as people you know. You learn not to follow people to their cars. You learn that being a guy doesn't exclude you from potential victimhood. It didn't exclude your father, after all.

You also learn that you are paranoid to think and feel these things. Honestly, I've thought and felt so much in the span of the past twenty-four hours that all I want to do is stop.

When Garth offers me a crumpled joint, I bite it between my teeth and breathe until I'm burning. Garth laughs and pounds me on the back as I hack up my heart.

"Where are we going?" I think I say it aloud. I'm already hazy, fuggy, fogged. I nearly drop my cane.

"I'm looking for something, Gus. Shouldn't take long. Are you cold?"

I'm not. I'm tingling and warm and confused and realizing that I left my new socks in the food court. I'm not keeping up at all now. Garth isn't changing his pace.

"There! Found one. You almost always do, when there are enough cars."

I lift woozy eyes from his boots and follow the line of his finger. "Oh."

Garth braces me against his body, his hand on my good elbow. He's pointing at a red Ford Taurus. It's a newer model than the one that swallowed Dad's corpse, but it does the trick. The rain's falling in earnest.

"You can't even get away from it if you try," Garth tells me.

KALYN

QUILLPOWER IS TOO awful a driver for anything *but* straight and narrow, so it's a good thing we're on the freeway. This nerd's pursuing light speed. I think our faces will be melded to the headrests by the time we get where we're going.

"Can I ask you something, Quillpower?"

"You'll ask notwithstanding."

"*Why* do you like me? I mean, really?"

He doesn't turn down the music. I do it for him.

"Gus says you've got me on some goddamn pedestal. That's as bad as being called white trash. I'm not your heroine. I didn't show up to *save* you."

"Why concern yourself with where I put you within my head? You're unattainable regardless."

"Fuck *yes* I'm unattainable. I'm a human being."

"Humans are categorical creatures. I'm only trying to adapt, Kalyn."

"You and everybody else. It's no excuse for objectifyin' people."

"Let's use an analogy. Visualize social categories as stacked boxes. The rows at the bottom of a *Tetris* heap are locked in from the start. There's no social mobility there. Gus and I? We occupy the bottom corners."

"You're *actually* comparing society to a game of *Tetris*."

Phil's not offended. "Exactly. I'm hopeless. *Unless* a block crashes in our vicinity, dismantling the infrastructure around us. Freeing us. A catalyst."

"How *nice* of me to be a *catalyst*, huh?"

Phil flicks his hazy eyes to the road. "You remain in motion. You could land anywhere you wish to. You're incapable of sympathizing."

"And *you're*— Jesus, you're incapable of using turn signals!" Phil swoops into the fast lane. "You don't know jack about my sympathies."

Bet Phil wishes I had a screen where my face is. "I know that every human being doesn't treat *you* despicably on principle."

Damn if he don't sound churlish. I think Phil's missed a pretty valuable point. He's missed the reason we're breaking speeding laws right now.

"*Gus* doesn't treat you despicably."

"Gus *can't*," Phil reasons, passing three cars in quick succession. "We only have each other for company."

"That's grade-A bullshit. Gus *has* other friends. Sure, some of them are online, or he only sees them at camp. But he's still got *you* featured front and center. Don't you wonder why? Aren't you grateful, for fuck's sake?"

Phil's eyelids flutter.

"You *aren't* Gus's last choice. You're his first, even though you're about as socially skilled as a stunted skunk."

It starts raining. We're both silent until we peel off down an exit ramp. Phil almost runs the red light at the bottom of the hill. I slap him on the arm.

"Gus thinks you're bad at understanding girls, but maybe you're bad at human beings." Saying more seems like betraying Gus. I don't need more reasons for Gus Peake to hate me. "Liking people isn't a game."

"Everything is a game," Phil argues, putting his foot on the gas. "Sometimes humanity just clouds that reality for other people."

"But not for you."

His answer is quiet. "No. Not for me."

Maybe Phil's got disabilities I can't see, and that's why he talks like a regurgitating computer. Gus talks about the branches that block his mind pathways, and maybe Phil's on a different path entirely.

If we could figure out how it feels to think like anybody else, there'd be fewer murders in the world.

Phil's wrong; I'm pretty sympathetic. Empathetic, even.

And if I'm complicated, so is *everyone* in Samsboro, seems like.

So much for the simple small town life.

By the time we reach the mall, the sky's pissing down. It's the kind of rain I haven't seen since summer, when thunderstorms beat the roofs of all the cars in the salvage yard like the worst percussion ensemble ever. We can barely see the lines in the lot. Soon we're going the wrong way down a parking aisle.

"Gus doesn't strike me as the shopping type," I say.

"You don't know him well."

"I know he's got better taste than this."

"Once more, with feeling: you don't know him as I do."

"Again with the competition." I hate that it stings.

The windows are fogging. I roll mine down, ignoring the drops. Phil glares, but water never hurt anyone and this vehicle could use a wash.

"Stop the van!" I've spotted something familiar—the pine-green truck Tamara picked me and Gus up in. There's a decal on its side: *Peake Landscaping.* "He's here!"

"Of course he is."

"If you're looking to get kicked, you're well on your way."

But Phil's staring past me so intently that for two seconds I assume King Lear himself must be standing behind me. "What?"

"Fuck," Phil spits, dropping any trace of that prudish accent. "*Fuck!*"

Phil throws himself outside before I can even turn.

About seven cars down, I spot what's got him riled. Two figures are standing in the downpour. There's this tall guy I've seen around school, one of the so-called Gagglers. Leaning against him is Gus, looking about ready to fall over.

I never thought I'd see Quillpower sprinting toward a fight. I never expected to see him make a lurching, fists-up beeline through two inches of water. Phil is made of sticks, but his arm doesn't snap when he decks the Gaggler in the cheekbone.

I'm outside now, caught in the chaos, not thinking about whether or not Gus'll want me there, or maybe *only* thinking about it. Phil lays another punch on the Gaggler.

The Gaggler's yelping like a pug by the time I reach them, and the pair of 'em are rolling in the puddles on the tarmac. Gus isn't watching any of this; his eyes are red and cloudy behind rain-streaked glasses, fixed on something beyond these two tussling idiots.

I steel myself and step into his line of vision. "Gus? You okay?"

He's staring at some random car. And before I can register why, Gus *sees* me.

A Spence and a red *Ford Taurus*. Me, wearing that stupid white dress.

To my horror, Gus starts giggling, way too hard, like something's scraping the sound out of his lungs, squeezing it like old glue from a blocked bottle. The wrongness of it makes me feel like *I'm* getting punched. It rises over the sound of splashing and cussing at our feet, over the rain and the rumble of engines.

I step around the idiots—Phil's in a headlock—and put my arms around Gus, wanting him to stop making that sound. Something burns my elbow, but I don't let go.

"Gus, hey, Gus. It's okay."

"It isn't." He won't stop giggling. I catch a whiff of his

breath—skunky, green, *way* too familiar. Now I clock the burning at my elbow, all right.

"Are you— *Jesus*, Gus? You're smoking pot?" I pluck the joint from his fingers and throw it into the mud.

He's still giggling, eyes unfocused. "You think cripples can't—can't get high, too?"

"Don't call yourself—"

"*Don't* tell myself what to call myself," he snaps.

"You're *asthmatic*, dumbass!" I'm nearly bowled over when Phil rolls into my calf. "Would you quit it? Christ!" I thrust a ballet flat into the nearest puddle, kicking water at the pair of them. Once, twice, and a third time, until I feel my foot hit flesh.

The Gaggler yelps and the two finally split. Phil's glaring, wiping his nose on his sleeve. The Gaggler scuttles backward, crablike, trying to get up. For some reason he's fumbling in his pocket. So help me, if he has a shiv—

But he pulls out a digital camera, of all things, and snaps a picture of us.

"What a reunion!" The Gaggler looks livid, but he's grinning. I've seen guys grin like that in prison. Dad warns me not to go near them.

"Delete that, Garth." Phil's voice is creepy-calm.

But this guy—Garth—tucks the camera away and buggers off, limping as water splashes at his ankles. Phil looks ready to chase him, but I put my arm out. We watch this asshole climb into a small sedan, watch it light up and pull away.

"*Timbbbbbberr.*" Gus is done laughing.

I'm shivering, but not just cold. Gus isn't looking at me, but he's not shoving my hand away. He's not as tense as usual. It's like the water's melting him. I don't know which version of me I am, but she's scared to speak.

"That motley-minded lout," Phil mutters. "That pox-marked puttock."

"Hey," Gus says, "I left my evil socks in the food court."

"Okay. Let's go get dry. At least on the outside." It's another one of my confusing jokes. I'm saying we're all sobbing on the inside. But it doesn't make any sense.

ACT FIVE
Enter PHIL WHEELER

PHIL

I CANNOT RECALL the last time I deigned to dine in an Orangee's restaurant. The food within ranks as barely adequate on the edibility spectrum. But within Orangee's, we are bombarded by blaring country-pop lyrics rather than icy dollops.

The greeter surveys we three misfits through tired eyes: Kalyn in pizza-stained, translucent garb; Gus, clutching a ridiculous pair of socks and hiccupping like a drunkard; myself, mud soaked and swollen faced, paper towel hastily shoved up my nostrils, leaning on Gus's cane because he refused to carry it.

"Table for three?"

A waitress sets a children's paper menu on my seat to spare the vinyl my ruin. Kalyn, thus far silent, asks the waitress for another children's menu and crayons.

My compatriots have elected to sit beside rather than across from each other. Gus is dissociating, presumably overwhelmed. Kalyn is as still as the proverbial grave.

Our waitress returns with waters and crayons on a tray, menus wedged beneath her arm. I order onion rings. "Would either of you like anything?"

Gus leans his head against the window glass. The light refracts on the water dribbling outside, casting mirrored shadows on his skin. Kalyn merely overturns her cup of crayons and draws a purple grid on the back of her menu.

I have never been socially adept. Even among my brothers, LARPers all, I struggle most in public and private. Yet in this merry company, the mere fact that I thank our waitress renders me the most capable in this booth.

"What fit of madness has taken the pair of you?"

Gus stares at his lap. Kalyn stares daggers at me.

"*Really*, Phil? Wanna explain why you decked the Gaggler?"

Intoxicated or not, this captures Gus's attention. I can scarce look at him. Not only because we have argued. Not only because I am questioning my treatment of him. Kalyn has asked me to consider Gus's treatment of me. I have much human thinking to do, which is no simple thing. My conscience is a carefully cultivated thing.

"Garth Holden is no friend to us. In no uncertain terms, he is a cream-faced loon."

If I were better at interpreting facial expressions, I could register the degree of hurt in Gus's eyes. Is it more or less than yesterday, when I left him in my van? Does it pertain at all to the bump beneath his forelock? Is it more or less than our first childhood argument, when I drained his chocolate milk and replaced his carton with an empty one?

Kalyn snorts. "What did he do? Beat you on a level of *Underlook?*"

"He could never." A basket of microwaved circles appears before us. "Would either of you like to partake?"

"No thanks."

" 'But if it be a sin to covet honor, I am the most offending soul alive.' " Frankly, I am surprised to find my knuckles bruised. I can't recall when last I engaged in violence.

Before I met Gus, I destroyed without consideration. I overturned desks and pinched classmates' skin. Children and animals knew to avoid me. When I speak to Kalyn of my baseness, she cannot fathom the depths from which I have climbed.

I struggle to empathize with people who aren't fictional.

At age five, I received an individualized education plan. I was tested for autism, but fell short of the spectrum and landed in some nether realm. I was intelligent, but not emotionally so. My father claims I was a conscientious toddler. I wept to see others weep.

"When you were three—and you won't remember this—you fell off your bike and smacked your head. You were hospitalized for a week, with damage to your temporal lobe. It happened while you were still growing. It stunted you, son."

It is strange to be called stunted when you are taller than anyone your age. It is stranger still to be called stunted by a parent who's crying tears you can't comprehend.

If I taught Gus words, Gus taught me the tenets of

humanity. If I cannot feel for others, I can mimic feeling. Gus is a living, breathing conscience, a so-called bleeding heart. Dad let him bleed on me, hoping it might stain me a better hue of human.

I haven't hurt a soul in years, until today.

Gus sobers as rain rails without. "Phil. Tell me why you hit Garth."

I tell them what they do not know about Garth Holden.

Gus idolizes anyone who seems comfortable in his own flesh. Garth has idolized Gus in return, in a manner of speaking. Garth has a morbid streak that goes beyond writing gothic poetry. Garth Holden once visited my home to be soundly beaten at video games. He was inquisitive about my best and only friend.

A number of people in the world are obsessed with true-crime stories. The obsession itself is not an issue. But Garth was not interested in Gus as a human being. He was interested in Gus as the son of a murdered man. He asked to be introduced to Gus. He asked if I'd seen the crime-scene photos. He asked whether I knew gory details.

Eventually he asked if Gus had received brain damage because his mother was shocked during pregnancy. That was the last time I used my fists. Garth then, Garth now. Gus has gazed longingly at Garth and his "Gaggle." I have glared them gone.

A crayon breaks in Kalyn's fist as I relay this. "Oh. Maybe I'll deck him next."

Gus tugs the menu closer. He selects a black crayon and scribbles. This perturbs me. One of Gus's greatest bugbears is the way outsiders infantilize him.

"Kalyn's dad killed my dad." He hiccups again. The crayon does not pause.

"Ah." It all comes together, a thing brought to fruition before me. "I *see*."

I assumed Kalyn's arrival signified the commencement of a coming-of-age romantic comedy. In truth, this is a murder mystery. Perhaps a tragedy. I wasn't wrong to think our lives a story. I was simply wrong about which genre we belong to.

"We should start researching immediately."

"Researching?" Kalyn lifts glassy eyes.

"If your father is innocent, then another culprit is responsible for the crime."

"He's not *innocent*," Gus says. "He can't be."

To my amusement, Kalyn nods. "I don't think Dad's innocent. But whether he was *justified* is another thing—"

"*Justified?*" Gus sputters. "I'm sorry, but? It was murder!"

"'*I'm sorry, but?*' Were *you* there?"

"The new evidence must be compelling. We could consider alternative suspects."

Neither of them looks thrilled by the suggestion, which baffles me.

"It's compelling, all right." Kalyn pulls her eyes from Gus's white face. "But Dad's *always* said he did the deed. Who lies about being *innocent?*"

"No one," Gus says, "except someone with, um, other bodies to hide."

"You don't know *anything* about my dad!"

"I know *he's* still breathing."

"Enough." I long to speak to the logical parts of them, but they are caught up in the minutiae of emotions. "This unhappy fate need not result in hatred. With you, Capulet, nor you, Montague. It's a cliché."

"Goddamnit, *Quillpower*—life ain't a Shakespearean tragedy!"

"So you say. Yet your stars are clearly crossed."

Gus closes his eyes.

"Gus," Kalyn says, "I told you to never come near my house. Now you know why. You're the match to my gunpowder."

"Not every explosion yields negative results," I suggest.

"If you're about to go off about *Tetris* rows again—" Kalyn warns.

"Sometimes you must raze a fortress before you can build anew. Today's headlines may trigger an explosion, yes. But what will come after, once the refuse is tidied away? The possibilities are fascinating."

"I'm sorry, Kalyn. Phil always . . . he does *this*."

"At least I do something." It is better than the alternative. It is better than throwing chairs.

When I was five, I hit my head and my soul flew out of me.

I will never remember who I was before, if I was anyone else at all.

John gave me my first Dungeons and Dragons handbook during my first school suspension. The book was dog-eared and stained with spaghetti sauce. The pages were stuck together with the glue of dried soda spills. But the font was legible. Laid out in plain writing were stats, a tangible system for weighing character attributes. Suddenly made measurable were concepts such as Wisdom and Constitution and Charisma. If it takes assigning numbers to my peers for me to see their value, isn't that preferable to seeing no value whatsoever?

The two of them are mum. To alleviate their stage fright, I remove the audience. "I'm going to the restroom. To change the tissues."

I duck behind a pillar. I do not wait long.

"Gus . . ."

"Kalyn."

"Phil is *so* much weirder than you let on."

"He's w-weirder than—than . . . yeah."

"He's weird, but he's got a point. Should we try and *solve* this?"

"I just met you, Kalyn," Gus replies after a beat.

"Yeah. I know. It's been less than a month, Gus. That's it. Our whole lives, our parents' lives, versus a month. I get it."

"I drove to Spence Salvage today. For the first time."

Clink. Kalyn sets down her drink. "Was it as trashy as you expected?"

". . . I don't know."

"Bullshit, Gus. I *saw* your house. Fucking mullet mansion."

"I don't know."

"D'you think it's worth the struggle? This *thing* we've got going here. Not that I like taking shit lying down—Spences don't."

"Your—your dad did. By confusing, I mean. Confessing."

Her exhale almost reaches me. "I know. I've got questions for Dad, believe me."

"Me too. For mine. But I can't ask them."

"Keep on guilting me, why don't you?"

"If your dad didn't do it, I'm *not* g-guilting *you*."

". . . okay, smartass."

". . . if he *did* do it. I'm still *not* guilting *you*."

". . . okay." Kalyn drops the epithet.

This conversation lacks the rhythm of poetry, but I have learned to lower my expectations of laymen. They may not see the symmetry of this, but I do.

"Gus. I don't expect you to wanna be in my life after . . . after all this."

"We've known each other one month."

"I heard you."

"One month—but, but I already, *you're* already, part of me."

"Because that's what I wanted! Gus, you don't really know me. I conned everyone, you included. Classic Spence."

"Yeah. You con people. I *still* like you."

"You're just high, Guslinda."

"No."

I hear nothing for a time.

"God help me, you're getting my hopes up here. I didn't know I *had* hopes deep down in me to begin with." Her laugh is minuscule. "It's not like me."

"Maybe it is like you."

". . . the wide and crooked, Gustier?"

I can hear his smile. "Maybe. The wild, I mean—*wide* and crooked. Maybe Phil's right. Maybe we can at least do better than our parents."

"*That* goes without saying. I don't plan on shootin' you anytime soon."

Gus isn't laughing. Kalyn isn't, either, though she mimics the sound.

"Sorry, that was . . . look, this could be *damned* impossible, Gus."

"Not impossible. Difficult. There's a difference."

"Is everything all right?" Our waitress appears beside me. I put a finger on my lips.

"My companions are reconciling a doomed friendship."

". . . Okaaay. I'll get y'all a second order of onion rings. On the house."

Both members of my troupe jump when I approach.

"More onion rings are coming." I note Gus's frown. "Yes?"

"I'm still p-pissed at you."

"No, you're not." I swat the air with a hand. "You're too overwhelmed with your world being rent asunder."

"Phil. You *ditched* me yesterday."

"Oh." If my moral compass says so, so be it. "I am here now, am I not?"

Gus cocks his head.

"Jesus, *Phil*, just tell him you're sorry." Kalyn's eyes bore into me. "You say a lot of words, but I know bullshit when I smell it."

I concede. "Apologies, Gus."

His frown persists. "Aren't *you* still pissed at me?"

I consider his set jaw. "Why should I be? It seems like a waste of energy."

Here is what Gus has never considered:

My dad didn't pair me with him to help Gus with his broken thought processes. He hoped Gus could repair *mine*. I don't expect Gus to find the work easy.

"We need to ask questions. Perhaps a stay in the library could benefit us—"

Kalyn folds her arms. "Weren't you going to go change those tissues?"

"Ah?"

"Phil, you're bleeding!"

I put a hand to my seeping nose. I am very *alive* today.

I need not be emotional to be invested. The role has never mattered so much to me as *having* one. It's about never being ignored in a classroom, never left alone to destroy my surroundings. Never being an NPC.

As the new lead investigator in the James Ellis murder, the single force that may keep Capulets and Montagues from clashing, it's fair to say:

Phillip Wheeler has entered this story at last.

GUS

BLACK-PEPPER CLOUDS GIVE way to a green-skied evening. The whole way back to Samsboro, Kalyn and I wait for a different storm to break.

The Death Van tailgates us from an unsafe distance. Phil got over yesterday so fast. After everything, where we stand now isn't any different than where we've always stood.

Pot is overrated. Hours later I'm too sober, with an aching head and a burning throat to show for it. Onion rings churn in my stomach.

Maybe Kalyn wants to escape Phil's driving. But maybe she wants to be near me.

I don't want to give up yet. There aren't many things worth keeping in the world. Maybe Kalyn and me, our friendship, isn't worth keeping, either. But almost every aspect of our lives has been decided for us. Trying to make this work is *our* decision.

"Gus, you're officially the best driver I know."

I jump. I thought Kalyn was sleeping. "Um. Thanks."

A minute passes.

"Phil and my mom drive like action villains."

My laugh sounds more like a long wheeze. I almost swerve into another lane.

"I take it back, I take it back! You suck, too!"

"*The Matrix.* That's what Phil says. He says you're like, um, the girl . . ."

"Trinity? Ha. I don't wear leather. Sci-fi's more my dad's thing. Only, he doesn't get to watch new movies in prison. I watch them and tell him about them."

"Oh." I wipe my eyes, letting my knee guide us. "So. What's his favorite movie?"

"Gus, you don't *want* to ask me about my dad. Stop being so damn nice."

"I'm not being . . . it's not nice."

"Then what the hell would you call it?"

"I have to think, I mean, I always thought . . ." Uncertain as I am, I'm not programmed to absorb a reality where Gary Spence didn't kill my dad.

The idea that Kalyn was raised in a totally different reality makes my heart shrink. And it bothers me, it really does, that Kalyn stands by her dad either way.

"I'm just . . . trying to figure it out. How you love him so much even though you think, you believed, the same thing I believe."

She sighs. "The murder thing has just . . . always been there.

I've known what Dad did. But to me he's *not* a murderer. He's my dad, who also murdered someone."

"And that makes him okay?"

"Hell no. He's *not* okay, locked up like a goddamn hamster. *I'm* not okay. And the way fucking Samsboro treats my grandma, my mom? *That's* not okay. Strangers talk like it's a *sin* for me to fucking exist—is *that* okay? The way *your* dad treated my dad, like shit on his shoe? Was *that* okay?"

"My dad didn't treat people like—like *shit*! He was a good person."

"Uh-huh. And how do you know that?"

"Everyone says so!"

"Everyone says so?" Her laugh is brittle. "Sorry, Gus, but you don't know what kind of person your dad was. You know your dad less than I know mine."

"People loved James Ellis." I think of those eternal eyes. "Every single person I've ever met has told me he was *good*."

"Think they could tell you anything different?" I shouldn't look away from the road, but I do. For the first time ever, Kalyn looks a little pitying.

I know what she's not saying. There's no way anyone can say anything awful about my poor, beautiful, dead father. Because clearly I don't need to suffer more, right?

"Fuck. I shouldn't have said . . . you know what, Gus?" Kalyn undoes her seat belt. "Pull over. I'll hitchhike home."

I blink stinging eyes. "No."

"Seriously, Gus. Let me out."

"I can't let you hitchhike!" I blubber. "You might get picked up by a murderer!"

Her response is a whimper. "Right, Gus."

We skate across a pothole puddle and hydroplane, weightless and terrified.

Forbidden words leave me. "You know, um, s-some people think I shouldn't have been born, too."

Kalyn puts a hand on my shoulder. "People suck, Gus."

"Yeah. But we don't have to."

She lets her hand fall away. Her warmth remains.

Seven mile-markers go by. The sky grows darker, threatening night instead of thunder. We're surrounded by bluish fields of grass.

"I knew it'd be all right." She finishes the thought minutes later, as we pass a crooked mailbox with a tin rooster tacked atop it. "Riding with you. Even though it's quiet. It's kind of nice, when it's just quiet."

Kalyn asks me to drop her off at the end of her driveway. "You've never seen this place after it rains. 'Flooding' doesn't do it justice."

Kalyn waves to me and then Phil, parked too close to my bumper. If he leaves a scratch, Tamara will want his blood.

Spence Salvage looks cleaner after the rain. The grass between the empty hulls is an almost glaring green. Years ago, Phil taught me about chloroplasts. Plants become greener as they collect water, opening up to the world right when most creatures close themselves off in shelters. Kalyn's a lonely gray figure, walking down her driveway.

It's hard to imagine things being okay.

KALYN

SPENCE SALVAGE COVERS forty acres. That's room for cars aplenty, especially if you don't mind them rubbing elbows, scraping side mirrors against each other.

The 1985 Taurus was impounded when the police pulled the body out of it. I know this. And even if most of the cars have been here for years, ever since the yard closed in '92, most of them haven't been here for actual *decades*.

But it's so dark, if I squint, these could all be coffin Tauruses.

"Fuck." I kick a puddle. The mud splashes high enough to fleck on my cheek.

I reamed Gus for not knowing what kind of person his dad was. But lots of people met Rose Poplawski, and most had no clue she was me.

Good thing Dad's calling tonight. Sure, there were reasons to lie to the press. Maybe there were reasons to take the fall, even.

But Dad didn't just confess to the police; he confessed to *us*. I can put up with him lying to everyone else, but to Mom and me?

"*Fuck*." Another puddle meets my boot. I stop.

Could this be the row? God knows I memorized the crime scene photos. But when your landmarks are cars that have shifted and vanished, well, angles are about as useful as belly buttons. And I hate thinking about angles.

Gus looked worried when he dropped me off. I've never seen my home from his angle. This'd be a scary place if you came here after dark, like James Ellis did.

When I reach the prefab, it's only six p.m. or so. Mom'll be pissed, because most weekdays I watch Grandma after school. There's rebelling like a good Spence, and then there's being a bad granddaughter.

Grandma's sitting at the kitchen table in semidarkness. The TV's muted but flashing bright, but she's facing the other way, still as the dead.

"Grandma?" She tilts her head toward me. "Where's Mom?"

Grandma tucks a cigarette between her papery lips.

"The hell? Quit that!" I'm a damn hypocrite. I reach for the cig, but Grandma finds the devil's quicksilver in her blood and whips it away before I can nab it.

"Small joys," she scolds. "*Small* joys."

"Great. *I'm* the one who's gonna get my ass roasted for it later. She at work?"

The TV shines white during a commercial, and I finally see what Grandma's up to. She's pulled an old shoebox full of yellowed photographs from the shed and overturned it on the table. She's using one unlucky photo as an ashtray, looks like, burning the face off a stranger.

"What you doin'?"

She takes a long drag and coughs like an engine. This time I'm quick enough to pluck the cigarette away. "You'll burn the house down."

"Claire—"

"Caught fire, yeah. So let's you and me not." I pull up a chair.

The photos look like a whole lot of nothing. People have familiar Spence faces, but I don't know my dead relatives. Here are barbecues and fishing trips, men and women posing with their bucks, grinning wide while deer bleed from the mouth.

Grandma's making piles of different people: there's Grandpa Ernest, who Mom never even met, because he got pancreatic cancer when Dad was in junior high. There's a pile for Uncle Rob, who committed suicide by car exhaust. A pile for Dad, too.

"Help me?" Grandma pleads.

I do my best. People like to joke about Spences dating each other, and honestly, I can't promise they didn't somewhere down the line because damned if we don't all have the same nose, same angry eyes, same "I *dare* you" lines in our foreheads. For all that, there are a lot of smiles here, too. People in blue bell-bottoms, laughing clouds of smoke. Jolly, drunken Christmases in cramped spaces.

What would all these people think of us?

"Grandma, don't you think it's about time for bed?" An hour's passed. I set down a picture of Dad sitting on an old sofa in the yard. A pretty girl leans against his armrest. Both of them are toasting tallboys. They look like kids.

But Grandma is pressing the end of her cigarette into a picture again, this time very deliberately. She's burning away the face of one of these familiar strangers, and by the time I snatch the photo from her, his face is completely gone.

I can't tell what kind of person he was, except that he was white and he had a prominent Adam's apple. He's wearing a denim jacket, and his arm is looped around a twelve-year-old Dad's bare, bony shoulders.

If Dad didn't kill James Ellis, could it have been the work of another Spence?

"Grandma, who is this? Why are you erasing him?" I look down, and she's blacked out at least five faces. I can't be certain, but the Adam's apple tells me it's the same guy, erased five times. "Who was this? An uncle? A brother?"

But she's not listening. Instead, she's eyeing the TV.

When I follow her gaze, I see Dad again, but now it's his mug shot.

"There's Gary," Grandma coos. When she's not looking, I scoop up all the photos marred by cigarette burns and tuck them into my lap.

A news anchor in a cheap-nails-red blazer fakes a look of concern.

I unmute the TV.

". . . developments of an unexpected nature. Earlier this week, we broke the news that Gary Spence, the thirty-seven-year-old man convicted of the first-degree murder of Samsboro teen James Ellis almost two decades ago, may be exonerated by new DNA evidence."

The screen switches to footage of a black woman in a pantsuit standing on the steps of a courthouse. A caption scrolling along the screen reads *Arlene Atkins, IFA Attorney: "Gary Spence could go free."*

The anchor continues: "Due to pressure from the Innocence Fighters Association, a nonprofit that has successfully exonerated more than thirty people since its inception in 1995, the prosecution is expected to agree to a retrial."

Arlene Atkins smiles. "Mr. Spence has been wrongfully convicted. If he's not back in court by Christmas, there's no justice in Kentucky."

It's going to be some phone call in twenty minutes, tell you what.

"Despite the support of IFA advocates, on a local level these developments are cause for controversy."

Now we're looking at downtown Samsboro, all the tiny businesses along Main Street. There's the ice cream place, the cinema, a diner, a real estate office, and a dive bar, too.

"Here in Samsboro, home of the Munch-O Mills cereal factory, the memory of James Ellis's murder remains painful."

The camera refocuses on a storefront. Hanging in the window

is a large poster picturing younger versions of Gus and his mom, and some pumpkins. Gus is in a wheelchair.

Who's "innocent"? the poster reads. *KEEP SPENCES BEHIND FENCES.*

The camera switches to an old man whose nostril hairs tickle his upper lip.

"Andrew Lewis, owner of Lew's Hardware and former coach of the Samsboro Eagles, has set a precedent for many downtown businesses by protesting the retrial."

"You go ahead," Andrew Lewis spits. "You go ahead and ask *anybody* in town, and they'll tell you." He scowls and points at the camera. "They'll tell you what I'm telling you. That family's got a reputation. Spence *confessed* to the murder. And I'm not talking in no police interrogation. In court, on live *TV*, that monster *confessed*. Said, 'Yeah, killed the running back, so what?' Just because he's feeling cowardly now doesn't mean we should set him free. Can James Ellis go free? No. I taught those boys in high school, so I know: Gary Spence is right where he belongs. Spences behind fences!"

I'm reeling, but we're back at the news desk. "Many citizens have strong opinions about the original trial. We here at WKZ News have received dozens of calls from listeners shocked and, in some cases, disturbed by the news. We would like to hear more from our listeners. Does Gary Spence really deserve the benefit of the doubt?"

It's a public trial already, I guess. I wonder if Gus is seeing this.

GUS

THE TV IS blaring. All the other lights are off.

I've never been good at tiptoeing. I set my cane against the wall and the keys back in the bowl. I'm dying for a glass of water, but more than that, I'm dying to get the next part over with. I'll be scolded and coddled and then it'll be over. When Phil pulled up behind me, he saluted but didn't step outside. He can't take this medicine for me.

"Mom . . . ? Tam?"

Mom's lying on the couch, almost exactly where I left her.

When I step into the living room, she looks at me and right past me at the same time. I was ready to face her anger, ready to argue my case despite feeling aching and wet and as old as the universe, but this silence is something else.

"Hey, Mom."

"Hey." There's a commercial break happening, but Mom's eyes remain glued to the screen. She's clutching a yearbook in her hands; I can tell from the dog-earing that it's Dad's from junior year, one she often pulls from the office. "How was school?"

Does she really think that I went to school? "Um. How was *your* day?"

She doesn't look at me.

"Where's T-Tam?"

"Around, probably," Mom says after a long pause. "I don't know."

"Mom. Are you okay?" I'm not used to being the one to ask that question. I feel guilty for that, for all of it, for leaving and everything that came before.

I'm not sure if I feel guilty about seeing Kalyn.

She doesn't answer my question. I limp to the kitchen entrance. I can't ask her how her abyss is. Not today.

The wind is picking up again, and the rain really hasn't quit yet; the grass looks more like a gray swishing ocean, and the Zen garden, with its sparse gingkoes and white stones, is an island in the tempest.

I find Tam on the bench near the stone garden. Despite the chill she's not shivering. I suppose it is a meditation garden, but seeing Tam so still has the opposite effect on me. Her stillness is as eerie as seeing a hummingbird rest in place.

"Hey, kid," she says. "Did you have a nice getaway?"

"It wasn't really a getaway," I say truthfully. "I ran into people I knew."

"Man, small towns. Friends, I hope?"

I think about telling her it was Kalyn. "Yeah and no," I say, and it's the truth.

"You're gonna need friends, I think." Beads of rain drip from her baseball cap.

I want to ask where her old friends are, but I think—no, I *know*—that part of living with her girlfriend in a small nowhere town means she doesn't have a lot of close friends nearby. Lots of people like Tam, but not a whole lot of people are there for her. Back when she lived in the city, I bet it was different. But now . . .

I take her hand and squeeze it. "What about you, Tam?"

"Well, your mom's my best friend. But I don't think she can really be that for either of us right now." She clears her throat. "You get dinner?"

"Kind of. Did you?"

"Not especially hungry. Why don't you head on in?"

"Why don't you?"

"Oh, I will. Gimme a minute." She smiles. "Who's the mom here?"

Something about her voice seems off, something about the way it cracks makes me tell her: "You are, Tam."

Before I head back inside, she squeezes me around the middle.

I do as she says and sit down to pull off my muddy shoes on the porch.

Inside, Mom's fallen asleep in front of the television. I lean over to kiss her good night and notice that the yearbook and some of the tissues have slid from her lap.

I lift Dad's yearbook off the floor. It's fallen open to the last pages, the space reserved for autographs. Every square inch of paper is covered with scrawling cursive, bubble letters, and clumsy signatures. It's a time capsule.

I take it upstairs with me. The stairs are where they've always been even if they feel like they're giving way. I glance out my window before collapsing onto my bed. Tam's still out there, statuesque in the darkness, but now her head is in her hands.

I rest the book on my knees, run my fingers across the letters. Usually I'd flip right to Dad's signature, but now I'm thinking about his classmates. About Mom and Gary Spence. All the kids who existed near him.

All these names, all these well-wishing empty words, and none of the writers knew what would happen just months later. Unless someone *did* know what was coming. Unless someone heard something, or *saw* something—

I wish I could leap to my feet. My finger freezes on the page. Lightning refuses to flash outside, despite the dramatic timing. The wind and rain have to be enough.

The message isn't long. The handwriting is messy and smeared:

> Jimmy my man! We did it! We survived the year. I won't say goodbye cause we're gonna hang out this summer, this is cheesy but it is good to finally know you man. come over to my place and we can shoot some potato guns. —GS

If I were at the library, I'd know for certain. I could look up statements available to the public, find somewhere in the records a picture of Gary Spence's handwriting.

Or I can ask Kalyn.

"Has it occurred to you, Gus, that this is precisely how your father got shot?"

"We don't know that," I reply, shivering in the passenger seat of the Death Van. It's almost impossible to make out the font on the Spence Salvage sign, backlit by the sunrise. "We don't know anything. That's why we're here."

Phil sighs, but I think some portion of him loves the thrill. I'm clutching Dad's yearbook in cold fingers. I'm grateful dawn is here, that these lines of vehicles on either side of us are looking less like a monstrous army and more like junk as the sky brightens. The rain left huge shining puddles in its wake. Kalyn was right to warn us, as even the indomitable Death Van is struggling to make headway here.

"This driveway is heinous." Phil has reason to grumble—I called him at midnight and asked him to embark on this insane mission with me at the crack of dawn. When I sneaked out, the house was hushed apart from my footsteps and water dribbling on the windows.

"How long is this nightmare?" Phil asks as we bump into another puddle.

"No idea." I try to swallow my heartbeat. "I've never been here before."

Finally the driveway curves and we can see the end of it—a circular loop where cars and refuse have been cleared away to reveal a large garage and a bedraggled little house covered in chipped yellow paint.

Kalyn's garage is bigger than her home.

"Do you think it happened here?" Phil says, cutting me with a worse thought. "The shooting? They never found out for sure."

I don't want to think about it, and that's when the driveway defeats us—the Death Van pitches forward into another puddle, but this time it doesn't come out the other side. For a minute Phil tries to fight the earth, letting the tires spin, cursing up a storm.

The revving of the engine terrifies me; it's shattering the quiet, and anyone in that house is definitely awake. "Quit it, Phil."

"As they say in films, 'There's no going back now.'" Phil switches off the ignition and climbs out of the van.

I have trouble getting out without sinking straight down into the muck, but I manage to soak only one shoe before joining Phil in front of the van. It's a cold morning and I'm sniffling from yesterday's rain, but that's not what chills me. I'm looking at the mess in the lawn—an overturned grill, a half-buried fire pit, empty beer cans scattered about, broken lawn chairs. I don't know that even Tam could do a lot for this yard.

I remember Kalyn's face when she saw our garden. Icy shame impales me.

There isn't a front step; only a cement block. I stop at the foot of it. I can't sense any movement inside the house, and suddenly it hits me that maybe Dad did stand here, maybe he did die *right* here.

I look at the yearbook, willing myself to breathe, reminding myself why I'm here: if Dad stood right here, maybe Gary stood next to him, like Phil's standing next to me.

We don't know.

I pull the screen open and tap on the door.

"Come now," Phil scoffs, and knocks five times, much harder.

I expect a pause; I expect eyes to appear between the plastic blinds of a window, but the door opens immediately. Kalyn appears in a waft of smoke and roses. She's wearing a holey Led Zeppelin hoodie and floral-print pajama bottoms. Her hair is a stormy nest atop her head, and she clutches a fresh egg in her upraised, bandaged fist.

"It's you," she says after a second, lowering her weapon.

I smile, just a little. Kalyn's posture relaxes a hair.

"The hell are you doing here?"

"Playing hooky," I say.

"Twice in one week?" Kalyn scowls. "They'll set the po-po on you."

But thinking of police doesn't make any of us feel better. "So have you been watching the news? Apparently Dad's guilty no matter what, at least in public opinion."

"The public opinion isn't *my* opinion. Can we please talk?"

Her cheeks flush. "Yeah, whatever. It's just me and Grandma right now."

The trailer smells warm and smoky, this mixture of

cigarettes and perfume that's not the best for my asthma. The wallpaper inside is peeling, and we're standing in a cramped kitchen attached to a living room. Mostly everything is brownish, but the card table in the center of the room is battered and pine green. A frail old woman sits in a wheelchair alongside it, poking at a piece of toast with one hooked finger.

"Grandma," Kalyn says, "these are some friends from school."

"Nice to meet you," I say; Phil's too busy peering at every corner to say a thing.

Grandma Spence is staring right through me, her mouth a tight line. I know she had a stroke, but I also know that having a hard time talking doesn't mean she isn't thinking all kinds of things. I start coughing.

"Sorry," I wheeze.

Kalyn's cheeks redden. "Oh, damn, right. We can talk outside; just give me a second to get Grandma settled."

Minutes later Grandma Spence is on the sofa with her eyes locked on the Food Network, and we're sitting at a picnic table out front. I didn't mention how cold my fingers are, but Kalyn brought out a cardboard box of mittens, hats, and scarves.

"Take your pick." I put on an orange beanie and camouflage mittens. Kalyn snorts. "Bet no one in your family's ever worn camo before."

"I'm not so sure." I set the yearbook on the table between us. "Kalyn. Last night. I *found* something." I flip it open to the back page and tap on it.

"That's *Dad's* handwriting," she says without even reading the words.

"I thought so," I breathe.

"This is James Ellis's—your dad's yearbook? Holy *shit*."

"I know."

"*Holy shit*. Does this mean our dads were *friends*? A Spence and an Ellis?"

"Suppose it's another thing that runs in the family." Phil shrugs.

Kalyn and I only look at each other.

"But . . . I mean, that changes things."

"I know."

Phil leans forward. "It's got the appeal of a classic mystery. Friends from different social strata, forced to vie against each other. With the addition of a modern, disturbing twist, of course."

"My dad being crammed in the trunk of a Ford, you mean."

"Precisely," Phil says. "Yes."

Kalyn punches him on the shoulder. "*Callous* much?"

"Yeah, but . . . I mean." Being sensitive won't actually help anything. Kalyn and Phil and me, *we* might help something.

"So what, Gus?" She holds up her hands. "So what does this mean? You know, once, *only* once, I told Dad I thought he was a good person. He was *not* a fan. You'd think I was slapping him. I used to think it was 'cause he couldn't see himself that way, but now I'm looking at everything we're seeing now . . ."

"He 'doth protest too much.'" Phil nods.

"What if my dad really didn't kill yours?" She tugs at her

hair. "But if he lied about that, the *single damnedest reality* of our lives, what *else* has he lied about?"

"That's not relevant," Phil says bluntly.

Kalyn's seething. "*What?*"

"I mean, certainly it's relevant to your relationship with your father. But the issue at hand is whether an innocent man should be in prison, and whether there's someone out there that should be there in his stead."

I shake my head. "Phil. You're not wrong, but sometimes you're so *wrong*."

But Kalyn closes her mouth, wiping at her eyes. "Fine. You want to play Scooby-Doo? Let's do it. Fuck it. And you know what? I found a clue, too."

She pulls a stack of photographs from the pocket of her hoodie and slaps them on the table. "Caught Grandma blanking out faces in old photos. She wouldn't tell me why, but someone's getting erased."

I stare at the pictures, all these nineties Polaroids and ash-stained Kodak moments.

"Is it all the same person?" Phil asks.

"I think so. But I don't know who he is. There are a lot of Spences I never met."

"It's the same person," I say, staring at the Adam's apples, the size ratio between Gary Spence and this faceless soul he's thrown his arm around in a dozen photos.

"Think he could be the *actual* murderer? Why would Dad take the fall for him?"

"Did your father have siblings, Kalyn?"

I'm staring at the pictures, piecing together the posture and the joy on Gary Spence's face. These two at a bonfire, these two kicking it in the back of a pickup truck, Gary and the faceless other. I've never thought of Gary Spence as a kid before.

"Dad had around five siblings, I think? But he *was* the youngest by, like, ten years. The next youngest was Uncle Greg, and he was working on an oil rig in Alaska around then. Not *all* Spences get stuck in Shitsboro." She shakes her head. "*Man*, have I got questions for Dad. He had *better* fucking call tonight."

"It's like—like." I sigh. "You hate your dad more now that he isn't a murderer."

"Well, isn't lying a little like murder, too, Gus?"

"No. It's really not." I set the photos down. "The guy in these photos can't be the murderer."

"How the hell do you know?" she says, standing up.

"Because the guy in these photos is *my* dad."

All this evidence of a friendship that no one ever thought was worth mentioning, all these photos of Gary Spence and my dad being best friends. Deleting Dad's face doesn't mean I couldn't recognize his posture, his height, his stance anywhere. I've spent a lifetime studying him, and I've never seen any of these photos.

"Ah," says Phil. "That's an alibi indeed."

"It doesn't help us," I spit. "It just makes everything feel worse."

Kalyn reaches out—I think she's reaching for the photos, but she takes my hand instead. "Look at me, Gus."

I lift my eyes. I recognize the expression in hers, the confusion and anger and betrayal and sadness. "Say our dads were good friends. It helps *me* to know that, in some type of way. Because I tell you what, I have a half-Ellis for a friend, and there's *no way* in hell I could ever kill you. You know?"

"Yeah. I know."

"Kalyn," Phil inquires, "if this evidence isn't pertinent to uncovering a new suspect, can you tell us what is? What DNA evidence has allowed the case to reopen?"

"My mom found a bloodstained jacket in the shed," Kalyn tells us, "and it proved that Dad was facing the other way when the gun went off. Like, he couldn't have shot it."

"The jacket was found in this shed?" Phil asks, pointing at the boxy little shack between the house and garage.

"Yeah, that's the one."

I wipe my eyes on my hand. "Did she find anything else in there?"

Kalyn's raising her eyebrows. "Y'all wanna pillage a shed, or what?"

KALYN

I COULD'VE CRIED when Gus appeared on my doorstep this morning.

Spending the morning tearing apart an old shed is less than awesome, but it beats school. At least I don't have to play nice after throwing pizza at my only fake friends yesterday. At least I don't have to see Sarah's disappointment or tell her the truth. Instead I get to see Gus's lovely face.

Now I'm confronted with busted old furniture being dragged into sunlight, the vision of Phil batting at cobwebs and Gus coughing on dust bunnies as we pull things from darkness. I can see the area Mom started clearing out, and we start there, because that's gotta be where the jacket was found.

I don't know what we're actually looking for. We're not going to find answers here, except Mom *did*, so at least this feels productive. It's at least a distraction.

Helping Gus move a tote of snow pants out of the musty darkness, I say, "You know, it's gonna be harder for us to meet up at school."

"Why?" Gus gasps as we plop the box down. He's wiping dirt from his glasses. God, his eyes are huge without those lenses, these deep orbs of gray that might woo the shit out of me if I were otherwise inclined. "Nobody knows who you are."

"They're bound to find out."

I have no idea why he's frowning at me.

"You sound like me," he says, "but before I met you."

I don't know how the hell to respond— I mean, wasn't Gus better off before he met me?—so maybe it's real lucky that Phil emerges from the shed, holding a pair of crutches and a filthy old comforter. "Kalyn, I haven't asked the obvious—could your grandmother have murdered Gus's dad?"

"Wonder what it's like to have a normal conversation," Gus says, wincing.

"Gus. *I* am not going to discount her merely because she's elderly and disabled, am I? That would be shortsighted and discriminatory."

Gus groans, but his cheeks flush as if he's pleased. He and Phil have a funny thing going, but it's some kind of actual understanding thing.

"Best not to discount Grandma in most things," I say, "because she'll kick your ass for it. But Grandma had an alibi. She was actually *at* the football game, working concessions with like a half-dozen church ladies."

Phil looks real disappointed, and I'm not sure whether to be offended. I have very confused thoughts about what constitutes a badass. Sure, murder ain't cool, but Grandma can hold her own in a tussle. I'm glad others can smell that on her.

After a few hours of sunshine that eats up a little of the puddles, the lawn surrounding the shed is a museum of someone else's memories. There's some genuinely nice, heavy furniture in the shed that we don't touch, and a dead snowmobile that should probably be parked elsewhere. Other than that, we've cleared things out pretty good. Most of the boxes are full of dusty old clothes, things belonging to bygone Spences. There are forgotten skis and junky Budweiser mirrors, dirty plates and ugly puppy statuettes, and the usual pile of car parts and crusty rags.

"Whole lotta crap," I say.

"No, it's not," Gus says awkwardly.

"Dear Rich Boy, I'm allowed to call my own crap 'crap.' Sincerely, Me."

That shuts him up pretty quick.

"What became of the murder weapon?" Phil asks, oblivious to the moment. "Locked in an evidence locker, I presume?"

"I guess so. It was Grandma's gun, technically."

Phil scratches his chin. "As your grandmother is not a murderess and her gun is elsewhere, presumably, I think I will journey into her midst and use the restroom."

"Check that she's breathing." I try to make it sound like a joke, but I have no idea when Mom came in last night, and she'd left again before I crawled out of bed.

Gus slumps atop a box, stretching his bad leg out in front of him. Sweat has left lines in the dirt around his face. He looks four times as tired as I feel.

"I thought we might find more photos of them." I get why he's disappointed—if Grandma blocked out all the faces of his father, maybe we'll never see real proof of the two of them spending time together. But that reminds me—

"Gus, there's a picture that was in the papers years back. Our dads were in the same shop class, and the class posed in front of a gazebo downtown. It's not exactly proof of friendship, but have you ever seen that?"

"No. I don't think so. Mom might have a copy of it, back home in the office."

"We should check out your place next."

"Yeah, maybe." Gus looks beyond uneasy. "I mean, for photos."

"Don't worry. I won't invite myself over."

"That's not what I mean," he says. "But lately Mom's . . . not okay."

"Your mom ever talk about my dad?" I ask, trying not to sound angry.

He blinks. "No. She didn't know him."

"She *must* have known him, right? If he and Gary were friends in high school. Funny if she never mentioned that, considering she was dating James and all."

I don't say it, not directly. I don't need to. A crease forms between his eyebrows.

"I bet no one knew they were friends," he reasons. "I bet they kept it a secret."

"What, like we do?"

Gus shakes his head. "Not like us. We're different."

But now my heart is pounding, and I can't believe we're sitting out here in the cold sun together, as if this can actually work. I don't want to hear Gus say we could be different from our parents. I want him to say that his parents could be the same as mine, in fact, that guilt doesn't belong only to the poor and trashy. I want Gus to consider, for one second, what *I've* always had to accept: "Who says your mom's not a murderer, Gus? Might have to ask her some questions. I don't think my dad's the only liar."

He's glaring at me, but how is that fair? "What? Don't like the shoe on the other foot? Easy to say anyone in *my* family is a murderer, but better not imply the same thing about yours, huh?"

"Because it's r-ridiculous!"

"Why? Because your family is so *wholesome*? Because your family wouldn't even want to be *seen* with mine, and everyone knows that?"

"It's not like—not that!" Gus sputters, fists clenched, climbing to his feet.

"Oh, really? You walked into my house today and felt bad for me. So what's it really like, Gus? How come you don't want me to come over?"

"Because—it's just—"

"How come we don't hang out at school, huh? *Really*, Gus?"

"Because you—you're too cool for me!" he blurts.

I'm left gobsmacked. "*What?*"

Gus's eyes are shining. "Because you are too cool to be seen with me. You say that Rose wouldn't mind, but I'm not exactly good for *your* image either, am I?"

"G-Gus," I stammer, "do—do you *really* think that?"

His expression makes my chest hurt. Gus has lived his whole life thinking people tolerate him. But I can't believe he still thinks that about me. And despite it all, I'm up and wrapping my arms around his stiff shoulders.

"Gus," I say, "I deserve more fucking credit than that. Maybe my family doesn't, fine. But I'm your fucking friend, you got that? You've gotta get out of your head."

I pull back. His expression crumbles. "Yeah. I know that . . . and maybe you're right. I can't think of my family like I think of yours. As the . . . bad guys."

"Yeah, well." I smirk. "It gets easier with practice."

"Ahem?" Something about the way Phil crops up like some wayward gopher lessens the tension. "Both of you are neglecting the idea that it could have been a complete outsider who committed this crime. Another classmate, a drifter, a stranger, unlikely though it seems."

"Coulda been a setup, even," I say, almost wanting to believe it.

Phil nods. "Many people had reason to dislike the Spence crowd. What if this was all part of an elaborate vendetta?"

But if that's the case, we'll never solve this, Scooby gang or not. And there's something in my bones that says otherwise. Dad wouldn't take the fall for a drifter. He wouldn't hide a body for a drifter, wouldn't go to prison for a drifter. No matter what the truth is, it's a lot closer to home. But which home? Mine, or Gus's?

The black clouds are returning. Gus eyes them uncomfortably.

"Kalyn, can you help us get the van out of the mud? I need to go home."

"What, right this minute?"

He looks at me. "After we clean up, I mean. I have some questions for my mom. I don't want to wait anymore."

By the time we're done it's late in the afternoon. Getting the van unstuck takes some doing, but after a little kitty litter and a lot of pushing, we free it from the mud and they wave goodbye.

I'm already waiting for the phone to ring.

GUS

ON THE WAY home, the rain returns with a vengeance. The Death Van's wipers can hardly keep up, and when Phil drops me in the driveway even he seems troubled. Home looks so very big, and unapproachable, almost.

"I mean, cinematically speaking, weather like this doesn't bode well for you."

The sunniest weather in the world wouldn't make this easy. "Wait here for me?"

Phil shrugs. "As you wish."

Inside, the living room couch is vacant.

The guest room is empty. The kitchen is too, and so is Mom's office on the opposite side. Her laptop's clamped shut. An abandoned, white-ringed cup of coffee chills on the desk.

I peer through the curtains at the backyard, just in case Tam is venting her feelings on the flowerbeds. Apart from rainwater rippling in new puddles and those radioactive blades of grass bending under heavy droplets, there's no movement.

I can feel my whole body tensing, chest and arms and legs and heart, too.

"Mom? Tam?"

I can't hurry up the stairs. I have to take my time. No running in tombs, kids!

I'm breathless when I reach the landing.

There's an inexplicable stack of flattened moving boxes leaning against the hallway bannister. My stomach knots.

My parents' bedroom door is open. The bed's unmade, the flowery quilt shucked and bunched at the foot of the mattress. When I step inside, the air feels icebox cold. The closet is gaping and so are some of the drawers.

Thump.

Something shifts on the other side of the wall.

Someone is in my room.

Mom and Tam have been murdered. It's not a rational thought, but I can't help it.

I pull a heavy, framed Dad from Mom's nightstand. This one shows him snowmobiling with friends. Mom's arms are wrapped around his waist. I wonder if Gary Spence is grinning under one of the other visors.

Thud.

I move slowly. I imagine a thousand things I *wish* my treacherous brain would block with branches. Mom splayed on the bed with her mouth slit at the corners, blood dripping through the mattress; Tamara stuffed in my closet between my polka-dotted raincoat and my overalls.

The floor doesn't creak. The carpet barely rustles.

My door is open just a crevice.

I peer inside.

I see very, very still shoulders.

Mom's washed her hair. She's balanced on my bed in an absolutely striking outfit. Her prized Vivienne Westwood blazer, usually reserved for author conferences. A pair of black, sharp-toed Fluevogs poke out from beneath the hem of her tailored pants. Mom looks nothing like her usual flowing self, buttoned up like this. I want to be relieved she's not vegetating, but it's wrong. Mom's wearing someone else's sharper skin.

"Hey, sweetie. How's the abyss today?" Mom smiles like this morning's catatonia never was. Her makeup can't hide the veins in her eyes.

I don't answer.

"I should have asked permission before coming into your room. I wanted someplace quiet."

"Um." The whole house is quiet. I don't ask about the boxes leaning against the banister, because obviously my exodus to the guest room is beginning at last. It's another something I can't process. "Sorry about . . . leaving. Today. Sorry about yesterday, too."

She waves a dismissive hand. "I don't blame you for wanting out. Gus, if driving away meant escaping, I'd have raised you on the road in a caravan." Mom yanks a constructed box closer. It's filled with my shoes. "You should keep these downstairs. It's rude to wear shoes in the house. We've both fallen into bad habits, haven't we?"

We haven't bothered with the "no shoes indoors" rule since Tamara moved in.

"*Mom*. Where's Tam?"

She glances at the Dad who watches me sleep. "Tam will be spending some time away. With her family."

"*We're* her, we are, the. Her." Why can't I say it? All these questions I wanted to ask, and they've left me stranded in the woods.

The boxes aren't for me moving downstairs. They're for Tam moving out.

"It's not permanent, sweetie. She's just upset. I met with Grandpa Ellis today. He's going to help us." Mom scoots over. "Come sit by me."

I can't holler words she won't hear. Like a good seven-year-old, I go crawling to my mother. Sitting feels like falling. I drop the snowmobiling Dad between us.

"God, that's an awful one." Mom pulls her finger across the glass. "I can't believe he convinced me to ride that thing. In my defense, I didn't know I was pregnant. But it was still a choice. I didn't think enough about my choices back then, Gus." She's looking right through me. "A single choice can make all the difference."

"Mom . . . ?"

Her eyes refocus. "Let's both really take the day off tomorrow, okay?"

I've got thoughts about that, trapped behind other thoughts. "Grandpa Ellis *hates* us. Why is he going to *help* us?"

Is it because Tamara's gone? I hope not. I hope there's no universe in which Mom would choose that scowling bastard over Tam.

"He doesn't hate you." She rests her head on mine. "He wants you to be safe; we have that in common. He's called that attorney again. We're putting together an entire team. I don't want you to worry, Gus. Gary Spence is never getting out of prison. I promise."

If there are words for the turmoil taking place inside my brain, I can't find them. There's been a hurricane. I can't clamber over the tangled debris.

Mom stares at the picture; why can't I ask who the other people were? "You're almost as old as James ever was now. A junior already."

As if that's a reminder I need. I focus on climbing over just one thought.

Something about the box of shoes—

No, not *that*. I try again.

"Mom, maybe . . . maybe we should let them do the retrial. If, um, Kalyn. I mean. If he's guilty. We'll just prove it for sure."

The temperature drops. "We *know* he's guilty. Gary Spence loathed your father. He drove him to his filthy junkyard and shot him in the head, Gus."

She never speaks this bluntly, unless I'm on the settee and she's on the sofa. And I realize that maybe what she's doing is *trying* to shove more trees down in front of me.

I speak a heresy: "Mom. What . . . if he *didn't?*"

Mom clenches her jaw. "Do you think your whole life is a lie? *My* whole life?"

"I don't . . ." The box of shoes plucks at me again. *Mom, did you know him?*

"*Please.*" She climbs to her feet. "*Please* enlighten me. Tell me about the innocence of a felon you've *never* met. Tell me what his daughter told you. I'm sure I'll change my mind about the evil man I knew."

I didn't even ask, and she said it anyhow. "You *knew* Kalyn's dad?"

"I knew him enough," she says stiffly.

So why was I raised believing they'd barely brushed shoulders? "Was he friends with you? With Dad?"

Her eyes widen. "Did she tell you that? I'm all ears, Gus!"

All ears? I might as well not have a mouth, for all the listening she does.

"I've spent all day being told I don't know what I know, but go on!"

How many times is someone called evil before it's true?

"We couldn't even have an open casket, but *you* think he deserves a second—"

"*Would you please let me talk!*" I scream.

Mom gapes. "I'm not stopping you."

But I'm breaking through a dozen branches at once; I'm an avalanche. "You are! You go—you are—you *stop me all the time!* You don't let me *think*, you *don't* listen. You don't *care* what I have to say!"

Her face contorts. "Do you want to repeat that?"

The box of shoes—one pair is *missing*. "Mom. Where are my Docs?"

"I threw them out."

"But those are—they were mine."

"You shouldn't be wearing shoes like that. You shouldn't be sleeping upstairs. And you shouldn't be going to school tomorrow."

"You can't treat me like I'm—I'm seven!"

"What do you think school will be like?" She's angry now, but not at me. "Gus, you try to embrace the world, and it slaps you down. Again and again!"

"I'm *seventeen*."

"*I am your mother*. I took care of you when you were a baby, and yes, when you were seven, and all the years before and after. You can bet your *life* that I'll take care of you for as long as I'm here. Seven or eighty-seven: it's inconsequential."

Mom might speak like Phil to win her arguments. But the way someone speaks doesn't determine the value of what they're saying. Kalyn talks with a twang, but she's cleverer than most people. I may use the wrong words. It doesn't make me wrong.

Details aren't inconsequential. The fact that Mom knew Gary Spence, the fact that Gary and Dad were friends, that's *not* inconsequential, and DNA evidence isn't inconsequential. *Innocence* isn't inconsequential.

I make myself stand. I'll never be as tall as she is, but I want to be closer to eye level. "I am *going* to school tomorrow. You don't get to lock me in the tomb with you."

"*Damn* it, Gus!" Mom spins around, and it's like those clothes have made her brittle, like the loss of her softness extends beyond what she's wearing. "You are the *only* child I'll ever have, and if that means I'm overprotective—well, Gus, being over-protective isn't something I'm ashamed of. Jesus, are there *reasons* to hover."

She tosses the picture frame onto the bed, and it slides onto the floor. "I know I'm not well. I *know* that. I've got the pre-scriptions to prove it. But you wouldn't be well either if you saw—if you went through what I—*no*. Gus. You would be worse in every way."

I am shrinking, aging backward as she cries.

"Can you *imagine* having a baby at your age? *I* couldn't. I was terrified. I didn't know what to do. I did it anyhow. I just did it."

"Why?" *A single choice*, my brain supplies. *A single choice can make all the difference.* What choice haunts Mom?

She blinks. "'*Why*,' Gus?"

"Why did you have me?" My brain's decided to clear away an enormous stump, one that's always been embedded in me, one I wish I could uproot forever. "You could have gotten an abortion."

Mom gives me a look so raw and horrible that it stops my breath.

She retreats without stepping away, flattening her shirt, squaring her shoulders. She holds out a hand. "Give me your phone."

I pass her my phone.

Mom closes the door. I slump back onto the bed.

In the span of forty-eight hours, I've broken and mended two friendships, met and abandoned an idol, smoked pot, lost one parent to moving boxes, cut my mother deeply.

I plan to stand up. By the time I actually put the plan into motion, my room's dark. A new storm rages outside, battering the windows.

I tap the touch lamp, bringing light back to my crypt. I stare at the snowmobiling photograph, wondering what memories have been blanked out of our lives.

A single choice, or many of them?

I'm still lost in the woods, staring right through the glass, when a stone shatters my bedroom window.

KALYN

IT'S KINDA AMAZING, how the entire world can shift while you're watching a screen.

After Phil and Gus depart, I go inside to find Grandma on the couch, but she's not watching the Food Network anymore. It's the news, dogging our lives as always.

I'm expecting the usual slew of speculation and fake updates on the Spence/Ellis case. What I'm not expecting is footage of Jefferson High and the chief Gaggler.

"Eighteen-year-old Garth Holden, a senior at Jefferson High, is almost the same age James Ellis was when he was shot and killed by a classmate. He's only a year younger than Gary Spence was when he went to prison for the crime."

The camera pans to the parking lot behind the football field. Preppy kids are milling about, painting posters and holding tarps up to hide trailers and wagons.

"Our field reporter, Anne Lemire, spoke to Garth after school. WKZ was already at Jefferson High, interviewing the student council, who are busy putting the final touches on their floats for tomorrow's homecoming parade."

Bullshit. Reporters aren't often allowed near schools or minors, but the parade would be a good excuse. No way Garth Holden stayed after school to make parade floats. He must have arranged this interview.

I let out a satisfied hoot when the camera reveals Garth. His nose is bulbous from Phil decking him yesterday; the skin under his eyes is swollen and purple. He looks damn near bee-stung to death. The reporter puts the mic in his face.

"You go to school with Gus Peake, the only son of the victim?"

"Yeah, we're good friends. Gus is having a hard time with all this. And considering all the challenges he's had to face—"

"He suffers from cerebral palsy, is that right?" Anne Lemire interjects.

He doesn't *suffer* from it. That's just Gus. I wish Willy Wonka would invent a way to punch people through TVs.

"Gus is one tough little guy. Always smiling, keeps his head up. But the truth is, he's really broken up." Garth puts on a sad face. "I'm worried about him, you know?"

"I imagine this must be gut-wrenching."

"Yeah. And Gus . . . he's making bad choices, you know? Skipping school—"

"Hypocrite!" I screech.

"—maybe trying drugs and stuff, I don't know."

"You gave him that joint!"

"Hear, hear!" Grandma cries.

"He's hanging out with some bad people."

The anchorwoman chimes in while the audio over Garth and Anne Lemire is muted. "It took some encouragement, but Anne convinced Garth to elaborate." We're treated to footage of Anne and Garth walking side by side around the football field, gesticulating as they talk. "More developments after the break."

I mute the TV, because if there's one thing worse than bullshit news it's lame-ass car commercials that try to make death machines look *sexy*.

"Well, Grandma, it's a real bullshit news day."

I bet I know what the developments are, and only the gossips are gonna like it. Well, that's half the town. Garth Holden, wreaking his petty revenge by ruining my life.

I'm on the edge of the couch, a human cliff-hanger, sucking Grandma's cigarette.

After one last commercial advertising a double-headed toilet brush, we're back to tonight's bullshit news.

"Before the break we spoke to a young man named Garth Holden, who shared revelations relating to the ongoing Spence/Ellis murder case. Back to you, Anne."

The newly risen wind whips Anne's hair up something fierce, just as it shakes Grandma's walls. "Revelations is right, Jennifer. Take a look."

The screen switches back to Garth.

"You're worried Gus might fall in with a bad crowd?"

"He already has. Gus made friends with the daughter of his daddy's murderer." The way he says it, adding a country accent to seduce his hometown, is so *rehearsed*. "Fell in *love* with her, maybe."

Oh, if I could *tan* his hide. What, you stick a guy and a girl together and automatically they've gotta be in love? Seriously, what year is it? No wonder we're all stuck on an ancient murder case. People can't get over their outdated notions.

"—an outlandish accusation, but Garth shared compelling evidence." Now we're looking at a photo, fresh off the fucking presses. I'd give Garth props for his photography, but I'd rather give him an impossible third black eye.

There's me with my arms around Gus, holding him up in the pouring rain with the Taurus beside us, captured in the frame like the one in the infamous photo that made the 1989 papers. My face is blurred out, but the vicious Moms of America will recognize my dress without trouble. Anyone at Jefferson High will recognize my pumpkin hair.

Gus isn't holding me, but the way I've got his head nestled against my neck, you'd think he's sucking my blood. It's that gross and intimate, and even if I know the truth, anyone might assume we were caught making out.

And Garth cropped Phil out of the photo.

I fucking *hate* the trickery of it, how we're all being *literally* framed, but this development is not actual *news* for me. We never get a say in how we're depicted.

But hell, is it even *legal* to air pictures of minors?

And while we're on it, do they have permission to show all of Gus's pictures? Maybe his family gave it years ago, to win a case they'd already won. How fucked is that, when you think about it? I mean, you *know* no one asked Gus for permission.

All these adults failing kids. It's blood-boiling.

"Turn on my baking program," Grandma demands. I bat her hand away.

To add insult to injury, WKZ flashes the old wedding photo beside the new photo.

"According to Mr. Holden, Spence's daughter registered for Jefferson High under a pseudonym earlier this fall. Interviewees tell us she has done well in school, gaining enough popularity to land a nomination for freshman homecoming court representative."

Well, *gee*, no one with two brain cells could *possibly* puzzle out my identity now. I'd roll my eyes, but they've been strained so far the strings at the back of them might snap, apple stems twisted too far along the alphabet.

"Anne," says the news anchor, "is it possible she's turned things around? How do we know she's actually 'a bad crowd'?"

I whistle. Could this be that rare unicorn, an unbiased Samsboro native?

"Jenn, I put that question to Garth Holden." The weather lifts Anne's lapels.

We switch back to daylight and Garth, who points at his black eyes. "She did this to me. What does that tell you?"

I'm used to getting blamed for hitting people, but usually because I *have* hit them.

Anne's microphone dips. "She did this to you? Really?"

"I was trying to tell Gus the truth. She's been lying to everyone, but I recognized her. There was always something kind of, I dunno, *fake* about her?"

"Pot, it's kettle calling," I spit.

"I called her out on it, and she really let me have it, as you can see. She's probably scared Gus into liking her. Maybe he *thinks* it's love, but it's not healthy. I'm super interested in true crime; it's kind of my thing. Sometimes violence is something you inherit." Garth adds sagely: "My cousin breeds pit bulls. Same dif. They play nice, and then they bite the face off your cousin."

Dog stereotypes aside—Stormy Wilson at the AMP used to have the nicest fucking pits—I'm ready to let Grandma put on her baking program after all if the alternative is me dropkicking the television and screaming our boxy house off its blocks.

"So you don't believe Gary Spence might be innocent? DNA evidence won't change your mind?"

Garth bats his eyelashes like Rose might, hand to god he does, almost like he can see me shaking on this doily-covered sofa. "Well, this is only *my* opinion."

"Anne Lemire, WKZ News."

Back to the news desk. "Is this the tale of a modern-day Romeo and Juliet, or a greater tragedy—history repeating itself on a small-town stage? Will tragedy befall a new generation of Samsboro youths?

"If the IFA's retrial request is granted and Judge Harcourt rules wrongful conviction, Spence could be returning home within a year. He may be disappointed to discover that home may not welcome him back."

Jennifer shifts her papers, just for show. "Up next: the fall food drive is kicking off again; learn what you can do to make sure everyone in your town has a wonderful Thanksgiving. Also: see what local businesses are doing to celebrate home-coming. Tomorrow the Jefferson Jaguars—"

I shut the TV off. I can see my reflection on the black screen. I don't look like any Southern Belle. All told, that report took fewer than five minutes.

But the news isn't really over. It's happening every minute. It's happening to me, and to Mom and Grandma and Gus and his folks, too. It's happening to Jefferson High. It'll happen even *more* tomorrow, when I show up for school.

Me and Grandma sit in the dark. I'm dying for the phone to ring.

Despite all the bullshit I've lived through, the screaming and the spitting white rage, dirt in my eyelashes and sand in my teeth—I've never been *outed* like this.

If Rose is made of paper like the terrible book that inspired her, well, the pages are curling up and kissing the bitter-sweet world goodbye. They're leaving behind a black, ashy husk. They're leaving what's really me, charred and stinking and red hot.

In some ways it's a relief, letting Rose die. I never really believed in her.

But it's hard to think a bunch of strangers killed her dead, because that's something that happens to Spences. Rose was never real, but she was a product of Spencehood. She was proof that not everything we put into the world is nasty.

I've seen Rose here in this house, in my family, when no one else has. There's Rose in Mom humming when she cooks macaroni, Rose in Grandma's baby-pure scalp and warm hands, Rose in the way Mom always smiled for real whenever her patients waxed nostalgic about sock hops of long ago.

Just because other people only see thorns in us, just because for so long *I* couldn't see anything else, doesn't mean we've got no petals.

That picture of me and Gus in the parking lot ain't romantic. But I can't look at that picture and honestly say that the way I've got all of myself protecting all of Gus's self isn't some kind of love.

I'll say it plain: you can love someone without wanting to fuck them. You can love someone without it being anything more or less than that. I don't know why some people can't see nuances like that, why they can't be happy that some relationships can be crooked but loving.

Dad won't call tonight, just like he didn't call yesterday. Either he killed James Ellis or he didn't, but maybe it wasn't about reasons. Maybe it was nuanced, too.

I don't know what's going on with my face. It's stupid, sitting here next to the phone with my eyes stinging. I don't know when Grandma moved over here to sit on the armrest, but her warm hand's on my arm.

"Oh, yeah, your show." I reach for the remote—

The door bursts open and I spin round, ready to chuck a chair if need be, but it's only Hurricane Mom. I'm so glad to see her that my chest hurts.

Mom kicks off sopping flip-flops. "Driveway's gonna be a bitch in the morning."

She leans over the kitchen sink, unwinds a dish towel from the rack, and starts wiping rain from her face. And then she can see clearly, and what she's seeing is me, dirty and teary, and Grandma, petrified by Mom's dramatic entrance.

Mom's face sags. "Hasn't your father called?"

I shake my head.

"Huh." She drops a damp canvas bag to the floor. "Think he got cold feet, hearing about old man Ellis trying to keep him in prison? Or do you think he heard about his daughter dabbling in assault? Maybe he thought you'd be visiting him in prison soon on your own steam, so where's the sense in calling?"

"You saw the news," I say.

"Oh, I saw plenty, behind the counter at work. They aired the picture at noon. Slapped your mug on TV just like that, like *you* were on trial!"

"Yeah."

Mom yanks her hair into a ponytail. Water droplets ricochet against my cheek. "For the love of Pete, I'm all for expressing yourself. But this is a *hot* mess."

"*Where* were you, Mom?"

She throws her hands up. "Where do you *think*? I was down

at that so-called news station, giving them hell for picturing a minor without parental consent. Sure, it was taken in public, but you're underage *and* they were giving out personal information. Which, as it happens, isn't legal. I did my research last time you wore that goddamn dress. Did they at least blur your face the second time?"

"Yeah," I murmur, "but my hair's pretty recognizable."

Mom looses another barrage of cusses and then breathes long and hard through flaring nostrils. "So we'll just have to sue them again."

"Again . . . ?"

"How do you think we paid rent before I got the caretaking gig? Sued the press and their sweet asses. There's a fine line between free speech and slander."

I'm hugging Mom tight before I can even think about doing it, trying to make my arms say how grateful I am for the shit she does for me, the shit she's *always* done for me. She tugs my braid. "Whoa there, darling."

I pull away, wiping my nose on my collar.

"They still implyin' you beat up that weasel-faced boy?" Mom wrings her ponytail out over the sink. "Because I'll add that to the list."

"How do you know I *didn't* beat him up? I mean, it's *me*."

"Bang," Grandma says.

"Lord knows it wouldn't be the first time." Mom slips into the third chair at the table and digs around in her bra for her cigarettes. "If you'd have beaten him up, sweetie, he wouldn't be doin' TV interviews. He'd be off somewhere licking his wounds."

I'm smiling, maybe because neither of us think I'm incapable of decking a guy if need be. I don't want to think about how that makes what Garth said about me being like a pit bull true. But even though I'm as dog-tired as I've ever been, sitting with Mom and Grandma Spence next to me, maybe my Rosiest bits have survived.

I'm glad I'm *not* just Rose Poplawski, petals and no thorns. Rose wouldn't have the guts to go to school tomorrow, but I do. I've got a righteous fire in me, a need to set Jefferson High off, for my sake and Gus's, too.

That's a whole nother thing. "When you saw the report before, did . . . I mean. So you know? About me and Gus."

Mom eyeballs me. "Gus *who*, Kalyn-Rose Tulip Spence?"

I swallow. "Gus Peake."

"Well." Mom considers the mud under her fingernails. "Don't know why I should care two figs about any Peake boys, 'specially since you're gay."

"But he's—his dad's *James Ellis*."

"Again," Mom says, "don't know why I should care *who* the hell he is, so long as you care about him and he cares about you."

My mouth is so agape that Grandma taps it closed for me.

"What, no comeback?"

Words spill out quick-sharp: "What about Spence pride, and justice, and—and revenge, and all that shit you raised me to care about—"

"Hold up. Those were your *father's* sermons, and I don't hold truck with any church, no matter who's standing at the front. If I preached for him, I'm sorry. But I gave you a new name and it didn't change you. Names don't change a person. If you like this boy, or whatever—"

"Mom, it's not romantic—"

"*Whatever*, who am I to say a thing?" Her smirk is so real. "I'm the batshit lady who fell in love with a murderer, remember?"

I can't stop shaking my head. "Well, fuck."

"Fuck indeed, sweetie, and one of these days we're both gonna wash our mouths out with Dial or something stronger."

"Damn straight," Grandma agrees.

"Mom. Did you know Dad and James Ellis were friends in high school?"

She takes a long drag. "It's news to me, but so is everything these days."

"But you always suspected something was off. You *believed* Dad didn't shoot James Ellis, no matter what he said." I shake my head. "How did you know?"

"Can't really say. Maybe it's just in my wiring. I can smell a liar. I wrote your Dad the day after his sentencing. I was in Arkansas, watching him volunteer for punishment, but I just felt . . . *this* was not the confession of a boy who's proud or vicious. It's a boy who looks *righteous* and *sad*. Your dad seemed like the opposite of the men I knew. I wanted someone to tell him so. So I got out my notepad. I didn't care about all that talk about girls who chase men on death row, didn't give a shit what other people were doing. I had faith in what I was doing."

I frown. "What you were doing."

"Yes. I wrote my way out of my father's house. Maybe it looks like I ran to another monster, but those letters got me away from a home that had covered me in bruises from the moment I had skin to bruise. You'll *never* meet your uncle or your grandpa, Kalyn. There's nothing *righteous* about the scars they left on me, the scars that killed my mother." She's glaring, but not at me. "That was a slow murder."

Grandma combs a hand through Mom's hair.

Her expression darkens. "And say I was wrong the whole time? Say your dad *is* a monster. Say Gary Spence *was* guilty, and my gut was just all twisted and wrong after being bruised too many times. Well, at least he's a monster in a cage. It's hard to put bruises on anyone from behind bars."

Mom's a madwoman, with all her peroxide and bullheaded convictions. I never questioned her motives for being with Dad, because I grew up loving him. It made sense that she loved him, too. Questioning it would be like questioning water being wet.

"You gonna tell me not to go to school tomorrow?"

"Hell no. You're going," she growls. "And *I'm* coming with you."

"'Kay."

Her tone changes: "Now the real issue: *Kalyn-Rose Tulip Spence*, how come you didn't tell me you've been nominated for freshman homecoming court representative?"

"What? You—I can't—I mean, just those words strung together are so stupid! I didn't tell you *because* it's stupid. And they didn't nominate me. They nominated the nice girl I was *pretending* to be."

"Oh, *sweetheart*." She cups my chin in her hand. "That's still you, like it or not."

PHIL

TAPPING WINDOWS WITH stones has never been among my favorite clichés.

But Gus said he would text me, and he has not done so, and an hour has passed.

The stone is not a large one. Yet I have the aim you'd expect of a Dungeon Master who has been eternally excused from PE thanks to the machinations of his school-employed father.

There is no reason this stone should hit Gus's window on the first attempt. There is *especially* no reason why this stone should shatter the glass of said window, rousing every fiend within the neighborhood, doubtless alerting Gus's mother to my presence.

Another person might have tried the front door. Before I made this foolhardy rescue attempt, I contacted Tamara.

Gus is home, I messaged. *But not replying to messages.*

Her reply arrived, quick and confounding: *I'm not there. had an argument with B. can you please check on him??*

Finally Gus appears beyond the curtain. I see the shoulders of his silhouette clench. Here I stand in the rain and dark, my face obscured from view. For all Gus knows, I am a serial killer. Cool droplets strike my brow and slide down the back of my neck. " 'Arise, fair sun, and kill the envious moon!' "

"*Phil*? You broke *my window*!"

"That was not my intention."

I scarce hear him over the downpour, but I see a sundering within him. Gus is never truly steady, but now he shakes from bow to stern.

"Mom . . . took . . . locked . . . in . . . room." He shouts and whispers every other word.

"Would that you could throw down your hair. Those curls are useless."

Gus retreats. I fear myself abandoned. I dislike the admission, but this story does not gain momentum with Phil Wheeler at the helm. When you are an empty person, you need others to occupy you.

I don't know what I will become if I am not reflecting Gus. It angers me to think of myself in the rain, trying to be human, while Gus in his tower wallows in humanity.

Gus reappears. He drops a duffel bag from his ivory tower. I pluck it from the earth before too much mud can seep into the fabric.

Gus thrusts a desk lamp through the window, popping the

screen loose. He pulls himself halfway across the frame. His good leg seeks purchase on damp roof tiles.

There is no piece of media in which this endeavor ends well, and most media does not bother to depict such struggles from the perspective of those with spastic muscles. Gus is doomed to snap his neck. By now his mother may have heard the ruckus.

Perhaps this thought propels Gus forward. He drags himself outside. His shoes brace against sloping tiles. I see him scrutinize the trellis—he's abandoned his glasses during this quest—but unlike convenient fictional trellises, this one is swamped in ivy and much shorter than the roof. Nevertheless, Gus inches sideways, bobbing as he goes.

His lopsidedness betrays him, and it is only by falling onto his stomach and allowing his body to drag that Gus spares himself sliding off the rooftop. He lodges his one foot in the gutter, sending up a mighty splash.

"Don't let go," I advise, and duck beneath the porch's overhang.

I free a cushion from the swinging chair, heedless of the tearing Velcro. I heave it down the ramp and onto the lawn. It is no trampoline, but it will suffice.

By the time I look toward the overhang again—Gus is no longer dangling.

I scan the ground for his body.

But Gus has reached the trellis. After a few jarring jabs of his foot during his descent, Gus falls from the height of only a yard.

"Well done." I hoist him to his feet.

Gus finds his unusual balance. He is breathless and slack faced. Exhaustion makes his eyes gleam under the porch light. He doesn't wipe the mud from his body.

"Do you think your mother heard us?"

Gus shakes his head. "She's vacuuming the g-g-guest room."

"How convenient!" I pull his duffel bag over my shoulder.

"Why are you whistling?" Gus asks as we near the Death Van.

I am having entirely too much fun. I suspect it's wrong to say so. "Am I?"

Gus pauses beside his mailbox. He treats me to a *look*. I'm not sure what it signifies. Perhaps he simply cannot see, but his prescription is not strong.

"Did you try the classic dummy-in-bed ruse?"

"No. But I blocked the door. With my, um, tabs. My *desk*."

"If only you'd had a filing cabinet to tip in front of it." I wipe water from my glasses. "In a sense, we've trained all our lives for scenes such as this."

Gus looks at his home. "Let's j-just go."

I hope for a chase scene, but the lights in Gus's home remain devoid of matronly silhouettes. The wipers squeak in double-time, matching my escalated heartbeat.

"What's the matter, Gus?" I ask after several blocks of irksome silence.

"You didn't ask me if I was hurt."

"When?"

"When I fell."

"You aren't hurt."

Gus doesn't reply. His eyes are larger without the boxy frames of his glasses. They are undeniably buggy organs. Nonsensically, he stares at me as Tam would.

Can it be that he's seeing me more clearly now?

John is unimpressed with our escapades. He fails to comprehend why Gus and I must climb inside through the minuscule basement window.

John scowls from his post on the sectional, watching our entrance with arms folded over his rotund stomach. He greets Gus with a smile and "Hey, man" before pushing Gus toward the downstairs shower, passing him a *Star Trek* towel, and shutting the door behind him.

John rounds on me. "Come *on*, Phil. Don't you think Dad heard the van pull in? What's the point of the dramatic entrance?"

"*Gus* isn't supposed to be here." I'm less concerned about the point, and more concerned about dramatics.

"You could have sent *Gus* through here and gone in through the front door yourself!" We listen to the pipes groan overhead as water starts spitting in the bathroom. "Or you could have come up with a scheme that didn't force Gus to do acrobatics!"

"Gus is capable."

"It's not about *that*." John tugs on his beard. "I wouldn't ask *any* guest to come in through the window!"

"You never have any guests. You don't have friends."

"You're grinning like an absolute jackass, and Gus looks like he's just been run over. I'm not the one who should be worried about losing friends tonight."

Before Gus came into my life, it was John who tried to raise me human. Before he had a beard, it was his hair that he tugged whenever he caught me drowning chipmunks or setting furniture aflame. John introduced me to D&D thusly: *"Phil, you'll be playing a cleric who cares about everyone, okay? Can you try that?"*

"The whole town's going nuts over the retrial thing. If Gus is caught in the middle of that, Phil, you've got to step up for a change."

"How do you know the town's 'going nuts'? You never leave the cellar."

John pinches the bridge of his nose. "Okay. Do whatever *you* want. *As you wish.*"

"Aaaaas, youuuu, wissssh!" I echo, paying homage to a mutual favorite film.

"Philip. Look at my face. Try, for once, to *read* what my expression is saying. Listen to what my *mouth* is saying: If you can't care about Gus? *Gus Peake*, of all people? A kid who loses to you on purpose no matter how many games of Betrayal at House on the Hill we play? Who else is going to care about *you*?"

This expends whatever energy John can spare toward my betterment. He settles behind his figurine-cluttered desk, downs a swig of Vault, pulls headphones over his ears, and immerses himself in a computer game.

I do not appreciate the atmosphere in this basement.

I climb the stairs. Alas, this is no time for a soliloquy: an audience awaits me at the kitchen table, huddled over another screen.

Dad launches to his feet. He's still wearing his work lanyard. There are marks on the bridge of his nose. Like John, he habitually pinches that place.

"Phil! When did you get home?"

"I've been home for a while." What constitutes "a while"?

"Must've dozed off before Matt left for work." Dad leans forward. "Dark happenings in Samsboro today, huh?"

"Dark happenings indeed."

"So . . . dare I ask? How *was* Gus today?"

"He didn't come to school." This is a truth.

Dad is no imbecile. "But did you speak to him on the phone?"

"No, in fact." Another truth.

"Maybe Beth's got the house on lockdown. I wouldn't blame her . . ." He doesn't end that thought with "this time," because he does not want to be seen judging another parent. The implication remains.

I retrieve a SunnyD from the refrigerator.

"I spoke to his SLP. She says Gus hasn't gone to his speech appointments."

"Should she have told you that? You aren't Gus's parent."

"Anything you'd care to tell me, Phil?"

I slam the fridge door. "I'd care to tell you he wasn't with me, Dad."

Dad's face creases. "Have you two had a falling out?"

More a falling off rooftops.

"I have homework."

"You have *tried* to check on him, haven't you, Phil? To see if he's okay? You're his best friend. Good to show a little empathy."

I pause, hand on the basement doorknob. How could I fail to develop a conscience in this household? Can I not belong to a story as what I am, holes and all?

"I'll do that, Dad. I'll ask Gus whether he's okay."

Dad stares, all-knowing. "Good, Phil. Be sure that you do."

When I reach the bottom of the stairs, Gus has emerged from his steam chamber. He's wedged on the sectional sofa, coiled up with his head resting against the cushions. He opens his eyes when I sit down across from him.

"Thanks," he says, seeing the SunnyD in my grip, "but I'm not thirsty."

"It wasn't for you." I peel the tab and empty the vessel in three swallows. My father's words, John's, Kalyn's: they infest my skull. I cannot help but wonder whether my "empathy" has any merit when others force it upon me.

Gus's large eyes are glazing. He may as well be another murder victim.

"What fate will tomorrow bring us, Gus Peake?"

He shudders. "I don't know. I just want to sleep."

"Ah, but *will* you?"

Gus shakes his head. It frustrates me immensely.

"Gus, this is the juncture in the story where you must rally and—"

"*Phil.*"

I do not know how to proceed. So I ask what's expected. "Gus. Are you okay?"

"I'm tired." He holds his bad arm tight against his chest, fingers curled.

"Yes. But are you, ah, okay?"

"No. But I'm going to school tomorrow." Gus speaks as clear as a bell. He is wont to do that when he is tired. Often it is his own awareness of speech that makes Gus falter.

"I'll go to school tomorrow, too." Gus may misinterpret this as loyalty.

Gus snorts. "We both know your dad won't, um. Let you go. Let you skip."

Perhaps Gus hasn't misinterpreted me. Perhaps he sees the hole where my heart should be. Perhaps he always has. If so, why has Gus tolerated me?

I consider Kalyn's words: *"Aren't you grateful?"*

Gus squeezes my shoulder. How? If you take the fiction from me, what is there left to hold? I never touch Gus if it can be avoided. I don't touch anyone.

"You really hit Garth hard yesterday," Gus ponders, pointing out the exception.

"My knuckles still twinge most profoundly."

"Do you really think it might have been a drifter who killed him?"

I answer the question he isn't asking. "Not really, but I doubt it was your mother."

His voice grows faint. Anxiety is no match for true exhaustion. "Yeah . . ."

He doesn't finish the thought. He doesn't have to, for I know Gus, or at least what he shows himself to be. As my father says, he's my best friend.

At what point does mimicking goodness make it so?

I know something Gus will never know, a great and tiny nothing: I did *not* grab the SunnyD for myself. I grabbed it for him, with nothing to gain from the effort.

When his breathing becomes slow and deep and even, the sure signs of slumber, I tug the duffel bag from his grip and replace it with a cushion. No phone is within.

A change of clothes, a bizarre pair of socks. The yearbook, old and worn.

"You're digging through his stuff?" John glares from afar.

"I'm digging for clues." It isn't a lie.

I open the yearbook and flip through its pages, absorbing the faces of strangers, looking for bruises on knuckles, seeking expressions inhuman and familiar.

ACT SIX
Happy Homecoming, Jefferson High

KALYN

WHAT AM I expecting, a picket line? The citizens of Samsboro, huddled outside Jefferson High, waving pitchforks and preaching the best ways to burn redneck witches?

All that greets us is the usual line of cars dropping kids off, the usual bodies kicking dust in the student parking lot. Mom parks our van in a spot marked *VICE PRINCIPAL*. Then the *actual* VP pulls up behind us. He thinks there's been a mistake, but Mom hollers about having a wheelchair user in the van. The VP starts off kind, telling her there are handicapped parking spots *closer* to the building. Mom tells him to go park there, since he's handicapped himself if he thinks it's in any way appropriate to call someone else handicapped (the hypocrisy here's a delicate work of Mom Art).

I'm on the defensive, and Mom isn't helping. I duck down, trying to hustle Grandma out as quick as possible while fifty-odd stares burn the back of my neck. I fight the itch to pivot and burn all rubberneckers with my laser eyes.

I get Grandma's chair unhooked and feel a hand brush my back. I whip round, ready to smack the bungee hook into my attacker's face—

Sarah looks at me like I've just shot her puppy. "Whoa, Rose!"

"What do you want?" There's no sugar left in me.

"I came to see if you needed help."

"So *you* haven't heard the news." Kalyn's been pulled too far back for too long. She's a branch snapping back into place with a whip crack.

"Claire caught fire," Grandma informs Sarah.

I snort despite myself, clambering into the van. "Go away, Sarah."

Sarah's wiping her hands down her jeans. "Sorry; I've got lotion on. Now just tell me where to grab, please." She stands there like a football player awaiting a pitch. I'd be laughin' under other circumstances, but Sarah's not seeing the whole picture. I'm a rabid cat and Sarah's still calling me kitten.

Mom's finally chased off the VP. She sizes Sarah up in one angry swoop. "Hey there, missy. You got cheerleading practice to get to, or what?"

"Mom—*don't*." Sarah's still squatting like a stubborn thing. "Look, I'd say we'll talk later, but you aren't gonna want to, so if you could just *go*—"

Sarah shakes her head. "You can't *shoo* me. I have six brothers."

I can't help but whistle. "*Six?*"

"Well, that's *nice*, Goldilocks. Please move." Mom puts herself between Sarah and the van. Grandma waves like royalty as we lift her. It's plain that it bothers Sarah something fierce to stand there watching while Mom and I lower her down.

"Please, let me—"

I slam the van door to drown her out.

Sarah looks past me. There's another bone-tired moment of suspense before I figure out she's reading the *Spence Salvage* van decal. She doesn't sound out the words, but the little flicker of understanding behind her eyes says plenty.

"See you, Sarah." I fall in with Mom and Grandma.

Sarah grabs my hand. "Why didn't you tell me?"

I spin on her, all blades and spit. "Why the hell *would* I? If you could see your own stupid, perfect face right now, you wouldn't ask me that."

She flinches at the second adjective. Sarah *does* seem perfect to me, but I know she can't be. I used to think it would be a compliment. Now the idea of anything as certain as perfection scares the living shit out of me.

"I'm not perfect. But I am your friend, Rose." Sarah narrows cornflower eyes. "I want to understand why you lied."

"Do me a favor? Be a *doll* and vote for me for homecoming court."

"I can't. I already voted for Rose Poplawski. Maybe you know her?"

I tear my hand away.

It's only when we're wheeling Grandma up the ramp to the

school that I get another good look at Mom. Mom never finished high school. She never even started it. I put my hand on her back, just for a sec. She blinks four times, but the shine doesn't go.

"Sorry you brought me?" she asks.

"Nah," I say, and then we're inside.

"I'm glad you came to see us today, Mrs. Spence." One of the qualifications for being principal is that you've gotta loathe it a little, tiny bit.

"I'm not here for your sake," Mom assures Principal Walton. "I'm here for Kalyn. I'm here to make sure y'all have some kind of plan for dealing with the situation."

"The situation."

Mom squints at her. "You've seen the news, right?"

"Yes. And let me assure you that WKZ did *not* have permission to interview students about the Ellis case. We're considering legal action. In the meantime, they've pulled the interview."

"Tell that to the internet," I say.

Principal Walton frowns. "Kalyn, if you want to take a few days off, we can arrange for take-home work with waived absences. These are unique circumstances."

Officer Newton, that familiar hulk of a truancy officer, must have squeezed silently into the doorway. He coughs at that.

Mom looks at me. "Kalyn?"

I'm thinking about photos in shoeboxes, about bloody shirts shoved into sheds and left to rot. I'm thinking of Gus, locked inside a box that looks like a mansion. The difference is, I've got a damn choice. And the easy one—staying out of the way—no matter who I am, I don't have that in me.

I aim for wild and crooked.

"I'm not going anywhere."

Mom smirks. "You heard the lady."

"Besides," I add, "I'm on the freshman homecoming court honor guard ballot."

Principal Walton's eyes dart to Officer Newton. "About that. You taking part in the parade might not be the best idea."

I present my pearliest smile. "Where's your school spirit, ma'am?"

"I'm not originally from Kentucky. I can't say I have any personal connection with the . . . *events* unfolding here. Yesterday was the first I heard of the trial."

"That damn news station," Mom snarls.

Principal Walton shakes her head. "No. I was actually eating dinner at Maverick's. The fifties soda shop downtown? Do you know it?"

"I'm not really up for six-dollar milkshakes," Mom says, "but I know the place."

"I was there with a friend last night. We overheard talk and saw—we got a good sense of the *mood* in Samsboro. Have you been downtown since yesterday?"

"Some of us have to work."

"Yes. *I'm* working right now." My respect for Principal Walton grows from nothing to a tiny beansprout. "That doesn't answer the question."

"No, we haven't been downtown."

I think about the signs in storefront windows.

"'*Spences Behind Fences*,'" I recall. "That the gist of it?"

Principal Walton nods. "People are *extremely* upset. And if Rose—"

"—it's Kalyn." Mom and I correct her in unison.

"If Kalyn *wins* the nomination, she'll be seated on a float during the parade. That doesn't seem like a good idea to me, considering the climate downtown."

"What, you expecting an assassination attempt?" I ask.

"That's not funny," Officer Newton scolds, but who cares what he says.

"Some citizens *will* recognize Kalyn. There's no way we can guarantee her safety if she takes part in the festivities. It's not a risk I'm comfortable taking."

"But you can't guarantee my safety here at school, either."

Officer Newton clears his throat.

"Officer Newton will accompany you to your classes today."

I'm torn between groaning and laughing. I lock eyes with Newton, who somehow scowls and winks at the same time.

"You're *that* worried? Because of a couple posters?"

Principal Walton meets me in an even stare. "I saw worse. Outside the cinema. Someone strung up a dummy with your father's face on it. People cheered."

We sit on that, for a second or twenty.

"Happy Halloween," I joke. No one laughs.

"People are emotional, which makes them irrational. They shouldn't blame you, Kalyn, but that doesn't mean they won't. While I believe our student body is largely conscientious, I can't say the same is necessarily true for the adult citizens of Samsboro."

"Preach." Grandma hears Mom and shouts "Hallelujah!" through the open door; she's been waiting outside under the watch of Ms. Patrick.

"Welp." I slap my knees. "Odds are I won't win anyhow."

"You might, Kalyn. The ballot boxes have been open in the library for weeks. Most students have already voted."

"Imagine a Spence winning a popularity contest." Mom whistles. "Tell you one thing, Kalyn. *If* you win that title and you *wanna* be in that parade, you're gonna be in it."

Who the hell knows what I want.

"If that's settled, I'm out of here. Grandma's got a doctor's appointment to get to, and I've gotta swing by the courthouse." Mom stops at the door. "Kalyn?"

"Yeah?"

"I hope you get that vote, girl." I hear Grandma trill goodbye to Ms. Patrick as she's wheeled outside.

The bell rings. It's just me, Principal Walton, and Officer Pits in here.

"You're gonna rig the vote so I lose, aren't you?"

Not even a blink. "I don't plan to. But I *do* plan to have you in here again soon, once this blows over."

"What, you like me that much?"

"You've got a truancy problem. That's the next conversation we'll be having."

"Why not have it now? There's a chance I'll be assassinated today, you know."

She shakes her head. "Get to class. And look after yourself, please."

Officer Newton shadows me as I step into the main office. I wonder if this is how Dad feels when guards lead him in handcuffs to the visitation room. I'm not wearing shackles, but I feel their ghosts on my wrists.

The office walls muffle most of the noise outside. Students churn and swell past the windows like a babbling brook. Once I leave this room, that river will heckle and jeer.

"I told her not to rig the nomination. I want you to know that."

I turn around. Ms. Patrick looks all teary. She's standing behind her desk and wringing her manicured hands.

"I mean it." She catches me eyeing her fingers and curls them into fists. "I'm the one who'll count the votes. If you win, I'll make sure you and everyone else know it, or there's really no justice in this town."

Brad leans out of his cubicle. Ms. Patrick doesn't bother sniping at him. Her eyes are on me. I bet her nails are cutting her palms.

"It's okay, Ms. Patrick. Really. I don't care about the parade."

"That's—that's not the point. It will be fair this time."

"This time?"

"I will *not* stand by and watch another good person get rail-roaded." It's not quite a shout, but it bursts from her like a confession. "I won't be part of it again."

"Ms. Patrick, how long have you worked here?" I take a step closer. "Did you know my dad?"

"You have to get to class." Her phone rings, and she's eager to answer it. I have a dozen more questions to ask, but she's right. Things are going to be bad enough without me being late to the slaughter. Plus, a giant pair of armpits is floating near my shoulders.

I push the door open and step into the hallway flood, letting the current whip me around. I should get big boots like Gus to anchor me. For now I'll just have to walk.

The attack comes from above. The cafeteria balcony.

Scrambled eggs slap me in the forehead and slip down my nose. They're followed by a shout from Officer Newton, and then a lunch tray smacks me on the crown, hard enough to make my legs crumple. I'm baptized with icy, sticky milk.

Well, I'll be damned. The sky is falling.

GUS

I WAKE UP wondering whether yesterday was a dream. I'm aching on the Wheeler sectional, no pictures of Dad in sight. Instead of pancakes, I eat Corn Pops. I do my daily PT exercises in the corner next to the water heater, rushing because I don't like to be seen doing them. Phil's picking his face in the bathroom mirror, rambling about D&D. We wait for his dad to leave for work, and I skirt John's worried glances.

Phil's awful driving is a comforting, familiar thing.

It's hot for October. The turning leaves are on fire in the sunlight as we pull up to Jefferson High. I wish I had edgy black sunglasses on, and not only to hide behind them.

I keep pulling at my socks. The mismatched OTKs are uncomfortable because the angelic and demonic wings tickle the backs of my knees when I walk. They aren't a good fit for me, especially with my leg throbbing.

But if I waited for things to fit me, I'd be waiting forever.

"Do you think Mom's called the police?" By now she'll have forced open my bedroom door. Will she come get me? Will she want to, after what I said to her? Will she wear the sharp jacket and shoes? I left a note, but maybe she won't read it.

Phil shrugs and gets out of the Death Van. He waits for me.

"'Cry havoc and let slip the dogs of war.'" Usually Phil's homages feel melodramatic. Today they feel about right.

"Do you . . . um. Kalyn?"

"I suspect she'll be in a mood. Who wouldn't be, upon seeing *that*?"

Phil points to a banner someone's hoisted up the flagpole. It's got bold, broken words on it, spray painted in red. *Spences Behind Fences.* I whisper out the words under my breath. When I drop my stare to ground level, the meandering morning crowd parts.

I hear a click—did someone snap a photo? I wonder how quickly it'll be online. Do I look half-dead? Did they get the banner in the shot, too?

You don't expect a potted plant to transform into a tragic figure. This is close to option *a*: The crippled side note with a tragic backstory who adds texture to a country setting.

Glances hit like hailstones. I'm still so tired that I can barely get my body to move, let alone hurry. I wore these fabulous socks, but no one is thinking about them.

My unappreciated socks. Phil's unappreciated hand-painted shoes. I wish people would see what we want to be instead of assuming what we are.

"*Excuse me!*" A sharp voice cuts through the middle of the crowd. There's a ripple of movement as people are jostled aside. "*Excuse me.* Are *you* in a wheelchair, young man? No. Get off the ramp, or get run down."

A plaid-clad lady pushing an old woman—no, pushing *Grandma Spence*—in a rattling wheelchair storms out of the crowd. This has to be Kalyn's mom. She's throwing very deadly stares at everyone, but she pauses when she sees me. The stubborn set of her jaw is familiar, and it means Kalyn probably came to school today.

Mrs. Spence's departure seems to snap some spell, or maybe the bell does that. Rubberneckers abandon the plant-boy spectacle and make for the school entrance.

"Can I help you with anything, Gus?" someone asks.

"No." I don't bother with eye contact.

"Well, anytime! I'm your guy! And I want you to know that skank isn't going to bother you today! None of us will let it happen." A clammy hand grips my shoulder. "Spences behind fences, man!"

"Hey, Gus." Another person I've never spoken to. "I heard about what's happening, and I want you to know that it's a crime that they're even considering putting your family through this. My dad was actually *friends* with your dad. He was in his PE class actually, and we think Gary Spence should probably get the chair."

"I—I don't—" I stammer, but Phil's ready this time.

"'Get thee to a nunnery!'" he bellows.

That's pretty low-hanging Shakespearean fruit. It proves Phil's feeling a bit overwhelmed, too. Beyond that, Phil's actually *touching* me. Just barely—two fingers on my back—but still.

Phil's stare is pointed as we ascend the steps that tripped me. It's *specifically* pointed to the left of the entrance, where the Gaggle is gathered. Today they're not singing songs about STDs. Garth crouches at their center. He waggles his fingers at me.

I can't believe I admired him. Why? Because he wears eyeliner and a kilt sometimes? Appearances aren't everything. Maybe I wanted to think they are. Believing appearances mattered let me justify feeling like *I* don't matter. But if appearances have little to do with worth, I'll have to figure out why I *really* feel worthless sometimes.

Phil clasps my shoulders and puts himself behind me like a lanky overcoat. "Let's get indoors. Recoup under cover."

We hear screaming as soon as we step into the foyer.

Phil draws himself up, using his height to pressure people out of the way. We press through the bodies spanning the hallway to discover the source of the commotion.

There's a mess on the floor beside the lockers that line the wall beneath the cafeteria ledge. A breakfast tray's been overturned. Chocolate milk and scrambled eggs are blown all over like brain matter. Orange juice, too, based on the smell. A rolling apple bumps against the toes of the crowd.

"Get to class!" Officer Newton roars.

He's crouched beside the supine form of Eli Martin, two meaty hands on Eli's shoulders. I've never seen Officer Newton's face this red, though his default is cherry tomato. I've never seen Eli Martin unconscious.

And I know what happened. It's more like instinct than solving a mystery.

"Where is she? Where's Rose?"

"She was just here." The reply comes from a girl with striking cheekbones. "It was *scary*, honestly. Eli dropped his tray on her *head*. Rose got back up and started *climbing* the lockers." The lockers aren't tall, but neither is Kalyn. "She grabbed Eli by the shirt while he was leaning over the ledge. Rose just yanked him down, and he hit the floor. It was just really . . . I don't know. It was really scary."

On the floor, Eli lets out a wheezing cough.

"Where did she go?"

"I don't know. It happened in like ten seconds. It was really—"

". . . scary. Okay."

Kalyn's fled the scene.

I can't run fast, but there are wings at my knees and they carry me her way.

Kalyn being in the kiln room might be predictable.

The truth is, she's not *always* unpredictable. She's not *always* fun, and she's not *always* tragic. She's Kalyn, and that's hard to categorize. Even thinking *that* seems wrong, because it's still thinking "of" her and not about her. That's not how people work.

I shove the door in and Phil follows.

I have to squint without my glasses, but clearly this is no sanctuary today. Remains of clay pots have been broken at her feet, sharp shards of glaze fallen to dust.

Kalyn's let her wild hair loose. The strands are wispier than I guessed, especially near the frizzy tips. They remind me of the tiny capillaries within lungs, the alveoli bristles that catch my eye on hospital waiting room posters. An egg swells on her forehead, white and purple and angry. She isn't a sci-fi heroine. She's Kalyn.

She's holding a long shard of pottery, some broken old bong or another.

Her hand is steady as she jerks it sharply sideways, shearing a huge portion of hair from the left side of her head. It falls like red water from her fingers.

"Kalyn!"

"Primscilla I ain't," she grumbles. "That's all."

Kneeling's not easy, but I put my hands on the dusty linoleum and feel tiny pieces of her there. The broken red threads of her hair make my hands lose purchase. Maybe that's why I fall against her, but it's not why I drape arms around her.

"Don't hurt yourself. Please."

"Hell, Gus. It's just a haircut," she whispers into my neck.

"And hey. If I *do* scalp myself by accident, it'll save the kids of Jefferson Fucking High some trouble."

"Not me."

Her laugh is damp with tears. "You *most* of all, Gussafras."

"My name's really just Gus. One syllable. Gus."

"What, *just* Gus?" Kalyn pulls back. "You've only got *half* a real name?"

"I get half a real everything." I mirror her tearful smirk.

"Crop off the other side, too," Phil blurts. "Shaved heads are a staple of badass science fiction protagonists. Ripley. Natalie Portman in *V for Vendetta*."

Kalyn rolls her eyes. "Fine, Phil. Go get me some real scissors."

"Kay . . ." I hesitate.

"What, Just-Gus?"

I don't know if Kalyn cherished her hair. It was always braided or rolled up and hidden away. But no one grows hair that long by accident.

"Your hair . . ."

"People around here are starting to get ideas about pumpkin-haired girls." A twinge enters her voice. "I'm getting ideas, too. Whoever *me* is, I don't want to be her."

"Maybe that's what happens when you're raised halfway."

"Again, while I understand 'halves' are among our story motifs," Phil pipes up, "your hair would be more appropriate if you cut it evenly."

Kalyn glares. "That's it. Please go away now, Phil."

Phil bristles. "You can't eject me from this story."

The past few days have tested us, and I'm not sure Phil's passing. "Phil. Just . . . just give us two minutes. *Please.*"

He departs, PSP at his fingertips. "'Hell is empty and all the devils are here.'"

"Keep an eye on that one," Kalyn says. "Not sure his heart's in the right place."

"I'm not always sure he has one. But he's not the one holding, um, cutter, I mean, a sharp object to his head."

She stares at the heap of hair in her lap. "Shit, man. You're right. We haven't even made it to class yet and my hair's been murdered. But your socks look dope."

"Thanks." I rest my back against the shelf beside her, like this was any other day.

"Also, you're super cute without your glasses."

"*Gross.*" I take her hand. "Did your dad call last night?"

She shakes her lopsided head. "Did you talk to your mom?"

"It . . . didn't go well," I say. "I sort of ran away from home."

"*You what?*"

"That's enough," says a booming voice. "Out you get."

Phil has returned, but not with scissors. With Officer Newton.

"Shit." Kalyn's hand tries tucking the ghost of her hair behind one ear.

"You *assaulted* another student."

"He assaulted me first, thank you kindly."

"Oh, I know," Officer Newton barks. "I was there."

"Time for another suspension, huh?"

"Wrong." Officer Newton unfolds his arms. "You aren't getting out of class that easy. Not for witnessing an accident."

Kalyn gapes and I frown. "I'm sorry, Officer Pi—Newton, but Eli getting snot-beaten was an accident? Who the hell's gonna buy that?"

Officer Newton's face is blank. "I have a witness."

The girl with striking cheekbones peers around the door. She spins a different story than the one she shared with me: "Eli dropped his tray on Kalyn, then fell over the ledge when he was craning over to mock her. I saw the whole thing."

"Sarah? Why would you . . ."

"My parents *never* met your parents," Sarah blurts, suddenly tearful, "but for some reason they've ordered *Spences Behind Fences* T-shirts. I asked them why. They said it's to support the community. But *you're* part of our community, too, aren't you?"

"Yeah," Kalyn says blankly. "I guess."

"So I'm just doing what's right," Sarah declares. "Defending my *friends*."

Kalyn wipes her eyes. "Okay, Sarah."

Officer Newton coughs. "Ready to return to class, or will I have to drag you?"

Phil's hung back in the hallway. I can't see his expression. Bringing Officer Newton here was either revenge or bad luck.

"No need." Kalyn stands. "I'm dyin' to go put some learning in people. I mean, *get* some learning in me."

She proffers her hand. I take it. "Same."

"Probably best you two aren't seen making eyes," Officer Newton suggests. "Cut your bodyguard some slack and call it quits for now, lovebirds."

We don't bother correcting him, although Kalyn sticks out her tongue.

We didn't come all this way to vanish.

PHIL

AS WE NEAR final announcements, the whole of Jefferson High is a wire pulled taut. If this is a guitar string, surely it will snap. Metaphors are not my strong suit.

Has today been decent entertainment? I do not know. Gus and I have spent hours dodging stares and bizarre attempts at human connection. I've been more shield than shadow, warding off ne'er-do-wells who want Gus to know they support him.

Here is an outline of the day, as we experienced it:

1st Hour, Homeroom: For the last ten minutes of homeroom, Gus and I completed homework in unusual quiet. Our teacher pretended to read with his feet on the desk. His eyes glanced frequently over the top of the book. He rarely turned a page. Gus was not studying so much as plotting, writing a long unknowable list in his notebook.

Before 2nd Hour: Gus and I visited his locker to fetch his textbooks. Lilies lay at his locker's foot. Valentine-like notes of condolences were pasted down its front.

"I'm not dead," Gus said.

Within his locker Gus discovered an anonymous hate letter, its angry scrawl incongruous against the backdrop of red hearts.

"'You're father would be ashamed,'" I read. "'Next time date hitler why dont you.' Not a correct apostrophe in evidence. Appalling."

Gus did not reply.

2nd Hour, AP Government: Our notoriously strict teacher, Mrs. Ollette, would not alter her method for something so measly as a murder scandal. She did not balk at discussing the intricacies of the judicial system. Eyes had a tendency to fall upon Gus whenever the word "jury" was uttered.

3rd Hour, AP English: Soft-hearted Mr. Alfonso *did* balk. Our test was canceled; we were granted the entirety of class to free read. He claimed it was a "homecoming treat," but when Gus shut his copy of *1984* after two pages and began scribbling down words on his mysterious notebook list again, he was not asked to stop.

Before Lunch: Gus was summoned to the office.

"Your mother stopped by," Ms. Patrick informed him.

Gus deflated. "Um. Do I have to leave?"

"No. She dropped this off for you."

Gus took the bag with his good arm and sagged under some surprising weight. He leaned against the glass window and pulled a large shoebox from the bag. Eventually he contrived to prop it open. We were treated to a vision of cherry-red leather boots.

Gus stared as if they were the most incomprehensible mystery of all.

I solved it. "Ms. Patrick, which mother was this?"

"Oh. It was, um . . . the gardener? Tammy, is it?"

"Tamara, the landscaper," I amended.

"I like your socks," Ms. Patrick told Gus as we left.

Lunch Hour, Speech Therapy: I'd met Gus's speech therapist before, at potlucks during which Dad invited coworkers to our home as if to say, "Yes, my wife left me, but I can still have dinner parties and raise our children well!" never mentioning that one son lives perpetually in the basement and another is devoid of human empathy. We walked in on the speech therapist gnawing on a peanut butter sandwich and watching cartoons on a portable DVD player.

"Gus, it's been a while! I wasn't expecting you. Avoiding the cafeteria?"

Gus nodded.

"Right. Here's the deal. We can start therapy today, or we can postpone that to next week and you can sit quietly and watch *Avatar: The Last Airbender* with me."

I watched a girl bend water to her will; Gus laced up his tall red boots and scribbled in his notebook.

Before 4th Hour: For the first time since parting this morning, we encountered Kalyn in the hallway. Officer Newton held a student, a member of Garth's Gaggle, by the scruff of her black tee while Kalyn wiped brownish spit from her face. Her unbound half head of hair was ever more tangled. She looked furious but also, perhaps, scared.

She marked Gus and her aspect shifted; immediately a mask fell into place. She smiled at his boots, then seemed to remember herself and looked away.

Gus wanted to go to her.

"Officer Newton is right," I reminded him. "Best not to engage."

Gus didn't argue.

4th Hour, The Pep Rally: We chose to take refuge in the library. The librarian led us into an empty computer lab and sat us in the carrel farthest from the door. "No one will come by during the rally."

We entered this bunker two minutes ago. I tucked the keyboard behind the desktop to allow us room to rest our heads.

Gus slides his cryptic notebook toward me with a sigh.

"These are the thinks, um. The thinks, the *things* I'm thinking about."

I stare at words transcribed in smeared lines. He has

ineptly titled the document "Clues?" As always, his penmanship leaves something to be desired.

Clues?

1. Gary Spence signed Dad's yearbook and appeared in photos with Dad, too. Good <u>friends</u>? If so, <u>why</u> would Gary Spence claim Dad bullied him?

At first I cannot fathom how he spent hours writing this entry; Gus turns the pages for me to reveal that each of the next several is dedicated to a numbered "clue."

2. Dad's body was found in the trunk of a red 1985 Ford Taurus at Spence Salvage. <u>Who found it?</u>

3. Gary Spence confessed to the murder immediately. <u>Why?</u>

4. New DNA evidence (a jacket) clears Gary Spence of guilt. <u>How?</u>

5. Mom said something like, "You wouldn't live through what I've seen." <u>What has she seen? Was it the murder? Is she involved?</u>

6. Dad was shot. <u>Why</u> was a knife belonging to Gary Spence found in the trunk with him?

7. Grandpa Ellis hates Mom. <u>Is this why? Or is it because she's gay or something else?</u>

"Um. Anything to add?"

"You spent all day on this? Gus, you need to better acquaint yourself with the internet." I amend the list with basic background knowledge, brushed up last night at John's desktop while Gus slept. I make impeccable additions with my fountain pen.

Clues?

1. Gary Spence signed Dad's yearbook and appeared in photos with Dad, too. Good <u>friends</u>? If so, <u>why</u> would Gary Spence claim Dad bullied him?
The two things are not mutually exclusive. Or, perhaps, like you and Kalyn, the general populace was not aware of the true nature of their friendship. There are social factors to consider. Spences and Ellises likely could not be seen together.

2. Dad's body was found in the trunk of a red 1985 Ford Taurus at Spence Salvage. <u>Who found it?</u>
Research reveals this was a woman named Kathy Sturluson. She was the Life Skills teacher at Jefferson High and would have known both boys. She is probably still alive. We can likely interview her.

3. Gary Spence confessed to the murder immediately. <u>Why?</u> Typically this sort of thing occurs when someone is protecting a secret or the true guilty party. You should be familiar with the idea of "taking the fall." The real question is not why, but <u>whom?</u> Whom did this behavior benefit?

4. New DNA evidence (a jacket) clears Gary Spence of guilt. <u>How?</u> This information will be revealed in court, if there is a retrial.

5. Mom said something like, "You wouldn't live through what I've seen." <u>What has she seen? Was it the murder? Is she involved?</u> This might explain some of her eccentricities. Is this why your mother is upset with you? Did you accuse her?

6. Dad was shot. <u>Why</u> was a knife belonging to Gary Spence found in the trunk with him? This is bizarre, agreed. Even if Spence was trying to frame himself, why plant a knife rather than the actual murder weapon?

7. Grandpa Ellis hates Mom. <u>Is this why? Or is it because she's gay or something else?</u> I fail to see why this is relevant.

Gus lingers on my amendment to number five. "I didn't accuse Mom of murder. I accused her of a thing, I mean. Something worse."

"Ah? How so?"

His face flushes. "Um. I asked her. I asked why she didn't abort me."

"Gus. You know I'm not especially adept at social interactions. But that hardly seems worse than a murder accusation."

"I know." He stares at the paper.

"Was it a genuine question?"

"I mean. Who wouldn't um . . . regret. I mean. Resent me. A little?"

I can't comprehend his thinking. "Nonsense. She's got nothing but blind, foolish affection for you. When you're in her vicinity, she tilts herself to orbit you. That's no act of resentment; it's a compulsion, gravity and motion. I study such things."

"But people don't have a choice, with gravity."

"Of course not. It was merely a metaphor. I don't know how to placate you."

"I know," Gus replies. "Thanks for trying."

I can hear riotous stomping from the gymnasium. Nothing so mundane as murder can put a damper on school spirit.

The door to the lab opens and the noise intensifies. Kalyn appears when she is not expected, and therefore appears now. Gus rises, but she attempts to bow out—

"Shit, I didn't—"

Officer Newton propels her inside. "Go on. I'm watching the door."

Scraps of paper speck the wilder side of her hair. She's tamed the tangle into a bun: half Princess Leia, half newborn. I can't retell scenes I did not witness, but Kalyn's face is bruised where it was not previously, and the red in her eyes is more pronounced.

"Kalyn," I ask, "care to regale us with your exploits?"

"That's a hard no, Quillpower." Kalyn scurries close to occupy the chair in the carrel beside ours. That's not enough proximity for Gus apparently, as he wheels his chair out and over so that he's aligned beside her.

"You okay-lyn?"

"Oh *gust* dandy. Same old shit. What's this?" Kalyn reviews Gus's list, whistles, frowns. "Lemme borrow your pen."

"Certainly not. This is a Faber-Castell. It's not for casual—"

Gus pulls it from my hand and gives it to Kalyn. She makes a point of licking the tip. "Thanks, Quillpower."

Her contributions are not insignificant.

Clues?

1. Gary Spence signed Dad's yearbook and appeared in photos with Dad, too. Good <u>friends</u>? If so, <u>why</u> would Gary Spence claim Dad bullied him?

The two things are not mutually exclusive. Or, perhaps, like you and Kalyn, the general populace was not aware of the true nature of their friendship. There are social factors to consider. Spences and Ellises likely could not be seen together. yeah, apart from the photos and the yearbook there's a picture where your mom and dad are on the hood of a car on fourth of july and to me it's always looked like it was taken ~~on grandma's property~~ @ spence salvage. I think they hung out.

2. **Dad's body ~~was~~ found in the trunk of a red 1985 Ford ~~Taurus~~ at Spence Salvage. <u>Who found it?</u>** Research reveals this was a woman named Kathy Sturluson. She was the Life Skills teacher at Jefferson High and would have known both boys. She is probably still alive. We can likely interview her. OK to Kathy Sturluson but I don't see how that'll help, not like she knows anything special just because she found him. Also we should interview the secretary here at JHS. She knows something too.

3. **Gary Spence ~~confessed~~ to the murder immediately. <u>Why?</u>** Typically this sort of thing occurs when someone is protecting a secret or the true guilty party. You should be familiar with the idea of "taking the fall." The real question is not why, but <u>whom</u>? Whom did this behavior benefit? This is my number 1 question and the question I'll be asking Dad next time he calls.

4. New DNA evidence (a jacket) clears Gary Spence of guilt. How? *This information will be revealed in court, if there is a retrial.* IFA is building a case because the jacket submitted as evidence proves Dad was facing the other way when the gun went off because of the way that the brain matter hit him. (graphic—sorry, Gus)

5. Mom said something like, "You wouldn't live through what I've seen." What has she seen? Was it the murder? Is she involved? *This might explain some of her eccentricities. Is this why your mother is upset with you? Did you accuse her?* No way. I'll ask her if you want. Your mom has no right to be upset with you gus so that's some bullshit and I won't say sorry this time. ☹

6. Dad was shot. Why was a knife belonging to Gary Spence found in the trunk with him? *This is bizarre, agreed. Even if Spence was trying to frame himself, why plant a knife rather than the actual murder weapon?* I don't know the answer to this except that maybe it wasn't a framing? GS and JE were in shop class together. So maybe it was like a borrowed knife or something, I don't think it has to do with the case.

7. *Grandpa Ellis hates Mom.* <u>*Is this why? Or is it*</u>
<u>*because she's gay or something else?*</u>
I fail to see why this is relevant. No idea, but fuck
him double if that's true.

Kalyn goes one further, adding an additional page.

8. Here's my big question. What's with the kidnapping
story? I mean my dad didn't kidnap your dad, your
dad left a football game at halftime. What made
him do that? <u>Who</u> made him do that?

"You think, um, *Ms. Patrick* knows something?" Gus asks.

"Likely many citizens have useful information," I supply.
"Perhaps the court will call them to the stand. At the very least,
Gus, your mother really is implicated now."

"This sucks," Gus says.

"Yeah, it does," Kalyn says.

"I fail to see why. We've made significant progress, considering we've spent less than two days investigating."

"Phil, you dope. That's exactly *why* it sucks." Kalyn knocks
my temple with her knuckles. "It *sucks* that the three of us figured all this out in a day. Because you know what? It wasn't
hard. It wasn't hard, but no one else has bothered doing it! It's
been two decades, but *no one* tried to sit down and put this shit
together. Fucking. *Shitsboro*."

Gus clutches his curls in his good hand as though attempting to puncture his scalp with his fingernails. "And also. It *sucks* that Mom is implicated."

"I know the feeling," Kalyn says, savagely or sagely.

Gus pulls his fingers upward until his curls unwind, puff out as if electrified. "It's been just two days. Two days, a single *choice*. How do we have this much bringing, *collected already*? Why don't the *police* have this much?"

"Perhaps they do but have not been inclined to say so." I adjust my glasses. "Oftentimes, police would rather have a tidy case than a correct one. 'Dirty cops' are a genre staple."

"Tidy." Gus clenches his fist. "But the world isn't tidy. People aren't tidy!"

"Color me unsurprised. Shitting on poor people. Bet that's a trope, too, hey, Phil?"

"Indeed, Kalyn. There are a thousand precedents. Read *The Grapes of Wrath*."

"Yeah. See. That bias I know about. But what I *don't* know? Why is *my dad* okay with framing poor people? And why the hell hasn't he called me?"

If this outburst feels as incongruous to Gus as it does to me, he does not say so. He leans back in his chair with his eyes closed. Perhaps he did not sleep well, having asked his mother why she did not abort him.

"We have a list of facts here. I would like to compile some theories." They stare at me. I forge ahead. "Why might Gary Spence murder his best friend? Or, if he did not, why would he assume the blame? The obvious notion—that he is covering for a mutual friend—seems to point directly at your mother, Gus."

"Mom's not a murderer," he says. "She'd have no motive."

"Then why has she lied about knowing him? Perhaps James and Gary had an affair, and she killed James in a jealous passion?"

Kalyn snorts. "I'm all about gay romance, but my dad's about as straight as a broomstick. Just doesn't seem likely."

Gus looks queasy.

"Maybe they really are covering for someone, though," Kalyn says. "But who?"

"The next suspect on my list is your grandfather, Gus."

Gus groans. "Grandpa Ellis is an asshole, but I can't camera, I mean, *picture* him murdering anyone. He'd hire someone else to do it."

"And there's no way in hell my dad would take the fall for that guy," Kalyn says. "Maybe it was all an accident. Maybe they were playing around and the gun went off and, I don't know . . ."

"And your dad just *accidentally* hid the body, too?" Gus whispers.

"Unlikely," I say. "No matter what theories we concoct, there's that notion to contend with: the body was found on Spence property, and a Spence willingly took the blame. As much as we might want to blame an outsider, aye, there's the rub."

"If by rub you mean fucking tragedy, then yeah," Kalyn spits.

"Do you know what I've never enjoyed about true-crime stories?" I ask.

"No, but you're going to tell us." Gus sounds distinctly unenthused. Kalyn snorts.

"They frequently lack resolution. The most infamous cases, JonBenet and Jakob Wetterling, the West Memphis Three, they've never been *resolved*. I've read stories that leave entire mysteries intact. Children who may or may not have fallen into lakes, husbands who may or may not have slit the throats of wives—"

"Enough examples," Gus interrupts.

"There are myriad questions but rarely answers. But then, there's a certain *sensationalism* to the unknown. Many audiences *prefer* unsolved mysteries."

"Because *they* aren't living them," Kalyn growls.

"Can we talk about something else?" Gus slumps. *"Anything* else?"

I suppose I'll allow them their humanity, but doing nothing is tedious. "Shall we plan a new campaign while we wait?"

Kalyn lays her head on Gus's shoulder. "Whatever. How does it work?"

"Well, you create characters by assigning them a race, a class, alignments. Your Dungeon Master—me—refers to the manual and oversees a storyline for them to occupy."

They close their eyes. My explanations of cantrips and character sheets are occasionally interrupted by echoes from the gym, but in here interruptions have ceased.

When I pause to ask if they've any questions, Gus's head is on his arm.

"On second thought," Kalyn says. "I've created enough characters this year."

The door opens. Enter: the girl from this morning, followed by Officer Newton.

Kalyn stands. "Sarah? What—"

She is breathless, ruddy cheeked. "Kalyn, you have to leave. Now. They announced homecoming court at the assembly."

"And?"

"And you won the nomination."

I cannot determine whether we are surprised. Kalyn clasps her hands under her chin and cries, mockingly, "Wow, I'm *popular.*"

"People are going nuts. Tearing down banners, chanting, stampeding, the works."

"The dogs of war indeed."

Officer Newton clears his throat. "Boy, you kids are theatrical. Come on, Spence. I'll give you a ride. You and your entourage."

"Kalyn," Gus says, "what are you going to do?"

"I don't know. Damned if I do or don't. Gus?"

"I'm not you. You do things I'd never do."

"Don't know about that." She smiles grimly. There's a mad gleam in her eye. Ophelia. "I *do* wanna give everyone in this town the finger."

"Then you should do it, Kay." Gus hoists himself to his feet.

"I don't blame you," Sarah says. "I'd feel the same way."

Kalyn rolls her eyes. "How do you know?"

"Because, for the hundredth time, you're my friend!"

"Er. Sorry." Our catalyst, taken aback?

I tally these interactions in my head, on character sheets unseen.

"Right. I'm gonna parade in front of a town full of angry hillbillies. Any plans about how we go about this? I don't want to be egged to death any more than I want to hear Phil ramble on about D&D."

"I'll be keeping an eye on you, for one," growls Officer Newton.

We gawp, collectively.

"But Principal What's-her-face said that the school couldn't ensure my safety—"

"Principal Walton isn't paying me. You won your damn pageant."

When Gus lifts his eyes from his cherry toes, the gleam has infected him. "Kalyn. Are you *sure* you're done inventing characters?"

"How do you mean?"

Gus divulges his plan in a single, mad sentence that feels almost out of character.

For a moment, silence. Then Kalyn, in a single graceful motion, swoops one arm around his neck and cuffs his ear. "It's got balls, Gustivus!"

"It's a little weird," Sarah says. "Where did you get the idea?"

"Um." Gus blushes. "Alexander McQueen?"

Sarah smiles. "I love it. And I have keys to the copy room, actually. Perks of being on the yearbook committee."

"As a storyteller I approve," I say, "but bodily harm seems probable."

Officer Newton sighs. "Well, kids. It's your funeral."

It may be, but it's fine entertainment. "'Cowards die many times before their deaths; the valiant never taste of death but once.'"

"No one's going to die," Gus says. "It's only a parade."

"Often funeral processions are," I retort.

"I don't plan on wearing black," Kalyn says, showing her teeth.

KALYN

"HOW DO I look?" I give a hideous twirl. It's hard to make heavy green robes look hot, but hey. Beggars can't be choosers, and honestly, the hood's doing my haircut a few favors.

"Positively shapeless." Phil isn't being mean. Shapelessness is sort of the whole point, and his bony ass is swamped in fabric, too, a field of royal purple.

"It's long on you, but it'll have to do." John, Quillpower's bearded older brother, is draping Sarah in pearly white cloth.

"Sarah looks like an angel, and the rest of us look like walking garbage bags."

"It's about actual ac-accessorizing." From the depths of the sectional couch, Gus gives me a thumbs-up. It's a funny thought to think when he's drowning in black robes, but I like looking at Gus, and I think he likes looking at me, too.

"What do you expect? We've been in the Fae guild for years,

and Matt's only just switched over to the royal family for next Faire. Wizardry garb's in short supply."

"I wouldn't worry so much," Officer Newton calls from his post on the stairs. "You all look ridiculous."

"You know, the more you talk, the more I don't like you," I tell him, but it's not true. I don't know why Officer Newton's helping us. I'm just glad he is.

Phil's basement smells faintly of boy feet, and friendly as John seems, it looks like he needs a shower. Still, I'll take this dingy space over Gus's house any day, and not just 'cause of the costume totes.

"Here's an idea." If Phil's self-conscious about the glittering golden stars on his robes, you'd never know. "Let's cosplay instead. Shave your head. Embrace Natalie Portman, Kalyn. Commit to the bit."

I flip him the bird. "Got the faces, Sarah?"

She passes me a stack of paper and a giant bottle of Elmer's. The printouts are still warm; they've got that weird water-melon-y wet-ink smell. Sarah sprinted to the copy room while we sneaked out of the library and met us in the parking lot within four minutes.

I stare at Dad's blown-up mug shot. "Honestly. He just looks *young*, doesn't he?"

"He could be anyone." I'm not sure when Gus got up, or how long I spent staring at that black-and-white face. "You okay?"

"Yeah. You, Wondergus?"

"It's just . . . I can't believe Mom didn't come after me today."

I called my mom once we got here, left a message explaining our whole plan. But Gus didn't call anyone. "Did you want her to?"

"No. I mean. What'll she say if she sees me doing this?"

I squeeze his shoulder. "Truth is, Gus, it doesn't really matter what she says."

Who knows if that's true. I've gone and said it anyhow.

Phil claps his hands. "John? Can you kit us out with headgear also?"

John digs through the totes again. He tosses two knights' visors, an army helmet, and a football helmet onto the couch. "Those are your options. Also, as an older sibling, I feel obligated to disapprove of all this."

Phil's stick arms are long enough to scoop up all four helmets. "But you *don't*?"

"I've got a soft spot for role-playing." He shrugs. "And it's good to see you doing something for someone else."

"See." I shove a football helmet over my head. "You're dressing me after all."

Gus smiles grimly and slaps my dad's glue-smothered face over my visor. The world goes dark, until Gus pokes Dad's eyes out. I'm not sure if Gus can tell through pencil holes, but I'm meeting his big, wiry eyes.

There just ain't much town to Samsboro. The parade route starts in the loading area behind Glen's grocery store, then winds around the front and turns right down Main Street. All told, it'll cover less than fifteen blocks.

All this morning's sunshine wore out the daylight's batteries. Sarah has Phil pull into the employee lot. He *just* manages not to run down any Rotary Club ladies. Sarah yanks off her robes and mask to go check things out. "People expect me to make an appearance, as a class rep. They won't think twice about me asking questions."

People swarm the back lot. The streetlights reveal bodies every so often, kids moving between papier-mâché monstrosities. The marching band waits in messy rows, warming up their instruments, while homecoming queen nominees are being propped up on old convertibles. They look pretty, in pastel colors and too-tight updos.

My hair's tucked away in an angry bird's nest, but strands keep slipping out of the helmet. I'd rip the damn thing off, except it took the combined efforts of Gus, Phil, and Sarah to hide it all away to begin with.

I sit in the back of the Death Van, trying not to sweat. Farther down the procession I spy the churning rabble of the football team, all rarin' to jog down a street before they've gotta jog around a field. I wonder if Eli is with them. Or did I *really* hurt him?

Teachers patrol the rows, looking high-strung—they *are* teachers—but excited. The whole scene's as Hicksville as you'd expect, and there's no hint that half these kids spat at me earlier today. I don't see any *Spences Behind Fences* signs.

We've got a sign, a message sprayed onto a bedsheet. John used some kind of special model primer to do it. He took the time to tell us it cost him eighteen bucks a can. "But it's made to prep *Warhammer* figures. Seems appropriate."

"It would seem no one expects you to make an appearance," Phil observes.

"Yeah." Gus landed a knight's helmet. He can lift his visor, but his face is lost in shadow. I hope he doesn't regret this yet.

There's a knock on the side of the van. Sarah looks twice back the way she came and slides the door shut behind her.

"The class floats will enter the procession right after the fire department and marching band. After the floats comes the football team and then the VFW reps. And finally, after all that comes the homecoming court on their convertibles, led by the underclassmen honor guard winners on a hayride pulled by a Munch-O Mills tractor."

"I don't get a convertible? Guess I'm less likely to get assassinated."

"That's not funny," Gus says.

"I know. I got enough death threats today."

"Did you really?" Phil, interest obviously piqued.

He's asked about my day a dozen times, but I'm not dyin' to relive it. Even if you're raised on a diet of persecution, it takes time to digest. Maybe one day I'll tell my friends about how I went into the bathroom for just one second without Officer Newton, and a girl I've never even *seen* called me a whore—as if that had anything to do with anything—and I retaliated by blowing her a kiss, and *she* retaliated by wrapping her skinny hand around what hair I had left and yanking it—

Sarah looks concerned. I can't tell what Gus looks, because he's got his visor pulled down. All I see when I look at him is Dad's decoupaged, warped face.

"I think it'd be better if we don't climb onto the hayride until the last second before it starts moving," Sarah says. "Otherwise, there's a good chance a teacher will see us and pull us off. Maybe they'll pull us off anyway, once the other honor guards see us."

"But I won the vote. Where's the *justice*?"

Sarah's lips twist. "Do you even think it exists?"

"Nah. Spy any dummies out there?"

Sarah opens her mouth and closes it again. "No. No *dummies*."

Gus groans.

"How ominous," Phil says.

I don't flinch. "Spill it, Sarah."

"Well . . . okay. It's *not* everyone. But I noticed kids in the marching band and on the football team are wearing blue buttons on their shirts. I asked around, and Kaleb told me they're supposed to represent solidarity with the Ellis family and the police department."

Officer Newton, lounging in the passenger seat, speaks up at last. "What the hell does any of this have to do with the police department?"

"Gus, the buttons have your dad's picture on them."

Gus is a statue, head and shoulder cocked.

I cackle. "It'll be a genuine *face-off*."

Sarah nods. "I spoke to Kara—she's on the junior honor

guard. She won't do anything if we show up. Neither will her boyfriend, Rob—he's the other rep. I can't speak for the sophomores. But one of them, Alex Rucinski? His dad's a cop."

Gus speaks right through the paper. "So why do we have to fly, I mean, go on the hayride? We can join the parade somewhere else."

"Where's a Trojan horse when you need one?" is Phil's useless contribution.

"Do we *need* a float?" Gus asks. "If the parade is slow enough that *veterans* can walk, we can, too."

The next pause is awkward as all get-out. Officer Newton doesn't seem to mind; he keeps flipping through a *Pathfinder* manual.

"I considered that," Sarah says, not looking at Gus, "but . . . I mean . . ."

"I can walk two miles. Don't look at me—don't *not* look at me like that."

"We *know* you can walk it," I tell Gus. "But . . . hell. There's no nice way to say this. Your gait is gonna be a big giveaway, Gus, even under robes like this."

"So? People will figure out it's me." Gus lifts his visor. "Maybe I want them to."

Freakin' Gus. "Wait, hold up—these masks were your idea!"

"They're not masks."

"Um, I think wearing a guy's mug shot on your head counts as a mask. I mean, it's not pantyhose or a Guy Fawkes head, but we could rob a bank like this—"

"Ah, but Gus never called them masks. He called them *costumes*." Phil holds up a finger. "Costumes are a form of disguise. Disguise plays a huge role in Shakespearean drama, and serves a variety of functions. In most masquerades, disguises are more a form of self-expression. Gus sees these robes as a *statement*. Not a deception. Yes?"

Gus nods. "This is a protest. I'm not hiding."

"So you *were* arranging a funeral procession." It's inappropriate as hell, how giddy Phil's getting. "Fantastic! Fine entertainment!"

I'm not sold. "Look, Gus. No. *No.* This isn't gonna play out like that."

"Yes, it is."

"What do you think'll happen when people figure you out? They'll realize that you're wearing the face of your dad's murderer—"

"*Supposed,*" they all say at once, and I can't believe how it swells my heart up.

"Okay. Your dad's *supposed* murderer. They'll believe the crap that Garth and the news have been shilling about you and me, and decide I've *voodooed* you into a *sinful heinous psycho love romance*—"

"Yeah! Because you have!"

Imagine the quiet that follows *that.*

"I mean." Gus isn't dodging this one. Bet my face is redder than his. "It's not heinous and it's not psycho and it's not romance, but I *do* love you, Kalyn."

"Isn't that *nice*," Officer Newton says. Guess we all needed his sarcasm, because Sarah giggles and Phil snorts.

"Fine, Gus. Love you, too, you weirdo. And that's why you are *not* getting shat on for my sake. I was okay with you guys doing the anonymous thing, tricking the rubes and whatnot, but I'm *so* not okay with you going down for my crimes."

"What crimes?" Sarah asks. "Maybe your dad's guilt is still debatable, but Kalyn, *you* didn't do anything."

"Aw, god. You guys know what I mean!"

"I'm sick of tricks!" Gus shouts. "I'm *sick* of pretending not to care, and people pretending to be what they aren't! I'm sick of fences! And you know what else, Kalyn? I'm sick of *lying* because my parents lied and your parents lied, and people in this town don't think past what they see. I won't lie this time. If we want to give Samsboro the middle finger, *we* have to do it. It has to be our damn finger!"

I close my mouth. "Loud and *clear*, Gus."

He pauses. "It was, wasn't it? No branches."

"Nope. So *why* the creepy decoupage Dads, then?"

"Dramatic flair, obviously," Phil says.

"Gary Spence's face will get attention. And if people realize it's *me*, the *poor*, *crippled* son of the dead guy, *maybe* a few will think twice before throwing eggs."

"It'll confuse them, at least," Officer Newton adds. "I *know* it's confusin' me."

"Gus, you aren't a *poor*, *crippled* son. Your family makes a respectable income."

"Shut up, Phil," Gus snaps.

"I'm a bad influence." I laugh. "I don't totally get it, but okay. I trust you, Gus."

"Thanks, Kay."

"I can limp, too, if you want." I grin like the devil.

"I can say 'shut up' to you, too," Gus says, but he doesn't.

Dad's worked a bunch of different jobs over the years. New inmates get stuck in the laundry, but maybe that's better than cleaning toilets. "I don't know," Dad argues. "Toilets aren't so personal as a guy's boxers, when you get down to the nitty-gritty."

No matter what job he got assigned, he said it could be worse, even after he worked in pots and pans for so long that his skin started to slough off. I figured that was his classic optimism, until Dad finally explained himself.

Off the coast of New York City, there's a place called Hart Island. It's what people used to call a potter's field. This island's where New York City buries all its unclaimed bodies. They've done it for more than a hundred years, and no one lives there, and they only allow visitors to take a ferry there once a month. Most graves on Hart Island don't have markers. There are hundreds of thousands of bodies there. Dead babies, homeless people, AIDS victims, and the used-up remains of medical school cadavers.

The people who stack and bury those bodies are inmates from a nearby prison.

"That doesn't sound *so* bad," I argued, trying to be tough.

"You'd get to work outside, and you'd be helping people, kind of."

"Oh, I'm sure it's not so bad—at first. But that kind of work would get in your head. It'd make you think about the meat of who you are and how little that meat matters. Bodies are heavier than what they weigh, Kalyn-Rose."

I thought Dad knew what he was talking about, having moved a body himself. And it did make for some heavy thinking. What's more awful? Being a nameless baby in a pinewood box, or being the guy paid pennies to stack nameless babies five deep in unmarked graves? How would it feel to know how little space baby coffins take up?

Until the morning of this homecoming parade, when I woke up really thinking Dad might be innocent, I'd never considered a third perspective:

How awful would it be movin' dead babies if you'd *never* moved a body before?

Here and now, the Jefferson High marching band starts playing the fight song and peels away down the road; I hear cheers of a crowd through the walls of the Death Van.

Here and now, we watch the procession move, watch floats and pretty people on convertibles fall into line as we climb through the sliding door. Here and now, we pull masks over our faces and hoods over our heads. Sarah takes my hand and I take Gus's hand and Phil steps in behind us. Officer Newton plays caboose.

Here and now, all eyes are on the parade, and as Sarah

pulls us through dawdlers in this emptying lot, we pick up our pace and suddenly, here and now, we're disrupting the flow of parade traffic, slipping into place just yards behind the football team.

Here and now, we yank our hoods down and unfurl our slapdash banner:

We Are People Beyond Fences, We Are People Beyond Spences

It's cryptic as hell, but I hope someone thinks it over. I hope they see us wearing mug shots and get that there are people underneath. Our lives aren't decided by shit people did before we were even around to do shit.

As we round the first corner and escape the shadow of the football team, maybe I shouldn't be worrying about folks stuck burying nameless babies on an island far away.

We go slowly. Not too slowly to keep up, but slowly enough to be noticed no matter how we walk. The faces lining the road quit smiling. Despite the cheering up ahead, a little patch o' quiet encases us.

At first people are confused, but soon they're shouting. We don't stop. It's chilly now that night's arriving, but Sarah's hand is warm and so is Gus's, for a change.

But you know what?

Wearing Dad's face isn't helping. If he couldn't stand up for himself, why are we standing up for *him*? I'm not sure what I'm protesting more, this town or his lies, because he couldn't do this first.

"Gus," I whisper, "I'm gonna take off this mask."

Gus is one step ahead. His visor is up, and you can see the person beyond that Spence. His face is flushed and he's limping. Before I know it I'm yanking off my helmet and letting my hacked hair unravel. People are booing, but I tuck Dad's face under one arm and show my face instead.

Here and now, I know why I'm thinking of Hart Island.

Gus and me?

We've been forced to move bodies for years, but we've never killed a damn one of them.

GUS

ONE OF PHIL'S Shakespeare quotes really appeals to me.

"We know what we are, but know not what we may be."

I used to have it sticky-tacked to the inside of my locker.

Between that, my favorite snaps from *Fruits*—the iconic Harajuku J-fashion magazine—a sketch of Edward Elric, a photo of Francesca Martinez, a family picture of our trip to Wisconsin, and the first character sheets Phil and I ever worked on, I had a collage of the things I loved in that tiny metal cupboard. I used to leave my locker open on purpose just in case someone happened to walk by and see *me*.

It never happened.

There're always more truths than one. Knowing who I am, or thinking I might know? That's only half a truth. Because my identity will always be halfway informed by the world. It has to be informed by *something*. Usually we define ourselves by loving things, Doc Martens or Shakespeare or music or whatever. But if the things we love are other people, those *people* define us. And then they're part of you, and *they* change what you know about yourself.

Who knows what we're becoming as we march down Main Street at dusk. People along the road jeer or fall silent. I'm panting at the effort or maybe with the adrenaline. Kalyn's hand is sweaty, but she's not letting go.

As the five of us walk through this town, clutching a spray-painted bedsheet, hot despite the cold, it's obvious that some people will never make the effort to *see* what we could be. If this is a locker we're leaving open, not everyone cares about looking inside.

This makes my feet heavy. The fact that a hollering, red-faced stranger just tried to break through the parade barrier makes my feet heavy. Officer Newton stomping toward another heckler makes my feet heavy.

So my feet are heavy; what else is new?

I'm starting to understand that people who don't care about us, who don't make that effort, shouldn't factor into who we are.

"We don't care what you think," I mutter under my breath. "We don't care."

Those words become our chant. I don't realize I'm repeating it until Kalyn and Sarah start repeating it, too. Phil doesn't take up the chant, but he's so wrapped up in the story that he's forgotten his paralyzing fear of public attention. He's still here.

Officer Newton spots another threat, a screaming woman— Who was James Ellis to her? What right does she have to claim my dad with her screams, this stranger who never came to see us?—and heads her off. Has he had that baton with him all day?

We pass Maverick's Diner. The patio is full of onlookers. Over their heads, the walls of the building are wallpapered with *Spences Behind Fences* posters.

One glance at the other side of the street proves we'll be seeing that pumpkin patch picture for the remainder of the parade. There are three blocks to go. The band marches on, oblivious to the booing that trails them. The booing can't bother me.

I've spent my whole life being stared at.

I look forward. My dead leg is trying to spasm. But I don't plan to stop, not yet.

I turn to Kalyn, too breathless to speak.

"If this is their worst?" She grins, showing every crooked tooth. "It's *nothin'*."

At the penultimate block stands Samsboro Cinema, old-timey and neon bright. I'm not surprised to see that three-worded phrase up on the marquee; it's clear that most of the downtown businesses have decided where they stand.

I *am* surprised to see the dummy dangling from the marquee, a dummy that would seem normal this close to Halloween, except it's wearing the same face we're wearing.

I take a step forward and a weight pulls me back. I've spent my whole life being stared at by a dead dad, but Kalyn hasn't.

The sound of the crowd is white noise, but the hiss of air that slips from between her teeth is anything but.

"'Death is a fearful thing,'" says Phil.

We stop for so long that the hayride kisses our heels.

"*Kay*." I repeat our chant: "We don't care what they think. We don't care."

She nods, shaken for once, and starts forward again—

Someone blocks our way. Mr. Lewis, owner of the hardware store.

"That's enough, kids. Get the hell off our street."

Officer Newton throws an arm across us. "Coach Lewis, this is a peaceful protest. Pull any stunts and we can have words at the station."

Mr. Lewis spits on the pavement. "They still let you in there, huh? You ain't a real cop, Earl Newton. The way you talk, you're still a picked-last freshman burnout. No wonder they demoted you to babysitting."

I shouldn't be surprised. Everyone in Samsboro knows everyone else.

"Mr. Lewis. You're holding up the procession."

"I'm defending the rights of a wounded family!" Mr. Lewis catches sight of me. "Son, did she threaten you? Come on, now. We'll get you to your mother."

I grit my teeth. "I'm not a damn baby."

Andy Lewis isn't listening. He's happy to feel righteous and feel people rallying with him. Townsfolk leak into the street, too many to stop, gathering behind him and around us. The parade marches on, but from here back it's a standstill.

"Raining on your parade, are we?" he continues. "Sorry I'm not inclined to listen to a cop who sides with criminals. You and Gary still best friends? Write him weekly?"

"Best friends?" Kalyn blurts. Her eyes cut Andy Lewis to ribbons.

"I went to school with your father," Officer Newton says, raising his voice in turn, "and so did half the people here, and most would have called him friend, too, before this turned into a goddamn crusade."

There are revelations happening, but it's hard enough to focus on standing with bodies pressing in on me. I'm being compressed like a tube of toothpaste—

Kalyn drops my hand when a Styrofoam cup smacks the back of her head. Cocoa splashes my visor and face, hot enough to singe my skin, and I can't help but yelp.

Kalyn yells and rounds on the crowd, looking for our attacker. Officer Newton is preoccupied with Andy Lewis.

I let go of Sarah's hand to pull my helmet off, and I manage it with Phil's help.

"Hey!" Sarah cries. "That's *not* okay!"

The cup came from the hayride. The sophomore boy leans over the wooden railing while the juniors pull on his jacket. Sarah breaks away from our chain to climb over the hay bales.

Someone grabs my hand. It's not Phil—he's craning his neck, distracted by some chaos I can't see.

A stranger wearing hoop earrings drags me away from my friends.

"It's all right, honey, I've got you—"

"Nnn!" I'm past coherence. I try to pull free, but I'm wobbly, and my jaw locks—

"Poor thing, this must be traumatizing for you—"

Mostly *she*'s traumatizing, and she's pulled me to the sidewalk—

And Phil's between the pair of us, hollering "Avast!" before severing the woman's grip with a single karate chop to her forearm. She lets go, but her squeal sets off a new surge of yelling.

"Exit, Gus. Exit!"

I anchor my feet in my cherry boots. "Where's Kalyn?"

"Don't worry, she's—"

A fist hits Phil hard enough to bowl him over. It's followed by a kick and then the screams of nearby witnesses. I don't recognize our attacker—some guy in khakis and a rugby polo. I don't care who he is, so long as he stops hurting my best friend. I fight my aching body and grab the stranger's arm.

The sirens wailing now aren't in the parade. It's hard to imagine how this plan could have gone worse. But it feels right, seeing my hometown fall apart like this. For so long it was just me and Kalyn living with the lies here. Now the struggle is everyone's.

I look beyond the terrible preppy outfit to the face of Phil's assailant.

"Gus, thank god, man!" Even with his face devoid of makeup and bruised to pieces, Garth's smile remains charming. "I'm here to save you!"

I can't hit him without letting go, so I settle for spitting on him.

Garth isn't what I dreamed he was, but it's still a shock when his face twists and he grabs my coiled right arm and pulls down on it. My shortened muscles scream and I do, too. It's the worst agony. My tendons are threads of string cheese being stripped apart.

"Sorry, Gus." Garth lets go of my bad arm—I whimper—then twists my good one behind my back. He pushes me forward, leaving Phil alone and bleeding at the feet of confused strangers.

I tell myself anyone would feel helpless in a situation like this. But as my right arm spasms, I have to wonder whether other people would have already *escaped*, whether others could be dragged toward the Maverick Diner's patio.

"Got him for you, Mr. E.," Garth says, like some comic book cliché.

"Thank you, Garth." An old man in a golf shirt stands up from his table. "These bones aren't what they used to be."

Garth beams wide. "Just trying to help."

The old man turns his cataracts on me. "Enough, Gus. Time to come home."

I stop, and I listen to the shouting and the sudden silence as the band finishes marching. I let the story take over. Grandpa Ellis is here to take me away, but that's not what numbs me.

Mom is with him, sitting at the table with fries in front of her, wearing that black blazer and absolutely no expression on her face.

PHIL

WHEN I EXPRESSED interest in becoming a vital character in the story unfolding in Samsboro, I did not account for the bruises I might sustain upon entering the spotlight.

Certainly, *nameless* characters die regularly in Hollywood films. The red shirts of *Star Trek*, the Jane and John Does of crime series.

Yet the maiming of main characters is generally managed with more care. A grave disfigurement often precludes the progression of plot or a character arc. Oedipus limps for a reason, a reason that contributes to solving an unsavory mystery. The loss of Frodo's finger is symbolic of a loss much greater.

Gus would deem this line of thinking *sickening*. He has cause to be critical. But like so many storytelling tropes, the idea that injury should serve a *purpose* comforts me.

I have nursed an invisible injury all my life, longing to find purpose within it.

Garth shoves me into the sidewalk. I see no poetry in it.

I cannot fathom how Garth's vengeance improves my character.

"'It will have blood they say,'" I mutter. "'Blood will have blood.'"

I could defer now. Retreat to the family basement, let the lens slip from me.

What says it of my burgeoning humanity that this thought is a brief one? Perhaps it is not humanity but anger that my tongue *will* tell. It propels me to my feet and through the crowd Garth has torn asunder.

I discover Garth leaning against the railing of Maverick's patio alongside the remnants of his Gaggle. They pluck fries from abandoned tables.

There's neither whisper nor whiff of our hero.

"Need something, Phil?" Garth licks salt from his fingers. His disaffection rivals my own on my coldest days, but his is so self-conscious. I think that Garth wishes he lacked a conscience, but cannot quite manage it.

Perhaps my maiming is not a sign of development, but evidence that I remain inconsequential. With Gus and Kalyn in absentia, what director would waste precious moments turning a camera upon Phil Wheeler?

"Guess not." Garth straightens.

I refuse to revert to empty space. I will not be the body in a basement, the unpleasant reminder that people are not guaranteed good souls when they are born, any more than they are guaranteed eyes or legs or hearts or brains.

If Gus is not here to make meaning of my existence, I must create it myself.

" 'Be great in act, as you have been in thought.' "

I see in Garth's eyes a reflection of myself. Except I have aligned myself with underdogs, not monsters. If I hurt him, will it be righteous?

"Where's Gus?"

Garth looks to his Gaggle. They are more than decorative; they bolster him. "I'm not going to tell you."

"I'd prefer a rational negotiation." When we used select video games on rainy days, I chose those with intricate plots. Garth chose those with the most decapitations. He was always captivated by the idea of violence, the shock of it.

"Because you're frightened?"

The crowd has dispersed, but this patio is an arena. I set my mask on a tabletop. A glass overturns. Ice skitters across its surface. No one moves.

Tell me we aren't gunslingers. Tell me we aren't worth watching.

"Garth. Negotiation is preferable to the alternative."

I know myself. I am well acquainted with my desires and limitations, have spent a lifetime defying and denying them. I can dismantle Garth and feel not the slightest remorse. Any Phil that might regret beating Garth over the head with my helmet died the day he fell off a bicycle.

I wonder if the crowd can smell the tension, as hounds smell an earthquake.

"Okay, Phil. What do you plan to negotiate with? Got knives in your pockets?"

"I've never seen you wear those clothes." Those stripes are wide and ugly.

"Just getting into character."

"Is it a character, or is it a disguise?"

"Same difference, Wheeler."

I take one step closer and reach beneath my robes. Garth's eyes track me. I retrieve my PSP and scrape my finger down the screen for effect. "Have you cleared your internet history of late? Do you believe your disguises there might be mistaken for characters? Wouldn't that be fortunate for you."

Garth blinks twice. "I don't know what you're talking about."

But I have him. "I think, Garth, that you value yourself more than you value this newfound attention. If the truth is made known, no number of rugby shirts will make you seem decent."

Garth watches me. On either side of him, Gagglers bear witness. "You don't have anything on me. You're full of shit."

"If you're certain, and you've nothing to hide, I suppose this negotiation is over. You win." I begin my retreat, willing dramatic timing to indulge me this once—

"Wait." Garth is ruffled now. "Fucking wait. He's with his grandpa. Not exactly news, and there's jack all you can do about it."

I put my PSP away. I tuck my helmet beneath my arm. "I see. Thank you."

Even as I turn away from him, I feel him bubbling over. I prepare for another blow, curling my bruised fist. *En garde.*

But I do not expect him to swing a patio chair at the back of my head. And when the leg of the chair grazes my skull, my first thought is nonsensical—

If Garth happened to hit the place I hit all those years ago, could I go back to being a normal, caring creature?

The answer seems to be no, because along with the stinging pain that knocks me into a table while Gagglers cry out, within me rises a rage that spreads from that spot to obscure all of me. It's as though I've sprung a leak in that place, and the container holding the cold reality of what I really am has broken asunder.

Perhaps I am only a red shirt, but that is not the only red part of me. All I see is red, all I feel is red when I whip my helmet against the side of his face.

Garth goes down with a yelp, but the red isn't finished yet. Perhaps I was never qualified to be an underdog. I have been trying very hard to miscast myself.

Garth gasps; I hit him again, with all my might. Somebody screams, and somebody else grabs the back of my shirt. I hit him again, with the flat of my left palm, but when I raise the helmet again, someone takes hold of my arm.

"Let him go, Phil!" It's not until she knocks me upside the head that I realize the person hollering at me is Kalyn, the catalyst.

I hit him again, and the pain in my hand mirrors the pounding in the back of my head. Kalyn yells and throws her arm around my neck, pulling me back.

But she's not the one who ultimately pins my arms—that's Officer Newton, who separates us in one sweeping motion. All humor is gone from his voice when he hollers profanities at us, kneels on my back, cuffs my hands behind me, and yanks me to standing. Garth groans on the ground, bruised and bloody.

The cuffs are cold, but they don't shock me. After all these years of trying to be other than what I am, they seem fated. Gus hates the idea of our lives being fictional. He felt certain of the role he would be stuck playing. Why did I never tell him that I felt it was the opposite—in a fiction, we could escape the futures prescribed for us.

"I can't believe you made me hit you," Kalyn gasps, glaring at me with tears in her eyes. She has abandoned her robes. Now she wears torn jeans and one of John's old *Gwar* T-shirts. "I've never had to hit a *friend*!"

Perhaps it's the pounding in the back of my skull, or perhaps her fist has loosened my jaw, because I laugh at this.

"What the hell is *funny* about this, Phil?" she demands.

"You think I'm your friend."

"I'll hit you again," she says, but her gaze wavers.

"You won't," Officer Newton growls. He glares at me. "I'm giving you a choice—you go straight to the hospital with this kid, or you go straight to the station."

I shrug.

"Fuck's sake, Phil." Kalyn shakes her head. "You think this is what Gus wants?"

I shrug. With a herculean effort, Kalyn hoists Garth to his feet. It's clear who the hero is here, and who the victim is, and I know where that leaves me. One of the main players has returned. And I welcome the eclipse.

KALYN

I WASN'T DOING so hot even before I caught Phil going batshit on the Gaggler, truth be told. I wasn't thinking about Hart Island or Dad or this shitty town.

I was thinking about how I let Gus go. I let him go because I got hotheaded, like I'm hotheaded now. I can't believe I dropped his hand so I could go scream at someone.

He'd take beef with my disbelief, say that I'm treating him like a little kid. But it's not that. Gus is my best friend, and I let someone take him away.

I wasn't alive to stop it when Dad was taken. There's nothing I could have done about the people of Samsboro then. But I'm alive now, so what's my excuse? When I gape at Phil, maybe I'm jealous—it's horrible the way he pummels Garth's face, but I understand the temptation. This jerk sold Gus down the river.

I don't know what to feel.

I guess that dummy shook me a little. Or a lot. By the time Officer Newton wrenched me away from Andy Lewis—I was trying to claw his skin off—Sarah was gone, Phil was gone, and Gus was gone, and we were surrounded by angry small-towners. A policeman with a megaphone called for the crowd to disperse, but our faction was already broken. Just like that.

"Took my eyes off you for *one second*—" Officer Newton hollered.

I was already sprinting, shoving more than one person over. Gus is short, and the crowd was tall and full of people who didn't want me going anywhere. I threw off the robe. October air numbed me, especially the bald half of my head, especially my heart.

Officer Newton got caught up talking to some police, but by the time I spotted Phil, pounding Garth's face into hamburger, he wasn't far behind me.

So here I am, with the pointless hollering and hitting, pointless like most things I do. I can't seem to change. If I'm *not* a murderer's daughter, why can't I change?

"Fuck's sake, Phil!" There's something dead about Phil's eyes. His glasses were knocked away in the scuffle. "You think this is what Gus wants?"

He shrugs. His eyes are stones.

"Thanks," Garth murmurs in my ear, and it makes me feel queasier.

"Shut up." I deposit him in a chair; two of the other Gagglers hurry forward to help him. "Where do you get off, you toddler-lookin' shit-monger?"

Garth has about as much face as a broken watch, but his eyes are *still* locked on Phil, and they look way beyond spooked. He doesn't answer.

"Toddler-looking is not especially profound, as insults go," Phil says dully, "but there is something Shakespearean about it."

"So what'll it be, Wheeler?" Officer Newton asks. "You gonna help get this young man to the ER?"

"Please don't make me go with him," Garth says, eyes wide between the blood.

"We'll take him," the girl says, hoisting him up. "He's our friend."

"Is he," Phil says, watching them retreat. "Lucky thing."

"Enough, Phil! Where's Gus?" *I let him go, what is* wrong *with me?*

He pulls his eyes from Garth. "With his grandfather. Mortimer Ellis."

"Mortimer Ellis?" I gasp. "Where does he live?"

"Worry about that after we get off this street." Officer Newton nods at one of the policemen waving the traffic away. While his big stature seems to discourage some rabble-rousers, one or two angry rednecks ogle us something fierce. "Wheeler, you're driving straight home. Spence, you're with me."

I dodge his grip and fall in alongside Phil, who looks calm as a damn stream despite the cuffs. How is he like that? I feel my gunpowder igniting, like I'm a collection of backyard firecrackers, and sparklers keep catching the others on fire.

I clap Phil's shoulder. "How did you get him to talk, Phil?"

"I told him I'd hacked his computer. That I'd expose his dull, dark secrets."

"What? Did you really hack it?"

"No. I merely assumed he would have things to hide."

"Why?" I won't ask about Gus.

"Because I have such things, too," Phil says, and I really don't doubt it.

"Hell, who doesn't," Officer Newton says.

"Wanna tell me about you and Dad being besties, then?" He doesn't look at me.

Officer Newton steers us down an alley behind Maverick's, away from Main Street and potential pitchforks. It'll be a small hike back to the van, but I won't let it pass silently. Silence allows too much time for thinkin'. There's also Sarah to wonder about. Last I saw her, she was climbing up onto that hayride like a Valkyrie.

"Sure, we've all got shit to hide." There I was, thinking too much. "What's bad enough to scare a human-shaped blister like Garth?"

"Considering Garth's nature, it's more likely to be watching snuff videos or questionable porn than actual crime. I doubt he could stomach real violence. Certainly he could not beat *me* senseless with a helmet."

Officer Newton steps out of the alley, but Phil's left me

stuck. All those hairs people say stand up when you're spooked? Mine are up, all right.

"Phil. Hold up."

Officer Newton hasn't seen us stop; he cuts across a credit union parking lot.

I look at Phil, in all his weird, pill-buggy glory. And I realize he's not just weird. He's talking about violence with less emotion than the printed Dad mug shots contain.

"That's . . . *Jesus*, Phil. You're really *off*, aren't you?" His expression shifts. "It's hard to tell when you're with Gus, but once you're by yourself . . ." Officer Newton's found a trail through the reeds, but I'm watching Phil like you'd watch alligators.

"When I was six, I fell off my bike. I hit my head, and my soul was knocked out of me." Phil's not quoting Shakespeare, but this line is obviously embedded in him. "Never tell Gus," he adds.

I don't know why I feel like laughing. "Oh, I think he knows."

"He knows that I am a soulless creature?" He sounds like a total mope, and suddenly he stops seeming so creepy. Melodramatic monsters are easier to deal with, in my experience. In tons of romance novels, Primscillas date vampires.

I don't hate Phil, though I'm not sure I buy the whole concussion-equals-sociopathy argument. There are a thousand reasons why people become who they are, and a thousand reasons they don't have to.

"Gus can't think you're soulless, you *ass*." We jaywalk to reach the credit union reeds. Not far off, sirens keep blaring. I put my icy fingers on Phil's shoulder. He's 3-D, all right. Maybe someone just has to remind him, and Gus ain't here. "I bet he knows that *you* think you are. But come on. Who've you killed?"

"Well, no one yet."

"Me neither, *yet*. So what's the difference?"

"*You* lack the capacity." His words are colder than the air.

"Maybe I do, but hell. Maybe I don't. Phil, the more time you spend worrying about being a sociopath, aren't you less likely to become one? We don't live in a *Minority Report* society where precogs decide our fate and punish us for future crimes. Why waste time hating yourself for crimes that haven't happened yet? Bad enough worrying about things that already have, dumbass."

Phil sucks air like he's got four extra lungs. "Did . . . did you just reference a Philip K. Dick story?"

"Love Spielberg. Freakin' hate Tom Cruise, though." I grab Phil's arm. We follow the path through the swampy ditch. Officer Newton's got a cell phone pressed against his ear. "Shakespeare talks about fighting your nature. Edmund, right?"

" 'Some good I mean to do, despite of mine own nature.' "

"Yeah. Just because you smacked your head and stopped caring about other people doesn't mean you can't learn to. You think I don't struggle to be a good person?"

"Sociopaths can't *learn* empathy. Extensive research has shown that—"

"I'm not talking about *sociopaths*, Phil. I'm talking about *you*. And if you really want to become better, you *should* talk to Gus. Tell him about the bike and your soul and all that crap." I grimace. "Gus'll accept you anyway. He accepts *me*, for chrissakes."

Officer Newton emerges from the reeds, boots soaked in mud, and stands on the shoulder. He looks like he's waiting on a taxi, but he's more likely to catch a tractor.

He grimaces at Phil. "I wasn't joking; I've called your brother, Wheeler, and he's expecting you home within half an hour. You've done enough for today."

"I'll return to the wings." Phil lets his shoulders rise and fall as Officer Newton undoes his cuffs. Like he couldn't care in the least.

But to me, someone who's been acting like someone not me for ages, it seems like a performance. Phil can shill whatever bullshit he wants about being an apathetic monster. Before he can make for the van, I grab his arm.

He stares at my hand like he can't comprehend it.

"Phil. You're saying you're not interested in saving your best friend?"

"That's the measure of it."

I shake my head. "Don't be a coward."

I want his eyes to flash, I want him to reference Shakespeare. But Phil stares at me levelly. "Rather a coward than what I am," he says, and pulls himself free.

He leaves me and Officer Newton standing on the corner.

I can't believe he's going until the van actually pulls away across the street, and then he's gone.

The wind's rising and the temperature's falling. Finally I turn to Officer Newton.

"Well, great. So what about us?"

"I called a ride."

"Who?" I pick burs from my jeans. "Mom? Isn't she working?"

Officer Newton doesn't answer.

"Or is it Tam?"

Officer Newton doesn't answer.

"Christ! Why can't any of the adults in this stupid town *talk*? *Adults* started this riot, *adults* shoved a teenager in prison, *adults* told Phil he's nuts, *adults* kidnapped Gus! What's wrong with you all? The fuck is *wrong*?"

Officer Newton doesn't look at me. "I *was* friends with your dad."

The fight falls out of me. The night seems to hug his next words.

"I'd say so, anyhow. We were classmates from first grade on up. Our families went to Sunday school together. Baptists, all of us, but we got up to some mischief. Once at church camp, your dad and me thought it'd be good to fill our squirt guns at the baptismal fountain. By the time we hit high school, couldn't say we were close, me and Gary. But we had classes together. Hung out some weekends, too."

"Was it bad?" I swallow. "The bullying?"

"From where I was standing, both kids gave as good as they got. They were pitted against each other from the get-go. Sure, James planted fruit flies in Gary's locker. But Gary poured rubber cement into James's baseball cleats."

"Doesn't mean it didn't get worse," I say, thinking of Dad's burn scars.

"I don't know. But there wasn't bad blood between Gary and James by the end. I took Tech Ed with 'em. Those two were thick as thieves. They worked on a semester project together. I was jealous, to be honest. I thought Gary might wanna work with me, help me finish up my dogsled. I had huskies back then, and Mr. Stroud would let you choose just about any project, so long as you could buy the wood."

My icy ears are ringing. "What project did they choose?"

"Don't remember."

I don't know what to say.

The car that comes is no tractor, but it's no great shakes, either. This station wagon would look right at home at Spence Salvage. The window rolls down and I cuss.

"Hey, folks." Ms. Patrick pushes an enormous, drooling dog out of her passenger seat. "Ready to go trail bombing?"

GUS

IF LIFE WERE a movie, Grandpa would sit in the back of a limo, hidden by tinted windows. As it is, he smiles and waves for us to follow like he's any other man in town, not the man who owns half of it.

Police are calling for order. The fuss is dying down. I'm dying down, too.

"Did that boy hurt you?" Mom searches my face.

I don't answer.

Her eyes are exhausted. "I know you're furious with me. I'm furious with me, too. But we have to go with him, Gus. Not a choice."

Suddenly I can't believe I marched all that way. I can't believe I thought I could keep up with Kalyn. I know that's the fatigue talking, but it's louder than anything. I want to run back to my friends. I don't want to move. As usual, I'm split in half.

Mom takes my arm—I can't even *look* at her—and leads me to Grandpa's Land Rover. He opens the door for us before heading around to the other side. Mom gives my hand a squeeze. It unlocks me, just a little.

"Gus. The abyss? Sometimes you have to face it."

"You aren't my abyss," I whisper. "You never were."

My body won't cooperate. My brain won't, either. If I went to Kalyn now, I'd be dead weight. But maybe if I give my brain a minute, I can stare down the abyss who's starting the engine, adjusting his lapels.

The Land Rover takes us beyond the outskirts of Samsboro. It's too dark to see much, but my stomach feels the moment we start going uphill. Houses grow larger as we ascend. This is where CEOs live, where wealthy people vacation.

We drive through a familiar wrought iron gate I thought we'd never see again. It takes a full minute to reach the end of the driveway and park in front of the quadruple garage. The air smells less like sugar here.

Grandpa's house is a rustic dream on steroids. It's too imposing to feel like a cabin at all. How many trees died to make this monster look quaint? The shiny grill on the deck, the Adirondack chairs overlooking the forest and lake—they scream money. Maybe they *just* scream. Motion-sensor lights glare at us, detecting our approach.

These polished wooden steps were always too high for me,

but I don't let it show. Grandpa isn't a super-villain, but there's a lot of gray area between that and being the sort of person you'd ever want to show weakness in front of.

He leads us into his living room, complete with a taxidermy grizzly bear and a fireplace big enough to swallow us. It's a kiln no one could bond beside. Mom and I sit on one side of an oak coffee table. Grandpa's on the other. Behind him is a trophy case filled with family accomplishments.

"Coffee? Tea? Whiskey?"

Mom shakes her head. I'd rather meet the grizzly's marble eyes than Grandpa's.

"Well, let me know. Got a dumbwaiter, if you can believe that."

He must have help hidden under our feet. Grandpa thinks relying on others makes you less of a person. I rely on Tam and Mom, and they rely on each other. I rely on my doctors and my friends, and they rely on me, too. I *know* that makes us all bigger people.

I *can* meet Grandpa's eyes.

"These aren't the best circumstances for a reunion," he grumbles. "I *should* be angry about that stunt, Gus. But it's nice, getting the whole family together."

"Tam's not here," I say. Mom glances at me.

"I *should* be angry," Grandpa repeats, like I never spoke. "It's appalling that you'd disparage your father's memory like this. Right when his name's at stake."

"I think . . . it's easy to be confused about all this," Mom says.

"Oh, *I'm* confused, Beth." His tone is as level as his stare. "You come to me begging for help, asking about lawyers, saying you're sorry for shacking up with that woman. Guess you've been *confused* for decades, eh?"

I can see anger in Mom's eyes, but her expression is neutral as water. No matter what brought her here, she's always been allergic to this house.

"Gus. I understand how *you* might be confused about what's right and wrong. Brain's a bit soft. That's not your fault." He taps his head. "You're following your mom's example. But come on, son. That Spence girl's not even much of a looker."

I imagine Kalyn's reaction. She'd punch him once for me, and twice for herself. What she looks like has nothing to do with it. The thought almost makes me smile.

"We'll all have to get along to make sure Spence stays behind bars. We'll have to play ball in court. But since when do you have sympathy for the devil?"

"Since always." "Devil" may as well mean "lesbian" or "disabled" to Grandpa.

His eyes bore into me. "I'd be disappointed if you didn't have a little fight in you. Guess that's why you marched. It's in the family. Rebellious, like me."

"Like my *moms*." I say the easiest words I've ever said: "You aren't my family."

"The hell I'm not. Who do you think pays for your health care? All those endless surgeries and appointments? That pediatrician from Pakistan, or what have you?"

My heart stutters. I don't have to look at Mom. I know he's telling the truth.

And it all makes sense. *This* is the reason Mom agreed to visit a man and a home she's allergic to. She isn't choosing a monster over Tam. She's choosing me. *Again.*

All this time, she's been locked in another tomb I never even noticed.

I have to break us both out.

I sit up straighter. "Gary Spence and Dad were close, weren't they?"

Grandpa stills. "There are school records that'll put you straight on that front, boy."

"Records about Dad *bullying* Gary Spence. Probably because you thought, um, you w-wanted Dad to. And they *still* ended up friends. You must have hated that. You must have hated Gary Spence."

"Hate's too strong a word. There's just a hierarchy. A food chain." Grandpa gestures at the grizzly. "That family's trash. Don't need more *why* than that."

Maybe Grandpa has another motive. Maybe decades ago, Kalyn's grandpa gave mine a bad deal on car repair. Maybe Grandpa fought with *him* in high school. But maybe *nothing* happened, beyond people pretending to be worth more than others.

"You *do* need more why. But you don't feel, I mean, you don't have it. Dad knew it. I bet he became friends with Gary *because* you bullied him not to."

"You don't know anything."

"Grandpa, did Dad even *like* you?"

I can read the answer in his face.

"He was, I mean, *probably dying* to know Gary Spence. At least Gary Spence wasn't *you*."

Grandpa places the full weight of his stare on Mom. "I never spared those rednecks a thought, until they *killed my son*."

"Unless they didn't."

"Gus," Mom warns, but I'm not finished.

"Unless DNA proves Gary Spence is innocent."

I half expect Grandpa to overturn the table, to come around and grab me.

I *don't* expect him to shrug. "You're right. The DNA *would* prove Gary Spence didn't do it. But we won't let them get that far."

I'm on my feet, thoughtless about getting there, but Grandpa doesn't seem to care.

"Listen here, son," Grandpa says, pouring himself a whiskey. "Best let this one go, now. Ain't that right, Beth?"

Mom's mouth is a firm line.

"Mom?"

She won't look at me.

"Your father was my only son." Grandpa shakes the glass in his hand. "My name died with him. He can't carry on a legacy. Can't keep up the house once I'm gone. He isn't here to inherit. In life, James was a failure in many ways. In death, at least he's a martyr."

"*Mom.*"

Tears slide down her cheeks.

"The hero, the widow, the son. Things are complicated enough, with the widow being a dyke and the son being damaged. Leave the rest alone, for god's sake."

Somewhere in there, Grandpa crossed a line. Mom stands. "Jimmy wasn't a hero. He was a screwed-up teenager, just like I was. I was wrong, Gus, to let you think he was anything else. Our home was supposed to be an apology, never an *altar.*"

I think of the faces on the wall, the tomb's icy chill.

"But I'm done with that. And we're done here. You called that march a rebellion, Mortimer? Like any rebellion worth its salt, it did its job. It woke people up. It woke *me* up. I won't let you *insult* my son, my *wife*, or our intelligence anymore."

"And the consequences?" Grandpa sets his glass down. "You're fine letting the truth come out?"

Mom laughs. "*I* haven't had trouble coming out for years. These aren't my skeletons. When I testify in court, I'll say what I never could. And maybe, finally, I'll sleep through the night." Mom looks at me. "We're leaving, Gus. Okay?"

"The hell you are," Grandpa snarls. "The hell you're going anywhere until we come to an agreement!"

"Go on, then. Hit me like you used to hit James. You think I never saw the bruises? We were *madly* in love, remember. Isn't that how you testified? 'Madly in love.' So hit me, old man, but know I'll hit back."

Grandpa tries to stand, maybe to hurt her after all, but his leg locks up.

By the time Mom and I reach the foyer, he's wheezing to keep up, and by the time I get down those deck steps and meet Mom at the bottom, he's fallen behind.

"Have fun with those medical bills!" he hollers. "Have fun in *prison!*"

"I could call Tam for a ride," Mom rasps as we walk down the driveway. When I look back, Grandpa's bracing himself in the door frame, backlit by amber light.

"It's not Tam's job to come, um. To save us."

"You're right." Her pace slows. "You're right. I wonder why. I wonder if I've been waiting for someone to stop bullets, ever since."

"Ever since what, Mom?"

She's not crying. She's not anything. "Ever since I watched your father die."

A gust of frigid wind blows hard, rising from the bottom of the driveway or beyond. Maybe it's come all the way here from Samsboro. Back in town, the homecoming game is probably starting, just like it started eighteen years ago. Maybe this is the same breeze Dad—and *Mom?*—felt that night at Spence Salvage, recycled around the world for two decades. I wonder if Kalyn feels it, and whether it smells as clean to her as it does to me.

PHIL

I PARK THE Death Van in our dark driveway. As anticipated, John waits in the kitchen, hands folded on the table. He is heavier and younger than our father, but they bear an uncanny resemblance. It's their eyes, the fullness and warmth within them.

I sit down at the table across from him, resigned to my fate.

"What the hell did you do, Phil?"

"Oh, of course. For I must have *done* something."

"Are you saying you didn't?"

I shake my throbbing head. "I beat a fellow student senseless. Surely Officer Newton informed you. *Of course* I did something."

"Why is it 'of course' with you?" John slams a palm on the table, and now I see the warmth in his eyes spill over, wetting his red cheeks. "Phil. Why do you think violence is an inevitability? Who taught you that? We never, ever did."

"You know what I'm like, John."

"I do know," he says, staring me down. "You're one of the smartest people I've ever met, Phil. Ever, and before I moved into the basement I studied at an Ivy League school. If you're not outthinking this, this *habit*, that's your own choice."

I think of all our points of reference. "You know how it is with some creatures. Goblins are sneaky, orcs brutal. The Balrog can only ever be fire and hatred."

He takes my hand. "You're not a fantasy creature, Phil. You're *here*, and you're my brother, and you deserve to give yourself a fucking chance."

These are altogether too similar to the words Kalyn gave me; I recoil from them. An ache forms in my chest, and maybe it is almost like feeling. How can people ever tell?

"Why? Why do I deserve that?"

John sighs. "Every single person on the planet deserves that, man."

I swallow. "Well, alas, for I have already lost my chance to partake in this story."

"Don't write yourself out. Where's Gus? Where's Kalyn?"

"On some noble quest, I imagine. Playing the heroes while I revert to an NPC."

He lifts up his hands. "Then change it. *Do* something, Phil."

"As though it's easy," I grumble. "You can't even leave the house."

"It's not me you're mad at. But nice try. How can you help Gus and Kalyn?"

"They sent me home. They're the leads in the play I no longer have a part in."

John taps his head. "What you're lacking in Charisma and Constitution, you make up for with Intelligence. You want life to come together in a story? I challenge you to pick a new role. How can you, Phil Wheeler, apathetic nerd and decent friend—"

"I'm not—"

"—*semidecent* friend: How can you help move the plot forward?"

I don't know if I'm capable of admiring my brother. Over the years, he has pulled my hands away from burners, he has held me back from knives. I have bitten his forearms, insulted his lifestyle, dismissed him as a dungeon dweller. But John is nothing if not a solid DM, a remarkable strategist. Perhaps, with his aid, there is a role yet to play.

"Mayhaps you can help me think of something." The gears within me start whirring. My eldest brother cuffs my ear with his hand, smiling through unfounded tears.

Maybe there is poetry in this.

KALYN

HONESTLY, I'M RELIEVED when Phil ditches us. Not because he's weirding me out. Not because I'm becoming a soggy dishrag as Officer Newton waxes nice about Dad.

I can't be puzzling out Phil when I'm trying to puzzle out *why* the school secretary has come to our rescue. And there'd be pretty much no room for Phil's scrawny skeleton in this car, what with me and the dog-monster crammed back here.

"Watch out for Angus." Ms. Patrick catches my eye in the rearview. She's driving a stick shift, and she's already stolen the best-driver title. "He might phlegm on you."

"It's cool." What harm can slobber do? I already look like the plague. "Thanks for the ride, Mrs. Patrick."

"Again, hon, it's Ms. Haven't been a Mrs. since the divorce. Hell, I don't think I was a *Mrs.* during the marriage. Never let a man pretend to own you, you hear me?"

"Loud and clear."

"And don't let any old broads tell you how to live," she adds, winking.

I'm grinning, despite everything, despite hell and the puddle of drool Angus has just dribbled onto my lap. "What if they're the only cool person in the school, though?"

"That's a whole nother story."

"Yeah, and not the story I need right now. Why are you helpin' us?"

"Well, that's a long—"

"If you're gonna say 'long story,' don't. Give me the abridged version, but *talk*."

She makes another turn. "Guess most people don't do you that kindness, huh?"

"They don't." I'm staring out the window, cracking my knuckles. "Except Gus and Mom. Dad didn't even bother calling last night."

"Whatever you're feeling, he must be feeling it times ten million."

"Is he feeling *innocent*, though?" I wipe my hand off on Angus's furry back. Big mistake. He thinks I'm petting him and responds by breathing putrid air up my nostrils.

"Gary never struck me as the kind to complain. Not that I knew him like you do. But he was real quiet, real serious sometimes. Back in those days, I was teaching. Life Skills. Your dad didn't even crack a smirk during the condom demonstration, and that's a doozy for most kids. If I remember right, *you* snickered like a damn buffoon, Earl."

"It's true," Officer Newton admits. "I was a real turd sometimes."

"Life Skills . . ." Something slides into place: the dog pictures on her desk, her tears in the office. Gus's clues and the part about Kathy Sturluson, the woman who—

"When I found James, I thought he was a *dummy*. Isn't that ridiculous? I mean, I was looking for him. But I didn't think he'd be dead. I felt guilty about creeping around Spence Salvage that day."

"Then why did you?"

"Why do you think?"

"Because Spences are guilty scum."

"Kalyn, if you keep telling people what you are without giving them the benefit of the doubt, you're helping those names stick."

There's nothing I can say to that.

"I got on just fine with your family. Used to take my car there for oil changes. That day I went to Spence Salvage to talk to James's best friend."

"Best friend," I echo.

"It was pretty common knowledge. Wouldn't you say, Earl?"

Officer Newton doesn't say a thing.

"If it was common knowledge, how come me and Gus never knew that? How come no one ever testified saying so?"

"Someone wanted it that way," she says. "An old man who's kept his dirty hands just out of reach for long enough, if you ask me."

I look out the window. It's so dark that I only see my own reflection.

"I knocked on the door and no one answered. Me and Spook walked around a bit, thinking they might be doing an oil change, and that's when I caught a whiff of that trunk. Mostly I was thinking 'it can't be,' but maybe I *did* suspect. This was a story I felt like I'd read before, you know?"

Yeah, I do know.

"We're four mastiffs on since then, but I remember what it felt like when I opened that trunk in the snow and saw him. You know what they don't tell you in the papers? Someone set him up, closed his eyes, tucked a fleece blanket around him like he was sleeping. You don't do that for someone you don't care about. James Ellis was missing for days. There were a thousand other places your dad could have put that body."

"Unless he cared too much to let him go," I breathe.

"Or," Officer Newton adds, "maybe Gary didn't know the body was there."

We let that one hang for a second.

"I think a lot about that day, Kalyn," Ms. Patrick says. "I wish I hadn't run to my car and called the police the minute I got home. I wish I'd spoken to your dad. I wish I hadn't listened to Mortimer Ellis. You see a body and you don't think straight."

"Most people would say you did exactly the right thing."

"So why do I regret it?" She's slowed the car to a halt in front of a gated driveway. There's no telling if she means to stop or if she's just overwhelmed.

She tells us to wait in the car.

She's in the wrong gang for that. Me and Officer Newton

get out—although it takes a minute to shove Angus off my lap. The temperature's dropped again.

Newton glares at me, but neither of us pretend I'm gonna get back in that car.

The gate is twice my height, black and forbidding. Funny how rich people are so scared about their privacy when they don't seem to recognize the existence of anyone else's. Ms. Patrick rings the buzzer, but I think it's pretty clear no one will answer. You don't put yourself in a mansion on a hill because you *wanna* associate with commoners.

"I'm pretty sure I can climb it."

"I'm pretty sure that's trespassing. You aren't doing that while I'm watching."

"Turn around, then, *Ocifer*," I grab the cold bars—

Ms. Patrick gasps. "Someone's coming."

"I don't hear an engine." Officer Newton draws his baton.

"No, they're *walking*."

"Are there bears in Kentucky?" I squint at the shadows. "Or do you think Mr. Ellis is coming to say hello?"

"The bear's more likely," Ms. Patrick says.

"Get back, Spence," Officer Newton warns.

But I'd recognize that gait anywhere.

"Gus!" I holler, and then he's wincing in the headlights' glare.

He looks more tired than ever, too tired to cover his eyes, but so far as I can see he's not hurt. When he hears me hollerin' he picks up his pace, leaving the other figure—his mom—behind.

"Kalyn!" he breathes at the gate, twisting his fingers around the metal.

"Behind bars at last," I joke. Gus laughs like he's been dying to. It kills me. "Tell you what, Gus, it's not much of a rescue if you've already escaped."

"We'll call it a jailbreak." Gus lets go of the bars and takes my hand instead. "Hopefully your dad'll be next."

And I realize something beautiful and horrible: *Gus* believes Dad isn't guilty.

So why can't *I* believe it yet? Why can't I let Dad be good? Let *us* be good?

"Sorry I let you go, Gus."

"Don't. And actually . . ." Those saucers widen. "I learned some things."

"Me too." We'll be editing his notes. "Think we might actually solve this thing?"

"Not sure it's the sort of thing that can be solved." I want to ask why he looks so sad and scared, but he changes the subject. "Where's Phil?"

I can't think how to answer that with Officer Newton looming behind us, and the image of Phil going apeshit looming inside me.

We're interrupted by the sound of Gus's mom losing her ever-loving shit: "Open the damn gate, or I *will* call the police and tell them everything, you hear me? I'll tell them about the bribes and the blackmail, and I'll tell them about jury members who've been living rich ever since they sent Gary Spence to prison, jury members who suspiciously donate to your causes! And if you've bought out the local police, well, I'll call national papers and I'll contact my publishers and I *will* put the truth out there!"

The gate clicks and eases open. I have a feeling she's still got more to say, because she looks almost mad about not having to scream anymore.

Gus and I don't fling ourselves on each other, because both of us would probably fall over, and as much as it sucks, I think both of us will always worry about whether people are watching us. But once that gate opens and Gus hobbles through, he loops his arm around my shoulders and that's enough.

Ms. Patrick glares at Mrs. Peake. "Beth."

"Mrs. Sturluson," she replies, just as stiffly.

"It's Patrick now," I say.

"And it's *Ms.*," Gus adds, because of course Gus noticed that.

"When you call the papers," Ms. Patrick says, "will you tell the whole story?"

"I will," Mrs. Peake replies, looking at Gus. "I'll tell them everything. But first, I'll tell all of you."

"Well, shit." My heart deflates. "Isn't that just too easy?"

I'm not really complaining. It doesn't *feel* easy. Me and Gus? We don't know the meaning of the word.

GUS

SOMEHOW WE ALL squeeze into that car. I joke that one of us could ride in the trunk. Only Kalyn laughs. We make it down the hill, back to the edge of Samsboro and home.

Tamara's truck idles in the driveway. She stands beside it with a box in her arms and freezes when the station wagon stops at her feet.

Mom clutches the seat in front of her. For a moment I think she's going to hyperventilate. Instead, she opens the door and runs straight for Tam.

I can't hear what they're saying. It's none of our business. But when Tamara sets the box down to wrap Mom in a hug, Kalyn reaches across the enormous dog to nudge me on the shoulder.

I climb out slowly. When Tamara sees me wearing those stupid cherry-red boots, she starts sobbing over Mom's shoulder.

I've only ever seen Tamara cry once before, on the day they got denied a marriage license. They knew they would get denied, but they tried and cried anyway. Their wedding was beautiful anyway.

Tamara shuffles forward because Mom's stuck to her like glue. She throws her other arm around me.

"They fit, then?"

"Perfectly," I say, hugging her back.

I call Phil and leave a message, telling him where we are, where *everyone* is.

"Kalyn won't say what happened," I say, "but you should be here, Phil."

It's his story, too, but he doesn't pick up the phone, and Kalyn just shakes her head, saying, "You two need to talk it out."

I head back to the kitchen and pause in the doorway. We've never had this many bodies in our home before. I never dreamed we would. When I catch Tamara's eye, I know she's thinking the same thing.

We've got enough chairs, but filling them is new. The house feels warmer, and not just because Angus is breathing hot air across my naked feet. A fire's been lit in here.

"Anyone want cocoa?" I ask, because someone should say something.

"Coffee," Officer Newton says.

"He didn't offer coffee, Earl," scolds Ms. Patrick.

Kalyn cackles, but I think she's nervous.

"Sit down, Gus." Mom lifts herself up. "I'll get it."

"I've got it."

"Tam, I don't want you—"

"Don't. This is my house, too, and I feel like making coffee for our guests. That's it." Tam gives Mom a look that probably says ten thousand things, but no one but the two of them knows what they are. "We'll talk later."

Kalyn cuts right to it. "*You've* got some talking to do now, Mrs. Peake."

Mom's eyes flit from our faces to Fridge-Dad. "I don't know where to start."

Kalyn taps my notebook. "Got anything to write with?"

Mom fetches the mug of multicolored pens that sits on her desk and overturns it. Kalyn assigns everyone a color. My notebook makes two rounds around our circle. Mugs are drained more than once.

"Should have used a poster board," Ms. Patrick says.

"Or gone traditional. Red strings and a photo wall," Kalyn says.

"Not bad work here, kids." As far as I can tell, Officer Newton's being serious.

"It's about time people cleaned up their messes," Ms. Patrick adds. "It shouldn't have taken children marching down Main Street."

Mom doesn't speak. Her hands look like mine, trembling on the table.

"Here, kids. It's all yours." Tam pulls the notebook from Mom's clutches. Mom puts both hands over her eyes.

Kalyn and I flip through rainbow-streaked pages. Purple for Ms. Patrick. Magenta for Mom. Green for Officer Newton. It reminds me of the yearbook signatures.

Until I start reading.

Clues?

1. Gary Spence signed Dad's yearbook and appeared in photos with Dad, too. Good _friends_? If so, _why_ would Gary Spence claim Dad bullied him?
The two things are not mutually exclusive. Or, perhaps, like you and Kalyn, the general populace was not aware of the true nature of their friendship. There are social factors to consider. Spences and Ellises likely could not be seen together. yeah, apart from the photos and the yearbook there's a picture where your mom and dad are on the hood of a car on fourth of july and to me it's always looked like it was taken ~~on grandma's property~~ @ spence salvage. I think they hung out. They started off on the worst foot as freshmen, but that was ancient history by senior year. Reports of bullying have been exaggerated. ∟—Ditto. they were friends plain and simple. Beth can confirm.

2. Dad's body ~~was~~ found in the trunk of a red 1985 Ford Taurus at Spence Salvage. _who found it?_

Research reveals this was a woman named Kathy Sturluson. She was the Life Skills teacher at Jefferson High and would have known both boys. She is probably still alive. We can likely interview her. OK to Kathy Sturluson but I don't see how that'll help, not like she knows anything special just because she found him. Also we should interview the secretary here at JHS. She knows something too. *He was tucked in like someone cared. After I found him I went back to my car, and I saw Beth Peake stepping into the Spence place. Why was Beth there?* again, why would gary leave a body to be found?

3. Gary Spence confessed to the murder immediately. Why? *Typically this sort of thing occurs when someone is protecting a secret or the true guilty party. You should be familiar with the idea of "taking the fall." The real question is not why, but whom? Whom did this behavior benefit? This is my number 1 question and the question I'll be asking Dad next time he calls. I believe he was covering for someone, a relative maybe. I think he knew about the body but not what to do about it.* I always got the feeling Gary would do almost anything for his crazy family and he had about half a dozen siblings as far as I could tell.

4. New DNA evidence (a jacket) clears Gary Spence of guilt. How? *This information will be revealed in court, if there is a retrial.* IFA is building a case because the jacket submitted as evidence proves Dad was facing the other way when the gun went off because of the way that the brain matter hit him. (graphic-sorry, Gus) *compelling, but I don't think that'll get him off without a good attorney. Couldn't the prosecution argue someone else was wearing the jacket? that would place another witness at the scene.*

5. Mom said something like, "You wouldn't live through what I've seen." What has she seen? Was it the murder? Is she involved? *This might explain some of her eccentricities. Is this why your mother is upset with you? Did you accuse her?* No way. I'll ask her if you want. Your mom has no right to be upset with you gus so that's some bullshit and I won't say sorry this time. ☹ *Pair this with number four. There's your witness. Beth?*

6. Dad was shot. Why was a knife belonging to Gary Spence found in the trunk with him? *This is bizarre, agreed. Even if Spence was trying to frame himself, why plant a knife rather than the actual murder weapon?* I don't know the answer

to this except that maybe it wasn't a framing?
GS and JE were in shop class together. So
maybe it was like a borrowed knife or something,
I don't think it has to do with the case. borrowed
friendship knife? Maybe. they were doing a shop project
together.

7. Grandpa Ellis hates Mom. Is this why? Or is it
because she's gay or something else?
I fail to see why this is relevant. No idea, but fuck
him double if that's true. Not much to contribute
here, except that man has been a plague on
Samsboro for years, and he's got his fingers in
every pie, as far as I'm concerned he's done
more evil in the world than any Spence. when I
was on the force, it was common knowledge that we
should turn a blind eye to whatever Mortimer Ellis got
up to. It's one of the reasons I left.

8. Here's my big question. What's with the
kidnapping story? I mean my dad didn't kidnap
your dad, your dad left a football game at
halftime. What made him do that? Who made him
do that? Who made him do that? More like
what. If there was something that could've
made a kid like James skip out on his
teammates, it had to be love. Where was Beth?
Exactly. Where was Beth?

There isn't a single magenta mark on the pages. Mom holds her pen like a sword, but she hasn't taken the cap off. The pages are passed around for a final read-through. They stop at her again.

"Please, Mom."

She uncaps the pen. Mom writes a single sentence on the last page. She pushes my notebook back to me. There in the margin, bright as an open wound:

you've never asked me about my locket, Gus.

I read it aloud. Based on faces around me, I'm not the only one taken aback.

"Your . . . locket?" It's always been a given that another Dad lives in there.

Mom pulls the chain off her neck. She sets the locket down on the notebook. I pick it up gingerly, as if it might burn me.

The doorbell rings, murdering the quiet. We all startle, cuss, or both.

Kalyn stands. "I mean, if no one else wants to get that—"

"No, I've got it." I don't know why, but I feel like if Mom gets up now, this story will break in two.

Kalyn leans shamelessly back in her chair, staring at the open doorway; Officer Newton does the same. I get the feeling that Fridge-Dad's eavesdropping. He might have been mischievous. He had forbidden friendships, after all. Maybe I'm finally getting to know him. Mom only blinks as I head for the foyer.

The faces on the front porch are familiar, and I don't really think they're unexpected. There's John, still poised next to the doorbell, and behind him lurks Phil, just out of reach. The relief I feel, seeing him here, is this big, blossoming thing, but it's dampened by the way he stares at anything but me. It's dampened by the presence of two other bodies on the porch.

"That ramp of yours is real handy." Mrs. Spence smells like cigarettes. "Gus, right? Nice to meet the man of mystery."

I have to switch hands on her; the right one is still throbbing and contains the locket. She recovers in a blink, and gives my arm a strong shake.

"Um, yeah. Thanks."

Mrs. Spence smiles a tired smile. I look at her face and wonder if she feels the way we all do: today's taken a lifetime. Grandma Spence, sitting beside her, looks a little worse for wear—her eyes are pinched shut and she's clutching the armrests of her wheelchair.

"My girl likes you an awful lot." Mrs. Spence bites her lip. "She in there?"

"Um, yeah, yeah she is. We're all just in the kitchen. Talking."

"Some conversation, I bet."

John elbows Phil, but Phil looks away. "Phil thought every player should be present for this. The conversation, revelations, et cetera."

"Yeah, yeah. Of course." I step aside. "Please come in."

"Sure we'd be welcome?" Mrs. Spence says, looking over my shoulder, and she sounds so uncertain that my chest hurts.

"It's my house, too," I say firmly. "Please. Please come in."

Any other week, I couldn't imagine these two women entering our home. But John leads the way to the kitchen, and then it's just me and my oldest friend.

I turn back to Phil, alone on the porch. His posture is all thorns, and he's never seemed as untouchable as he does now. Something unseen and large has shifted.

"Thank you for this, Phil." I want to hug him, but he might run.

"Never thank me," he mumbles. "I merely thought . . . I . . . I have often believed that if only the Montagues and Capulets might have spoken more, negotiated sooner . . . the deaths of their loved ones need never have happened. It's imbecilic, not communicating."

"Okay," I say, "so come in and talk with us."

"Surely you have spoken to Kalyn," he whispers.

I take his hand. "Phil. I *want* you in here. Please."

"Why?" he asks, finally looking at me. "I have no part to play."

I pull him inside. "Because I *want* you. All right?"

He doesn't reply, but squeezes my hand back, nodding once. "Okay."

In the kitchen, the Spences stand awkwardly in the doorway. Everyone else in the room is wide-eyed, awaiting a possible explosion.

Mom stands, flattening her blouse. "Um. You must be Kalyn's mother."

"That's a nice way to say it, yeah," Mrs. Spence says. She pushes the chair through the door and reaches out her hand. When Mom takes it, I think we all exhale. Kalyn looks entirely gobsmacked. "Louise Spence. You're softer than you look in the papers. And this here's Grandma Spence."

"We've met," Mom admits. "How are you, ma'am?"

If there's a reply, it's too quiet to overhear.

"'Claire caught fire,'" Kalyn mutters. "That's what she probably said."

"Yes. Poor Claire." Ms. Patrick sighs. "Another damn tragedy."

"Crappy way to die," Officer Newton says. "For sure."

"Wait—what?" I have no idea why Kalyn's eyes are bulging. "*What?*"

"I was just admiring your ramp," Mrs. Spence says. "Who built it? I'll recommend them to my patients."

"Oh, it was . . . my partner, actually."

"Oh, yeah? Well, damned if that ain't good craftsmanship." Mrs. Spence looks right at Tam and says again: "Damned if that isn't good craftsmanship, er . . . ?"

"Call me Tam," Tam says with a small smile.

"Just don't call you late for dinner!" Mrs. Spence parks Grandma Spence and leans over to kiss Kalyn's shorn head. "You run into a helicopter, Kalyn-Rose?"

Kalyn touches her scalp. "Somethin' like that. What the hell you doing here?"

"You think I shouldn't be here?" she says, and her raised

eyebrow is an eerie twin of Kalyn's. "Surprised you didn't call me over yourself."

"Yeah, well," Kalyn says as her mom settles into an empty chair, "it's been a day. You watch the parade, Mom?"

"Nah, missed it, but it's probably already airing on the news. Was at the courthouse again. Might just have to get a bunk there. We've got actual paparazzi swarming the salvage yard. I was seeing about a cease and desist order. That's not how you get one, usually, but squeaky wheels and grease. Our driveway is private property. *Trespassers will be shot*. But now the news vans are just lining the road instead. Looks like you're finally famous, Kay."

"An actress after all." Kalyn reaches for the locket in my hand. "Mrs. Peake?"

Mom lingers on her feet.

"Open it, Gus," she tells me.

I hesitate. "Is this really all we. I mean, all it takes?" Faces surround me, friends and photos and family and strangers, too. "This random group of gaggle, um, of people. That's all it takes to solve a murder? Just . . . putting them in a room together?"

"That's not all it took," Tam says. "It took you two caring. It took asking."

"It took only the smallest effort," Phil says bluntly. "Minuscule, even."

There's a darkness to Kalyn's words. "He's right. You've all been in Samsboro this whole time. If you'd've talked . . . if *any* of you had made the *effort*? If you could have grown up, we wouldn't have had to."

I look at Mom. "We wouldn't have been raised half-dead."

Mom breathes deep. "I wanted things to be *better* for you. As parents, all you want is for things to be easier on your children, for them to face fewer hardships than you had to. I thought this was the way."

"That's nice and all, but just because we popped out kids doesn't mean we suddenly know more about right or wrong." Mrs. Spence is *definitely* Kalyn's mom.

Kalyn offers me the locket.

I shake my head. "You do it."

It pops open easily. Kalyn peers inside. Her eyes narrow as she tilts the locket my way. I see two images:

My sixth-grade school photo. A picture of Tam in her wedding tux.

"Well," Kalyn says, "I don't get it."

Mom puts out a fragile hand. "Here."

Mom plucks Tam's photo from its frame. "I'm sorry. I didn't see how it could hurt, leaving her there, Tam. Underneath. It's been thirteen years since—"

"Oh, it hurts, but not for the reasons you think. It hurts you never told me, Beth."

She returns the locket to Kalyn, who sets it on the table with a gentle *thunk*. The adults crane their necks. No one utters a syllable.

Within the frame I see the photo of a stranger. She's young, maybe sixteen or so, with ashy blond braids. Maybe she needs braces, but her smile is likable.

"Let me guess," Mrs. Spence says. "That'll be Claire, right?"

Kalyn's almost yelling: "*Fuck's* sake, who the hell is Claire?"

The answer comes from the last place I expect it. The wispy woman in the wheelchair raises her hand. "Claire was my baby girl. My daughter."

"And she died in a fire? For real?" Kalyn's not laughing. "Gran, I'm sorry."

"Claire was the girl I loved," Mom whispers. "When I was your age."

That likable smile, it's familiar. This is an alternative version of Kalyn.

The final branches break. My thoughts fall out at last, but it's Phil who says it:

"*Claire* was the Spence who killed your dad."

KALYN

STORYTELLING IS ANOTHER Spence tradition, or it used to be. Dad and I might not see each other much, but we've had hundreds of conversations. He never hangs up sooner than he has to. Every week of my life, I've spoken to him for thirty minutes straight. Minus my toddler years, that adds up to more than three hundred hours of talk.

Most kids get that much time with their dads over just a few months, but still. We make the most of it. You can tell a lot of stories over three hundred hours.

"Have I told you about the time your uncle Hank dropped firecrackers down the church organ? Jiminy Christmas, that was hilarious." Not that all the stories are hilarious, but Dad tells them anyhow. He talks about overpriced obituaries and tragedies, too.

Dad's *never* mentioned the funeral of a sister named Claire.

He's *never* mentioned her existence.

And Dad's *definitely* never mentioned, oh, you know, that his sister Claire committed the crime that defines all our lives.

That's the story we're hearing now, in this crowded kitchen. Every eye is fixed on Gus's mom as she tells us something true.

There are parts that make me want to yell and interrupt.

But there's also this feeling hanging around, like the smell of burning sugar, that if anyone stops Mrs. Peake, she won't finish. This lady's hidden truths in her house for longer than I've breathed air. This feels like some kind of exorcism.

People say you should pull a Band-Aid off all at once.

Give Gus's mom credit: she's not a writer for nothing. She might not be funny like Dad, but she can spin a yarn. I bet she's been writing this in her head for years.

"I was raised in a religious home. It doesn't really matter what religion; it only matters that it was the kind of religion that gave my devout parents permission, upon walking in on their fifteen-year-old daughter kissing her best friend, to beat their daughter with a belt, send her to a delightful summer camp for conversion therapy, and then move the whole tainted family to a brand-new town. Everyone needed 'a fresh start.'

"I've spent the second half of my life trying to forget the first half. I pretend that camp had no lasting effect. I ended up working my dream job, married to my dream girl, and we've raised a son who is better than any I could have dreamed. But there are days when I can't get dressed, and days when I treat my loved ones like they're temporary."

Tamara wipes her eyes.

"In Samsboro, I made a point of dating boys. I made it a *spectacle*. A parade of handsome young men visited our refurbished farmhouse. I made mistakes. Once I brought home a slender boy with a soft smile and a passion for horticulture. I could see what my father thought when he gazed at this boy from across the dinner table: *His waist is so narrow, his face is so* pretty. *Do I need to call the camp counselors?*

"I won't pretend my motives for dating James were pure. I'd tried not dating for a while, tried making friends and focusing on college applications. But I wasn't allowed to attend sleepovers or join study groups. My father stared at the empty chair. *Do I need to call the camp counselors?*

"When James asked me to Winter Carnival, I kissed him on the spot.

"I won't say 'I was young,' because I know that young people are capable of great and terrible things. And I did care about James. He was genuinely talented and gradually he became *genuinely* kind. James sat at our table, and my father's noose loosened.

"James was always trying to become better than his father. That was relatable. We'd both done awful things in the name of our fathers. The difference was, James stopped bullying people by the time I met him. I was still doing an awful thing to James.

"Maybe my eyes wandered. Maybe my laughter faltered. The closer friends we became, the more James probably suspected we were only ever going to be that. Whenever I saw doubt in his eyes, I kissed him harder."

It sounds so Rose-y. Maybe every generation is made of tragic little pretenders.

"Even before we agreed to pretend she never existed, Claire had an atmosphere of absence about her. She was in half my classes and I never noticed. I didn't meet Claire so much as become aware of her, like waking up and finding a body warm and breathing next to me.

"James and I were spending more and more time at Spence Salvage. Gary wasn't allowed to go to the Ellis mansion. I met Mr. Ellis all of once and understood that Spences and Ellises were a caustic combination.

"Gary and James really were an odd couple. James was this shining star. Gary looked like he needed a bath, and burn scars mottled his arms. Teachers berated Gary on principle. Yes, the Spences were poor, but it went deeper. Spences looked perpetually ready to catch fire. Spence faces were built for mug shots.

"I have no idea how they became so close. They were inseparable by the time I moved to Samsboro, a buddy-cop duo. You rarely saw one without the other. If James noticed the looks people gave him for hanging out with Gary, it never stopped him. James was so popular that people couldn't actually say a word. Eventually they saw Gary as comic relief, the hillbilly jester. James *never* treated Gary that way."

"Because he *wasn't* that way." Gus presses his fingertips to mine.

I want to wipe my eyes, but I don't want his fingers to move.

"One day Gary came to class with two black eyes. James

wanted to punch the entire universe, but Gary wouldn't let James near his uncle. The more I saw of Spences, the more I understood their reputation, but also their strange loyalty to one another."

How many Spences will I never know about? How many of us hit each other?

"Claire and I never spoke where anyone might *see* us. We cracked jokes around bonfires. Soon my ribs were cracking as my heart pressed against them, watching how she tucked her hair behind her ears.

"Claire wasn't nice. Not to me, and *definitely* not to James— she remembered his bullying days. But she treated her mother like a paper rose. Claire was a chronic shoplifter. She painted stolen lipstick on like warrior paint. If I had to pinpoint the first reason I loved her, it may have been that I wanted to *be* her. If Claire sat at a table with my father, she'd kick the chairs over. She'd bite through the phone cord before he could call counselors." Beth smiles. "When I met you, Kalyn, I saw Claire. I saw her in red.

"During one of our bonfires, Claire waited for James and Gary to head out into the salvage yard with baseball bats in tow, looking to bash windows—"

Windshield wrecking is another Spence tradition.

"—and then she sat on my lap and asked when I was going to make out with her, already. I couldn't have kissed James hard enough to redeem the way I kissed Claire. I slept with him for the first time that night."

If this talk bothers Gus, you'd never know. Maybe he inherited his dad's face, or maybe this story feels like it belongs to strangers.

"That fall, James and Gary took Tech Ed. Claire and I took Drama. James and Gary were whittling picture frames, and Claire and I were tangled up between the curtains. I didn't know I was pregnant. By the time I did, Claire was begging me to leave *Shitsboro* with her."

Same stupid nickname, same stupid town.

"James's smile grew so *goofy* and *young* when I told him about you. I don't know what I hoped for." For the first time in all this, she looks at her son, lets his eyes envelop her. "Gus, I'm going to answer the question you asked me."

"Okay," he says, but I'd say he's anything but.

"I *wanted* James to ask for an abortion. I couldn't think that way myself. If there was one thing that scared my father more than me being gay, that was it."

Gus's eyes are closed, his lips stretched shut over his crooked teeth.

"Had James suggested . . . I'm not proud, but I wanted an *out*. But your dad was *thrilled*. He already loved you." Tears speckle the tablecloth. "I'm so sorry, Gus."

Gus opens his eyes. "I wasn't there. Don't apologize to me."

"That's not something you ever need to apologize for." Tam's voice is so firm that it almost takes shape in the air. "Don't you dare."

"On principle, I understand that. I support the right to choose.

But it's hard to think of those principles when your son is sitting right in front of you."

Ms. Patrick clears her throat. "I don't know what to say, as it's not my place. But you kids *really* should have listened more in my Sex Ed class."

It's insane, but we laugh like freakin' donkeys.

Hearing this stupid, sad story is leaving us all parched. There's no way this story can ever be satisfying. I get why Gus looked scared about hearing the truth. The truth doesn't necessarily make things any better. It doesn't *solve* things.

Beth can't carry on so easily after our outburst. She takes a big breath. "So I agreed to leave. With Claire. It was naive, but that's the only escape I thought we had. My father never let me go anywhere unless he knew James was with me. We needed to wait for a night when we wouldn't be missed, and James would be preoccupied."

"Homecoming," Gus whispers.

"The only person who could have made Gary betray James was Claire. He wasn't happy, but he wasn't surprised. I don't think Gary cared for 'lesbians' as a concept, considering the bigotry he was raised on, but he doted on his little sister. When she asked for his help repairing one of the cars, he handed her the keys to his truck instead.

"The night before the game, my parents went out to dinner. I told them I'd be with James. In reality, Claire drove over to my house and we took this opportunity to load up the truck. But my parents ran into James at Maverick's. He covered for me, telling them I was waiting in the car. Then James drove straight to my place to see if I was okay. He thought I might have 'morning sickness or something.'

"James saw Gary's truck in the driveway. James was not the type to assume the worst of anyone, but the sight must have confused him. And what must have confused him more was my reaction when he asked me about this at school the following day. I was blindsided; I stammered about 'Gary helping me with something.'

"What must have confused James *most* was talking to Gary during Tech Ed. Gary denied the truck ever having been there. I know he did, because he confronted Claire and me after school. He was so angry. 'I *hate* you for making me do this. James is the only friend I've got, and you're making me do this.'"

I don't know which of us around this table winces hardest.

"James was lied to by both of his friends. What was he supposed to think?"

"He could have *trusted* you," I say. "He could have gotten over himself."

She shakes her head. "James tried to be a good person, but he was far from perfect. He *was* possessive at times, and he had that temper. He was petrified of becoming his father. For a year, I *had* lied to him, and maybe he felt that. James was nice, but he wasn't stupid. When none of us showed up at the game, that was it.

"I don't know what James was thinking when he walked out on his team at halftime. Did he scan every inch of the stands before he got in the car, or did he simply know we weren't there? They said he was kidnapped. James kidnapped himself. And yes, he brought a knife with him. It was Gary's whittling knife, a gift he couldn't bear to keep."

"A friendship knife after all," I say. "These days kids give each other necklaces."

"It sounds stupid."

"It doesn't sound stupid," Gus says. "It just sounds, um, *childish*."

He's right. Every inch of this story is childish as hell. We dreamed of drifters, of conspiracies and plots. But the truth is so much *smaller*.

Mrs. Peake keeps talking, faster now, barreling downhill with no bungees to hold her. "James pulled into Spence Salvage. There was Gary's truck, filled with my stuff, and there was Gary, helping me heft a suitcase into the back, and James just . . . lost it."

She closes the locket. "I never saw James bully anyone. That was the first time I could imagine what that looked like. He started pulling things from the truck, throwing them to the ground. Then he started screaming.

"Gary was furious because James wouldn't listen, appalled that James would throw his fists whenever Gary got close. But Gary couldn't betray Claire by saying what was really going on. Claire was in the trailer, gathering the last of her things."

Next to me, Grandma's shoulders tremble.

"If Claire had been outside, maybe she'd have told him the truth. I couldn't.

"I've forgotten most of what was said. I only remember that we were all shouting. At one point James asked me to leave with him. I refused. I wasn't scared so much as humiliated, like I was back on a bunk bed in a cabin where a priest was forcing me to look at pictures of naked men—men doing—"

This is the exact moment that my mom gets up, walks around the table, and wraps Mrs. Peake in her arms. "It's all right, hon. You're almost there."

"Thank you." Mrs. Peake looks at Grandma Spence. "Mrs. Spence. Claire insisted two girls on the road had better be prepared to meet trouble. You kept that gun under your nightstand, didn't you?"

Grandma has been crying softly, breaking my heart. She shakes her head, but it's not the "no" headshake. It's a heavier thing, another damn confession.

"It feels almost *clinical* now, how things unfolded. The more often people recall a memory, the less accurate it becomes. The more the brain reinvents details."

The part Gus and me needed, maybe we've needed to hear our whole lives? It's just one blunt paragraph, shorter than a news article.

"James held the whittling knife out to Gary, telling him to take it back. Gary shook his head, took me by the shoulders, and turned us around to go. Claire stepped out of the trailer with her grandma's gun in tow. She saw James, screaming, following us with a knife upraised. Unlike me, Claire *had* seen James hurt people. She'd sat at Gary's bedside after James pushed him into that bonfire. I think Claire meant to scare him. I'll never know. She jumped down from the porch and pulled the trigger twice."

Hatred and misunderstanding, passed down over decades.

"The moment James hit the ground, Gary was there to catch him. But we could tell." Her voice shakes. "We could tell an ambulance wouldn't help. But I could also tell, even then, the very second Claire started weeping. The way Gary looked at her. He wasn't going to let her suffer for it."

"Why not?" I say, and anger brings me to my feet. "Why the hell not let her take the fall? She made her own stupid choices. Why should Dad pay for it?"

"To protect everyone, sounds like," Phil reasons. "To not out Beth. To not out Claire. To not bring the wrath of Ellis down on everyone."

"She was his baby sister," Officer Newton reasons, though he looks furious.

"That's fucking *condescending*. Claire was the criminal. Why the *hell* did *any* of you let Dad sink like that?"

"What would you do," Gus asks quietly, "if it were me?"

"I'd tell your ass to tell the truth and go to fucking prison! I'd call you an idiot and tell you to face the damn music, and sayonara, Gus, because no one person is ever worth giving up your whole life for, you idiot!"

"But you wouldn't. You'd hurt yourself first every time." Gus has never sounded this certain. "How many blows have you already taken for me?"

"That's not the same."

"Maybe it is. Maybe you're your father's daughter." Gus smiles, but it's a painful thing to see, what with his eyes leaking. "You're *still* holding my hand, Kay."

And suddenly I'm a sopping mess of salt water and snot, leaning into his shoulder.

"What I don't know," Gus says while his heart beats against my cheek, "what—what I don't *get* is how you could all just erase her. It's awful. Like Claire didn't exist."

I exhale. That's who Grandma was looking for, in all those family photos.

"It was for her sake," says Mrs. Peake.

"Maybe, when she was still alive," Gus chokes. "But now . . . it's only because she's inconvenient, right? Because she doesn't fit into the lies you all told."

No one can answer that.

Officer Newton breaks the hiccupping quiet. "We lost that homecoming game."

"Mrs. Peake."

"Yes, Kalyn." She seems more alive without that bile inside her.

"Why *didn't* you and Claire skip town? After it all panned out? I mean, I get you sticking around for the trial and everything, but afterward . . . why weren't you together?"

She doesn't answer. Gus slowly raises his hand.

"Because of me, right? Because you were pregnant. Grandpa Ellis didn't want a source, I mean, a *scandal* on top of a murder.

And he probably, um, offered to help you escape your parents. Am I right?"

Officer Newton says, "More solid police work."

"He probably just wanted a replacement, um, for James. An heir. Must've been a big disappointment when I came out."

"Don't say that about yourself." That comes from every adult here.

"Let him speak," I mutter.

"It might not be what *you* think about me. It's not what *I* think about myself. But it's what that jerk thought. If we can't talk about it, how will we ever resolve it?"

Mrs. Peake nods. "I don't know how Mortimer knew I was pregnant. James would never have told him. James never even told Gary. Things might have been so different, if he had."

"Old man Ellis has a reputation for bribing cops," Mrs. Spence reasons. "Wouldn't be surprised if he'd bribed some doctors, too."

Angus whines. No one asks what happens next.

"*Shit*." Everyone stares at me. "I've gotta be home by eight."

"Getting ready for the dance?" Phil smirks halfway.

"I'm expecting a call from Dad. Boy, what a call it'll be. Anyone wanna join?"

Nobody wants to, but Gus stands up first.

GUS

OUR CARAVAN HEADS for Spence Salvage under starlight.
Mrs. Spence's van takes the lead, followed by the station wagon,
followed by us. Tamara put us three in her truck without a
word, probably so we could have a few minutes of peace.

"You okay?"

Tam stares at me. "You *kidding* me right now? You're asking *me*?"

"Yeah."

"Oh, Gus. You should be worried about your own self."

"No." There's not a lot of room in the truck, so Kalyn's
pressed against me, thighs and of course fingers. "People worrying only about themselves leads to lies and murder."

"Fair point."

Main Street is still cordoned off—guess a riot leaves more of
a wreck than a parade does—so the caravan takes bumpy back

roads to the edge of town. Ms. Patrick's car kisses the lips of potholes.

"I wasn't expecting the whole Scooby Gang to volunteer," Kalyn grumbles. The clock under the dashboard reads 7:41 p.m.

It took too long to get us out of the house. Three people offered to do the dishes before Ms. Patrick elbowed her way to the sink. No one stayed behind.

"Don't get me wrong," Mrs. Spence told Mom while we gathered in the driveway. "You'd better testify and help get my husband out, now we're kind of family."

Can families really be broken and made so easily? I don't know. But Kalyn is on one side of me, and Tam is on the other, and Phil is just behind me, and I love them all.

"Are you really moving out?" I ask Tam.

"I don't know, Gus. It's been a wild night, and not in a good way." She eases the truck onto a road cutting through fields; we've already reached Harrison Farm. A blob of Angus's spit smacks our windshield as we pick up speed. "All these years I've been with your mom, she never mentioned being with anyone else. I figured she must've been, because we've all got the sadness of something in us. I never cared. It's not like I didn't have my own drama. But this . . ."

"Did you really spend last night with your family?"

We slam into a puddle.

"I've only got one family these days. I stayed in a Super 8 last night."

It's not nice of me to feel relieved. But if you can make and break a family, I like to think you wouldn't keep trying to remake a seriously broken one. I'd rather think you'd keep the ones made on purpose.

"I'm proud of you, sticking up for that dead girl," Tam says suddenly. "I remember reading about it. When she died. I didn't know anything about her. It was just such an awful thing."

"What happened?" Kalyn asks.

"I think it was a freak accident. She pulled an aerosol can from a firepit, and it blew up in her face. Not the kind of obituary you forget."

"She can't have been old."

"Older than either of your dads were before their lives were taken away from them." There's something silencing about the way Tam refers to both dads as casualties.

Harrison Farm is more than decrepit. The back of the barn has collapsed in on itself, a splintered shipwreck in tall grass. This penultimate road is more like a trail, pocked with puddles, but our caravan barely slows. We hit the M-12, cars coated in mud. It's 7:49.

As the caravan starts up the last hill, my phone buzzes. The number seems familiar, but I can't place it until I pick up.

"Gus? It's Mr. Wheeler. Is Phil with you? He hasn't been answering his phone."

I glance at Phil in the rearview. "Yeah, he's here. John, too."

"Where are you? Not trapped downtown?"

"No, we're okay." I put him on speakerphone.

"Hello, Dad," Phil drones. "Let me reassure you that I have killed no one."

His sigh of relief becomes a burst of static. "And no one is hurt?"

Phil *seems* off, in some indefinable way, and we're all a little hurt, but Tam speaks up, "They're fine, Colin."

"Thank you, Tamara. Have you seen the news? The parade, no, the *protest*, is being replayed on national television. Partly because of the controversial nature of the case, partly the mock hanging, and partly the dramatic costuming, I'd say. Please promise me you'll all stay in tonight."

"Darn," Kalyn scoffs, "guess we'll have to miss the game." It's 7:52.

"Haven't you heard? They canceled the game."

Tam whistles. "The people of Samsboro won't like that one bit."

"They don't, and that's why you *have* to stay safe. Downtown's a wreck, and based on the coverage, Spence Salvage looks like a war zone."

"Um," Kalyn says as we crest the hill.

It isn't quite pitchforks. It isn't quite the whole town. But I feel, actually and really, that we might finally be stuck in one of Phil's dystopian movies.

Stretched along the road, vehicle after vehicle spans the length of Spence Salvage. Some are news vans, but most aren't. A huge pickup blocks the driveway. People sit on the hoods of cars or congregate with posters in the ditches. I don't need to hear what they're hollering.

The first vehicles in our caravan have rolled into it.

"You know," Tam says, hitting the brakes and switching into reverse, "something tells me we shouldn't be running into that mess."

"What's going on?" Mr. Wheeler demands. "I thought you said you were at home?"

"Yeah, well," Kalyn growls, "guess home is relative. Tam, turn the car around."

I gape at her. "But—your dad—"

"Thanks, Gus. But *he's* not going anywhere. Dad can call tomorrow. Mr. Wheeler, we've got other calls to make, but can you handle a sleepover tonight?"

"Well, I suppose so, but who is this? And—"

She hangs up the phone before he can argue.

"Let's go back," she says as we stare out at her home in ruins. It strikes me that our entire lives have been invaded by strangers, and this is just another illustration of the point, this swarm of people who know nothing laying claims on our lives.

"That's very rational of you," Phil observes quietly.

"Yeah, well," she says, leaning her head on my shoulder, "I've had enough for now."

"Enough of what?" I ask.

"Everything, I guess."

"For now and always," Tam says.

KALYN

I WON'T PRETEND I don't notice the exact moment eight
o'clock passes.

There's a big part of me wondering how Dad feels, calling
and getting no reply, if he feels anything like how I felt last
night when he didn't call. There's a small part of me relieved to
let the phone ring in the empty prefab.

I don't know how to talk to an innocent man, a giant kid.
I know he's not different, but it feels different. Like I've been
talking to a Rose all along, or talking to someone not realizing
there was a Rose underneath.

PHIL

I REMAIN UNCONVINCED that I'm a character worth saving.

They save me all the same. When at last the chaos has died down and proven itself less chaotic than a kitchen conversation, when at last we three are camped out in my basement on the dirty old sectional, we collapse like medieval lovers, arms wide or curled inward.

"When will it all be over?" Gus asks.

"Octogus, it's *never, ever* over."

"At least we aren't alone," Gus says, to both of us.

"Gus." I perceive this as a moment for corrections. "What would you say if I told you I am always alone?"

"I'd say that you're being more play, um, *melodramatic* than usual."

"Gus. I am inhuman. I have always been. Kalyn insists I tell you."

"I don't know why I thought you'd be more tactful about it, Phil."

I'm not awaiting her response. I await his. I have awaited it for years.

When next I open my eyes, I am staring into the stars of his. "Shut up, Phil."

"I am not speaking in jest. I have antisocial personality disorder."

"Oh. Okay." I wish he would look away. "Thanks for telling me."

"This is not a *coming out*, fool. I am telling you I am better left to the flames. I am as heartless as any murderer, most likely. Today . . . today I beat Garth senseless."

"That's not cool, but you did that for me, right?"

"That was scary shit, but the dude was swinging a chair at you," Kalyn adds.

"No, but I—listen—I am telling you I *feign* my humanity."

"That's weird." Gus puts his palm on my heart. "You look like a real person."

"Would you stop making a mockery of this?" I pull myself upright so quickly that he falls back in the blankets, catching himself ungracefully on Kalyn's knees. "I have hurt you and will hurt you again. I have only ever pretended to be your friend."

"I'd say you're a good actor, then. Which is basically, um, the same."

"It is *not* the same. One day I may harm someone as easily as help them—"

Without warning, Gus's arms are around my neck and his

breath is at my throat. His heartbeat matches mine. "Me too, Phil, if you don't shut up. Whatever this is, however you are, we'll work through it. It's not our first dangerous campaign."

I don't know what I'm feeling, or if I'm feeling, but there is something. Something like relief or warmth, unfamiliar in this familiar, dark space beneath my home. I can't fathom why, but I hug him in turn. Perhaps we do become the roles we adopt. Perhaps thinking makes it so.

"Bad as things are," Gus says, "I think it could be worse."

"Indeed; we could be falsely imprisoned for murder," I supply.

"Or we could *be* murdered," Kalyn adds, "or raised by shittier parents."

We quiet at that.

"Welp. Since we're all being optimists now," Kalyn says, "who wants to go to the dance tomorrow?"

"Not really dressed for it." Gus pulls away from me. "And there's something deep and dark that Phil hasn't told you."

"I have just unveiled the greatest secret of my existence. What else must I divulge?"

"Phil can't dance. Not even a little bit."

It occurs to me now that there are no finales. There is no such thing as catharsis. Our story will not end with us joking in a basement as sirens blare and motors rev and strangers battle nonsensically far beyond us, removed from us, in newsrooms and on forums and in fields they don't belong in.

It is enough, for an instant, to pretend it might. It is enough to believe in no ending at all. Sometimes you must be satisfied with dissatisfaction. It is the most human thing.

EPILOGUE
Love, Kalyn Spence

KALYN

THINGS ALL FUNNEL downward.

I let Mom buzz the rest of the hair off on Sunday night. I look like 1980s Sinéad O'Connor, sans orthodontist.

After all the weekend drama—the dance was canceled, too—I figure I'll be facing fists at Jefferson. It takes every god-given centimeter of my self-control not to bring another egg to school. Maybe it always will. Maybe I'll always consider violence. But if it's my first thought and not my first action, that's progress. I don't bring the damn egg.

I'm hitching a ride today so Mom can stay on the phone with the IFA and the lawyers and the press all morning.

See, tides are turning. Turns out all those rioters who thought they could trample our property are criminals now. Half the older men in town got caught on national television vandalizing our precious old junk. When Tam turned our truck around,

Mom and Mrs. Peake decided to carry on down the hill, which is crazy and amazing. There's a new picture making rounds, featurin' Mom and Mrs. Peake facing down a line of protestors. The way those ladies are hollerin', frozen on film, they could be related.

"They're alllll getting served," Mom tells me, gleeful as punch. The IFA has hooked us up with some good lawyers.

Now the whole world's looking at Samsboro, and according to the world, things here aren't so black and white. People are demanding the retrial. I wonder if any of the hateful moms of America have changed their tune. Probably not. Most people would rather be stubborn than right.

All that matters, at least to Gus and me, is that one of those people making demands is Gus's mom. I don't know what changed in that crowded kitchen. Maybe she's glad to see that splinter gone. Maybe she's done carrying on a legacy she never asked for, one she doesn't want to pass down to Gus and me. She's gonna testify. Combined with new evidence, that might be enough to exonerate Dad.

"It would help if your grandmother would testify, too," she adds, but that's not happening. All this stuff has done a real number on her. She's been coughing nonstop since Friday, and she's started calling me Claire. There's no such thing as easy medicine.

So the retrial will happen; god knows what will come after.

Phil pulls the Death Van up our driveway. Mud attacks the Death Star. Considering everything, Phil looks the same as always. Can't gauge a guy by lookin' at him.

"Natalie Portman at last," he says as I climb in. I punch him nicely.

We head back into town. Gus is waiting on the porch in that swinging chair, and he's wearing practical shoes today. I notice, but that's his business, not mine.

Gus and I agree to hold hands on the way into Jefferson High. I don't know what it means except it feels better to walk on four legs than two. Dogs like Angus know what's up, I guess. Humans have to work harder to be good.

For every kid who seems ready to spit, there's another kid who offers a high five. Garth doesn't show up for school, and Eli Martin doesn't meet my eyes, but he nods when I pass. I don't know how much of this is genuine goodwill and how much of it is awe at the national attention. Everyone's slipped out of their usual faces today, lost their petals.

Sarah spends the whole day fielding our encounters, laying out strategies for dealing with drama, making sure I "stay out of trouble."

"I thought you liked me being trouble." It's weird, this little lunch table with the four of us—well, five, if you count Officer Newton, looming against the wall.

"I like you being you. You're the only one who thinks that has to mean trouble."

Phil shakes his head. "I think it also, but I am sure that's a comfort to you both."

Officer Newton is actually great at origami, which is something I never knew I wanted to learn until he started folding frogs in the desk next to mine, bored stupid by American History.

Origami's got me thinking about all sorts of things I want to create.

I've never been artistic, or I've never known whether I am. Truth is, I've never thought a lot about the future. Now I can't seem to stop. Feels like it really exists.

I think growing up is relative, but I also think that no matter what, I don't have to be more or less than a Spence; I've just got to be more or less me.

When I share this notion with Gus, we aren't next to a dark kiln or cloud gazing on steps. It's November, and we're sitting on his porch even though it's cold as . . . you know. Tam and Mrs. Peake are raking leaves onto flowerbeds again. Me and Gus are sharing hot cocoa and lukewarm chatter. The sky's the kind of gray that means nothing at all.

"Well," Gus says, setting down his mug, "I could've told you that."

"Gimme a break," I say, poking him.

"I mean it. I'm two years older than you, and I never, *ever* struggle with my identity."

He can't keep a straight face, but I would never want him to.

"I'm officially older than Dad ever was," he tells me.

A second or ten passes. "Congratulations on surviving."

"You too, Kalyn," he says quietly. "Congratulations."

It's a stupid thing to cry about, but what the hell else is new?

GUS

I THOUGHT WHEN the moving van showed up Mom might panic, but it's Tam who spends the whole morning finding excuses to blow her nose in the bathroom.

I need another surgery. Those pesky muscles in my upper arm have started pulling my right shoulder forward, and they threaten to slowly twist my spine. Maybe it has to do with Garth yanking on my arm, or maybe it doesn't. Dr. Petani referred me to a specialist who thinks an operation will help me stand taller in the future.

She was more upset than I was. "Sometimes these things happen after a growth spurt. You should stop growing up so quickly, Gus."

"Thanks, Dr. Petani, but I'm good."

We're moving into an apartment near Hardwick General, a hospital that specializes in orthopedic surgeries. The doctor there is super young and super enthusiastic. It's hard to be excited about meeting people who can't wait to cut you up. But people don't always come across the right way when you first meet them. If I'm going to be seeing this guy for six months of rehab, I want to like him.

"If anyone will like a sadist," Phil reassures me, rolling for initiative, "it's you. I imagine you're more cowed by the prospect of attending a new school full of oglers and necks of rubber."

"It'll be okay," I say, and I think it mostly will be. After marching down the street with all the eyes of Samsboro on me, it's hard to care about a few more strangers' stares. "And we're going to move back for senior year."

"Yes, you'll be fine. Even without your Mercutio."

I put my hand on his shoulder, just for a moment. "You'll be fine, too."

"Obviously."

It's my last afternoon in Samsboro, and we're playing a short campaign in his basement. Phil's cleric attacks the warg who bit me during my last turn. He rolls a fifteen and adds a plus-five modifier, soundly wounding our foe.

There's nothing but packets of paper and dice on the table between us, but it feels like so much more than that.

"Phil. I'll call you constantly."

"Oh, please not constantly. I may be preoccupied." He's jotting notes on his character sheet. "I'm going to attend therapy that doesn't involve my own father. 'Some good I mean to do, despite of mine own nature.'"

I want to tell him that's great. I shove the popcorn bowl his way.

After we move, we'll be three hours from Samsboro. Once the trial begins, Mom's going to have a long commute on her hands. But I'm going to join her on that commute whenever I can.

"It's your roll," Phil says.

I want to tell Phil how much I'll miss him. Instead, I roll the dice and attack, finishing off that goblin.

Kalyn's family hosts a farewell barbecue. Mom seems nostalgic as we approach, commenting on the rusted *Spence Salvage* sign. "That was here even back when I was a kid, Tam."

Mom's still anxious about being outside, but she's started writing thought pieces. When Grandpa stopped paying for my health care, Mom wrote an article about his years of abuse and blackmail. People started a fund-raiser. My surgery might not cost us a penny. It's a surreal, scary, happy, guilty thought.

A couple days after her kitchen confession, I sat down across from Mom while she was working and waited for her to look at me.

"Can I ask you about s-something?"

"Anything, Gus. From now on, anything."

"I want to know about Claire."

So Mom told me. She told me about their first secret date, when they rode to Tittabawassee Creek and went fishing, even though neither of them knew the first thing about it. Claire sometimes bit not her fingernails but the skin around them, and thought it was a sign of her future schizophrenia. Claire could be sarcastic about even the most serious things, but sincere about the silliest. Claire adored "those hideous Precious Moments statues. She had no taste, but she loved me. I had no integrity, but I loved her."

I said, "When we get to the new place, we could hang a picture of her, too."

It's a rollicking ride down the Spence driveway, but not nearly as rollicking as that moment. I wasn't sure if Mom was going to sob or hold me. She did both.

When we reach the bedraggled prefab, Kalyn's waiting with two baseball bats in her hands. She gets up from her perch on the ramp Tamara installed and holds them up over her head like rabbit ears.

"WonderGus," she says, "wanna take part in a Spence tradition?"

"That's not your best idea ever, sweetie," Mrs. Spence calls from behind the grill. Tamara hands her a plate of tofu. Mrs. Spence cackles before dipping the entire block in barbecue sauce and slapping it down alongside the sausages. Grandma Spence, sunk into her chair beside the picnic table, makes a tittering noise.

"Oh, but it is a lot of fun," Mom says. "If you've got helmets?"

Kalyn pulls two welding masks from a lawn chair behind her.

"You can come, too, Beth! Got another bat in the shed

somewhere. Apparently we hoard baseball bats as well as DNA evidence."

Mom laughs, something that seems no less amazing for happening more these days. "Oh, no. I'm going to hang back and reminisce."

Kalyn and I beat the life out of a busted windshield, watching the glass pearl and bounce away. Phil would enjoy this more than I do, especially with my arm acting up. But we give it our all, in oven mitts and long sleeves.

It's only after we're done that I recognize the car we've wrecked is a Taurus.

"What?" she says. "I've still got angry feelings, you know."

I kick the hubcap. "Yeah, me too."

Dad's a loss I'll always feel, but like my arm and leg and Kalyn and my family, that loss is part of me. Dad didn't die for any good reason. I'm sorry about what happened to him, and sorry I'll never know him. But who knows who I would have been if I hadn't lived my whole life without him. I wouldn't know Kalyn. I wouldn't be me.

It would be another great tragedy.

So I can't really be entirely sorry.

KALYN

I SIT DOWN next to the phone. It's definitely too early.

I haven't spoken to Dad for a month. At first I was overwhelmed, and then I was angry. For weeks, Dad refused to participate in a retrial. All this work from all these people, and *Dad* wasn't cooperating.

I think Mom put him straight, there.

Now I've had time to think about what to say.

The phone rings at exactly 8:00 p.m. I hear good ole sentient Judy, the same robot she's always been, and then Dad's voice, soft and gravelly like I remember.

". . . that you, Kalyn?"

"Hey, Dad. A lot's been going on."

"So I've heard, baby girl. Proud of you."

"You too. General consensus is you aren't a murderer."

He clears his throat. "Well, the word is often wrong."

"Dad, I *know* you aren't a murderer. So can you grow up and stop being a liar, too? I've heard what happened. I know about Aunt Claire. You shoulda just let her go to jail. How could you forget her like that?"

For half a minute, I can only hear him breathing and the echoes of life beyond the phone line, other convicts making phone calls home. Bodies far away.

"I think of Claire every day. Part of me thinks she's still alive out there."

"She's not, Dad." I sigh.

"Kalyn," he says, "at a certain point you live with something for so long it becomes your world. And then it's what you know, and where you feel comfortable, and you can't imagine trying to escape it. I can't imagine trying to make it in the world. With you, your mom. I can't imagine coming home to a place where Claire's dead. I can't imagine getting a job. I only ever worked at a gas station. I can't imagine growing up. I've been in here since I was a kid, honey. It's my only reality."

It hurts to hear it, in the same way pulling a splinter hurts. You know it'll be better once it's out. I know we'll be better once Dad's out, or at least we can try to be.

"You know the best movies take place in different realities. *Gattaca*."

"*Dark City*." A dry chuckle. "But those are some pretty dark examples."

"*Mad Max*." I smirk. "Dad, I thought I was betraying you by pretending to be something other than me. These past few months, I wondered what you'd think of me. But it doesn't matter, not so much."

He just waits. That's something I like about him, something I want to learn to do one day. You know, when *I* grow up.

"I was betraying me, and that's worse. I'm going to work on it. And for the love of god, I want you to work on it, too, okay. I want you to work on it and learn to quit lying to yourself all the damn time, so that we can all stop lying to each other."

"All right, Kalyn."

"That's not a good enough start," I tell him, eyes burning. "Try again, dammit."

"I didn't kill him, sweetie," he tells me, and it's the first time the story we heard in that kitchen feels real to me. "I hated him and he hated me, but the minute someone else pushed me into the fire, James pulled me out again." His voice cracks. "He pulled me out and called an ambulance and decked the guy in the face for good measure, and I couldn't hate him after that. I could never, ever kill him. I loved him, honey."

"Once more, with feeling." I pass the phone to the boy who's sitting beside me.

Gus lets go of my hand—not for forever—and takes the phone.

I can tell the very instant Dad repeats himself, because Gus pulls off his glasses to wipe his eyes. He looks nothing like his dad and everything like Gus, especially when he shares his crooked smile with me.

He's Gus, and I'm Kalyn, and it's enough for now and always.

And you know what? When Gus hangs up the phone, I'm going to tell him so.

I'm going to tell him something true.

ACKNOWLEDGMENTS

Wild and Crooked is my first novel in the contemporary genre, my first book without fantastical science or aliens or monsters beyond the human kind. Still, it demanded more of my imagination than my previous books, and would not be the story that it is without the insight of other, wiser people.

As ever, many thanks to my infallible editor, Mary Kate Castellani, who always sees my characters first and genre second. Thanks also to all the proofreaders and copyeditors and the entire team at Bloomsbury, who tolerate my foibles and misquotes and provide wonderful guidance.

This book deals with some sensitive issues, and for that reason it would have been impossible to write it in good conscience without referring to expert readers. Any remaining errors are on me! Endless gratitude to Chloe Smith, an amazing talent in her own right, who helped make Gus as real as possible and also offered fantastic encouragement. Thanks also to my sister, Erin Thomas, a kick-ass speech-language pathologist (my sister is seriously the coolest, and I really should have incorporated more of her advice), and other early readers!

I also have to give ultimate kudos to Karen Kilgariff and Georgia Hardstark, the amazing hosts of *My Favorite Murder*, for humanizing true-crime stories and always putting an emphasis on valuing the victims over the villains. They are too good for this world. SSDGM.

I need also to thank my parents, Kathryn Thomas and Haydn Thomas, social workers who raised my siblings and me to value others regardless of their differences, disabilities, or limitations. I am so grateful for all the perspective they have given us.

Finally, thanks again to my darling egg-carton of fans. Your support has meant so much on dark days, and your fan art makes me cry with joy. Sorry about Blunderkinder Book Three, y'all. It's still a flame in my heart (I can't give it up).

In so many ways, *Wild and Crooked* is a reflection on rural upbringing. I was raised in the woods of Michigan, but there are woods everywhere, and I think I will always write stories about trying to find a way through them.